PENGUIN BOOKS

PRETTY GIRLS

Karin Slaughter is one of the world's most popular and acclaimed storytellers. Published in 120 countries with more than thirty-five million copies sold across the globe, her twenty-one novels include the Grant County and Will Trent books, as well as the Edgar-nominated *Cop Town* and the instant *New York Times* bestselling novels *Pretty Girls*, *The Good Daughter* and *Pieces of Her*.

Slaughter is the founder of the Save the Libraries project – a non-profit organisation established to support libraries and library programming.

For more information visit KarinSlaughter.com

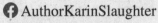 AuthorKarinSlaughter

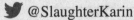 @SlaughterKarin

D1339818

Also by Karin Slaughter

Blindsighted

Kisscut

A Faint Cold Fear

Indelible

Faithless

Skin Privilege

Triptych

Fractured

Genesis

Broken

Fallen

Criminal

Unseen

The Kept Woman

Cop Town

Pretty Girls

The Good Daughter

Pieces of Her

The Last Widow

False Witness

Girl, Forgotten

eBook originals

Snatched

Busted

Karin Slaughter

THE INTERNATIONAL NO. 1 BESTSELLER

PRETTY GIRLS

PENGUIN BOOKS

PENGUIN BOOKS

UK | USA | Canada | Ireland | Australia
India | New Zealand | South Africa

Penguin Books is part of the Penguin Random House group of companies
whose addresses can be found at global.penguinrandomhouse.com

First published in the UK by Century in 2015
Published in paperback by Arrow Books in 2016
Reissued in Penguin Books 2023
026

Copyright © Karin Slaughter, 2015

The moral right of the author has been asserted

Lines from 'Closer to Fine' by Indigo Girls, words and music by Emily Saliers
and Amy Ray, published by Universal/MCA Music Ltd; Lines from 'Justify My
Love' by Madonna, written by Lenny Kravitz, Ingrid Chavez, with additional lyrics
by Madonna, published by Universal Music Publishing Group, REACH MUSIC
PUBLISHING, Warner/Chappell Music, Inc.; Lines from 'We Are Never Ever
Getting Back Together' by Taylor Swift, written by Taylor Swift, Max Martin and
Shellback, published by Sony/ATV Music Publishing UK Ltd.

Typeset in 10.81/15.6 pt Times LT Std
by Integra Software Services Pvt. Ltd, Pondicherry

Printed and bound in Great Britain by Clays Ltd, Elcograf S.p.A.

The authorised representative in the EEA is Penguin Random House Ireland,
Morrison Chambers, 32 Nassau Street, Dublin D02 YH68

A CIP catalogue record for this book is available from the British Library

ISBN: 978-0-099-59943-2

www.greenpenguin.co.uk

MIX
Paper | Supporting
responsible forestry
FSC® C018072

Penguin Random House is committed to a sustainable future for
our business, our readers and our planet. This book is made from
Forest Stewardship Council® certified paper.

For Debra

A particularly beautiful woman is a source of terror.

Carl Jung

i.

When you first disappeared, your mother warned me that finding out exactly what had happened to you would be worse than never knowing. We argued about this constantly because arguing was the only thing that held us together at the time.

"Knowing the details won't make it any easier," she warned me. "The details will tear you apart."

I was a man of science. I needed facts. Whether I wanted to or not, my mind would not stop generating hypotheses: Abducted. Raped. Defiled.

Rebellious.

That was the sheriff's theory, or at least his excuse when we demanded answers he could not give. Your mother and I had always been secretly pleased that you were so headstrong and passionate about your causes. Once you were gone, we understood that these were the qualities that painted young men as smart and ambitious and young women as trouble.

"Girls run off all the time." The sheriff had shrugged like you were any girl, like a week would pass, a month, maybe a year, and you would come back into our lives offering a half-hearted apology about a boy you'd followed or a friend you'd joined on a trip across the ocean.

You were nineteen years old. Legally, you did not belong to us anymore. You belonged to yourself. You belonged to the world.

Still, we organized search parties. We kept calling hospitals and police stations and homeless shelters. We posted fliers around town. We knocked on doors. We talked to your friends. We checked abandoned buildings and burned-out houses on the bad side of town. We hired a private detective who took half of our savings and a psychic who took most of the rest. We appealed to the media, though the media lost interest when there were no salacious details to breathlessly report.

This is what we knew: You were in a bar. You didn't drink any more than usual. You told your friends that you weren't feeling well and that you were going to walk home and that was the last time anyone ever reported seeing you.

Over the years, there were many false confessions. Sadists rallied around the mystery of where you'd gone. They provided details that could not be proven, leads that could not be followed. At least they were honest when they were caught out. The psychics always blamed me for not looking hard enough.

Because I never stopped looking.

I understand why your mother gave up. Or at least had to appear to. She had to rebuild a life—if not for herself, for what was left of her family. Your little sister was still at home. She was quiet and furtive and hanging out with the kind of girls who would talk her into doing things she should not do. Like sneak into a bar to hear music and never come home again.

On the day we signed our divorce papers, your mother told me that her only hope was that one day we would find your body. That was what she clung to, the idea that one day, eventually, we could lay you down in your final resting place.

I said that we might just find you in Chicago or Santa Fe or Portland or some artistic commune that you had wandered off to because you were always a free spirit.

Your mother was not surprised to hear me say this. This was a time when the pendulum of hope still swung back and forth between us, so that some days she took to her bed with sorrow and some days she came home from the store with a shirt or a sweater or a pair of jeans that she would give you when you returned home to us.

I remember clearly the day I lost my hope. I was working at the veterinary office downtown. Someone brought in an abandoned dog. The creature was pitiful, obviously abused. He was mostly yellow Lab, though his fur was ashen from the elements. Barbs were clumped in his haunches. There were hot spots on his bare skin where he'd scratched too much or licked too much or done the things dogs try to do when they are left alone to soothe themselves.

I spent some time with him to let him know he was safe. I let him lick the back of my hand. I let him get used to my scent. After he calmed, I started the examination. He was an older dog, but until recently, his teeth had been well kept. A surgical scar indicated that at some point an injured knee had been carefully and expensively repaired. The obvious abuse the animal suffered had not yet worked its way into his muscle memory. Whenever I put my hand to his face, the weight of his head fell into the palm of my hand.

I looked into the dog's woeful eyes and my mind filled in details from this poor creature's life. I had no way of knowing the truth, but my heart understood this was what had happened: He had not been abandoned. He had wandered off or slipped his leash. His owners had gone to the store or left for vacation and somehow—a gate accidentally left open, a fence jumped, a door left ajar by a well-meaning house-sitter—this beloved creature had found himself walking the streets with no sense of which direction would take him back home.

And a group of kids or an unspeakable monster or a combination of all had found this dog and turned him from an adored pet into a hunted beast.

Like my father, I have devoted my life to treating animals, but that was the first time I had ever made the connection between the horrible things people do to animals and the even more horrific things they do to other human beings.

Here was how a chain ripped flesh. Here was the damage wrought by kicking feet and punching fists. Here is what a human being looked like when they wandered off into a world that did not cherish them, did not love them, did not ever want them to go home.

Your mother was right.

The details tore me apart.

ONE

The downtown Atlanta restaurant was empty except for a lone businessman in a corner booth and a bartender who seemed to think he had mastered the art of flirty conversation. The pre-dinner rush was starting its slow wind-up. Cutlery and china clashed in the kitchen. The chef bellowed. A waiter huffed a laugh. The television over the bar offered a low, steady beat of bad news.

Claire Scott tried to ignore the endless drum of noise as she sat at the bar nursing her second club soda. Paul was ten minutes late. He was never late. He was usually ten minutes early. It was one of the things she teased him about but really needed him to do.

"Another?"

"Sure." Claire smiled politely at the bartender. He had been trying to engage her from the moment she sat down. He was young and handsome, which should've been flattering but just

5

made her feel old—not because she was ancient, but because she had noticed that the closer she got to forty, the more annoyed she was by people in their twenties. They were constantly making her think of sentences that began with "when I was your age."

"Third one." His voice took on a teasing tone as he refilled her glass of club soda. "You're hittin' 'em pretty hard."

"Am I?"

He winked at her. "You let me know if you need a ride home."

Claire laughed because it was easier than telling him to brush his hair out of his eyes and go back to college. She checked the time on her phone again. Paul was now twelve minutes late. She started catastrophizing: carjacking, hit by a bus, struck by a falling piece of airplane fuselage, abducted by a madman.

The front door opened, but it was a group of people, not Paul. They were all dressed in business casual, likely workers from the surrounding office buildings who wanted to grab an early drink before heading home to the suburbs and their parents' basements.

"You been following this?" The bartender nodded toward the television.

"Not really," Claire said, though of course she'd been following the story. You couldn't turn on the TV without hearing about the missing teenage girl. Sixteen years old. White. Middle class. Very pretty. No one ever seemed quite as outraged when an ugly woman went missing.

"Tragic," he said. "She's so beautiful."

Claire looked at her phone again. Paul was now thirteen minutes late. Today of all days. He was an architect, not a brain surgeon. There was no emergency so dire that he couldn't take two seconds to text or give her a call.

She started spinning her wedding ring around her finger, which was a nervous habit she didn't know she had until Paul had pointed it out to her. They had been arguing about something that had seemed desperately important to Claire at the time but now she couldn't remember the topic or even when the argument had occurred. Last week? Last month? She had known Paul for eighteen years, been married to him for almost as long. There wasn't much left that they could argue about with any conviction.

"Sure I can't interest you in something harder?" The bartender was holding up a bottle of Stoli, but his meaning was clear.

Claire forced another laugh. She had known this type of man her entire life. Tall, dark, and handsome with twinkling eyes and a mouth that moved like honey. At twelve, she would've scribbled his name all over her math notebook. At sixteen, she would've let him put his hand up her sweater. At twenty, she would've let him put his hand up anything he wanted. And now, at thirty-eight, she just wanted him to go away.

She said, "No thank you. My parole officer has advised me not to drink unless I'm going to be home all evening."

He gave her a smile that said he didn't quite get the joke. "Bad girl. I like it."

"You should've seen me in my ankle monitor." She winked at him. "Black is the new orange."

The front door opened. Paul. Claire felt a wave of relief as he walked toward her.

She said, "You're late."

Paul kissed her cheek. "Sorry. No excuse. I should've called. Or texted."

"Yes, you should've."

He told the bartender, "Glenfiddich; single, neat."

Claire watched the young man pour Paul's Scotch with a previously unseen professionalism. Her wedding ring, her gentle brush-offs, and her outright rejection had been minor obstacles compared to the big no of another man kissing her cheek.

"Sir." He placed the drink in front of Paul, then headed toward the other end of the bar.

Claire lowered her voice. "He offered me a ride home."

Paul looked at the man for the first time since he'd walked through the door. "Should I go punch him in the nose?"

"Yes."

"Will you take me to the hospital when he punches me back?"

"Yes."

Paul smiled, but only because she was smiling, too. "So, how does it feel to be untethered?"

Claire looked down at her naked ankle, half expecting to see a bruise or mark where the chunky black ankle bracelet had been. Six months had passed since she'd worn a skirt in public, the same amount of time she'd been wearing the court-ordered monitoring device. "It feels like freedom."

He straightened the straw by her drink, making it parallel to the napkin. "You're constantly tracked with your phone and the GPS in your car."

"I can't be sent to jail every time I put down my phone or leave my car."

Paul shrugged off the point, which she thought was a very good one. "What about curfew?"

"It's lifted. As long as I stay out of trouble for the next year, my record will be expunged and it'll be like it never even happened."

"Magic."

"More like a very expensive lawyer."

He grinned. "It's cheaper than that bracelet you wanted from Cartier."

"Not if you add in the earrings." They shouldn't joke about this, but the alternative was to take it very seriously. She said, "It's weird. I know the monitor's not there anymore, but I can still feel it."

"Signal detection theory." He straightened the straw again. "Your perceptual systems are biased toward the monitor touching your skin. More often, people experience the sensation with their phones. They feel it vibrating even when it's not."

That's what she got for marrying a geek.

Paul stared at the television. "You think they'll find her?"

Claire didn't respond. She looked down at the drink in Paul's hand. She'd never liked the taste of Scotch, but being told she shouldn't drink had made her want to go on a week-long bender.

This afternoon, out of desperation for something to say, Claire had told her court-appointed psychiatrist that she absolutely despised being told what to do. "Who the hell doesn't?" the blowsy woman had demanded, slightly incredulous. Claire had felt her cheeks turn red, but she knew better than to say that she was particularly bad about it, that she had landed herself in court-appointed therapy for that very reason. She wasn't going to give the woman the satisfaction of a breakthrough.

Besides, Claire had come to that realization on her own the minute the handcuffs were clamped around her wrists.

"Idiot," she had mumbled to herself as the cop had guided her into the back of the squad car.

"That's going in my report," the woman had briskly informed her.

They were all women that day, female police officers of varying sizes and shapes with thick leather belts around their chunky waists carrying all manner of lethal devices. Claire felt that things would've gone a lot better if at least one of them had been a man, but sadly, that was not the case. This is where feminism had gotten her: locked in the back of a sticky squad car with the skirt on her tennis dress riding up her thighs.

At the jail, Claire's wedding ring, watch, and tennis shoe-laces had been taken by a large woman with a mole between her hairy eyebrows whose general appearance reminded Claire of a stink bug. There was no hair growing out of the mole, and Claire wanted to ask why she bothered to pluck the mole but not her eyebrows but it was too late because another woman, this one tall and reedy like a praying mantis, was already taking Claire into the next room.

The fingerprinting was nothing like on TV. Instead of ink, Claire had to press her fingers onto a filthy glass plate so the swirls could be digitized into a computer. Her swirls, apparently, were very faint. It took several tries.

"Good thing I didn't rob a bank," Claire said, then added, "ha ha," to convey the humor.

"Press evenly," the praying mantis said, chewing off the wings of a fly.

Claire's mugshot was taken against a white background with a ruler that was clearly off by an inch. She wondered aloud why she wasn't asked to hold a sign with her name and inmate number.

"Photoshop template," the praying mantis said in a bored tone that indicated the question was not a new one.

It was the only picture Claire had ever taken where no one had told her to smile.

Then a third policewoman who, bucking the trend, had a nose like a mallard, had taken Claire to the holding cell where, surprisingly, Claire was not the only woman in a tennis outfit.

"What're you in for?" the other tennis-outfitted inmate had asked. She looked hard and strung out and had obviously been arrested while playing with a different set of balls.

"Murder," Claire had said, because she had already decided that she wasn't going to take this seriously.

"Hey." Paul had finished his Scotch and was signaling the bartender for a refill. "What are you thinking about over there?"

She let out a long sigh. "I'm thinking your day was probably worse than mine if you're ordering a second drink." Paul rarely drank. It was something they had in common. Neither one of them liked feeling out of control, which had made jail a real bummer, ha ha.

She asked him, "Everything all right?"

"It's good right now." He rubbed her back with his hand. "What did the shrink say?"

Claire waited until the bartender had returned to his corner. "She said that I'm not being forthcoming about my emotions."

"That's not like you at all."

They smiled at each other. Another old argument that wasn't worth having anymore.

"I don't like being analyzed," Claire said, and she could picture her analyst offering an exaggerated shrug as she demanded, "Who the hell does?"

"You know what I was thinking today?" Paul took her hand. His palm felt rough. He'd been working in the garage all weekend. "I was thinking about how much I love you."

"That's a funny thing for a husband to say to his wife."

"It's true, though." Paul pressed her hand to his lips. "I can't imagine what my life would be like without you."

"Tidier," she said, because Paul was the one who was always picking up abandoned shoes and various items of clothing that should've been put in the laundry basket but somehow ended up in front of the bathroom sink.

He said, "I know things are hard right now. Especially with—" He tilted his head toward the television, which was showing a new photo of the missing sixteen-year-old.

Claire looked at the set. The girl really was beautiful. Athletic and lean with dark, wavy hair.

Paul said, "I just want you to know that I'm always going to be here for you. No matter what."

Claire felt her throat start to tighten. She took him for granted sometimes. That was the luxury of a long marriage. But she knew that she loved him. She needed him. He was the anchor that kept her from drifting away.

He said, "You know that you're the only woman I've ever loved."

She invoked her college predecessor. "Ava Guilford would be shocked to hear that."

"Don't play. I'm being serious." He leaned in so close that his forehead almost touched hers. "You are the love of my life, Claire Scott. You're everything to me."

"Despite my criminal record?"

He kissed her. Really kissed her. She tasted Scotch and a hint of peppermint and felt a rush of pleasure when his fingers stroked the inside of her thigh.

When they stopped for air, she said, "Let's go home."

Paul finished his drink in one swallow. He tossed some cash onto the bar. His hand stayed at Claire's back as they left the restaurant. A cold gust of wind picked at the hem of her skirt. Paul rubbed her arm to keep her warm. He was walking so close to her that she could feel his breath on her neck. "Where are you parked?"

"Parking deck," she said.

"I'm on the street." He handed his keys to her. "Take my car."

"Let's go together."

"Let's go here." He pulled her into an alley and pressed her back against the wall.

Claire opened her mouth to ask what had gotten into him, but then he was kissing her. His hand slid underneath her skirt. Claire gasped, but not so much because he took her breath away as because the alley was not dark and the street was not empty. She could see men in suits strolling by, heads turning, eyes tracking the scene until the last moment. This was how people ended up on the Internet.

"Paul." She put her hand to his chest, wondering what had happened to her vanilla husband who thought it was kinky if they did it in the guest room. "People are watching."

"Back here." He took her hand, leading her deeper into the alley.

Claire stepped over a graveyard of cigarette butts as she

followed him. The alley was T-shaped, intersecting with another service alley for the restaurants and shops. Hardly a better situation. She imagined fry cooks standing at open doors with cigarettes in their mouths and iPhones in their hands. Even without spectators, there were all kinds of reasons she should not do this.

Then again, no one liked being told what to do.

Paul pulled her around a corner. Claire had a quick moment to scan their empty surroundings before her back was pressed against another wall. His mouth covered hers. His hands cupped her ass. He wanted this so badly that she started to want it, too. She closed her eyes and let herself give in. Their kisses deepened. He tugged down her underwear. She helped him, shuddering because it was cold and it was dangerous and she was so ready that she didn't care anymore.

"Claire . . ." he whispered in her ear. "Tell me you want this."

"I want this."

"Tell me again."

"I want this."

Without warning, he spun her around. Claire's cheek grazed the brick. He had her pinned to the wall. She pushed back against him. He groaned, taking the move for excitement, but she could barely breathe.

"Paul—"

"Don't move."

Claire understood the words, but her brain took several seconds to process the fact that they had not come from her husband's mouth.

"Turn around."

Paul started to turn.

"Not you, asshole."

Her. He meant her. Claire couldn't move. Her legs were shaking. She could barely hold herself up.

"I said turn the fuck around."

Paul's hands gently wrapped around Claire's arms. She stumbled as he slowly turned her around.

There was a man standing directly behind Paul. He was wearing a black hoodie zipped just below his thick, tattooed neck. A sinister-looking rattlesnake arced across his Adam's apple, its fangs showing in a wicked grin.

"Hands up." The snake's mouth bobbed as the man spoke.

"We don't want trouble." Paul's hands were in the air. His body was perfectly still. Claire looked at him. He nodded once, telling her it was going to be okay when clearly it was not. "My wallet's in my back pocket."

The man wrenched out the wallet with one hand. Claire could only assume a gun was in the other. She saw it in her mind's eye: black and shiny, pressed into Paul's back.

"Here." Paul took off his wedding ring, his class ring, his watch. Patek Philippe. She had bought it for him five years ago. His initials were on the back.

"Claire," Paul's voice was strained, "give him your wallet."

Claire stared at her husband. She felt the insistent tapping of her carotid artery pulsing in her neck. Paul had a gun at his back. They were being robbed. That's what was going on. This was real. This was happening. She looked down at her hand, the movement tracking slowly because she was in shock and terrified and didn't know what to do. Her fingers were still wrapped around Paul's keys. She'd been holding on to them the entire time. How could she have sex with him if she was still holding his keys?

"Claire," Paul repeated, "get your wallet."

She dropped the keys into her purse. She pulled out her wallet and handed it to the man.

He jammed it into his pocket, then held out his hand again. "Phone."

Claire retrieved her iPhone. All of her contacts. Her vacation photos from the last few years. St. Martin. London. Paris. Munich.

"The ring, too." The man glanced up and down the alley. Claire did the same. There was no one. Even the side streets were empty. Her back was still to the wall. The corner leading to the main road was an arm's length away. There were people on the street. Lots of people.

The man read her thoughts. "Don't be stupid. Take off the ring."

Claire took off her wedding ring. This was okay to lose. They had insurance. It wasn't even her original ring. They had picked it out years ago when Paul had finally finished his internship and passed his Registration Exam.

"Earrings," the man ordered. "Come on, bitch, move."

Claire reached up to her earlobe. Her hands had started to tremble. She hadn't remembered putting in the diamond studs this morning, but now she could see herself standing in front of her jewelry box.

Was this her life passing before her eyes—vacant recollections of *things*?

"Hurry." The man waved his free hand to urge her on.

Claire fumbled with the backs on her diamond studs. The

16

tremble made her fingers thick and useless. She saw herself at Tiffany picking out the earrings. Thirty-second birthday. Paul giving her a "can you believe we're doing this?" look as the sale-slady took them back to the special secret room where high-dollar purchases were made.

Claire dropped the earrings in the man's open hand. She was shaking. Her heart beat like a snare drum.

"That's it." Paul turned around. His back was pressed against Claire. Blocking her. Protecting her. He still had his hands in the air. "You have everything."

Claire could see the man over Paul's shoulder. He wasn't holding a gun. He was holding a knife. A long, sharp knife with a serrated edge and a hook at the point that looked like the sort of thing a hunter would use to gut an animal.

Paul said, "There's nothing else. Just go."

The man didn't go. He was looking at Claire like he'd found something more expensive to steal than her thirty-six-thousand-dollar earrings. His lips tweaked in a smile. One of his front teeth was plated in gold. She realized that the rattlesnake tattoo had a matching gold fang.

And then she realized that this wasn't just a robbery.

So did Paul. He said, "I have money."

"No shit." The man's fist hammered into Paul's chest. Claire felt the impact in her own chest, his shoulder blades cutting into her collarbone. His head snapping into her face. The back of her head banged against the brick wall.

Claire was momentarily stunned. Stars fireworked in front of her eyes. She tasted blood in her mouth. She blinked. She looked down. Paul was writhing on the ground.

"Paul—" She reached for him but her scalp ignited in white-hot pain. The man had grabbed her by the hair. He wrenched her down the alley. Claire stumbled. Her knee grazed the pavement. The man kept walking, almost jogging. She had to bend at the waist to alleviate some of the agony. One of her heels broke off. She tried to look back. Paul was clutching his arm like he was having a heart attack.

"No," she whispered, even as she wondered why she wasn't screaming. "No-no-no."

The man dragged her forward. Claire could hear herself wheezing. Her lungs had filled with sand. He was taking her toward the side street. There was a black van that she hadn't noticed before. Claire dug her fingernails into his wrist. He jerked her head. She tripped. He jerked her again. The pain was excruciating, but it was nothing compared to the terror. She wanted to scream. She needed to scream. But her throat was choked closed by the knowledge of what was coming. He was going to take her somewhere else in that van. Somewhere private. Somewhere awful that she might not ever leave again.

"No . . ." she begged. "Please . . . no . . . no . . ."

The man let go of Claire, but not because she'd asked him to. He spun around, the knife out in front of him. Paul was up on his feet. He was running toward the man. He let out a guttural howl as he lunged into the air.

It all happened very quickly. Too quickly. There was no slowing of time so that Claire could bear witness to every millisecond of her husband's struggle.

Paul could've outrun this man on a treadmill or solved an equation before the guy had a chance to sharpen his pencil, but his opponent had something over Paul Scott that they didn't teach in graduate school: how to fight with a knife.

There was only a whistling noise as the blade sliced through the air. Claire had expected more sounds: a sudden slap as the hooked tip of the knife punctured Paul's skin. A grinding noise as the serrated edge sawed past his ribs. A scrape as the blade separated tendon and cartilage.

Paul's hands went to his belly. The pearl handle of the knife stuck up between his fingers. He stumbled back against the wall, mouth open, eyes almost comically wide. He was wearing his navy-blue Tom Ford suit that was too tight across his shoulders. Claire had made a mental note to get the seam let out but now it was too late because the jacket was soaked with blood.

Paul looked down at his hands. The blade was sunk in to the hilt, almost equidistant between his navel and his heart. His blue shirt flowered with blood. He looked shocked. They were both shocked. They were supposed to have an early dinner tonight, celebrate Claire's successful navigation of the criminal justice system, not bleed to death in a cold, dank alley.

She heard footsteps. The Snake Man was running away, their rings and jewelry jangling in his pockets.

"Help," Claire said, but it was a whisper, so low that she could barely hear the sound of her own voice. "H-help," she stuttered. But who could help them? Paul was always the one who brought help. Paul was the one who took care of everything.

Until now.

He slid down the brick wall and landed hard on the ground. Claire knelt beside him. Her hands moved out in front of her but she didn't know where to touch him. Eighteen years of loving him. Eighteen years of sharing his bed. She had pressed her hand to his forehead to check for fevers, wiped his face when he was sick, kissed his lips, his cheeks, his eyelids, even slapped him once out of anger, but now she did not know where to touch him.

"Claire."

Paul's voice. She knew his voice. Claire went to her husband. She wrapped her arms and legs around him. She pulled him close to her chest. She pressed her lips to the side of his head. She could feel the heat leaving his body. "Paul, please. Be okay. You have to be okay."

"I'm okay," Paul said, and it seemed like the truth until it wasn't anymore. The tremor started in his legs and worked into a violent shaking by the time it reached the rest of his body. His teeth chattered. His eyelids fluttered.

He said, "I love you."

"Please," she whispered, burying her face in his neck. She smelled his aftershave. Felt a rough patch of beard he'd missed with the razor this morning. Everywhere she touched him, his skin was so very, very cold. "Please don't leave me, Paul. Please."

"I won't," he promised.

But then he did.

TWO

Lydia Delgado stared out at the sea of teenage cheerleaders on the gym floor and said a silent prayer of thanks that her daughter was not one of them. Not that she had a thing against cheerleaders. She was forty-one years old. Her days of hating cheerleaders were well over. Now, she just hated their mothers.

"Lydia Delgado!" Mindy Parker always greeted everyone by their first and last names, with a triumphant lilt at the end: See how smart I am for knowing everyone's full name!

"Mindy Parker," Lydia said, her tone several octaves lower. She couldn't help it. She'd always been contrary.

"First game of the season! I think our girls really have a chance this year."

"Absolutely," Lydia agreed, though everyone knew it was going to be a massacre.

"Anyway." Mindy straightened out her left leg, raised her arms over her head and stretched toward her toes. "I need to get Dee's signed permission slip."

Lydia caught herself before she asked what permission slip. "I'll have it for you tomorrow."

"Fantastic!" Mindy hissed out an overly generous stream of air as she came out of the stretch. With her pursed lips and pronounced underbite, she reminded Lydia of a frustrated French bulldog. "You know we never want Dee to feel left out. We're so proud of our scholarship students."

"Thank you, Mindy." Lydia plastered on a smile. "It's sad that she had to be smart to get into Westerly instead of just having a lot of money."

Mindy plastered on her own smile. "Okay, well, cool beans. I'll look for that permission slip in the morning." She squeezed Lydia's shoulder as she bounced up the bleachers toward the other mothers. Or Mothers, as Lydia thought of them, because she was trying really hard not to use the word motherfucker anymore.

Lydia scanned the basketball court for her daughter. She had a moment of panic that nearly stopped her heart, but then she spotted Dee standing in the corner. She was talking to Bella Wilson, her best friend, as they bounced a basketball back and forth between them.

Was this young woman really her daughter? Two seconds ago, Lydia had been changing her diapers, and then she had turned her head for just a moment and when she looked back, Dee was seventeen years old. She would be heading off to college in less than ten months. To Lydia's horror, she'd already started packing. The suitcase in Dee's closet was so full that the zipper wouldn't close all the way.

Lydia blinked away tears because it wasn't normal for a grown woman to cry over a suitcase. Instead, she thought about the permission slip that Dee had not given her. The team was probably going to a special dinner that Dee was afraid Lydia couldn't afford. Her daughter did not understand that they were not poor. Yes, they had struggled early on as Lydia tried to get her dog grooming business off the ground, but they were solidly middle class now, which was more than most people could say.

They just weren't Westerly Wealthy. Most Westerly Academy parents could easily afford the thirty grand a year to send their kid to private school. They could ski at Tahoe over Christmas or charter private planes down to the Caribbean, but even though Lydia could never provide the same for Dee, she could pay for her daughter to go to Chops and order a fucking steak.

She would, of course, find a less hostile way to convey this to her child.

Lydia reached into her purse and pulled out a bag of potato chips. The salt and grease provided an instant rush of comfort, like letting a couple of Xanax melt under your tongue. She had told herself when she put on her sweatpants this morning that she was going to the gym, and she had gone *near* the gym, but only because there was a Starbucks in the parking lot. Thanksgiving was around the corner. The weather was freezing cold. Lydia had taken a rare day off from work. She deserved to start it with a pumpkin caramel spiced latte. And she needed the caffeine. There was so much crap she had to cram in before Dee's game. Grocery store, pet food store, Target, pharmacy, bank, back home to drop everything off, back out by noon to see her hairdresser, because Lydia was too old to just get her hair cut anymore, she had to go through the tedious process of coloring the gray in her blonde hair so that she didn't look like Cruella De Vil's lesser cousin. Not to mention the other new hairs that required maintenance.

Lydia's fingers flew to her upper lip. Potato chip salt burned the raw skin.

"Jesus Christ," she mumbled, because she had forgotten that she got her mustache waxed today, and that the girl had used a new astringent and that the astringent had caused an angry rash to come out on Lydia's upper lip so that instead of the one or two stray hairs she had a full-on, red handlebar mustache.

She could only imagine Mindy Parker conveying this to the other Mothers. "Lydia Delgado! Mustache rash!"

Lydia crammed another handful of chips into her mouth. She chewed loudly, not caring about the crumbs on her shirt. Not caring that the Mothers could see her gorging on carbs. There was a time when she used to try harder. That time had been before she hit her forties.

Juice diets. Juice fasts. The No-Juice Diet. The Fruit Diet. The Egg Diet. Curves. Boot Camp. Five-minute Cardio. Three-minute Cardio. The South Beach Diet. The Atkins Diet. The Paleo Diet. Jazzercise. Lydia's closet contained a veritable eBay of failures: Zumba shoes, cross-trainers, hiking boots, bellydancing cymbals, a thong that had never quite made it to a pole-dancing class that one of her clients swore by.

Lydia knew that she was overweight, but was she really fat? Or was she just Westerly Fat? The only thing she was certain of was that she wasn't thin. Except for a brief respite during her late teens and early twenties, she had struggled with her weight her entire life.

This was the dark truth behind Lydia's burning hatred for the Mothers: She couldn't stand them because she couldn't be more like them. She liked potato chips. She loved bread. She lived for a good cupcake—or three. She didn't have time to work out with a trainer or take back-to-back Pilates classes. She had a business to run. She was a single mother. She had a boyfriend who occasionally required maintenance. Not just that, but she worked with animals. It was hard to look glamorous when you'd just come from aspirating the anal glands of a slovenly dachshund.

Lydia's fingers hit the empty bottom of the potato chip bag. She felt miserable. She hadn't wanted the chips. After the first bite, she didn't even really taste them.

Behind her, the Mothers erupted into cheers. One of the girls was doing a series of handsprings across the gym floor. The movement was fluid and perfect and very impressive until the girl threw up her hands at the finish and Lydia realized she wasn't a cheerleader, but a cheerleader's mother.

Cheerleader's Mother.

"Penelope Ward!" Mindy Parker bellowed. "You go, girl!"

Lydia groaned as she searched her purse for something else to eat. Penelope was heading straight toward her. Lydia brushed the crumbs from her shirt and tried to think of something to say that wasn't strung together with expletives.

Fortunately, Penelope was stopped by Coach Henley.

Lydia exhaled a long sigh of relief. She pulled her phone out of her purse. There were sixteen emails from the school noticeboard, most of them dealing with a recent plague of head lice wreaking havoc in the elementary classes. While Lydia was reading through the posts, a new message popped up, an urgent plea from the headmaster explaining that there really was no way to find out who had started the lice pandemic and for parents to please stop asking which child was to blame.

Lydia deleted them all. She answered a few text messages from clients wanting to make appointments. She checked her spam to make sure Dee's permission slip hadn't accidentally gone astray. It had not. She emailed the girl she'd hired to help with paperwork and asked for her again to submit her time card, which seemed like an easy thing to remember because that was how she got paid, but the child had been hand-raised by an overbearing mother and couldn't remember to tie her shoes unless there was a Post-it note with a smiley face physically attached to the shoe with the words TIE YOUR SHOE. LOVE MOM. PS: I AM SO PROUD OF YOU!

That was being ungenerous. Lydia was no stranger to Post-it mothering. In her defense, her helicoptering tended to revolve around making sure that Dee could take care of herself. LEARN HOW TO TAKE OUT THE TRASH OR I WILL KILL YOU. LOVE MOM. If only she had been warned that teaching this sort of independence could lead to its own set of problems, such as finding an over-packed suitcase in your daughter's closet when she had ten whole months before she was supposed to leave for college.

Lydia dropped her phone back into her purse. She watched Dee pass the ball to Rebecca Thistlewaite, a pale British girl who wouldn't be able to score if you put her face through the basket. Lydia smiled at her daughter's generosity. At Dee's age, Lydia had been fronting a really terrible riot girl band and threatening to drop out of high school. Dee was on the debate team.

She volunteered at the YMCA. She was sweet-natured, generous, smart as hell. Her capacity for detail was astounding, if not
highly annoying during arguments. Even at a young age, Dee had
had an uncanny ability to mimic back whatever she heard—especially if she heard it from Lydia. Which is why Dee was called
Dee instead of the beautiful name Lydia had put on her birth
certificate.

"Deedus Christ!" her sweet little child used to scream, legs and
arms kicking out from her highchair. "Dee-dus Christ! Dee-dus
Christ!"

In retrospect, Lydia could see it had been a mistake to let her
know it was funny.

"Lydia?" Penelope Ward held up a finger, as if to tell Lydia
to wait. Instantly, Lydia checked the doors. Then she heard the
Mothers tittering behind her and realized she was trapped.

Penelope was something of a celebrity at Westerly. Her
husband was a lawyer, which was typical to a Westerly dad, but
he was also a state senator who had recently announced he was
going to make a run for the US House of Representatives. Of all
the fathers at the school, Branch Ward was probably the most
handsome, but that was largely because he was under sixty and
still had a clear view of his feet.

Penelope was the perfect politician's wife. In all of her
husband's promos, she could be seen looking up at Branch with
the googly-eyed devotion of a border collie. She was attractive,
but not distracting. She was thin but not anorexic. She'd given
up a partnership at a top law firm to pop out five fine, Aryan-
looking children. She was president of Westerly's PTO, which
was a pretentious and unnecessary way of saying PTA. She ran

the organization with an iron fist. All of her memos were bullet-pointed to perfection, so concise and focused that even the lower Mothers had no trouble following. She tended to speak in bullet points, too. "Okay, ladies," she would say, clapping together her hands—the Mothers were big clappers—"refreshments! Party favors! Balloons! Table dressings! Cutlery!"

"Lydia, there you are," Penelope called, her knees and elbows pistoning as she jogged up the bleachers and plopped down beside Lydia. "Yum!" She pointed to the empty bag of chips. "I wish I could eat those!"

"I bet I could make you!"

"Oh, Lydia, I adore your dry sense of humor." Penelope pivoted her body toward Lydia, establishing eye contact like a tense Persian cat. "I don't know how you do it. You run your own business. You take care of your home. You've raised a fantastic daughter." She put her hand to her chest. "You're my hero."

Lydia felt her teeth start to gnash.

"And Dee's such an accomplished young lady." Penelope's voice dropped an octave. "She went to middle school with that missing girl, didn't she?"

"I don't know," Lydia lied. Anna Kilpatrick had been one year behind Dee. They'd been in the same PE class, though their social circles never overlapped.

"Such a tragedy," Penelope said.

"They'll find her. It's only been a week."

"But what can happen in a week?" Penelope forced a shudder. "It doesn't bear thinking about."

"So don't think about it."

"That is such fantastic advice," she said, sounding both

relieved and patronizing. "Say, where's Rick? We need Rick here. He's our little shot of testosterone."

"He's in the parking lot." Lydia had no idea where Rick was. They'd had a hideous fight this morning. She was pretty sure he never wanted to see her again.

No, that was wrong. Rick would show up for Dee, but he would probably sit on the other side of the gym because of Lydia.

"Rebound! Rebound!" Penelope screamed, though the girls were still warming up. "Gosh, I've never noticed before, but Dee looks just like you."

Lydia felt a tight smile on her face. This wasn't the first time someone had pointed out the resemblance. Dee had Lydia's pale skin and violet-blue eyes. Their faces were shaped the same. Their mouths smiled in the same way. They were both natural blondes, something they had over every other blonde in the gym. Dee's hourglass figure only hinted at what could happen later in life if she sat around in sweatpants inhaling potato chips. At that age, Lydia, too, had been just as beautiful and just as thin. Unfortunately, it had taken a hell of a lot of cocaine to keep her that way.

"So." Penelope slapped her hands on her thighs as she turned back to Lydia. "I was wondering if you could help me out."

"Oka-a-ay." Lydia drew out the word to convey her great trepidation. This was how Penelope sucked you in. She didn't tell you to do things; she told you that she needed your help.

"It's about the International Festival next month."

"International Festival?" Lydia echoed, as if she had never heard of the week-long fundraiser where the whitest men and women in North Atlanta sat around in Dolce & Gabbana sampling perogies and Swedish meatballs made by their children's nannies.

"I'll resend you all the emails," Penelope offered. "Anyway, I was wondering if you could bring some Spanish dishes. *Arros negre. Tortilla de patates. Cuchifritos.*" She pronounced each word with a confident Spanish accent, probably picked up from her pool boy. "My husband and I had *escalivada* while we were in *Catalonia* last year. Ah-mazing."

Lydia had been waiting four years to say, "I'm not Spanish."

"Really?" Penelope was undaunted. "*Tacos*, then. *Burritos*. Maybe some *arroz con pollo* or *babacoa*?"

"I'm not from *Meh-i-co*, either."

"Oh, well, obviously Rick's not your husband, but I thought since your name is Delgado that Dee's father—"

"Penelope, does Dee look Hispanic to you?"

Her shrill laughter could've shattered crystal. "What does that even mean? 'Look Hispanic.' You're so funny, Lydia."

Lydia was laughing too, but for entirely different reasons.

"Goodness." Penelope carefully wiped invisible tears from her eyes. "But tell me, what's the story?"

"The story?"

"Oh, come on! You're always so private about Dee's father. And yourself. We hardly know anything about you." She was leaning in too close. "Spill it. I won't tell."

Lydia ran a quick P&L in her head: the profit of Dee's undetermined heritage making the Mothers cringe with anxiety every time they said anything mildly racist vs. the loss of having to participate in a PTO fundraiser.

It was a difficult choice. Their mild racism was legendary.

"Come on," Penelope urged, sensing weakness.

"Well." Lydia took a deep breath as she prepared to sing the Hokey-Pokey of her life story, where she put the truth in, pulled a lie out, added an embellishment and shook it all about.

"I'm from Athens, Georgia." *Though my Juan Valdez mustache may have fooled you.* "Dee's father, Lloyd, was from South Dakota." *Or South Mississippi, but Dakota sounds less trashy.* "He was adopted by his stepfather." *Who only married his mother so she couldn't be compelled to testify against him.* "Lloyd's father died." *In prison.* "Lloyd was on his way to Mexico to tell his grandparents." *To pick up twenty kilos of cocaine.* "His car was hit by a truck." *He was found dead in a truck stop after trying to snort half a brick of coke up his nose.* "It happened fast." *He choked to death on his own vomit.* "Dee never got to meet him." *Which is the best gift I ever gave my daughter.* "The end."

"Lydia." Penelope's hand was over her mouth. "I had no idea."

Lydia wondered how long the story would take to circulate. "Lydia Delgado! Tragic widow!"

"What about Lloyd's mother?"

"Cancer." *Shot in the face by her pimp.* "There's no one left on that side." *Who isn't in prison.*

"Poor things." Penelope patted her hand over her heart. "Dee's never said anything."

"She knows all the details." *Except the parts that would give her nightmares.*

Penelope looked out at the basketball court. "No wonder you're so protective. She's all you have left of her father."

"True." *Unless you counted herpes.* "I was pregnant with Dee when he died." *White-knuckling detox because I knew they would take her away from me if they found drugs in my system.* "I was lucky to have her." *Dee saved my life.*

"Oh, honey." Penelope grabbed Lydia's hand, and Lydia's heart sank as she realized that it had all been in vain. The story had obviously moved Penelope, or at least interested her, but she had come here with a task and that task was going to be assigned. "But, look, it's still part of Dee's heritage, right? I mean, stepfamilies are still families. Thirty-one kids at this school are adopted, but they still belong!"

Lydia took a millisecond to process the statement. "Thirty-one? As in exactly thirty-one?"

"I know." Penelope took her shock at face value. "The Harris twins just got into preschool. They're legacies." She lowered her voice. "Lice-carrying legacies, if you believe the rumor."

Lydia opened her mouth, then closed it.

"Anyway." Penelope blasted another smile as she stood up. "Just run the recipes by me first, okay? I know you like Dee to take on special skills projects. You're so lucky. Mom and daughter cooking together in the kitchen. Fun-fun!"

Lydia held her tongue. The only thing she and Dee did together in the kitchen was argue about when a mayonnaise jar was empty enough to be thrown away.

"Thanks for volunteering!" Penelope jogged up the bleachers, pumping her arms with Olympic vigor.

Lydia wondered how long it would take for Penelope to tell the other Mothers about the tragic death of Lloyd Delgado. Her father always said that the price for hearing gossip was having someone else gossip about you. She wished that he were still alive so she could tell him about the Mothers. He would've wet himself with laughter.

Coach Henley blew his whistle, indicating the girls should wind down their warm-up drills. The words "special skills projects" kept rolling around in Lydia's head. So, here was confirmation that the Mothers had noticed.

Lydia would not feel bad for making her daughter take a basic car maintenance class so that she would know how to change a flat tire. Nor did she regret making Dee enroll in a self-defense course over the summer, even if it meant that she missed basketball camp. Or insisting that Dee practice how to scream when she was scared, because Dee had a habit of freezing up when she was frightened and being silent was the worst thing you could possibly do if there was a man in front of you who meant to do you harm.

Lydia bet that right now, Anna Kilpatrick's mother was wishing she'd taught her daughter how to change a flat tire. The girl's car was found in the mall parking lot with a nail in the front tire. It wasn't a big leap to think that the person who'd driven in the nail was the same person who had abducted her.

Coach Henley gave his whistle two short blasts to get the team moving. The Westerly Women ambled over and formed a half-circle. The Mothers stamped their feet on the bleachers, trying to build excitement for a game that would unfold with the same drama as a mime's funeral. The opposing team hadn't even bothered to warm up. Their shortest player was six feet tall and had hands the size of dinner plates.

The gym doors opened. Lydia saw Rick scan the crowd. And then he saw her. And then he looked at the opposing side's empty bleachers. She held her breath as he considered. Then she let it out as he made his way toward her. He slowly climbed the bleachers. People who worked for a living didn't tend to sprint up bleachers.

He sat down beside Lydia with a groan.

She said, "Hey."

Rick picked up the empty bag of chips, leaned back his head, and let the crumbs fall into his mouth. Most of them went down his shirt into his collar.

Lydia laughed because it was hard to hate someone who was laughing.

He gave her a wary look. He knew her tactics.

Rick Butler was nothing like the fathers at Westerly. For one, he worked with his hands. He was a mechanic at a gas station that still pumped gas for some of their elderly customers. The muscles in his arms and chest came from lifting tires onto rims. The ponytail down his back came from not listening to the two women in his life who desperately wanted it gone. He was either a redneck or a hippie, depending on what kind of mood he was in. That she loved him in both incarnations had been the surprise of Lydia Delgado's life.

He handed back the empty bag. There were specks of potato chips in his beard. "Nice 'stache."

She touched her fingers to her raw upper lip. "Are we still fighting?"

"Are you still being grumpy?"

"My instinct tells me yes," she admitted. "But I hate when we're mad at each other. I feel like my whole world is upside down."

The buzzer sounded. They both winced as the game started, praying the humiliation would be brief. Miraculously, the Westerly Women managed to get the tip off. Even more miraculously, Dee was dribbling the ball down the court.

Rick yelled, "Go, Delgado!"

Dee obviously saw the looming shadows of three giant girls behind her. There was no one to pass to. She blindly heaved the ball toward the basket, only to watch it bounce off the backboard and drop into the empty bleachers on the other side of the gym.

Lydia felt Rick's pinky finger stroke her pinky finger.

He asked, "How did she get so amazing?"

"Wheaties." Lydia could barely get the word out. Her heart always swelled when she saw how much Rick loved her daughter. She could forgive the ponytail for that alone. "I'm sorry I've been such a bitch lately." She amended, "I mean, for the last decade."

"I'm sure you were bitchy before that."

"I was a lot more fun."

He raised his eyebrow. They had met at a Twelve Step meeting thirteen years ago. Neither one of them had been a lot of fun.

"I was thinner," she tried.

"Sure, that's what matters." Rick kept his eyes on the game. "What's gotten into you, babe? Every time I open my mouth lately, you howl like a scalded dog."

"Aren't you glad we're not living together?"

"We gonna have that fight again?"

She almost started to. The words, "but why do we need to live together when we live right next door to each other?" were right on the tip of her tongue.

The effort didn't go unnoticed. "Nice to see you can keep your mouth shut when you really want to." He whistled as Dee tried for three points. The ball missed, but he still gave her a thumbs-up when she glanced his way.

Lydia was tempted to tell him that Dee wouldn't give a rat's ass about his approval if they lived together, but decided to save it for the next time they were yelling at each other.

Rick sighed as the opposing team got the ball. "Oh Lord, here we go."

The dinner-plate girl was blocking Dee. She didn't even have the decency to raise her arms.

Rick sat back against the bleachers. His boots rested on the seat in front of him. There were oil stains on the cracked brown leather. His jeans had grease spots. He smelled faintly of engine exhaust. He had kind eyes. He loved her daughter. He loved animals. Even squirrels. He had read every book Danielle Steele had ever written because he got hooked in rehab. He didn't mind that most of Lydia's clothes were covered in dog hair or that her only regret about their sex life was that she couldn't do it wearing a burqa.

She asked, "What do I need to do?"

"Tell me what's going on in that crazy head of yours."

"I'd tell you but then I'd have to kill you."

He thought it over for a moment. "All right. Just don't mess up my face."

Lydia stared at the scoreboard. 10–0. She blinked. 12–0. "I just . . ." She didn't know how to say what she needed to say. "It's just history coming back on me."

"That sounds like a country music song." He looked her in the eye. "Anna Kilpatrick."

Lydia chewed her lip. He wasn't asking a question. He was giving an answer. He'd seen all the clippings she'd kept on Anna Kilpatrick's disappearance, the way Lydia's eyes filled with tears whenever the girl's parents were on the news.

He said, "I heard the police found a new clue."

"All they can do now is hope they find the body."

"She might be alive."

"Optimism is a sliver of glass in your heart."

"That from another song?"

"From my father."

He smiled at her. She loved the way the lines around his eyes crinkled. "Babe, I know I asked you to stay away from the news, but I think you should know something."

Rick wasn't smiling anymore. She felt her heart lurch in her chest.

"Is she dead?" Lydia put her hand to her throat. "Did they find Anna?"

"No, I would've told you right off. You know that."

She did know that, but her heart was still racing.

"I saw it in the crime blotter this morning." Rick was visibly reluctant, but he pushed on. "It happened three days ago. Paul Scott, architect, married to Claire Scott. They were downtown. Got robbed. Paul took the wrong end of a knife. Died before they got him to the hospital. Funeral's tomorrow."

The Mothers erupted into another round of cheering and clapping. Dee had somehow managed to get the ball again. Lydia watched her daughter sprint down the court. Dinner-Plate Hands snatched away the ball. Dee didn't give up. She chased after the girl. She was fearless. She was fearless in every aspect of her life.

And why wouldn't she be? No one had ever slapped her down. Life hadn't had a chance to hurt her. She had never lost anyone. She had never known the sorrow of having someone taken away.

Rick asked, "You gonna say something?"

Lydia had a lot to say, but she wasn't going to let Rick see that side of her; that angry, brutal side that she'd anesthetized with coke and when the coke was too much, pushed down with food.

"Liddie?"

She shook her head. Tears streamed down her face. "I just hope he suffered."

ii.

It's your birthday today, the fourth birthday that has passed without you. As usual, I set aside some time to go through our family photos and let all of the memories wash over me. I only allow myself this pleasure once a year, because doling out these precious memories is what gets me through the countless, endless days without you.

My favorite photograph is from your first birthday. Your mother and I were far more excited than you were, though you were generally a happy baby. To you, this birthday was just another day. Nothing remarkable except the cake, which you immediately destroyed with your fists. There were only two of us on the guest list. Your mother said it was silly to publicly mark an event that you would never remember. I readily agreed, because I was selfish, and because I was never happier than when I had my girls all to myself.

I timed myself as the memories ebbed and flowed. Two hours. No more. No less. Then I carefully placed the pictures back into the box, closed the lid, and put them on the shelf for next year.

Next, as is my routine, I walked to the sheriff's office. He stopped returning my calls long ago. I could see the dread in his eyes when he saw me through the glass partition.

I am his challenger. I am his failure. I am his pathetic pain in the ass who won't accept the truth that his daughter walked away.

Our first birthday without you, I went to the sheriff's office and calmly requested to read all of the files pertaining to your case. He refused. I threatened to call the newspaper. He told me to go ahead. I went to the payphone in the lobby. I slotted in a quarter. He came over and hung up the phone and told me to follow him back into the squad room.

We performed this same kabuki theater year after year until finally, this year, he gave up without a fight. A deputy led me back to a small interrogation room where they had laid out copies of all the files pertaining to your investigation. He offered me a glass of water, but I pointed to my lunch box and thermos and told him I was fine.

There is no clear narrative to a police report. Your file has no beginning, middle, and end. There are summaries of witness statements (most of their names unhelpfully blacked out), handwritten notes from detectives that use a language I have yet to master, statements that have proven to be false and others suspected to be false (again, blacked out) statements that have proven to be true (everybody lies to some degree when questioned by the police) and interview notes with a paltry list of suspects (yes, their names are all blacked out like the others).

Two different types of maps have been taped together, one showing downtown and the other showing the campus, so that your last known footsteps can be traced across town.

There are also photographs: your dorm room with favorite clothes unaccounted for, toiletries mysteriously gone, textbooks abandoned, reports half finished, a missing bicycle (though it was later found).

The first sheet of paper in your file is the same sheet of paper I saw on the first anniversary of your birthday, then the second, the third, and now the fourth.

CASE PENDING UNTIL FARTHER LEADS.

Your mother would've used a red pen to correct the word to FURTHER, but I take craven pleasure in knowing that from the very first page, they are wrong.

This is what the weather was like on Monday, March 4, 1991:

The high was 51 degrees. The low was 37. The skies were cloudless. There was no precipitation. The dew point was 34 degrees. Winds came out of the northwest at sixteen miles per hour. There were twelve hours and twenty-three minutes of visible daylight.

These were some of the items in the news that week:

The murder trial of Pamela Smart began.

Rodney King was beaten by members of the Los Angeles Police Department.

A United Airlines flight went down near Colorado Springs.

President Bush declared the Iraq War was over.

You disappeared.

Here are the sheriff's explanations for why he thinks you left us:

You were angry with us because we wouldn't let you live off campus.

You were furious that we would not let you drive to Atlanta for a concert.

You had been arguing with your sister about the provenance of a straw hat.

You had stopped speaking to your grandmother because she had implied that you were gaining weight.

The sheriff has no children of his own. He does not understand that these high states of emotion are simply a by-product of being a nineteen-year-old young woman. These disagreements were such minor storms in our family ecosystem that at the start of the investigation, we failed to mention even one of them.

Which, to his thinking, meant that we were trying to hide something.

In fairness, you were no stranger to the police. You had been arrested twice before. The first time, you were caught in a secure lab at the university protesting the research of genetically modified organisms. The second time, you were caught smoking pot in the back of Wuxtry, the record store where your friend Sally worked.

Here are the so-called clues the sheriff cites to support his runaway theory:

Your toothbrush and hairbrush were gone (or maybe you'd accidentally left them in the communal shower).

A small leather satchel was missing from your roommate's closet (or maybe she'd let a friend use it for Spring Break).

Some of your clothes seemed to be missing (or borrowed without your permission).

Most damningly, you had left an unfinished love letter on your desk—*Kiss you in Paris...hold your hand in Rome...*

Here, said the sheriff, was proof that you were planning to leave.

Here, said your sister, was proof that you were writing a music review of Madonna's "Justify my Love."

There was a boy, though any father of a teenage girl can tell you there is always a boy. He had ruffled hair and rolled his own cigarettes and talked about his feelings far too much for my comfort. You were interested in him, which meant you weren't really dating yet. There were notes being passed back and forth. Records of late-night phone calls. Soulful mix tapes delivered. You were both so young. This was the beginning of something that might lead to everything or nothing at all.

To answer the obvious question, the boy was camping with his family when you were taken. He had an airtight alibi. A park ranger had seen him with the family. The man had stopped by their campsite to warn them that a coyote had been sighted in the area. He sat with the family by the fire and discussed football with the father because the boy was not a fan.

The park ranger's contribution to the case did not stop there. He offered the sheriff a possible explanation, an explanation the sheriff later presented as fact.

That same week, the ranger had come across a band of stragglers camping in the woods. They had been moving around the state for a while. They dressed in dark clothing. They cooked their meals on an open fire. They walked down country roads with their hands clasped behind their backs and their heads down. Drugs were involved, because with these sorts of characters, drugs are always involved.

Some called them a cult. Others said they were homeless. Many said they were runaways. Most called them a nuisance. You, my sweet girl, were heard by many of your friends sympathetically referring to them as free spirits, which is why the sheriff assumed that, lacking any other leads, you had simply run off to join them.

You volunteered at the homeless shelter and you drank alcohol even though you were underage and you were caught smoking pot, so it only made sense.

By the time the runaway theory became cemented in the sheriff's mind, the group of stragglers, the cult, the free spirits—whatever they were called—had moved on. They were eventually located in North Carolina, too stoned and too disbanded to say who had been among them.

"She looks very familiar," one of the few remaining original members had written in his statement. "But we all have eyes and noses and teeth, so doesn't that mean that everybody looks familiar?"

This is why we know you were abducted:

You were mad at your mother, but you still came home the day before and talked to her in the kitchen while you did your laundry.

You were furious with your sister, but you still let her borrow your yellow scarf.

You despised your grandmother, but you still left a card to be mailed the following week for her birthday.

While it is not entirely out of the realm of possibility that you would run into the woods and join a group of aimless, wandering vagabonds, it is completely impossible that you would ever do so without telling us first.

This is what we know you did on the day you were taken:

At 7:30 on the morning of Monday, March 4, you joined some friends from the homeless shelter and went to Hot Corner to pass out food and blankets. At 9:48 a.m., Carleen Loper, the desk monitor at Lipscomb Hall, was on duty and recorded your return to the dorm. Your roommate, Nancy Griggs, left for the pottery lab at 10:15 a.m. She said you were tired and had gone back to bed. Your English professor remembers you from his noon workshop. He offered you some editorial suggestions on your Spenser paper. He recalls a lively discussion. (He was later ruled out as a suspect because that evening, he was teaching a class on the other side of campus.)

Around 1:00 p.m., you went to the Tate Student Center where you ate a grilled cheese sandwich and a salad that you shared with Veronica Voorhees.

The next part is less specific, but based on interviews, the sheriff managed to put together a likely list of your activities. At some point, you dropped by the *Red & Black* offices to deliver your story on UGA's attempt to privatize meal services. You returned to the student center and played a game of pool with a boy named Ezekiel Mann. You sat on the tweed couches in the lounge with another boy named David Conford. He told you that he'd heard Michael Stipe, the lead singer of REM, would be at the Manhattan Cafe that night. Friends in the vicinity claim that Conford asked you to go with him, but he insists that he did not ask you out on a date.

"We were just friends," he said in his statement. The deputy who interviewed him made a note that the boy had obviously wanted to be more. (Witnesses place both Mann and Conford in the student center later that evening.)

On or around 4:30 p.m. that afternoon, you left the Tate. You walked home, leaving your bike outside the student center, likely because it was getting colder and you didn't want to freeze going down Baxter Hill. (Two weeks later, your bike was found chained to the rack outside the center.)

According to the desk monitor, by 5:00 p.m., you were back in your dorm room. Your roommate Nancy recalls your excitement when you told her that Michael Stipe was going to be at the Manhattan. You both decided you would get a group together and go later that night. You were all underage, but you knew John MacCallister, a townie who worked the front door, from high school. Nancy made several calls to friends. A meeting time of 9:30 p.m. was arranged.

Since your psych professor had scheduled an exam before Spring Break, you and Nancy went to the North library to study. Around 8:30 p.m., you were both seen at the Taco Stand, a restaurant catty-corner from the black iron arch that stands at the main campus entrance. You took the food back to Lipscomb Hall. You entered through the back door, which was propped open, so the night desk monitor, a woman named Beth Tindall, did not record your entry.

Upstairs, both you and Nancy showered and dressed for the evening. You were wearing saddle loafers, black jeans, a man's white button-up shirt, and an embroidered silver and gold vest. You had silver bangles on your wrist and a locket that belonged to your sister around your neck.

Later, Nancy could not recall whether or not you brought

back from the communal showers the wire basket you kept your toiletries in (they were not found in your dorm room). Nancy mentions in one of her statements that abandoned items in the bathrooms were generally either stolen or thrown away.

At 9:30 p.m., you met your friends at the Manhattan Cafe, where you were told that the Michael Stipe rumor was false. Someone mentioned that the band was touring in Asia. Someone else said they were in California.

There was an overall sense of disappointment, but it was agreed that you all might as well stay for drinks. It was Monday night. Everyone but you had classes the next day, a fact that later worked to your disadvantage, because Nancy assumed you had gone home to finish your laundry and we assumed that you were at school.

The first round was Pabst Blue Ribbon, which the Manhattan served for a dollar each. At some point later, you were seen holding a Moscow Mule, a cocktail that sold for four dollars fifty and featured vodka, Blenheim ginger ale, and lime. Nancy Griggs indicated that a man must have purchased the drink because all the girls had a habit of asking for the expensive cocktail whenever a man was paying.

A song you liked came on the jukebox. You started dancing. Someone said the song was by C+C Music Factory. Others said it was Lisa Lisa. Regardless, your enthusiasm was contagious. Soon, what little floor space there was in the club was taken up with dancers.

That night, there was no particular boy you seemed to favor. All of your friends told the sheriff that you danced because you loved dancing, not because you were trying to attract men. (So, you weren't an evil temptress, though the sheriff tried his best to make that part of your story.)

At exactly 10:38 p.m., you told Nancy that you had a headache and were going to return to the dorm. She knows this was the time because she looked at her watch. She asked you to stay until eleven, at which point you could walk back to the dorm together. You told her you couldn't wait that long, and to try to be quiet when she got in.

The sheriff must have asked Nancy about your level of intoxication, because he writes in his notes that Nancy said you were not showing a high level of intoxication, but that you kept yawning and seemed unfocused.

The last sentence in Nancy's signed statement simply reads: After 10:38 p.m., I never saw her again.

No one saw you after that. At least no one who didn't mean you harm.

Nancy's last sentence is on the last page in your file. There is nothing more we know. As the sheriff might say, we don't have anything farther.

Here is something the sheriff does not know and that your mother refuses to believe: I remember looking at my watch that night. It was a few minutes later, closer to eleven, most likely the time you were taken.

We were having a late dinner at Harry Bissett's Grill on Broad Street, roughly five blocks away from the Manhattan. Your mother was downstairs using the restroom. The waiter offered to bring the check. I looked at my watch—that was when I noted the time. Your little sister was home studying with a friend, but she was old enough to put herself to bed, so I decided to order your mother's favorite dessert.

I remember watching her walk back up the stairs. I couldn't stop smiling, because your mother was particularly beautiful that night. Her hair was pulled back. She was wearing a white cotton dress that curved around her hips. Her skin glowed. There was so much life in her eyes. When she smiled at me, I felt like an explosion had gone off inside my heart. I could not possibly love her more than I loved her in that moment: my wife, my friend, the woman who had given me such kind, thoughtful, beautiful children.

She sat across from me at the table. I took both her hands in mine.

"Why are you smiling?" she asked.

I kissed the inside of her wrists and answered what I felt at that moment was the absolute truth. "Because everything is perfect."

This is what I know that I am:

A fool.

THREE

She had just buried her husband.

Claire kept repeating the words in her head as if she were narrating a story rather than experiencing the event in her actual life.

Claire Scott had just buried her husband.

There was more, because the service had been long, with many moving parts that Claire recalled with her cold narrator's eye.

The casket was gunmetal gray with a blanket of white lilies covering the closed lid. The smell of wet earth was pungent as the machine lowered his body into the grave. Claire's knees went weak. Her grandmother stroked her back. Her mother offered her arm. Claire shook her head. She thought of strong things: Iron. Steel. Paul. It was not until they were climbing into the back of the black limousine that Claire truly understood that she would never see her husband again.

She was going home—back to their home, the home that

they had shared. People would meet her there, parking their cars along the curving driveway and spilling into the street. They would make toasts. They would tell stories. In his will, Paul had requested a wake, though Claire had been too hung up on the derivation of the word to call it that. She asked herself: Wake as in, maybe Paul will wake up? Wake as in, the disturbed trail of water left behind a boat?

Claire felt the second wake made the most sense. The calm had been disturbed. She was trapped in turbulent waters. Swimming against grief. Drowning in sympathy.

There had been so many phone calls and cards and flower arrangements and notices of donations that had been made in Paul's name. Architecture for Humanity. Habitat for Humanity. The American Cancer Society, though Paul had not died of cancer.

Was there a charity for murder victims? Surely this was something Claire should've looked into. Was it too late? Four days had passed since that awful night. The funeral was over. People she hadn't seen or heard from in years had already sent their respects. They kept telling her that she was in their thoughts, that Paul was a good man, that they were there for her.

Claire nodded when they said this—at the police station, at the hospital, at the funeral home, at the graveside service—though she wasn't quite sure where *there* was.

"How are you holding up?" they asked. "How are you feeling?"

Disembodied.

That was the word that best described Claire's feelings. She had looked up the definition on her iPad last night to make sure she had it right.

Existing without or separated from the body.

Lacking any obvious physical source.

Again, the second definition fit best, because Paul had been her physical source. He had given weight to her life, tied her down to the world when her natural inclination had always been to float above everything as if it were happening to someone else.

She had felt this intense disembodiment for the last four days, really from the moment the Snake Man had told them to turn around. And then the police, the undertaker, asking if she wanted to see the body one last time and Claire blanching at the word "body" and sobbing like a child because she had spent every single second since they had taken Paul from her arms trying to remove the image of her lifeless, murdered husband from her mind.

Claire Scott wanted to see her husband again.

She did not want to see his *body*.

She stared out the window. They were inching forward in dense Atlanta traffic. The funeral procession had been truncated two lights back. Only their limo stayed out ahead. This wasn't like the country, where strangers respectfully pulled over to the side of the road to let mourners pass. They ignored the police officers riding ahead on their motorcycles. They ignored the yellow FUNERAL flags that people had stuck on their cars. They ignored everyone but Claire, who felt like the world was staring into the back of the car trying to catch a glimpse of her grief.

She struggled to remember the last time she'd ridden in a stretch limousine. Certainly decades had passed since she rode in any type of car with both her mother and grandmother. That last limo ride must have been a trip to the airport with Paul. The car service had given them an upgrade from the usual sedan.

"Are we going to the prom?" Paul had asked.

They had been on their way to Munich for an architectural conference. Paul had booked them into the Kempinski. For six blissful days, Claire swam laps in the pool, had massages and facials, ordered room service, and shopped alongside wealthy Middle Eastern wives whose husbands were in Germany for healthcare. Paul would join her in the evenings for dinners and late-night strolls along the Maximilianstrasse.

If she thought about it hard enough, she could remember what it felt like to hold his hand as they passed the darkened windows of all the closed shops.

She would never hold his hand again. She would never roll over in bed and rest her head on his chest. She would never see him come down for breakfast wearing those God-awful velour shorts she hated. She would never spend her Saturdays on the couch with him, reading while he watched football games, or go to another corporate dinner party or wine tasting or golf tournament, and even if she did, what would be the point if Paul wasn't there to laugh with her about it?

Claire opened her mouth for air. She felt as though she was suffocating in the closed limo. She rolled down the window and took great gulps of cold air.

"We'll be there soon," her mother said. She was sitting across from Claire. Her hand was wrapped around the liquor decanters in the side console because the sound of the rattling glass was the proverbial fingernails on a blackboard.

Her grandmother, Ginny, buttoned up her coat, but said nothing about the cold.

Claire rolled up the window. She was sweating. Her lungs felt shaky. She couldn't think beyond the next few hours. There were going to be over one hundred people at the house. Paul's partner at the firm, Adam Quinn, had turned the guest list for the wake into a corporate event for Quinn + Scott. A US Congressman; several captains of industry and their trophy wives; a handful of hedge fund managers, bankers, restaurateurs and real estate developers, and countless blowhards Claire had never met before and, frankly, had never wanted to, would soon be tracking through the house.

Their house.

They lived in Dunwoody, a suburb just outside of Atlanta. The lot had a gentle slope; at its crest had been a small cottage with a tire swing in the back yard that the bulldozers had razed the first day of construction. Paul had designed their home from the ground up. He knew where every nail and screw was. He could tell you where every single wire led and what it was supposed to control.

Claire's contribution to the infrastructure had been to give Paul a label maker because he loved labeling things. He'd been like Harold with his purple crayon. The modem said MODEM, the router said ROUTER. The cut-off for the water supply had a giant, labeled tag. Every appliance had a label telling the date it had been installed. There were laminated checklists for everything, from winterizing the outdoor spigots to troubleshooting the a/v system, which more closely resembled a NASA control board.

Managing the house was arguably a part-time job. Every January, Paul gave Claire a list of contractors so she could set up the annual appointments for maintenance on the generator, the geothermal units, the garage doors, the copper gutters, the composite roof, the irrigation system, the well for the irrigation system, the outdoor lighting, the elevator, the gym equipment, the pool equipment, and the security system.

And those were just the tasks she could recite off the top of her head. January was less than two months away. Who was she supposed to call? Claire always threw away the list after the last workman left. Did Paul have the file somewhere? Would she even know how to find it?

Her hands started shaking. Tears filled her eyes. She was overwhelmed by all the things she did not know she needed to do.

Her mother asked, "Claire?"

Claire wiped away her tears. She tried to logic down the panic. January was next year. The wake was right now. Claire didn't have to be told how to throw a get-together. The caterers would've arrived an hour ago. The wine and liquor had been delivered this morning. As Claire had gotten dressed for the funeral, the gardeners were already out in the yard with their leaf blowers. The pool had been cleaned yesterday evening while the tables and chairs were being unloaded. There were two bartenders and six servers. Black-eyed pea cakes with shrimp. Zucchini and corn fritters. Coriander-spiced beef fritters. Burgundy beet risotto tarts. Lemon-spiced chicken with dilled cucumbers. Pigs in a blanket with mustard, which Claire always threw in as a joke but was invariably the first thing the caterers ran out of because everyone loved tiny hotdogs.

Her empty stomach soured at the thought of all that food. She stared blankly at the liquor decanters in the limo. Her mother's hand rested lightly on the stoppers. Her yellow sapphire ring was a gift from her second husband, an affable man who had quietly died of a heart attack two days after retiring from his dental practice. Helen Reid was sixty-two years old, but she looked closer to Claire's age than her own. Helen claimed her good skin came from being a librarian for forty years, which had kept her out of the sun. The fact that they were often mistaken for sisters had been the bane of Claire's younger existence.

"Did you want a drink?" Helen asked.

Claire's mouth formed a reflexive no, but she said, "Yes."

Helen pulled out the Scotch. "Ginny?"

Claire's grandmother smiled. "No thank you, dear."

Helen poured a generous double. Claire's hand shook as she took the glass. She'd taken a Valium this morning, and when that hadn't seemed to work, she'd taken some Tramadol left over from a root canal. She probably shouldn't put alcohol on top of the pills, but Claire probably shouldn't have done a lot of things this week.

She threw back the drink. Her mind flashed up the image of Paul throwing back his Scotch in the restaurant four nights ago. She gagged as the liquid hit her stomach and burned back up her throat.

"Goodness." Ginny patted Claire's back. "Are you okay, dear?"

Claire winced as she swallowed. She felt a sharp pain in her cheek. There was a small rash of scraped skin where her face had grazed the brick wall in the alley. Everyone assumed the injury had happened during the robbery, not before.

Ginny said, "When you were a little girl, I used to give you Scotch and sugar for your cough. Do you remember that?"

"Yes, I do."

She smiled at Claire with genuine affection, which was something Claire could not quite get used to. Last year, the old woman had been diagnosed with something called pleasant dementia, which meant that she had forgotten all the perceived slights and neurotic obsessions that had made her such a nasty bitch for the first eight decades of her life. The transformation had made everyone wary. They were constantly waiting for the old Ginny to rise up phoenix-like and burn them all anew.

Helen told Claire, "That was nice that your tennis team showed up."

"It was." Claire had been shocked that they'd made an appearance. The last time she'd seen them, she was being shoved into the back of a police car.

"They were dressed so impeccably," Ginny said. "You have such lovely friends."

"Thank you," Claire said, though she wasn't sure whether they had attended Paul's funeral because they were still her friends or because they couldn't pass up a juicy social event. Their behavior at the cemetery had offered no clues as to which was the truth. They had kissed Claire's cheek and hugged her and told her how sorry they were, and then they had all wandered off while Claire was greeting other mourners. She couldn't hear them, but she knew what they were doing: picking apart what everyone was wearing, gossiping about who was sleeping with whom and who had found out and how much the divorce would cost.

Claire had found herself having an almost out-of-body experience where she floated like a ghost over their heads and heard them whispering, "I heard Paul was drinking. Why were they in that alley? What did they think would happen in that part of town?" Someone, invariably, would make the old joke, "What do you call a woman in a black tennis dress? A Dunwoody widow."

Claire had been friends with these types of mean girls all of her life. She was pretty enough to be the leader, but she'd never been able to engender the type of fearless loyalty it took to marshal a pack of she-wolves. Instead, she was the quiet girl who laughed at all the jokes, straggled behind them at the mall, sat on the hump in the backseat of the car, and never, ever—ever—let them know that she was secretly fucking their boyfriends.

Ginny asked, "Which one were you charged with assaulting?"

Claire shook her head to clear it. "She wasn't there. And it wasn't assault, it was disorderly conduct. That's an important legal distinction."

Ginny smiled pleasantly. "Well, I'm sure she'll send a card. Everyone loved Paul."

Claire exchanged a look with her mother.

Ginny had hated Paul. And she had hated Claire with Paul even more. Ginny had been a young widow when she raised Claire's father on a paltry income from a secretarial job. She wore her struggles like a badge of honor. Claire's designer clothes and jewelry and the big houses and the pricey cars and the luxury vacations had come as a personal affront to a woman who had survived the Great Depression, a world war, the death of a husband, the loss of two children, and countless other hardships.

Claire could vividly recall the time she'd worn red Louboutins to visit her grandmother.

"Red shoes are for toddlers and whores," Ginny had quipped.

Later, when Claire had told Paul about the exchange, he'd joked, "Is it creepy that I'm fine with either?"

Claire put her empty glass back in the console. She stared out the window. She felt so out of time and place that she momentarily didn't recognize the scenery. And then she realized that they were almost home.

Home.

The word didn't seem to fit anymore. What was home without Paul? That first night when she got in from the police station, the house seemed suddenly too big, too empty, for just one person.

Paul had wanted more. He had talked about children on their second date and third date and countless dates thereafter. He had told Claire about his parents, how wonderful they were, how he had been devastated when they'd died. Paul was sixteen when the Scotts were killed in a car accident during a freak ice storm. He was an only child. The only relative he'd had left was an uncle who passed away while Paul was in high school.

Her husband had made it clear that he wanted a big family. He wanted lots and lots of kids to inoculate himself against loss and Claire had tried and tried with him until finally she had agreed to go see a fertility expert who had informed Claire that she couldn't have children because she had an IUD and was taking birth control pills.

Of course, Claire hadn't shared that information with Paul. She had told her husband that the doctor had diagnosed her with something called an "inhospitable womb," which was true because what was more inhospitable than a pipe cleaner stuck up your uterus?

"Almost there," Helen said. She reached over and touched Claire's knee. "We'll get through this, sweetheart."

Claire grabbed her mother's hand. They both had tears in their eyes. They both looked away without acknowledging them.

"It's good you have a grave to visit." Ginny stared out the window with a pleasant smile on her face. There was no telling where her mind was. "When your father died, I remember standing at his grave and thinking, This is the place where I can leave my grief. It wasn't immediate, of course, but I had somewhere to go, and every time I visited the cemetery, I felt like when I got back into my car, a tiny little bit of grief was gone."

Helen brushed invisible lint from her skirt.

Claire tried to summon good memories of her father. She was in college when Helen called to say that he was dead. At the end of his life, her father had been a very sad, very broken man. No one had been surprised when he'd committed suicide.

Ginny asked, "What's that missing girl's name again?"

"Anna Kilpatrick."

The limo slowed as it made the wide turn into the driveway. Helen shifted in her seat to look out the front window. "Is the gate supposed to be open?"

"I guess the caterers—" Claire didn't finish the sentence. There were three police cars parked behind the caterers' van. "Oh, God. What now?"

A policewoman motioned for the limo to park on the pad down from the main house.

Helen turned to Claire. "Have you done something?"

"What?" Claire couldn't believe the question, but then she thought about the Valium and the Tramadol and the Scotch and her heartless parole officer who'd said Claire's smart mouth was going to get her in trouble one day, to which Claire had told him that day had come and gone or she wouldn't have a parole officer.

Would he really drug-test her on the day of her husband's funeral?

"For the love of God." Helen slid toward the door. "Claire, do something about your expression. You look guilty as hell."

"I didn't do anything," Claire said, resurrecting a whiny tone she hadn't deployed since the ninth grade.

"Let me handle this." Helen pushed open the door. "Is there a problem, Officer?" She was using her librarian voice, low and terse and highly annoyed.

The cop held up her hand. "You need to step back, lady."

"This is private property. I know my rights."

"I'm sorry." Claire edged in front of her mother. No wonder she had a problem with authority. "I'm Claire Scott. This is my house."

"Can I see some ID?"

Helen stamped her foot. "Oh, for Godsakes. Are you really here with three police cars to arrest my daughter on the day she put her husband in the ground?" She threw a hand toward Claire. "Does she look like a criminal?"

"Mother, it's all right." Claire didn't remind her that technically, she *was* a criminal. As part of her parole, the police could trespass all they wanted. She opened her purse to look for her wallet. And then she remembered that the Snake Man had taken her wallet.

Claire saw the tattoo again, the gold-plated fang. The Snake Man's skin was white, a detail that had startled Claire when she'd relayed it to the detective at the police station. Was it racist to assume that rich white people were only robbed by black or Hispanic gang members, or had Claire listened to too much rap music in spin class? It was the same thinking that had made her conjure the image of a shiny black gun when it was actually a knife being held to Paul's back. A knife that didn't even look real, but had still managed to murder her husband.

The earth started to tremble. Claire felt the vibrations move up from her feet and into her legs.

"Claire?" Helen said.

They'd been in Napa a few years ago when an earthquake hit. Claire had been thrown from bed, Paul on top of her. They'd grabbed their shoes but little else as they ran past broken water pipes and shattered glass.

"Insufficient shear reinforcement mode," Paul had said, standing in the middle of the crowded, broken street in his boxers and undershirt. "A newer building would have base isolation bearings, or a quake-resistant sill-anchoring system that could buffer the shearing effect."

Listening to him drone on about seismic loading was the only thing that had calmed her.

"Claire?"

Claire blinked open her eyes. She looked up at her mother, wondering why their faces were so close.

"You fainted."

"I didn't," Claire argued, though evidence pointed to the contrary. She was lying on her back in her own driveway. The policewoman was standing over her. Claire tried in vain to think of an insect the woman resembled, but honestly, she just looked overworked and tired.

The cop said, "Ma'am, just stay there. There's an ambulance ten minutes out."

Claire forced away the image of the paramedics who had rushed down the alley with their gurney in tow, the way they had spent less than a minute examining Paul before shaking their heads.

Had someone actually said, "He's gone," or had Claire said the words herself? Heard the words. Felt the words. Watched her husband go from being a man to being a body.

Claire asked her mother, "Can you help me up?"

"Ma'am, don't sit up," the cop ordered.

Helen helped her sit up. "Did you hear what the cop said?"

"You're the one who helped me sit up."

"Not that. Someone tried to rob the house."

"Rob the house?" Claire repeated, because it didn't make sense. "Why?"

"I imagine they wanted to steal things." Helen's tone was patient, but Claire could tell she was unsettled by the news. "The caterers walked in on the burglars."

Burglars. The word sounded antiquated in her mother's mouth.

Helen continued, "There was a fight. The bartender was badly hurt."

"Tim?" she asked, because she thought knowing the details might make her understand that this had really happened.

Helen shook her head. "I don't know his name."

Claire looked up at the house. She was feeling disembodied again, drifting in and out of the wake of Paul's absence.

And then she thought of the Snake Man and snapped back into the present.

Claire asked the cop, "There was more than one burglar?"

"There were three African American males, medium builds, mid-twenties. They were all wearing masks and gloves."

Helen had never had much faith in police officers. "With that description, I'm sure you'll find them in no time."

"Mother," Claire tried, because this wasn't helping.

"They were in a silver late-model four-door." The cop gripped the baton handle on her belt, likely because she longed to use it. "We've got a state-wide BOLO on the vehicle."

"Young lady, to me a bolo is a garish string tie." Helen was in full librarian mode again, taking out all the angst that she couldn't direct toward Claire. "Could you trouble yourself to speak English?"

Ginny provided, "Be-on-the-look-out. Am I right?" She smiled sweetly at the cop. "I have a color television in my sitting room."

Claire said, "I can't sit in the driveway like this." Helen grabbed her arm and helped her stand. What would Paul do if he were here? He would take charge. Claire couldn't do that. She could barely keep her legs underneath her. "Did the burglars take anything?"

The cop said, "We don't think so, ma'am, but we need you to walk through with the detectives and check." She pointed toward a group of men standing by the mudroom door. They were all wearing *Columbo* trench coats. One of them even had a cigar clenched between his teeth. "They'll give you a checklist to generate an inventory. You'll need a thorough report for your insurance company."

Claire felt so overwhelmed that she almost laughed. The woman might as well have asked her to catalog the Smithsonian.

"I've got people coming. I need to make sure the tables are set up. The caterer—"

"Ma'am," the cop interrupted, "we can't let anyone into the house until the scene is cleared."

Claire put her fist to her mouth so she wouldn't tell the cop to stop calling her fucking "ma'am."

"Ma'am?" the cop said.

Claire dropped her fist. There was a car stopped at the bottom of the driveway. Gray Mercedes. Headlights on. Yellow FUNERAL flag hanging out of the window. Another Mercedes slowed to a stop behind it. The funeral procession had finally caught up. What was she going to do? Falling to the ground again seemed like the simplest solution. And then what? The ambulance. The hospital. The sedatives. Eventually, she would be sent home. Eventually, she would find herself standing in this same place again with the detectives and the inventory and insurance and the bullshit. This was all Paul's fault. He should be here. He should be taking care of all of this. That was his job.

Claire Scott was furious at her dead husband for not being there to solve her problems.

"Honey?" Helen asked.

"I'm okay." Claire had realized a long time ago that if you lie with enough conviction, you can usually fool yourself. All that she had to do now was generate a to-do list. That's what Paul would have done. He had always said there was nothing that a list couldn't solve. Conquer the details and you conquer the problem. "I'll go walk the detectives through the house. We'll need to cancel the wake." She turned to the limo driver, who'd been discreetly standing to the side. "Can you take my grandmother back to the home, please?" She told the cop, "Please cancel the ambulance. I'm fine. There are over a hundred people on their way here. Unless you want them coming into the house, you need to post someone at the bottom of the driveway to stop them."

"Will do." The cop seemed happy to get away from them. She practically ran down the driveway.

Claire felt some of her bluster dissipate. She looked at her mother. "I'm not sure I can do this."

"You're already doing it." Helen looped her hand through Claire's arm and walked with her toward the men in trench coats. "Did you hurt your head when you fainted?"

"No." Claire felt the back of her head. The bruises from the alley were still tender. Another lump wouldn't make much of a difference. "Have I ever fainted before?"

"Not that I know of. You should try to do it in the grass next time. I thought you'd cracked open your noggin'."

She squeezed her mother's arm. "You don't have to stay here."

"I'm not leaving until I know you're all right."

Claire pressed together her lips. There had been a time when her mother had been incapable of being present for anything. "Listen, I know how you feel about the police, but you need to cool it."

"Huckleberries," Helen muttered, her word for incompetent policemen. "You know, it's occurred to me that I'm just about the only person in our family who hasn't gone to prison."

"Jail, Mother. Prison is for after you're convicted."

"Thank God I didn't use the wrong word with my book club."

"Mrs. Scott?" One of the trench-coated men walked over with his badge in his hand. He reeked of cigar smoke because it wasn't enough of a cliché to wear a trench coat. "I'm Captain Mayhew, Dunwoody Police Department."

"Captain?" Claire asked. The man she'd talked to after Paul's murder was only a detective. Was a burglary more important than a murder, or were murders so common in the city of Atlanta that they relegated them to detectives?

"I'm real sorry for your loss." Mayhew dropped the badge into his coat pocket. His mustache was bushy and untrimmed. Hairs climbed down from his nostrils. "The Congressman asked me to handle this personally."

Claire knew who the Congressman was. Johnny Jackson had been Paul's benefactor almost from the start, awarding him government contracts that should've gone to more experienced architects. The man's early investment had been rewarded over the years. Every time Quinn + Scott was given a new government job, Paul's personal Amex bill was riddled with charges for chartered planes he never flew in and five-star hotels where he never stayed.

She took a deep breath and asked, "I'm sorry, Captain. I'm feeling a bit discombobulated. Can you please start from the beginning and tell me what happened?"

"Yeah, I can imagine with the funeral and all, this is the last thing you want to be dealing with right now. Like I said, my condolences." Mayhew took his own deep breath, his far more raspy. "We've got a nutshell, but we're still filling in some blanks. You're not the first person in the county to have this kind of thing happen. We suspect it's a gang of young males who read the obituaries, find out when the funerals are, then Google Earth the house and figure out whether it's worth robbing."

"Good Lord," Helen said, "that really is beyond the pale."

Mayhew seemed just as outraged. "We think the burglars only had a minute or so before the catering van pulled up. They saw the broken glass from the side door." He pointed to the glass, which was still scattered on the bluestone steps. "The bartender went inside—probably not the best idea. He took a beating, but he managed to stop the gang from cleaning you out."

Claire looked up at the house again. Paul had been drawing variations of the plans since architectural school. The only thing that changed was the amount of money they could spend. Neither one of them had grown up rich. Claire's father had been a college professor. Paul's parents had owned a farm. He loved having money because it made him feel secure. Claire loved having it because once you paid for something, no one could ever take it away from you.

Had she not paid enough for Paul? Had she not worked enough, loved enough, been enough? Is that why she had lost him?

"Mrs. Scott?"

"I'm sorry." Claire didn't know why she kept apologizing. Paul would've cared more about this. He would've been outraged by the violation. Their window broken! Burglars rifling their belongings! One of their employees attacked! Claire would've been right beside him, just as outraged, but without Paul, she could barely force herself to go through the motions.

Helen asked, "Can you tell us if the bartender is okay? Tim, was it?"

"Yeah, Tim." Mayhew nodded and shrugged at the same time. "Most of the wounds are superficial. They took him to the hospital to stitch him up."

Claire felt some of the horror penetrate. Tim had been

bartending for them for years. He had a son with autism and an ex-wife he was trying to win back and now he was being stitched up at the hospital because of something horrible that had happened inside her home.

Helen asked, "But you still need Claire to go through the house to see if the burglars took anything?"

"Yes, eventually. I know this is really bad timing, but what we need from Mrs. Scott right now is to know where the set-up is for the security cameras." He pointed to the black globe on the corner of the house. "We're pretty sure that one got them coming and going."

"I'll take you to it." Claire didn't move. They were all staring at her, waiting. There was something else she needed to do. Lots of something elses.

The list. She felt her brain flip back on like a light switch.

Claire turned to her mother. "Can you ask the caterers to donate the food to the shelter? And let Tim know we'll take care of the hospital bill. I'm sure it's covered under our homeowner's policy." Where was the paperwork? Claire didn't even know who their agent was.

"Mrs. Scott?" There was another man standing beside Captain Mayhew. He was a few inches taller and dressed slightly better than the rest of the group. His trench coat was nicer, his suit was better tailored, and his face was clean-shaven. His easy manner should've put Claire at ease, but there was something about him that felt deeply unsettling, not least of all because he was sporting a nasty-looking black eye.

The man indicated his bruised eye with a chuckle. "The wife doesn't like it when I talk back."

Helen said, "Domestic violence is so funny." She noted Claire's wary expression. "I'll be in the kitchen if you need me."

The black-eyed man tried again. "Sorry, Mrs. Scott. My name is Fred Nolan. Maybe we can talk while you take us to the guts of the security system?"

He was standing close enough that Claire felt the need to step back. "This way." She started walking toward the garage.

"Hold up." Nolan put his hand on her arm. His thumb pressed against the soft underside of her wrist. "The control board for the security system is in the garage?"

Claire had never taken such an instant, visceral dislike to another human being. She looked down at his hand, willing the skin to freeze to the bone.

Nolan got the message. He released her arm.

"As I said, it's this way."

Claire suppressed a shudder as she continued walking. Mayhew walked beside her. Nolan followed closely at her heels. Too close. The man wasn't just unsettling, he was creepy. He looked more like a mobster than a cop, but he was obviously good at his job. Claire hadn't done anything criminal—at least not lately—but he'd managed to make her feel guilty anyway.

Nolan said, "Usually all the security stuff is in the main part of the house."

"Fascinating," Claire mumbled. She could feel a headache working into her temples. Maybe the burglary was a godsend. Instead of spending the next four hours entertaining Paul's mourners, she would spend half an hour with this asshole before she kicked them all out of the house and took a handful of Valium to bed.

For complicated reasons Paul had tried to explain, all the security mainframes were in the garage, which was a two-story detached structure built in the same style as the house. Paul's office on the top floor had a kitchenette, two walk-in closets, and a full bathroom. They had laughed about the space being nicer than a hotel if she ever kicked him out of the house.

"Mrs. Scott, do you mind my asking why the alarm wasn't on?" This was from Mayhew. He had taken out a notebook and pen. His shoulders were hunched as if someone had asked him to mimic a character from a Raymond Chandler novel.

Claire said, "I always leave the alarm off for the caterers. The gate was closed."

His mustache twitched. "The caterers have the front gate code?"

"And a key to the main house."

"Anyone else have a key?"

The question struck her as odd, or maybe she was annoyed by the way Fred Nolan was still breathing down her neck. "Why would the burglars break the glass in the door if they had a key?"

Mayhew looked up from his notebook. "It's just a routine question. We'll need to talk to anybody who had access to the house."

Claire felt a tickling sensation at the base of her throat. She was starting to feel overwhelmed again. This was the sort of thing Paul would know. She tried, "The housecleaners, our handyman, Paul's assistant, his partner, my mother. I can look for names and numbers."

"Your mom," Nolan said. "She's quite the pistol."

Claire pressed the code into the keypad beside the four-bay garage. The heavy wooden door slid silently up its tracks. She watched the men's eyes take in the diamond-plate wainscoting and matching storage cabinets. The floor was a racetrack-white and black rubber tile. There was a bracket for everything—hand tools, extension cords, tennis rackets, golf clubs, basketballs, sunglasses, shoes. Paul's custom workbench took up one side of the room. He had a charging station, a mini fridge, a flat-panel TV, and an air conditioner for hot summer days.

Then, of course, there was Claire's BMW and Paul's Porsche Carrera and Tesla Model S.

"Holy shit." Nolan's tone was reverential. Claire had seen men get harder over Paul's garage than they ever got over a woman.

"It's through here." Claire entered the four-digit code into another keypad and led them downstairs to the basement. She had loved that Paul loved his garage. He spent hours in here working on his models. Claire had teased him that the only reason he constructed them at home instead of at work was because here, he got to clean up after himself.

"Kind of a neat freak," Nolan said, as if reading her mind.

"I got lucky," Claire told him. Paul's mild obsessive–compulsive disorder had never stopped their lives or made him do odd things like touch a doorknob twelve times. Actually, his compulsions manifested themselves in acts that any wife could appreciate: putting down the toilet seat, folding all the clothes, cleaning up the kitchen every night.

At the bottom of the stairs, Claire entered another four-digit code into the keypad on the door. The lock clicked open.

Mayhew said, "Never seen a basement under a garage like this."

Nolan said, "Kind of *Silence of the Lambs*-y."

Claire flipped on the lights and the small, concrete room came into stark relief. Paul had designed the space to double as a tornado shelter. Metal shelves held food and supplies. There was a small TV, a weather radio, a couple of camping cots, and plenty of junk food, because Claire had told Paul that in the event of the apocalypse, she was going to need lots of chocolate and Cheetos.

She was glad she still had on her coat. The temperature was kept low because of all the computers. Everything was controlled from inside this room, not just the security cameras but all the audio-visual systems, the automation for the blinds and fixtures, and whatever else made the house run like magic. There were banks of components with flashing lights and a small desk with four flat-screen monitors mounted on articulating stands.

Nolan asked, "Does your husband secretly work for the NSA?"

"Yes." Claire was tired of his questions, which were made even more grating by his flat, Midwestern accent. The most expedient thing would be to just give them what they wanted so they would go away.

She opened a desk drawer and found the laminated checklist that explained how to work the security cameras. Paul had tried to walk her through the steps but Claire's eyes had glazed over and she'd worried she was going to have a seizure.

She tapped the computer keyboard and entered the access code to the system.

"Lots of passwords to remember." Nolan was standing too close again.

Claire slid away from Nolan. She handed Mayhew the directions. "You'll have to take it from here."

Nolan asked, "Are all of your houses like this?"

"We only have one house."

"'Only.'" Nolan laughed.

Claire had reached her limit. "My husband is dead and now my house has been broken into. Is there something you find funny about this situation?"

"Whoa." Nolan held up his hands like she'd tried to scratch out his eyes. "No offense, lady."

Mayhew's mustache twitched again. "Hard to offend someone if you keep your fucking mouth shut."

Claire gave Nolan a look before turning away from him. She knew how to shut down a man. He didn't leave, but he took a few steps back to let her know the message had been received.

She watched the monitors as Mayhew followed Paul's checklist. The views were split so that each screen showed four different aspects from sixteen different cameras. Every entrance, every bank of windows, the pool area, and several sections of the driveway were monitored. Claire could see that the caterers were in the motorcourt turning around their truck. Helen's silver Ford was parked on the other side of the garage. She was talking to one of the detectives outside the mudroom door. Her hands were on her hips. Claire was glad there was no sound.

Mayhew flipped through the pages of his notebook. "Okay. We've got a basic time frame for the break-in based on when the caterers called 911." He pecked at some keys and Helen disappeared from the monitor. The catering van went from making a sharp turn to pulling into the motorcourt. Mayhew skipped back the footage until he found what he wanted. Three individuals at the bottom of the driveway. They were far enough away to be indistinct, just dark, menacing blurs making their way toward the house.

Claire felt every hair on the back of her neck rise up. This was actually something that had taken place at her home.

She noted the time on the video. While the burglars were passing the parking pad in front of the house, Claire had been standing by the small, non-denominational chapel in the cemetery wondering why she hadn't died in that alley with her husband.

"Here we go," Mayhew said.

Claire felt a sharp pain in her chest as the blurs turned into men. Seeing it made it real, something she had to deal with. It was just as she had been told: three African American males in ski masks and gloves jogged up the driveway. They were all dressed in black. Their heads scanned left and right in a coordinated pattern. One of them held a crowbar in his hand. Another had a gun.

Nolan said, "Looks pretty professional to me."

Mayhew agreed. "This ain't their first rodeo."

Claire studied the men walking so confidently toward her mudroom door. Paul had ordered all the doors and windows from Belgium. They were solid mahogany with four-point locks that were easily bypassed when a crowbar smashed the leaded glass and one of the burglars stuck his arm through the window and turned the thumb latch.

Her mouth went dry. She felt tears come into her eyes. This was her mudroom. This was her door, the same door she used countless times every day. The same door Paul came through when he got home from work.

Used to come through.

She said, "I'll be upstairs if you need me."

Claire walked up the stairs. She wiped her eyes. Her mouth opened. She forced herself to draw in breath, to let it go, to fight the hysteria living in the pit of her stomach.

Paul's stairs. Paul's workbench. Paul's cars.

She went through the garage. She kept going to the stairs in the back and climbed them as quickly as her heels would allow. She didn't realize where she was going until she found herself standing in the middle of Paul's office.

There was the couch he napped on. There was the chair he sat in to read or watch TV. There was the painting she'd given him for their third wedding anniversary. There was his drafting table. There was his desk, which he'd designed so that no cords were hanging down. The blotter was pristine. The outbox held neatly stacked papers with Paul's angular handwriting. There was his computer. There was his pencil set. There was a framed photograph of Claire from more years ago than she could count. Paul had taken it with a Nikon that had belonged to his mother.

Claire picked up the picture. They were at a football game. Paul's jacket was wrapped around her shoulders. She could recall thinking how warm it felt, how reassuring. The camera had captured her laughing, mouth open, head tilted back. Ecstatically, irrevocably happy.

They'd both gone to Auburn University in Alabama, Paul because it had one of the top architectural programs in the country, Claire because it was far enough away from home to be meaningful. That she ended up with a boy who had grown up less than twenty miles from her childhood home was just further proof that no matter how far you ran, you always ended up back where you started.

Paul had been a breath of fresh air compared to the other boys Claire dated in college. He was so sure of himself, so sure of what he wanted to do and where he was going. His undergrad had been paid by a full ride scholarship and graduate school was taken care of by the money he inherited when his parents died. Between a small life insurance policy, proceeds from the sale of the farm, and the out-of-court settlement from the trucking company that had owned the eighteen-wheeler that killed the Scotts, there was more than enough money for tuition and living expenses.

Still, Paul had worked the entire time he was in school. He had grown up on a working farm, where he was expected to do chores at the crack of dawn. In ninth grade, he'd won a scholarship to a military boarding school in southeast Alabama. Between the two home lives, routine had been drilled into his system. He was incapable of being idle. One of his jobs during college was at Tiger Rags, a university bookstore. The other was as a tutor in the math lab.

Claire was an art history major. She had never been good at math. Or at least she'd never tried to be, which was the same thing. She could vividly remember the first time she'd sat down with Paul and gone over one of her assignments.

"Everyone knows you're beautiful," he'd told her, "but no one knows that you're clever."

Clever.

Anybody could be smart. It took a special somebody to be clever.

Claire returned the photograph to its spot. She sat down at Paul's desk. She rested her arms where his arms used to rest. She closed her eyes and tried to find a trace of his scent. She took a deep breath until her lungs ached, then slowly sighed it out. She was almost forty years old. She didn't have any children. Her husband was dead. Her best friends were probably drinking margaritas at the bar down the street and gossiping about how washed out she had looked at the funeral.

Claire shook her head. She had the rest of her life to think about how lonely she was. What she needed to do right now was get through today. Or at least the next hour.

She picked up the telephone and dialed Adam Quinn's cell phone number. Paul had known Adam longer than he'd known Claire. They'd been dorm-mates their first year at Auburn. They'd gotten their architectural degrees together. Adam had been best man at their wedding. More importantly, Adam and Paul tended to use the same people to manage their lives.

He picked up on the first ring. "Claire? Are you all right?"

"I'm fine," she told him, but only now that she had something concrete to do did she feel that way. "Listen, I'm sorry to bother you, but do you know who our insurance agent is?"

"Oh. Yeah. Okay." He sounded confused, probably because this was the last question he expected from Claire on the day of her husband's funeral. "Her name is Pia Lorite." He spelled the last name. "I can text you her info."

"I don't have a cell phone," Claire realized. "The Snake Man took it. I mean, the guy who—"

"I'll email it to you."

Claire was about to tell him she couldn't access her email, either, but then she remembered her iPad. It was an older model. Paul kept threatening to replace it with a laptop and she kept saying it was fine and now she would probably pack it up to take with her in thirty-odd years when she went into a nursing home.

"Claire?" Adam's voice was muffled. She gathered he was walking into another room. How many phone calls had there been between them where Adam had gone into another room? Half a dozen, maybe.

So meaningless. So stupid.

He said, "Listen, I'm really sorry about this."

"Thank you." She felt tearful again, and she hated herself for it because Adam was the last person she should be tearful with.

"I want you to know if you need anything . . ." His voice trailed off. She heard a scratching sound and guessed he was rubbing his fingers along his face. Adam was one of those men who had a perpetual five o'clock shadow, even right after he'd shaved. Claire had never found hairy men particularly attractive, but she'd still managed to sleep with Adam anyway.

She couldn't even console herself by saying it had happened a long time ago.

"Claire?"

"I'm here."

"I'm sorry to bring this up, but Paul should have a file on his computer for work in progress. Can you email it to me? I hate to ask, but we've got a really important presentation first thing

Monday morning and it would take hours to duplicate Paul's work."

"It's fine. I understand." She reached under Paul's desk and pulled out the keyboard. "I'll send it from his email."

"You've got his password?"

"Yes. He trusted me." Claire was conscious that she and Adam both knew he shouldn't have.

What a stupid, pointless mistake.

She said, "You'll have it in a few minutes."

Claire hung up the phone. She thought about the hours she had spent with Adam Quinn. Hours she should've spent with her husband. Hours she would kill to have back now.

There was no going back. She had to keep moving forward.

Paul's iMac desktop was a blank field of blue with the dock at the bottom. Beside the icons listing Paul's applications were three folders: Work, Personal, House. She clicked House and quickly found the January to-do list. She also saw a file titled "insurance" that contained not just the name of their insurance agent, but a PDF with descriptions, photographs, and serial numbers of everything in the house. Claire sent all 508 pages to the printer.

Next, she opened the Work folder. This was far more complicated and confusing. There was no "work in progress" folder, just a long list of files with numbers instead of names. Claire assumed these were project numbers, but she couldn't be certain. She clicked on the date field to list them chronologically. There were fifteen recent files he'd been working on in the last two weeks. The last one had been opened the night before Paul died.

Claire clicked on the file. She expected to find a schematic or scope of work, but all that happened was the little iMovie icon on the dock started bouncing.

"Oh," she said, because at first she didn't understand what she was seeing. And then she smiled for the first time since the Snake Man had told them not to move.

Paul had been looking at porn on his computer.

Not just any porn.

Kinky porn.

A young woman in a leather bustier was chained to a concrete-block wall. She wore a studded dog collar. Her arms and legs were spreadeagled, giving her crotchless leather panties a workout. She was making squeaky, fearful noises that sounded more 1970s horny than present-day scared.

Claire shot a guilty glance at the open doorway to Paul's office. She muted the sound, but let the movie play.

The woman was in a filthy room, which made it all the more shocking that Paul was interested. She was obviously young, but not alarmingly so. Her brunette hair was cut in a chic pixie. Heavy mascara ringed her eyes. Bright red lipstick made her lips seem bigger than they were. Her breasts were small, but she had fantastic legs. Paul had always liked Claire's legs, even when she had on the ankle monitor.

Actually, he'd especially loved the ankle monitor, which was the kinkiest thing she'd ever gotten out of him until he'd turned inexplicably rough with her in the alley.

And now, of course, because this movie was pretty out there.

Suddenly, a man's head filled the screen. He was wearing a leather ski mask with open zippers at the mouth and eyes. He smiled into the camera. There was something disturbing about the way his red lips showed against the metal teeth of the zipper, though Claire doubted Paul had been looking at the man.

The focus blurred, then sharpened. The smile disappeared. And then the man started walking toward the girl. Claire saw his erect penis jutting out from his tight leather briefs. There was a machete in his hand. The long blade glinted in the overhead light. The man stopped a few feet away from the girl.

The machete arced into the air.

Claire gasped.

The machete came down on the woman's neck.

Claire gasped again.

The man wrenched out the blade. Blood sprayed everywhere— onto the walls, onto the man, onto the camera.

Claire leaned forward, unable to look away.

Was this real?

The woman's body convulsed, arms and legs pulling at the chains, head jerking. Blood poured down her chest, pooled at her feet.

The man started fucking her.

"Mrs. Scott?"

Claire jumped back so hard that the chair slammed into the wall.

"Are you up there?" Fred Nolan was walking up the stairs.

Claire banged on the keyboard, blindly searching for a way to stop the movie.

"Hello?" Nolan's footsteps were getting closer. "Mrs. Scott?"

She held down the control button and furiously tapped on the Q to quit the program. Error messages started popping up. Claire grabbed the mouse and clicked each one closed. The rainbow wheel started to spin. "Shit!" she hissed.

"Mrs. Scott?" Fred Nolan was standing in the open doorway. "Something wrong?"

Claire looked back at the computer. Sweet Jesus. The desktop was blank again. She willed her voice not to shake. "What is it?"

"Just wanted to say that I'm sorry about before."

Claire nodded. She didn't trust herself to speak.

Nolan let his gaze travel around the room. "Nice office."

She tried not to blink because every time her eyes closed, she saw the woman. The man. The blood.

"Anyway," he tucked his hands into his pockets, "I wanted you to know that I talked to Detective Rayman about your husband's case."

She had to clear her throat a few times before she forced out, "What?"

"Detective Rayman with the Atlanta Police? You spoke to him the night your husband was murdered?"

She held her breath, trying to calm it. "Yes."

"I want you to know that we looked at all possible connections, and there doesn't seem to be one between what happened to your husband and what happened today."

Claire nodded. She felt a sharp jab of pain in her jaw from clenching her teeth.

Nolan let his eyes slowly take another tour of the office. "Your husband was a tidy guy."

Claire didn't respond.

"Kind of a control freak?"

She shrugged, though Paul had never tried to control her.

Except when he jammed her face into that brick wall in the alley.

Nolan indicated the digital lock on the door. "That's some pretty serious security."

She echoed the words that Paul had often told her. "Doesn't really matter if you don't set the alarm."

Nolan smiled his deeply unsettling smile. He wasn't standing over her, but he might as well have been. "We'll need to send a crew up here anyway."

She felt her heart stop. The computer. The files. The movie. "That's not necessary."

"Better safe than sorry."

Claire tried to think of a good excuse to contradict him. "Did the security cameras show the men breaking into the garage?"

"You can never be too sure."

She summoned a weak copy of her mother's librarian voice. "I would think sixteen cameras would make you as sure as possible."

Nolan shrugged. He was smiling at her again.

"Not to mention half a million dollars' worth of automobiles that are still parked in the garage."

He kept smiling, and Claire realized that she was talking too much. Her hands were sweating. She gripped the arms of the chair.

Nolan asked, "Something up here you don't want us to see?"

Claire forced herself not to look at the computer. Instead, she looked at his lips and tried not to think about the red, wet lips behind the zippered mask.

He said, "I'm curious, Mrs. Scott, did your husband say anything to you before he was murdered?"

She remembered the alley, the rough texture of the brick, the burn of skin being scraped from her cheek. Was Paul suddenly into that kind of thing? Was that why he had this movie on his computer?

"Mrs. Scott?" Nolan mistook her silence for embarrassment. "Don't worry. Detective Rayman told me why you and your husband were in the alley. No judgment here. I'm just curious about what your husband said."

She cleared her throat again. "He promised me he wasn't going to die."

"Anything else?"

"I already told all of this to Detective Rayman."

"Yeah, but that was a few days ago. Sometimes it takes some perspective to jog your memory." He pressed a little harder. "Sleep usually does it. I've dealt with a lot of victims of violent crime. There's this adrenalin rush that gets them through the hard parts, and then they have to tell their story to old gumshoes like me, and then they go home and they're alone and they start to crash because the adrenalin's gone and there's no forward momentum and they fall into a heavy sleep and then suddenly they wake up in a sweat because they remembered something."

Claire swallowed again. He was perfectly describing her first night alone, but the only revelation that had come when she'd woken up with the sheets soaked in sweat was that Paul was not there to comfort her.

Comfort.

How could the man who looked at such vile filth possibly be the same gentle man who had comforted her for eighteen years?

"So," Nolan said, "did you remember anything? Doesn't have to seem useful. Just a stray comment he might have made, something unusual that he did. Before or after the attack. Anything you can think of. Maybe not even something he said, but his demeanor."

Claire's hand went to her thigh. She could almost feel the missing streaks of skin where Paul had raked his fingers up her leg. He'd never marked her like that before. Had he wanted to? Had he been fighting the impulse all those years?

"General demeanor," Nolan prompted. "Anything he said."

"He was shocked. We were both shocked." Claire clasped her hands together on the desk so that she wouldn't start wringing them. "It's called Masters of the Universe Complex." She sounded like Paul, and in fact the phrase had come from her husband. "It's where people think that status and money insulate them against tragedy."

"Do you think that's true?" Nolan asked. "Seems like you've seen more tragedy than most."

"That's a keen bit of detective work on your part." Claire forced herself to stay in the present. "Are you a detective? Because when I met you in the driveway, you didn't give your title or show me your credentials."

"You're right."

He didn't volunteer the information, so she said, "I'd like to see your identification."

Nolan was apparently unflappable. He reached into his coat pocket as he walked toward her. His wallet was a cheap bifold. Instead of a detective's shield, there were two laminated cards behind plastic sleeves. Everything on the top card was in gold ink—the words Federal Bureau of Investigation, the blind Lady Justice, and the bald eagle. The bottom card was in blue ink and showed Fred Nolan's color photograph, his name, and revealed that he was a special agent from the Atlanta field office on West Peachtree.

The FBI. What was the FBI doing here?

She thought about the file on Paul's computer. Had the FBI tracked the download? Was Fred Nolan here because Paul had stumbled across something he shouldn't have? What Claire had seen could not be real. It was a made-up movie designed to appeal to a sick fetish.

A sick fetish that, apparently, her husband had either stumbled across by mistake or kept hidden from her for the last eighteen years.

"Satisfied?" Nolan was still holding out his wallet. He was still smiling. He was still acting like this was a casual conversation.

Claire looked at the credentials again. Nolan had fewer gray hairs in the photograph. "Does the FBI routinely investigate foiled burglaries?"

"I've been doing this job long enough to know that nothing's routine." He flipped the wallet closed. "The gang who robbed your house crossed county lines. We're helping coordinate between the police forces."

"Isn't that the job of the Georgia Bureau of Investigation?"

"You're certainly up on your law enforcement hierarchy."

Claire had to put a stop to this before she gave everything away. "It's just occurred to me that you never answer my questions, Agent Nolan, so maybe I should stop answering yours."

Nolan chuckled. "I forgot you've had experience with the justice system."

"I'd like you to leave now."

"Sure." He indicated the door. "Open or closed?"

When she didn't answer, he closed the door behind him anyway.

Claire ran to the bathroom and threw up.

FOUR

Lydia tried to concentrate on the road as she drove her daughter to an away game. She had lasted twenty-four hours before the full impact of Paul Scott's death hit her. The hangover from her ensuing breakdown was breathtakingly awful. All day, she'd felt weepy and exhausted. Her head throbbed with every heartbeat. The coffee she'd gulped down to stave off the headache had made her fidgety. She hated the feeling of being punch-drunk and she hated it even more that her first thought when she opened her eyes this morning was that a bump of coke would even her out.

She wasn't going to give up seventeen and a half years of sobriety for that asshole. She would throw herself off a bridge before she did something so stupid.

But that didn't stop her from hating herself for even thinking of using. And it didn't stop her from crying like a baby last night.

She had wept in Rick's arms for over an hour. He'd been so

sweet to her, stroking her hair and telling her that she had every right to be upset. Instead of making her talk it out or driving her to a meeting, he'd put on John Coltrane and fried some chicken. The chicken was good. The company was better. They had started arguing about which was the best Coltrane solo, "Crescent" or "Blue in Green," and right in the middle of it Dee came out of her room and gave Lydia the greatest gift a teenage daughter can ever give her mother: She had agreed with her.

The cordiality had been short-lived.

Dee was currently slumped in the minivan's passenger seat in what Lydia thought of as her Phone Posture (automobile). Her sneakers were on the dashboard. Her elbows and forearms were flat to the seat like a kangaroo's feet. She held her iPhone two inches from her nose. The seatbelt would probably decapitate her if they were in an accident.

"OMG!" Dee would text as they waited for the ambulance. "Decapd in car ax!"

Lydia thought about all those times her own mother had told her to stand up straight, stop slouching, hold the book away from her face, moisturize, wear a bra to bed, always suck in her stomach, and never hitchhike, and she wanted to slap herself for not following every single stupid piece of advice that had ever come out of the woman's mouth.

Too late for that now.

Rain started to spit onto the windshield. Lydia turned on the wipers. The rubber part of the blades skittered across the glass. Rick had told her last week to come by the station and get the wiper blades changed. He'd said the weather was looking bad, and Lydia had laughed because no one could predict the weather.

Metal scraped glass as the shredded rubber flopped in the wind.

Dee groaned. "Why didn't you get Rick to change those?"

"He said he was too busy."

Dee gave her a sideways glance.

Lydia turned up the radio, which is how she used to fix strange car noises before she dated a mechanic. She shifted in the seat, trying to get comfortable. The seatbelt insistently pushed against her gut. The plump rolls of fat reminded her of a popped can of biscuits. This morning, Rick had gently suggested that she might want to go to a meeting. Lydia had agreed this was a good idea, but she'd ended up going to Waffle House instead.

She'd told herself that she wasn't ready to share what she was feeling because she hadn't had time to process Paul Scott's death. And then she reminded herself that one of her more unsung talents was that she was really, really good at denial. Maintaining a three-hundred-dollar-a-day coke habit took a certain level of self-delusion. Then there was the short-sighted conviction that she was never to blame for the consequences of her own actions.

The addict's credo: It's always somebody else's fault.

For a while, Paul Scott had been that fault for Lydia. Her touchstone. Her mantra. "If only Paul hadn't . . ." prefixed every excuse.

And then Dee had come along and Lydia had righted her life and she'd met Rick and Paul Scott had gotten shoved into the back of her mind the same way she had pushed back all the awful things that had happened during what she thought of as The Bad Years. Like the many times she'd found herself in county lock-up. Or the time she'd woken up with two skeevy guys in a Motel 8 and convinced herself that trading sex for drugs wasn't the same as doing it for money.

At the Waffle House this morning, she'd almost ignored Rick's call on her cell phone.

He had asked, "You feel like using?"

"No," she'd told him, because by then, the desire had been stifled by a tall stack of waffles. "I feel like I want to dig up Paul's body and kill him all over again."

The last time Lydia had seen Paul Scott, she was practically crawling out of her skin from withdrawal. They were in his stupid Miata that he cleaned every weekend with cloth diapers and a toothbrush. It was dark outside, almost midnight. Hall and Oates were playing on the radio. "Private Eyes." Paul was singing along. His voice was terrible, but then any noise had felt like an ice pick in her ear. He seemed to sense her discomfort. He smiled at Lydia. He leaned over and turned down the radio. And then he put his hand on her knee.

"Mom?"

Lydia looked over at her daughter. She feigned a double-take. "I'm sorry. Are you Dee? I didn't recognize you without a phone in front of your face."

Dee rolled her eyes. "You're not coming to my game because we suck, right, not because you're still mad about the permission slip?"

Lydia felt awful that her daughter could even think such a thing. "Honey, it's all about your poor performance. You're just too painful to watch."

"Okay, as long as you're sure."

"Positive. You are terrible."

"Question answered," Dee said. "But since we're being brutally honest, I have something else to tell you."

Lydia couldn't handle one more piece of bad news. She stared at the road thinking, *pregnant, failing biology, gambling debts, meth habit, genital warts.*

Dee said, "I don't want to be a doctor anymore."

Lydia felt her heart seize. Doctors had money. They had job security. They had 401(k)s and health insurance. "You don't have to decide anything right now."

"But, I kind of do because of the undergrad of it all." Dee slid her phone into her pocket. This was serious. "I don't want you to freak out or anything—"

Lydia started to freak out. *Sheep herder, farmer, actress, exotic dancer.*

"I was thinking I want to be a veterinarian."

Lydia burst into tears.

"Deedus Christ," Dee mumbled.

Lydia looked out the side window. She had been fighting tears off and on all day, but this time she wasn't upset. "My dad was a vet. I wanted to be a vet, but . . ." She let her voice trail off, because that's what you did when you were reminding your daughter that a felony drug conviction prevented you from being licensed in any state. "I'm proud of you, Dee. You'll be a great vet. You're so good with animals."

"Thanks." Dee waited for Lydia to blow her nose. "Also, when I go to college, I want to start using my real name."

Lydia had been expecting this, but she still felt sad. Dee was making a new start. She wanted a new name to go with it. She told her, "I went by the name 'Pepper' until I changed high schools."

"Pepper?" Dee laughed. "Like Salt-N-Pepa?"

"I wish. My dad said it came from my grandmother. The first time she looked after me, she said, 'That child has hell and pepper in her hair.'" Lydia saw this required further explanation. "I was a handful when I was a kid."

"Wow, you've really changed a lot."

Lydia poked her in the ribs. "Julia's the one who started calling me Pepper."

"Your sister?" Dee's head had turtled down her neck. Her voice sounded tentative.

"It's okay to talk about her." Lydia willed her lips to turn up into a smile, because talking about Julia was always hard. "Is there anything you want to know?"

Dee obviously wanted to know more than Lydia could tell her, but she asked, "Do you think you'll ever find her?"

"I don't know, sweetheart. It was a long time ago." Lydia rested her head in her hand. "We didn't really have DNA back then, or twenty-four-hour news cycles, or the Internet. One of the things they never found was her pager."

"What's a pager?"

"It's like text messaging, but you can only leave a phone number."

"That sounds stupid."

"Well." Maybe it sounded stupid to someone who could hold a tiny computer with access to the entire world's knowledge in her hand. "You look like her. Did you know that?"

"Julia was beautiful." Dee sounded dubious. "Like, really beautiful."

"You're really beautiful too, sweetheart."

"Whatever." Dee took out her phone, ending the conversation. She slowly sunk back into the Posture (automobile).

Lydia watched the wipers valiantly battle the rain. She was crying again, but not the humiliating, sobby cries that she'd been struggling against all morning. First Paul Scott and now Julia. Today was apparently her day to be overwhelmed by old memories. Though, admittedly, Julia was never far from Lydia's mind.

Twenty-four years ago, Julia Carroll had been a nineteen-year-old freshman at the University of Georgia. She was studying journalism, because in 1991 there was still such a thing as having a career as a journalist. Julia had gone to a bar with a group of friends. No one remembered a particular man paying closer attention to her than the others, but there must have been at least one, because that night at the bar was the last time anyone ever reported seeing Julia Carroll again.

Ever. They'd never even found her body.

This was why Lydia had raised a child who could change a flat tire in three minutes and who knew that you never, ever let an abductor take you to a second location: because Lydia had witnessed firsthand what can happen to teenage girls who are raised to think that the worst thing that can happen to them is they don't get asked to the prom.

"Mom, you missed the turn."

Lydia tapped the brakes. She checked the mirrors and backed up. A car swerved around her, horn blaring.

Dee's thumbs blurred across the bottom of her phone. "You're gonna end up killing yourself in a car accident and I'm gonna be an orphan."

Lydia had only herself to blame for this kind of hyperbole.

She drove around the school and pulled into a parking space in the back. Instead of the Valhalla that was the Westerly Intramural Sporting Complex, the gym behind Booker T. Washington High School in downtown Atlanta was a 1920s red-brick structure that more closely resembled the Triangle Shirtwaist Factory.

Lydia scanned the parking lot, because that's what she always did before she unlocked the doors.

"I'll get a ride home from Bella." Dee grabbed her gym bag off the back seat. "See you tonight."

"I need to go in."

Dee looked horrified by the prospect. "Mom, you said—"

"I need to go to the bathroom."

Dee got out of the car. "You pee all the time."

"Thank you for that." Between thirty-two hours of labor and the looming specter of menopause, Lydia was lucky her bladder wasn't hanging between her knees like a cow's udder.

She turned around to retrieve her purse from the back seat. Lydia stayed there, making sure Dee went into the building. And then she heard the click of the driver's-side door opening. Instinctively, Lydia swung around with her fists up, screaming, "No!"

"Lydia!" Penelope Ward had her arms over her head. "It's me!"

Lydia wondered if it was too late to punch her.

Penelope said, "Gosh, I didn't mean to scare you."

"I'm fine," Lydia lied. Her heart was down by her bladder. "I was just dropping off Dee. I can't talk right now. I have a funeral to go to."

"Oh, no. Whose?"

Lydia hadn't thought that far ahead. "A friend. An old teacher. Miss Clavel." She was really talking too much. "That's all there is. There isn't any more."

"Okay, but a quick word." Penelope was still blocking the open door. "Remember how I told you about the International Festival?"

Lydia bumped the gear into reverse. "Just send me whatever recipe you want and I'll—"

"Super! You'll have it by three o'clock today." Penelope was good about setting her own deadlines. "But, listen, are you still in touch with the band?"

Lydia edged her foot toward the gas.

"It jogged my memory when you said you grew up in Athens. I went to UGA."

Lydia should've guessed by the pastel sweater sets and blow-jobby pucker to her lips.

"I saw you perform a zillion times. Liddie and the Spoons, right? God, those were the days. Whatever happened to those gals? Probably ended up married with a ton of kids, am I right?"

"Yep." *If you mean incarcerated, divorced four times and keeping a punch card in her wallet from the Women's Health Center so she can get her tenth abortion for free.* "We're all just a bunch of old ladies."

"So," Penelope was still blocking the door, "you'll ask them, right? What a kick Dee would get out of seeing her mom on stage."

"Oh, she'd be thrilled. I'll email you about it, okay?" Lydia had to get out of here with or without the minivan door intact.

She eased her foot off the brake. Penelope walked alongside her. "Need to go now." Lydia motioned for her to get out of the way. "Need to close the door." She tapped her foot on the gas.

Finally, Penelope stepped back so she wouldn't get knocked down. "I look forward to receiving your email!"

Lydia hit the gas so hard that the minivan lurched. God, this really was her day to have her shitty past dredged up and thrown like a pile of steaming cow manure at her feet. She'd love to get Penelope Ward and the band together. They would eat her alive. Literally. The last time the Spoons had been in the same room together, two of them ended up in the hospital with severe bite marks.

Was that the first time Lydia had been arrested? It was definitely the first time her father had bailed her out of jail. Sam Carroll had been equal parts mortified and heartbroken. Of course, at that point in his life, there were very few pieces of his heart left that were big enough to shatter. Julia had been gone for five years by then. Her father had had five years of sleepless nights. Five years of suspended grief. Five years of filling his head with all the terrible things that might have been done to his eldest daughter.

"Daddy," Lydia sighed. She wished that he had lived long enough to see Lydia straightened out. She really wished that he'd met Dee. He would've loved her dry sense of humor. And maybe knowing Dee, holding his granddaughter in his arms, would've kept his poor, broken heart beating a few more years.

Lydia stopped at a red light. There was a McDonald's on the right. Lydia still needed to go to the bathroom, but she knew if she went inside, she'd order everything on the menu. She stared at the light until it turned. Her foot went to the gas.

Fifteen more minutes passed before she pulled into the Magnolia Hills Memorial Gardens. She'd told Penelope Ward that she was going to a funeral, but she felt more like she was going to a birthday party. Her birthday party. The Lydia who didn't have to worry about Paul Scott anymore was officially four days old.

She should've brought a hat.

The rain picked up as soon as Lydia stepped out of the van. She popped open the back and found an umbrella that would open. The hem of her dress wicked up rainwater. She scanned the cemetery, which was gardenlike and hilly with lots of magnolias, just as advertised. She pulled a sheet of paper out of her purse. Lydia loved the Internet. She could Google Earth the Mothers' houses, look up how much they'd paid for their idiotic designer outfits, and, more important to today's task, print out a map leading to Paul Scott's gravesite.

The walk was longer than she had anticipated, and of course the rain got worse the farther she got from her van. After ten minutes of following what turned out to be a very inaccurate map, Lydia realized she was lost. She took out her phone and Googled the information again. Then she tried to map her location. The flashing blue dot said she needed to go to the north. Lydia turned north. She walked a few feet and the blue dot indicated she needed to go south.

"For fucksakes," Lydia mumbled, but then her eye caught a headstone two rows over.

SCOTT.

Paul had grown up just outside of Athens, but his father's

people were from Atlanta. His parents were buried alongside Scotts going back several generations. He had once told Lydia that Scotts had even fought on both sides of the Civil War.

So, he came by his duplicity honestly.

Paul's grave had a tiny marker that looked more like a stake you'd use to label a vegetable garden. Sugar Snap Peas. Cabbage. Sadistic Prick.

Lydia supposed his headstone had been ordered. Something large and garish made of the finest marble and phallic-shaped because being dead didn't stop you from being a dick.

Last night while Lydia was watching TV with Rick, she had zoned out, picturing herself standing by Paul's grave. She hadn't anticipated the rain, so in her mind, the sun was happily shining in the sky and bluebirds sat on her shoulder. Likewise, she had never considered the freshly dug red Georgia clay would be covered by Astroturf. The fake grass was the kind of thing you saw at a putt-putt course or on the balcony of a cheap motel. Paul would've hated it, which is why she couldn't help smiling.

"Okay," Lydia said, because she hadn't come here to smile. She took a deep breath and slowly let it go. She pressed her hand to her chest to still her heart. And then she started talking.

"You were wrong," she told Paul, because he had been a pedantic asshole who thought he was right about everything. "You said I would be dead in a gutter by now. You said I was worthless. You said that no one would believe me because I didn't matter."

Lydia looked up at the dark sky. Drops of rain tapped insistently against the umbrella.

"And I believed you for so many years because I thought I'd done something wrong."

Thought, she repeated silently, because she knew that no one could punish her as viciously as she punished herself.

"I didn't lie. I didn't make it up. But I let myself think that you did it because I asked for it. That I'd sent you the wrong signals. That you only attacked me because you thought I wanted it." Lydia wiped tears from her eyes. She had never in her life wanted anything less than Paul's advances. "And then I finally realized that what you did wasn't my fault. That you were just a cold, psychotic motherfucker, and you found the perfect way to push me out of my own family." She wiped her nose with the back of her hand. "And you know what? Fuck you, Paul. Fuck you and your stupid piece-of-shit Miata and your Goddamn graduate degree and your blood money from your parents' car accident and look who's standing here now, asshole. Look who got gutted in an alley like a pig and look who's dancing on your fucking grave!"

Lydia was practically breathless from finally getting it all out. Her heart was pounding in her chest. She felt hollow, but not from her outburst. There had to be something else. For so many years, she'd dreamed of confronting Paul, taking him down, beating him with her fists or kicking him with her feet or stabbing him with a rusty knife. Words were not enough. There had to be something more to do than just scream at his grave. She looked out at the cemetery as if an idea would strike her like lightning. Rain was coming down so hard that the air had taken on a white haze. The ground was saturated.

Lydia dropped her umbrella.

The ground could probably be wetter.

Her bladder was still full. Nothing would give her greater pleasure than pissing on Paul's grave. She yanked back the green carpet. She hiked up her dress and bent over so she could pull down her underwear.

And then she stopped because she wasn't alone.

Lydia noticed the shoes first. Black Louboutins, approximately five thousand dollars. Sheer hose, though who the hell wore pantyhose anymore? Black dress, probably Armani or Gaultier, at least another six grand. There were no rings on the woman's elegant fingers nor a tasteful tennis bracelet on her birdlike wrists. Her shoulders were square and her posture was ramrod straight, which told Lydia that Helen's admonitions had been followed by at least one of her daughters.

"Well." Claire crossed her arms low on her waist. "This is awkward."

"It certainly is." Lydia hadn't seen her baby sister in eighteen years, though in her wildest imagination, she had never dreamed that Claire would turn into a Mother.

"Here." Claire snapped open her two-thousand-dollar Prada clutch and pulled out a handful of Kleenex. She tossed the tissues in Lydia's general direction.

There was no graceful way to do this. Lydia's underwear was down around her knees. "Do you mind turning around?"

"Of course. Where are my manners?" Claire turned around. The black dress was tailored to her perfect figure. Her shoulder blades stuck out like cut glass. Her arms were toned little sticks. She probably jogged with her trainer every morning and played tennis every afternoon and then bathed in rosewater milked from a magic unicorn before her husband came home every night.

Not that Paul Scott was ever coming home again.

Lydia pulled up her underwear as she stood. She blew her nose into the tissue, then dropped it on Paul's grave. She kicked the Astroturf back in place like a cat in a litter box.

"This was fun." Lydia grabbed her umbrella and made to leave. "Let's never do it again."

Claire spun around. "Don't you *dare* slink off."

"*Slink?*" The word was like a match to kindling. "You think I'm *slinking* away from you?"

"I *literally* stopped you from pissing on my husband's gave."

Lydia couldn't talk in italics anymore. "You'd better be glad I didn't take a shit."

"God, you're so crass."

"And you're a fucking bitch." Lydia turned on her heel and headed toward the van.

"Don't walk away from me."

Lydia cut between the graves because she knew Claire's heels would sink into the wet grass.

"Come back here." Claire was keeping up. She had taken off her shoes. "Lydia. God dammit, stop."

"What?" Lydia swung around so fast that the umbrella swiped Claire's head. "What do you want from me, Claire? You made your choice—you and Mom both. You can't just expect me to forgive you now that he's dead. It doesn't change anything."

"Forgive *me*?" Claire was so outraged that her voice trilled. "You think I'm the one who needs forgiveness?"

"I told you that your husband tried to rape me and your response was that I needed to get the fuck out of your house before you called the police."

"Mom didn't believe you either."

"*Mom didn't believe you either*," Lydia mocked. "Mom thought you were still a virgin in the eighth grade."

"You don't know a Goddamn thing about me."

"I know you chose a guy you'd been screwing for two seconds over your own sister."

"Was this before or after you stole all the cash from my wallet? Or from under my mattress? Or from my jewelry box? Or lied to me about 'borrowing' my car? Or told me you didn't pawn Daddy's stethoscope, but then Mom got a call from the pawnshop because they recognized his name?" Claire wiped rain out of her eyes. "I know it was before you stole my credit card and ran up thirteen grand in debt. How was Amsterdam, Lydia? Did you enjoy all the coffee shops?"

"I did, actually." Lydia still had the little canal house souvenir the KLM stewardess had given her in First Class. "How did you enjoy knowing you turned your back on the last sister you have left?"

Claire's mouth snapped into a thin line. Her eyes took on a heated gleam.

"God, you look just like Mom when you do that."

"Shut up."

"That's mature." Lydia could hear the immaturity in her own voice. "This is idiotic. We're having the same argument we had eighteen years ago, except this time we're doing it in the rain."

Claire looked down at the ground. For the first time, she seemed uncertain of herself. "You lied to me all the time about everything."

"You think I'd lie about *that*?"

"You were stoned out of your mind when he drove you home."

"Is that what Paul told you? Because he picked me up from jail. You're not usually stoned in jail. That's kind of a no-no."

"I've been to jail, Lydia. People who want to get high find a way to get high."

Lydia snorted a laugh. Her goody-two-shoes baby sister had been to jail like Lydia had been to the moon.

Claire said, "He wasn't even attracted to you."

Lydia studied her face. This was an old line of reasoning, but she was saying it with less conviction. "You're doubting him."

"No, I'm not." Claire pushed her wet hair back off her face. "You're just hearing what you want to hear. Like you always do."

Claire was lying. Lydia could feel it in her bones. She was standing there getting soaked in the rain and lying. "Did Paul hurt you? Is that what this is about? You couldn't say it when he was alive, but now—"

"He never hurt me. He was a good husband. A good man. He took care of me. He made me feel safe. He loved me."

Lydia didn't respond. Instead, she let the silence build. She still didn't believe her sister. Claire was just as easy to read now as when she was a little kid. Something was really bothering her, and that something obviously had to do with Paul. Her eyebrows were doing a weird zig, the same way Helen's did when she was upset.

They hadn't spoken in nearly two decades, but Lydia knew that confronting Claire always made her dig in her heels deeper. She tried a diversion. "Are you following this Anna Kilpatrick thing?"

Claire snorted, as if the answer was obvious. "Of course I am. Mom is, too."

"Mom is?" Lydia was genuinely surprised. "She told you that?"

"No, but I know she's following it." Claire took a deep breath, then let it go. She looked up at the sky. The rain had stopped. "She's not heartless, Lydia. She had her own way of dealing with it." She left the rest of the sentence unsaid. *Dad had his own way of dealing with it, too.*

Lydia busied herself with closing her umbrella. The canopy was white with various breeds of dogs jumping in circles around the ferrule. Her father had carried something similar back when he could still hold down his job teaching vet students at UGA.

Claire said, "I'm Mom's age now."

Lydia looked up at her sister.

"Thirty-eight. The same age Mom was when Julia went missing. And Julia would be—"

"Forty-three." Every year, Lydia marked Julia's birthday. And Helen's. And Claire's. And the day that Julia had disappeared.

Claire let out another shaky breath. Lydia resisted the urge to do the same. Paul hadn't just taken away Claire all those years ago. He'd taken away the connection that came from looking into someone else's eyes and knowing that they understood exactly what you were feeling.

Claire asked, "Did you have kids?"

"No," Lydia lied. "You?"

"Paul wanted to, but I was terrified of . . ."

She didn't have to put a name to the terror. If family planning was the sort of thing Lydia had been capable of in her twenties, there was no way in hell she would've had Dee. Watching how the loss of a child had pulled her parents apart—not just pulled them apart, but destroyed them—had been enough of a caution- ary tale.

Claire said, "Grandma Ginny has dementia. She's forgotten how to be mean."

"Do you remember what she said to me at Dad's funeral?"

Claire shook her head.

"'You're fat again. I guess that means you're not taking drugs.'"

Claire took in Lydia's shape, leaving the obvious question unspoken.

"Seventeen and a half years sober."

"Good for you." There was a catch in her voice. She was crying. Lydia suddenly realized that despite the designer outfit, her sister looked like hell. Her dress had obviously been slept in. She had a cut on her cheek. A black bruise was under her ear. Her nose was bright red. The rain had soaked her through. She was shivering from the cold.

"Claire—"

"I have to go." Claire started walking toward her car. "Take care of yourself, Pepper."

She left before Lydia could think of a reason for her not to.

iii.

The sheriff arrested me today. He said that I was interfering with his investigation. My defense—that I could not interfere with something that did not exist—left him unmoved.

Years ago, to help raise money for the local humane shelter, I volunteered myself to be pretend-arrested at the county fair. While you and your little sister were playing skee ball (Pepper was grounded for mouthing off to a teacher) all of us villains were held in a roped-off part of the fair while we waited for our significant others to bail us out.

This time, as with the pretend-time, your mother bailed me out.

"Sam," she said, "you can't keep doing this."

When she's anxious, your mother twists her new wedding ring around her finger, and every time I see this I can't help but feel she is trying to twist it off.

Have I ever told you just how much I love your mother? She is the most remarkable woman I have ever known. Your grandmother thought she was a gold-digger, though there was hardly a scrap of silver in my pocket when we first met. Everything she said and did delighted me. I loved the books she read. I loved the way her mind worked. I loved that she looked at me and saw something that I had only ever glimpsed in myself.

I would've given up without her—not on you, never on you, but on myself. I suppose I can tell you this now, but I wasn't a very good student. I wasn't smart enough to just get by. I wasn't focused enough in class. I rarely passed exams. I skipped assignments. I was constantly on academic probation. Not that your grandmother would ever know, but at the time, I was thinking of doing what you were later accused of doing: selling all my belongings, sticking out my thumb, and hitchhiking to California to be with the other hippies who had dropped out and tuned in.

Everything changed when I met your mother. She made me want things that I had never dreamed of wanting: a steady job, a reliable car, a mortgage, a family. You figured out a long time ago that you got your wanderlust from me. I want you to know that this is what happens when you meet the person you are supposed to spend the rest of your life with: That restless feeling dissolves like butter.

I think what breaks my heart the most is that you will never learn that for yourself.

I want you to know that your mother has not forgotten you. Not a morning passes that she does not wake up thinking about you. She marks your birthdays in her own way. Every March 4, the anniversary of your disappearance, she walks the same path you might have walked when you left the Manhattan Cafe that night. She leaves a nightlight burning in your old room. She refuses to sell the house on Boulevard, because, despite her protests, she still holds out the slim hope that one day, you might come walking back up the sidewalk and find your way home.

"I want to feel normal again," she once told me. "Maybe if I pretend I am long enough, it might actually happen."

Your mother is one of the strongest, smartest women I have ever met, but losing you cleaved her in two. The vibrant, caustic, witty, contrary woman I married splintered off into silence. She would tell you she gave in to mourning you for too long, let the pity and self-hate drag her into that black pit that I still crawl around in. If she did, her stay there was temporary. Somehow, she managed to wrench a piece of her former self out of the ground. She tells me that the other, miserable half, the chipped-off, cast-off half, still follows at a respectful distance, ready to take over the second she stumbles.

Only through sheer strength of will does she manage to never stumble.

When your mother told me she was marrying another man, she said, "I can't sacrifice the two daughters I have left for the one that I'll never see again."

She didn't say that she loved this man. She didn't say that he moved her, or that she needed him. She said that she needed the things that he could offer: stability, companionship, a glass of wine at night without the drowning sense of sorrow.

I do not resent this other man for taking my place. I do not hate him because I do not want your sisters to hate him. It is remarkably easy for a divorced parent to make remarriage a smooth transition for his or her children. You just keep your mouth shut and let them know that everything is going to be all right.

And I really feel that it will be—at least for the remaining part of my family.

Your mother has always been a good judge of character. This man she chose is kind to your sisters. He goes to Pepper's riotous, perplexing concerts and pays attention to Claire. I cannot begrudge him attending PTA meetings and carving pumpkins and putting up Christmas trees. They visit your sisters once a month in Auburn (I know, sweetheart, but they couldn't go to UGA because it reminded them too much of you). I cannot blame your mother for moving on while I stayed rooted in the past. I have widowed her. I would just as soon ask her to stay with me as I would ask her to lay with me in my grave.

I suppose the sheriff called her to bail me out because left to my own devices, I would've stayed in the cell until he was forced to either arraign me or let me go. I was trying to make a point. Your mother agreed, if I meant that the point I was making was that I am a stubborn asshole.

You of all people will know that this exchange means that she still loves me.

But she has also made it clear that this is it for her. She no longer wants to hear about my wild goose chases or my crazy searches or my meeting strangers in dark corners and interrogating young women who knew you back then but are now married and gainfully employed and trying to start families of their own.

Should I fault her for this? Should I blame her for giving up on my windmills?

Here is why I was arrested:

There is a man who works at the Taco Stand. He's the manager now, but he was bussing tables the day you disappeared. The sheriff's men cleared his alibi, but one of your friends, Kerry Lascala, told me that she'd overheard this man at a party talking about how he saw you on the street the night of March 4, 1991.

Any father would seek out this man. Any father would follow him down the street, let him know what it felt like to have someone behind you who was stronger and angrier and had an agenda that involved taking you somewhere more private.

Which sounds like harassment, but feels like investigating a crime.

Your mother pointed out that the Taco man could hire a lawyer. That the next time the huckleberries come, it could be with a warrant.

Huckleberries.

This was one of your mother's words. She gave Sheriff Carl Huckabee the nickname during the third week of the investigation, and by the third month, she had extrapolated it to everyone in uniform. You might remember the sheriff from that day at the carnival. He is a clumsy Barney Fife type with a stiff mustache he keeps trimmed in a straight line and sideburns he grooms so often you can see the furrows left by the teeth of his comb.

This is what Huckleberry believes: The Taco man was with his grandmother at her nursing home the night you went missing.

There was no sign-in sheet at the front desk. No log. No cameras. No other witnesses but his grandmother and a nurse who checked the old woman's catheter around eleven that evening.

You were last seen at 10:38 p.m.

The nurse claims that the Taco man was asleep in the chair beside his grandmother's bed when you were taken.

And yet, Kerry Lascala says that she heard him say otherwise.

Your mother would call this kind of thinking crazy-making, and maybe she's right. I no longer tell your sisters about my leads. The Taco man, the garbage man who was arrested for flashing a grade-schooler, the gardener peeping Tom, the night manager at the 7-Eleven who was caught molesting his niece, are all strangers to them. I have moved my collection of clues into the bedroom so they won't see it when they visit.

Not that they visit much, though I cannot blame them. They are young women now. They are building their lives. Claire is around the same age as you were when we lost you. Pepper is older, though not wiser. I see her making so many mistakes (the drugs, the uncaring and unavailable boyfriends, the anger that burns so hot she could light an entire city), but I feel like I don't have the authority to stop her.

Your mother says that all we can do is be there for Pepper when she falls. Maybe she's right. And maybe she's right to be worried about this new man in Claire's life. He tries too hard. He pleases too much. Is it our place to tell her? Or will she figure it out on her own? (Or will he? She has your Grandma Ginny's wandering eye.)

It's strange that your mother and I are only ever whole when we talk about your sisters' lives. We are both of us too wounded to talk about our own. The open sores of our hearts fester if we are together too long. I know your mother looks at me and sees play-houses I built and touch-football games I played and homework I helped with and the millions of times I lifted you in my arms and swung you around like a doll.

Just as when I look at her I see the growing swell of her belly, the gentle look on her face when she rocked you to sleep, the panic in her eyes when your fever spiked and you had to have your tonsils out, and the vexed expression she would get when she realized that you had out-argued her.

I know that your mother belongs to another man now, that she has created a stable life for my children, that she has managed to move on, but when I kiss her, she never resists. And when I hold her, she holds me back. And when we make love, it is my name she whispers.

In that moment, we are finally able to remember all of the good things we had together instead of everything that we have lost.

FIVE

Claire was still soaking wet from her graveside confrontation with Lydia. She sat shivering in the middle of the garage holding a broken tennis racket in her hand. Her weapon of choice. It was the fourth tennis racket she had broken in as many minutes. There wasn't a cabinet or a tool or a car in the garage that hadn't met the hard edge of a graphite tennis racket. Bosworth Tennis Tour 96s, custom designed to Claire's stroke. Four hundred bucks a pop.

She rolled her wrist, which was going to need ice. The hand was already showing a bruise. Her throat was raw from screaming. She stared at her reflection in the side mirror dangling from Paul's Porsche. Her wet hair was plastered to the shape of her skull. She was wearing the same dress she'd worn to the funeral yesterday afternoon. Her waterproof mascara had finally given up the ghost. Her lipstick had long been chewed off. Her skin was sallow.

She could not remember the last time she had lost her shit like this. Even on the day she'd ended up in jail, Claire had not lost this volume of shit.

She closed her eyes and breathed in the silence of the large room. The BMW's engine was cooling. She could hear it clicking. Her heart was giving six beats for every one click. She put her hand to her chest and wondered if it was possible for your heart to explode.

Last night, Claire had gone to bed expecting nightmares, but instead of dreaming about being chained to a concrete wall, the masked man coming for her, Claire's brain had given her something far worse: a highlight reel of some of her most tender moments with Paul.

The time she'd twisted her ankle in St. Martin and he'd driven all over the island looking for a doctor. The time he'd scooped her up with the intention of carrying her upstairs, but because of his bad back ended up making love to her on the landing. The time she'd woken up from knee surgery to find a smiley face drawn on the bandage around her leg.

Could the man who still, almost twenty years into their marriage, left notes on her coffee cup with an actual heart with their initials inside really be the same man who'd downloaded that movie onto his computer?

Claire looked down at the broken racket. So much money, and the sad truth was that she really preferred a sixty-dollar Wilson.

Back when she and Paul were students, they always made lists when they couldn't figure out what to do. Paul would get a ruler and draw a line down the center of the page. On one side they would list reasons they should do something, buy something, try something, and on the other side they would write the reasons not to.

Claire pulled herself up to standing. She tossed the racket onto the Porsche's hood. Paul kept a notepad and pen on his workbench. She drew a line down the center of a blank page. Paul would've broken out into a sweat over that line. It veered to the left toward the bottom. The pen had skipped off the page, curling up the edge.

Claire tapped the pen on the side of the bench. She stared at the two empty columns. There were no pros and cons. This list was for questions and answers.

The first question was: Had Paul really downloaded the movie? Claire had to assume that he had. Accidentally downloading files with viruses and spyware was Claire's thing. Paul was too careful to accidentally download anything. And if by some off chance he had downloaded the movie by mistake, he would've deleted the file rather than storing it in his Work folder. And he would've told Claire about it, because that's the kind of relationship they had.

Or at least it was the kind of relationship she'd thought they'd had.

She wrote the word "Accident?" in one column and "No" in the other.

Claire started tapping the pen again. Could it be that Paul had downloaded the movie for the sado-masochism, then not realized until he got to the end that it was more than that?

She shook her head. Paul was so straitlaced that he tucked his undershirt into his boxers before he went to bed at night. If someone had told her last week that her husband was into SM, after she choked down her laughter, Claire would have assumed that Paul would be a bottom. Not that he was passive in their sex life. Claire was the one more likely to just lie there. But sexual fantasies were projections of opposites. Paul was in control all of the time, so his fantasy would be to let someone else take over. Claire certainly had daydreams about being tied up and ravished by a stranger, but in the cold light of day, that sort of thing was terrifying.

And besides that, a few years ago when she'd read Paul several passages from *Fifty Shades of Grey*, they'd both giggled like teenagers.

"The biggest fantasy in that book," Paul had said, "is that he changes for her in the end."

Claire had never thought of herself as an expert in male behavior, but Paul had a point, and not just about men. People did not change their basic, core personalities. Their values tended to stay the same. Their personal demeanors. Their world outlook and political beliefs. One need only go to a high school reunion to verify the theory.

So, going by this, it made no sense that the man who had cried when their cat had to be put down, who refused to watch scary movies, who joked that Claire was on her own if an ax murderer ever broke into the house, would be the same man who derived sexual pleasure from watching horrible, unspeakable acts.

Claire looked down at the notepad. She wrote, "More files?" Because that was the dark thought lurking in the back of her mind. The file name had been a series of numbers, and all of the files she'd seen in the Work folder were similarly numbered. Had Paul downloaded more of these disgusting movies? Was that how he spent his time when he told Claire he'd be working late in his office?

She wasn't a Pollyanna about these things. She knew men watched pornography. Claire herself wasn't adverse to the soft-core sex of a pay-cable show. The thing was that their sex life had been fairly tame. They'd tried different positions or variations on a theme, but after eighteen years, they knew what worked and they stuck with the old standards. Which was likely why Claire had ended up taking Adam Quinn up on his offer last year at the company Christmas party.

Claire loved her husband, but sometimes, she craved variety.

Was Paul the same? She had never considered the possibility that she wasn't enough for him. He had always been so smitten with her. Paul was the one who reached down to hold her hand in the car. He was the one who sat close to her at dinners and put his arm around her at movies and watched her cross the room at parties. Even in bed, he was never pleased until she was. He rarely asked Claire to use her mouth on him, and he was never an asshole about it. Back when she still had friends, they had jealously teased her about Paul's devotion.

Had that been for show? Through all the seemingly happy years of their marriage, had Paul yearned for something more? And did he find that something more in the disgusting contents of that movie?

Claire wrote down another question: "Is it real?"

The production had an amateurish feel, but that could've been on purpose. Computers were capable of amazing things. If they could make it look like Michael Jackson was dancing on stage, they could make it look like a woman was being murdered.

The pen was tapping again. Claire watched it bounce between her fingers. The workbench top was bamboo. The damn thing had proven to be indestructible. She'd been half tempted to take a page from Lydia's book and piss all over it.

Lydia.

God, what an unexpected slap in the face to see her sister after all these years. She would not be telling her mother about the meeting, mostly because Helen had enough to fret over between Paul's murder and the burglary. Besides, the irony was not lost on Claire that less than a year after her family broke ties, Lydia had finally managed to get herself clean. Between looking for Julia and paying bail bondsmen and lawyers and rehab clinics for Lydia's upkeep, Sam Carroll had been nearly bankrupt when he'd finally taken his life.

For that sin alone, Claire should've cut off her sister, but then she'd accused Paul of trying to rape her, and that had been the final straw.

Did Paul hurt you? Lydia had asked, standing less than ten yards from Paul's grave. *Is that what this is about?*

Claire knew what the "this" was. It was doubt. She was doubting her husband because of what she'd found on his computer. Her mind had made the leap from Paul watching violence to actually committing it, which was a stupid connection because millions of young men played violent video games but only a handful went on spree killings.

Then again, Paul had once told her that there was no such thing as coincidence. "The Law of Truly Large Numbers provides that given a large enough sample size, any outrageous thing can happen."

Claire looked down at the three items on her list:

Accident?

More files?

Is it real?

At the moment, only one of those outrageous questions could be answered.

Claire went up the stairs before she could stop herself. She keyed in the code to open the door to Paul's office. Agent Nolan had made a comment about all the codes needed for the house, but Paul had made it easy for Claire by making all the door codes a variation on their birthdays.

The office looked the same as it had been the day before. Claire sat down at the desk. She hesitated as she reached out to tap the keyboard. This was a red pill/blue pill moment. Did she really want to know if there were more files? Paul was dead now. What was the point?

She tapped the keyboard. The point was that she had to know.

Claire's hand was surprisingly steady as she moved the mouse to the dock and clicked on the Work folder.

The rainbow wheel spun, but instead of a list of files, a white box popped up.

CONNECT TO GLADIATOR?

There was a YES and NO button underneath. Claire wondered why she hadn't been prompted to log in the day before. She had a vague recollection of clicking CLOSE on several messages yesterday when Agent Nolan was creeping his way up the stairs. Apparently, one of the things she'd closed was the connection to whatever this Gladiator was.

She leaned her elbows on the desk and stared at the words.

Was this a sign that she should stop? Paul had trusted her completely—too completely, going by her affairs, because of course Adam Quinn wasn't the first. Or the last, since she was being brutally honest; there was a reason Tim the bartender was estranged from his wife.

She tried to summon yesterday's crushing guilt, but the remorse had been sanded down by the rough images she'd found on her husband's computer.

"Gladiator," Claire said. She didn't know why the word sounded familiar.

She rolled the mouse over and clicked on the YES button.

The screen changed. A new message popped up: PASSWORD?

"Fuck." How much harder was this going to get? She tapped her finger on the mouse as she stared at the prompt.

All of the system passwords were a combination of mnemonics and dates. She typed in YALAPC111176, which stood for "You Are Looking At Paul's Computer," followed by his birthday.

A black triangle with an exclamation point in the center told her that the password was incorrect.

Claire tried a few more variations, using her birthday, their wedding anniversary, the date they first met in the computer lab, the date they first went out, which was also the same day they'd first had sex because Claire never played hard to get when she'd made up her mind.

Nothing worked.

She looked around Paul's office, wondering if she was missing something.

"You Are Looking At The Chair Where Paul Reads," she tried. "You Are Looking At The Couch Where Paul Naps." Nothing.

"You Are Looking At The Computer Where Paul Jerks Off."

Claire slumped back in the chair. Directly across from Paul's desk was the painting she had given him for their third wedding anniversary. Claire had painted it herself from a photograph of his childhood home. Paul's mother had taken the picture standing in their back yard. The picnic table was set with birthday decorations. Claire wasn't good with faces, so a tiny blob represented a young Paul sitting at the table.

He'd told her that the farmer who'd bought the Scott land had torn down the house and all the surrounding structures. Claire couldn't blame the man. The house had a home-built look to it, the wooden paneling ran up and down instead of left to right. The barn in the back yard loomed like the *Amityville Horror* house. It cast such a dark shadow over the picnic table and old well house that Claire had been forced to guess the colors. Paul had told her she'd gotten them exactly right, though she was fairly certain the little structure over the well should've been green instead of black.

Claire typed some more guesses into the computer, speaking aloud so she could get the first letters of each word in the correct order. "You Are Looking At Claire's Painting." "You Are Looking At The House Where Paul Grew Up." "You Are Looking At An Old Well House That Should Be Green."

Claire slammed the keyboard tray back into the desk. She was angrier than she'd thought. And realizing she was angry made her realize where she'd seen the word Gladiator.

"Idiot," she whispered. Paul's workbench had a giant metal logo on the side that said GLADIATOR, the company that had custom-made the piece. "You Are Looking At Paul's Workbench."

Claire added Paul's birth date, then pressed enter.

The drive connected. The Work files came up.

Claire's hand stayed still on the mouse.

Helen had told her a long time ago that knowing the truth wasn't always a good thing. She had been talking about Julia, because that was all her mother was capable of talking about back then. She would stay in bed for weeks, sometimes months, mourning the unexplained disappearance of her oldest child. Lydia had taken over the parenting for a while, and when Lydia had checked out, Grandma Ginny had moved in and terrorized them all into shape.

Would Helen want to know where Julia was now? If Claire handed her mother an envelope and inside was the story of exactly what had happened to Julia, would she open it?

Claire sure as hell would.

She clicked on the second file in the Work folder, which, according to the date, Paul had watched the same night as the first. The same woman from the first movie was chained in the same way to the same wall. Claire took in the details of the room. She was definitely looking at an older basement. It was nothing like the pristine, smoothly formed walls in Paul's dream basement. The cinderblock wall behind the woman looked dank and wet. There was a stained mattress on the concrete floor. The trash came from fast-food restaurants. Old wires and galvanized pipe hung from the ceiling joists.

Claire turned the sound back on, but low. The woman was whimpering. A man entered the frame. Claire recognized him as the same man from the other movie. Same mask. Same tight leather briefs. He wasn't hard yet. Instead of a machete, he had an electric cattle prod in his hand. Claire waited until he was about to use it, then she paused the movie.

She sat back in the chair. The man was frozen. His arm was out. The woman was shrinking away. She knew what was coming.

Claire closed the movie. She went back to the files and opened the third one from the top. Same woman. Same set-up. Same man. Claire studied his naked back. She didn't tell herself why until she confirmed there was no constellation of moles under his left shoulder blade, which meant that the man could not be Paul.

The relief was so overwhelming that she had to close her eyes and just breathe for a few minutes.

Claire opened her eyes. She closed the movie. The file names were in sequences, so she gathered there were ten more files of the woman in various scenes of torture before the death shot. According to their dates, Paul had watched them all the night before he'd died. They were each around five minutes, which meant he'd spent almost an hour watching the vile images.

"No way," Claire mumbled. She was lucky if Paul lasted more than ten minutes. Was he watching these movies for something other than sexual pleasure?

She scrolled down to the next sequence of files. There were only five in this series. Paul had watched the first one ten days ago, the next was nine days ago, and so on until the night before Paul had died. She clicked open the most recent movie. Another girl. This one even younger. Her long, dark hair covered her face. Claire leaned in closer. The girl was pulling at the restraints. She turned her head to the side. Her hair fell away. Her eyes went wide with fear.

Claire paused the movie. She didn't want to see the man again.

There was another question she should've put on the list: *Is this legal?*

Obviously, that all depended on whether or not it was real. If the police could arrest you for watching fake gore, every cinema in America would be part of a sting operation.

But what if Paul's movies *were* real?

Agents from the FBI didn't just show up at burglaries for no reason. When Julia first went missing, Helen and Sam had raised hell trying to get the FBI involved, but it was explained to them that by law, a state agency had to request federal help before the feds could review the case. Given that the sheriff thought Julia had run off in a fit of rebellion, there had been no request sent up the chain.

Claire opened the web browser and pulled up the FBI's home page. She went to the FAQs. She scrolled through questions about all the various crimes the agency investigated until she found what she was looking for.

Computer-related crime: In the national security area, the FBI investigates criminal matters involving the nation's computerized banking and financial systems. Examples of criminal acts would be using a computer to commit fraud or using the Internet to transmit obscene material.

Claire had no doubt these movies were obscene. Maybe she'd been right about Agent Fred Nolan yesterday. The FBI had tracked the downloaded files to Paul's computer. Claire had seen a *60 Minutes* story where a government whistleblower had said connecting your computer to the Internet was tantamount to jacking yourself directly into the NSA. They probably knew that Paul had looked at the movies.

Which meant that they knew that Claire was looking at them, too.

"Jesus!" The Mac was hardwired to the Internet. She grabbed at the cords plugged into the back of the computer. She yanked on the cables so hard that the monitor twisted around. Thin wires stripped away from the plastic plug, severing the Internet connection. Claire nearly passed out with relief. Her heart was beating so hard that she could feel it in her neck.

Her parole officer had made it clear that he would send her to jail for even the smallest violation. Was it illegal to look at these movies? Had Claire broken the law without even realizing?

Or had she overreacted like an idiot?

She turned the monitor back around. All of the web pages said she was not connected to the Internet. The movies were still frozen on-screen. Another error message had popped up.

WARNING! DISK "GLADIATOR" NOT PROPERLY EJECTED. SOME FILES MAY HAVE BEEN LOST.

Claire looked at all the cables she had unplugged. She wasn't completely ignorant about computers. She knew that movie files were large and required a lot of storage. She knew that the lightning symbol on the back of the computer was for a Thunderbolt connection, which transferred data twice as fast as USB.

She also knew her husband.

Claire knelt down on the floor. Paul had designed his desk so that all the cables were concealed inside. Everything electrical, from the computer to the desk lamp, connected into a battery back-up tucked inside the desk. She knew the large black box was the battery back-up because Paul had labeled it: BATTERY BACK-UP.

She pulled out the drawers and checked inside and behind them. There didn't appear to be an external hard drive inside the desk. The power cord for the back-up was concealed inside the front right desk leg. The plug came out at the bottom and connected to a floor outlet.

Nothing was labeled GLADIATOR.

Claire pushed on the desk. Instead of the whole thing rolling straight back, it went lopsided, like an excited dog wagging its entire butt. There was another cable threaded through another leg. It was white and thin, the same as the Thunderbolt cable that she'd yanked out of the back of the computer. That end was still on top of the desk. The other end disappeared into a hole drilled into the hardwood floor.

She went downstairs into the garage. Paul's Gladiator work-bench took up an entire wall. Smaller rolling cabinets with drawers were on either side with an open span of about ten feet in between. Claire pulled out all of the cabinets. No stray cables trailed from the back of the drawers. She looked underneath the bench. Claire had driven into the garage thousands of times, but she'd never noticed that the diamond-plate paneling behind the bench wasn't the same paneling that was on the wall. She pressed against the metal and the sheet flexed under her hand.

Claire stood up. Thanks to her tennis racket, Paul's 3-D printer and CAD laser cutter were in pieces strewn across the bamboo worktop. She swept them onto the floor with her arm. She turned off the lights. She leaned over the workbench and looked down though the narrow crack between the bench and the wall. She started at the far left end. At what she knew was the exact center, she saw a flashing green light behind the workbench.

She turned the lights back on. She found a flashlight in one of the rolling cabinets. The workbench was too heavy to move, and even without that, it was bolted to the floor. She leaned back over the bench and saw that the green flashing light was on a large external hard drive.

None of this was an accident. Claire couldn't come up with any good excuses. This set-up had been designed into the house when it was built eight years ago. Paul hadn't just watched those movies. He had collected them. And he had gone to great lengths to make sure that no one found them.

Tears filled her eyes. Were the movies real? Could she possibly have evidence of the torture and killing of perhaps dozens of women?

Yesterday, Fred Nolan had asked Claire about Paul's demeanor before he died. For the first time since it happened, Claire let herself consider what her own demeanor had been. She was shocked when Paul pulled her into that alley. Excited when he made it clear what he wanted to do. Thrilled when he'd been so forceful, because it was sexy and completely unexpected.

And then what?

Claire knew she'd been terrified when she realized they were being robbed. Had she been scared before that? When Paul spun her around and crushed her against the wall, hadn't she been a little afraid? Or was she revising her memory because the way he'd kicked her legs apart and pinned her wrists to the wall was oddly reminiscent of the spreadeagled young girls in the movies?

Those poor creatures. If the movies were real, then Claire owed it to their families to do everything she could to make sure they knew what had happened to them. Or what might happen, because there was the slim possibility that the young girl in the second movie was still alive.

Claire moved quickly because she knew that if she stopped to think about it, she would do the wrong thing.

Paul always bought two of everything for the computers. There was an extra twenty-terabyte hard drive in the garage basement. Claire leveraged the heavy box off the shelf and lugged it up to the office. She followed the directions to set up the drive using the computer, then she plugged in the Gladiator cable. She highlighted all of the files and dragged them to the new drive.

DO YOU WANT TO COPY GLADIATOR ONTO LACIE 5BIG?

Claire clicked YES.

The rainbow wheel started spinning as the computer calculated the amount of time it would take to transfer all of the files. Fifty-four minutes. She sat down at Paul's desk and watched the progress bar inching across the screen.

Claire looked at the anniversary painting again. She thought about Paul as a child. She'd seen pictures—his winsome, toothy grin; the way his ears poked out from his giant head when he was six and seven; the way everything started to catch up when puberty hit. He wasn't dashing or flashy, but he was handsome once she'd talked him into wearing contacts and buying nice suits. And he was funny. And he was charming. And he was so damn smart that she just assumed he knew the answer to everything.

If only he were here now to answer her questions about this.

Claire's eyes blurred. She was crying again. She continued crying until the message came up that all the files had been successfully copied.

A toppled cabinet was blocking her BMW. She drove Paul's Tesla because it was getting dark and the Porsche's headlights were shattered. Claire did not question herself about what she was doing until she pulled into the parking lot in front of the Dunwoody police station. The hard drive was belted into the seat beside her. The white aluminum box weighed at least twenty pounds. The passenger airbag had turned off because the sensors assumed a toddler was in the seat.

Claire looked up at the police station, which resembled a 1950s office supply store. Fred Nolan was probably the person she should be giving this to, but yesterday, Nolan had been an asshole to Claire, and Mayhew had basically told him to shut the fuck up, so she was going to give it to Captain Mayhew.

Did she trust him to take this seriously? Unlike Fred Nolan, Claire had not gotten a clear vibe off Captain Mayhew, other than to think that he looked like a cop out of central casting. His mustache had thrown her off because Sheriff Carl Huckabee, the original Huckleberry, had sported an impotent-looking mustache that he kept trimmed in a straight line rather than grooming it to follow the natural curve of his upper lip. Claire had been thirteen the first time she'd met the man. She could still recall looking up at the strange pushbroom over his lip and wondering if it was fake.

Which mattered not one bit in her current situation, because facial hair was not a universal indicator of incompetency.

She looked down at the hard drive in the seat beside her.

Red pill/blue pill.

Mayhew wasn't the concern here. It was Claire. It was Paul's reputation. There was no such thing as anonymity anymore. This would get out. People would know what her husband was into. Maybe people already did.

And maybe the movies were real, which meant that the second girl might still be alive.

Claire forced herself to get out of the car. The hard drive felt heavier than before. Night was falling fast. Thunder rumbled in the distance. The overhead lights came on as Claire walked across the parking lot. Her funeral dress had dried, but it was stiff and chafing. Her jaw hurt from grinding her teeth. The last time she was at the Dunwoody police station, she was in a tennis dress and being escorted in through the back doors.

This time she found herself in an extremely narrow front lobby with a large piece of bulletproof glass separating visitors from the office area. The receptionist was a burly man in uniform who didn't look up when Claire entered.

She put the hard drive down on an empty chair. She stood in front of the window.

The burly officer reluctantly looked up from his computer. "Who're you here to see?"

"Captain Mayhew."

The name elicited an immediate frown. "He's busy, ma'am."

Claire hadn't expected this. "I need to leave this for him." She pointed to the hard drive, wondering if it looked like a bomb. It sure as hell felt like one. "Maybe I can write a note explaining—"

"Lee, I got this." Captain Mayhew was standing behind the glass. He waved for Claire to go to a side door. There was a buzzing sound, then the door opened. Instead of seeing just Mayhew, she found Mayhew and Adam Quinn.

"Claire." Adam seemed tense. "I didn't get that email."

"I'm sorry." Claire had no idea what he was talking about. "What email?"

"The work-in-progress file from Paul's laptop."

Paul's laptop. God only knew what he had on the MacBook. "I don't—"

"Just get it to me." Adam walked past her and out the door.

She stared at his back long after he'd gone. She didn't understand why he seemed so angry.

Mayhew told Claire, "Guy does not like being in a police station."

Claire suppressed the first response that came to mind: *Who the hell does?*

Mayhew said, "We're talking to everybody who has a key to your house."

Claire had forgotten Adam was on the list. He and his wife Sheila lived five streets over. He checked on the house when Claire and Paul were out of the country.

Mayhew asked, "What can I do you for, Mrs. Scott?"

"I have something you need to see." She started to lift the hard drive.

"I got that." Obviously, he wasn't expecting the box to be so heavy. He almost dropped it. "Whoa. What is this thing?"

"It's a hard drive." Claire felt herself getting flustered. "It was my husband's. I mean, my husband—"

"Let's go back to my office."

Claire tried to pull herself together as she followed him down a long corridor with closed doors on each side. She recognized the open area for processing prisoners. Then there was another long corridor, then they were in an open office space. There were no cubicles, just five desks with five men all hunched over their computers. Two rolling whiteboards were at the front of the room. All were filled with photographs and scribbled notes that were too far away to make out.

Mayhew stopped outside his office door. "After you."

Claire sat down. Mayhew put the drive on his desk, then took a seat.

She stared at him. More to the point, she stared at his mustache so that she wouldn't have to look him in the eye.

He asked, "Do you want something to drink? Water? Coke?"

"No, thank you." Claire couldn't drag this out any longer. "There are movies on that drive of women being tortured and murdered."

Mayhew paused for a moment. Slowly, he sat back in his chair. He rested his elbows on the arms, folded his hands together in front of his stomach. "Okay."

"I found them on my husband's computer. Well, hooked up to my husband's computer. An external hard drive that I found—" She stopped to catch her breath. He didn't need to know the lengths Paul had gone to in order to hide the movies. He just needed to know that they were there. Claire pointed to the hard drive. "That has movies that my husband watched of two different women being tortured and killed."

The words hung between them. Claire could hear how awful they sounded.

She said, "I'm sorry. I just found them. I'm still . . ." She didn't know what she still was. Shaken? Grieving? Furious? Terrified? Alone?

"Just a sec." Mayhew picked up the phone and punched in an extension. "Harve, I need you in here."

Before Claire could open her mouth again, another man came into the room. He was a shorter, wider version of Mayhew but with the same type of shaggy mustache.

Mayhew said, "Detective Harvey Falke, this is Mrs. Claire Scott."

Harvey gave Claire a nod.

Mayhew said, "Hook this up for me, will ya?"

Harvey looked at the back of the drive, then he looked at the back of Mayhew's computer. He opened one of the desk drawers. There was a tangle of cables inside. He fished out the one he needed.

Mayhew asked Claire, "Sure you don't want some water? Coffee?"

Claire shook her head. She was scared that he wasn't taking her seriously. She was also scared that he was. They were down the rabbit hole now. There was no turning back.

Harvey made quick work of the connections. He leaned past Mayhew and started typing on the keyboard.

Claire looked around the room. Mayhew posed in the requisite framed photos of him shaking hands with city officials. A golfing trophy for the police league. Numbers from various marathons. She looked at the plaque on his desk. His first name was Jacob. Captain Jacob Mayhew.

Harvey said, "There ya go."

"Thanks." Mayhew turned the keyboard back around as Harvey left the room. He straightened the mouse, then clicked on one of the files. "Let's see what we've got here."

Claire knew what he had. She looked away while he clicked open a handful of movies and watched them. The sound on his computer was turned off. All she could hear was Mayhew's steady breathing. She supposed you didn't get to the rank of captain by being surprised by what humanity could throw at you.

Several minutes passed. Finally, Mayhew let go of the mouse. He settled back in his chair again. He pulled at his mustache. "Well, I wish I could tell you I haven't seen stuff like this before. Much worse, being honest."

"I can't believe . . ." Claire could not articulate the things she could not believe.

"Listen, ma'am, I know it's shocking. Trust me. The first time I saw this kind of stuff, I couldn't sleep for weeks, even though I knew it was fake."

Claire felt her heart leap. "It's fake?"

"Well, yeah." He stopped mid-chuckle. "It's called snuff porn. It's not real."

"Are you sure?"

He turned the monitor so she could see for herself. One of the movies was frozen on-screen. He pointed out, "See this shadow here? That's the connection for the squib. Do you know what a squib is?"

Claire shook her head.

"It's a Hollywood thing, like a little plastic bladder filled with fake blood. They hide it under clothes or stick it on your back. The bad guy comes along and supposedly shoots you, or in this case machetes you, and then another guy off-camera presses a button and the squib explodes and the blood pours out." He traced his finger along a shadow at the woman's side.

"This dark line here is the wire that connects to the squib. They got remote-controlled ones now, so I guess this was low budget, but—"

"I don't understand."

"It's fake. Not even good fake."

"But, the girl—"

"Yeah, I know what you're thinking. She looks just like Anna Kilpatrick."

Claire hadn't been thinking that at all, but now that he'd said it, the resemblance was uncanny.

"Lookit," Mayhew said, "I know about your past. Your sister."

Claire felt a warm sensation rush through her body.

"If I had a sister who disappeared like that, I'd probably be quick to make these kinds of connections, too."

"That's not what I—" Claire stopped herself. She had to appear calm. "This has nothing to do with my sister."

"You look at this girl in the movie, and you think, *Brown hair, brown eyes, young, pretty. It's Anna Kilpatrick.*"

Claire's eyes went to the frozen image on-screen. How had she not noticed before? Every time he said the girl's name, the resemblance became more obvious.

"Mrs. Scott, I'm gonna be honest because I feel for you." He patted his hand on the desk. "I really feel for you."

Claire nodded for him to continue.

"This has to stay between us, all right? You can't tell nobody else."

She nodded again.

"The Kilpatrick girl." He slowly shook his head side to side. "They found blood in her car. A lot of blood. You know what I

137

mean? The kind of blood that you need inside your body if you're going to stay alive."

"She's dead?" Claire felt a weight crushing her chest. She realized that somewhere, somehow, she had been hoping the girl was alive.

"Mrs. Scott, I really am sorry about your loss. And I'm sorry that you had to see this side of your husband. Men are pigs, all right? Take it from a pig who knows." He tried to smile. "Guys can look at some hard-core shit, excuse my language, but that doesn't mean they're into it or even want to do it. This kind of stuff is all over the Internet. And as long as it's not kids, it's legal. And it's disgusting. But that's kind of what the Internet is for, right?"

"But . . ." Claire grasped for words. The more she thought about it, the more the girl looked like Anna Kilpatrick. "Don't you think it's an odd coincidence?"

"No such thing," Mayhew said. "There's something called the Law of Truly Large Numbers. Get a big enough sample size, outrageous things are bound to happen."

Claire felt her eyes widen, her lips part, in a textbook example of shock.

"Is something wrong?"

She worked to return her expression to some semblance of normal. He might as well be quoting Paul, which begged the question, had he ever met Paul?

"Mrs. Scott?"

"I'm sorry." Claire forced some calm into her voice. "It's just—the way you said it. I hadn't thought about it that way, but now that I hear it, it makes sense." She had to clear her throat before she could continue. "Where did you hear that phrase, the Law of Truly Large Numbers?"

He smiled again. "I dunno. Probably a fortune cookie."

She tried to steady herself. Every ounce of her being was telling her something was wrong. Was Mayhew lying? Or was he trying to protect her from something more dangerous at play?

She asked, "Can you tell me why Agent Nolan was at my house yesterday?"

Mayhew huffed out some air. "Being honest with you again? I got no idea. Those FBI guys are like flies around our cases. The minute it looks like we've got something good, they snatch it away so they can get all the credit."

"They can take a case away from you? They don't have to be asked?"

"Nope. They just walk in and take over." He unplugged the hard drive. "Thanks for bringing this in. Of course I'm gonna have my people look at it, but like I said, I've seen this kind of thing before."

Claire realized he was dismissing her. She stood up. "Thank you."

Mayhew stood up, too. "The best thing you can do for yourself is forget about this, all right? Your husband was a good guy. You had a solid marriage. Almost twenty years and you still loved each other. That's something to hold on to."

Claire nodded. She was feeling sick again.

Mayhew placed his hand on the hard drive. "Looks like you took this right from his computer."

"Sorry?"

"The drive. It was connected directly to his computer, right?"

Claire didn't hesitate. "Yes."

"Good." Mayhew put his hand to her back and led her out of the office. "We wouldn't want any copies floating around. Like on a back-up? Or another computer?"

"I checked. It was only on the hard drive."

"What about his laptop? Didn't Quinn say something about Paul's laptop?"

"I already checked it." She had no idea where the damn thing even was. "There's nothing else."

"All right." His fingers curved around her waist as he steered her toward the last corridor. "You let me know if anything else comes up. Just give me a call and I'll head right over and take it off your hands."

Claire nodded. "Thank you for your help."

"Any time." He walked her across the small lobby and held open the glass door.

Claire held on to the railing as she navigated her way down the stairs. The overhead lights sent a glimmer through the rain as she crossed the parking lot. The entire time, she felt Mayhew's eyes on her. She didn't turn until she had reached the Tesla.

The doorway was empty. Mayhew was gone.

Was she being paranoid? Claire wasn't sure about anything anymore. She opened the car door. She was about to get in when she saw the note on the windshield.

She recognized Adam Quinn's handwriting.

I really need those files. Please don't make me do this the hard way. AQ

SIX

Lydia lay on the couch with her head on Rick's lap. Two dogs were on the floor in front of her, a cat was curled into her side, and the hamster was either running a marathon on its wheel or the parakeet in Dee's room was scraping its beak on the side of the cage. The fish in the fifty-gallon tank were blissfully quiet.

Rick absently ran his fingers through her hair. They were watching the ten o'clock news because they were both too pathetic to stay up until eleven. The police had released a composite drawing of a man seen in the vicinity of Anna Kilpatrick's disabled car. The drawing was almost laughably vague. The guy was either tall or medium height. His eyes were blue or green. His hair was black or brown. There were no tattoos or identifying marks. His own mother probably wouldn't recognize him.

The report cut to a taped interview with Congressman Johnny Jackson. The Kilpatrick family was from his district, so by law, he had to milk their personal tragedy for every political ounce possible. He droned on about law and order for a few seconds, but when the reporter tried to pull Jackson into speculation about the girl's well-being, the man fell uncharacteristically silent. Anyone who'd ever read an airport paperback knew that the chances of finding the missing girl alive dwindled with each passing hour.

Lydia closed her eyes so she wouldn't see images of the Kilpatrick family. Their haggard expressions had become painfully familiar. She could tell they were slowly coming to accept that their little girl would not be coming home. Pretty soon, a year would pass, then another year, then the family would quietly mark the decade anniversary, then two decades, then more. Children would be born. Grandchildren. Marriage vows would be made and broken. And behind every single event would lurk the shadow of this missing sixteen-year-old girl.

Every once in a while, a Google alert on Lydia's computer found a story that mentioned Julia's name. Usually it was because a body had been found in the Athens area and the reporter had reached into the archives to find past open cases that might be relevant. Of course, the body was never identified as Julia Carroll. Or Abigail Ellis. Or Samantha Findlay. Or any of the dozens of women who had gone missing since then. There was a depressingly large number of hits for "missing girl + University of Georgia." Add in "rape" and the tally climbed into the millions.

Had Claire performed these same types of searches? Did she feel the same kind of nausea when an alert came up that a body had been found?

Lydia had never checked the Internet for information on her

baby sister. If Claire had a Facebook page or Instagram account, she did not want to see it. Everything that had to do with Claire had to do with Paul. The association was too painful to invite onto her computer screen. And honestly, the anguish of losing Claire was almost more overwhelming than losing Julia. Whatever had happened to her older sister had been a tragedy. Her rift with Claire had been a choice.

Claire's choice.

And Helen's, too. The last time Lydia had talked to her mother, Helen had said, "Don't make me choose between you and your sister."

To which Lydia had responded, "I think you already have."

Though Lydia hadn't spoken to her mother since, she still kept tabs on her. The last time she'd checked the Athens-Clarke County tax records, Helen still lived in their old house on Boulevard, just west of campus. The *Banner-Herald* ran a nice story when Helen retired from the library after forty years of service. Her colleagues had said that their grammar would never be the same. The obituary for Helen's second husband mentioned that she had three daughters, which Lydia thought was nice until she realized that someone else had probably written it. Dee hadn't made the list because they didn't know she existed. Lydia would likely never remedy the situation. She could not bear the humiliation of having her daughter meet people who held her mother in such low regard.

Lydia often wondered if her family ever looked online for her. She doubted Helen used Google. She had always been a strictly Dewey Decimal kind of gal. There were so many different sides of Helen that Lydia had known. The young, fun-loving mother who organized dance contests and *Sweet Valley High* sleepovers. The much-feared, cerebral librarian who humiliated the school board when they tried to ban *Go Ask Alice* from the library. The devastated, paralyzed woman who drank herself to sleep in the middle of the day after her oldest daughter went missing.

And then there was the Helen who warned, "Don't make me choose," when she had clearly already made her choice.

Could Lydia blame them for not believing her about Paul? What Claire had said at the cemetery today was mostly true. Lydia had stolen from them. She had lied. She had cheated. She had exploited their emotions. She had banked on their fear of losing another child and basically extorted them for drug money. But that was the thing. Lydia had been a junkie. All of her crimes had been in the service of getting high. Which begged the obvious question that Helen and Claire had apparently never bothered to ask: What could Lydia possibly gain from lying about Paul?

They hadn't even let her tell the story. Separately, she had tried to tell each of them about riding with Paul in the Miata, the song on the radio, the way Paul had touched her knee, what had happened next, and they had each had the same response: I don't want to hear it.

"Time to wake up." Rick muted the TV when a commercial came on. He slipped on his reading glasses and asked, "What is the groundnut better known as?"

Lydia carefully rolled onto her back so the cat wouldn't be disturbed. "The peanut."

"Correct." He shuffled through the Trivial Pursuit cards. They were cramming for the Westerly PTO Parent/Teacher Trivia Night. Lydia barely had two years of college. Rick had three.

They took a perverse pleasure in beating the doctors and lawyers of the Westerly Chosen.

Rick asked, "Who is buried in an Argentine cemetery under the name Maria Maggi?"

"Eva Perón. Give me something harder."

Rick shuffled through the cards again. "Where is the tallest mountain on earth?"

Lydia put her hand over her eyes so she could concentrate. "You said tallest, not highest elevation, so it can't be Everest." She made some thinking noises that caused the dogs to stir. The cat started making biscuits on her stomach. She could hear the clock ticking in the kitchen.

Finally, Rick said, "Think ukulele."

She peeked through her fingers. "Hawaii?"

"Mauna Kea."

"Did you know the answer?"

"I'm gonna say yes because you have no way of knowing."

She reached up and pretended to smack his cheek.

He bit at her hand. "Tell me what your sister's like."

Lydia had already told him about surprising Claire at the cemetery that afternoon, though she'd left out the unseemly bit about squatting over Paul's grave. "She's exactly how I thought she would be."

"You can't just say she's a Mother and leave it at that."

"Why not?" The words came out sharper than Lydia intended. The cat sensed her tension and moved to the arm of the couch. "She's still thin and beautiful. Obviously she works out all the time. Her outfit cost more than my first car. I bet she has her manicurist on speed dial."

Rick stared down at her. "That's all there is to her? A gym membership and designer clothes?"

"Of course not." Lydia bristled, because Claire was still her sister. "She's complicated. People look at her, and they see how beautiful she is, but they don't realize that underneath she's smart and funny and . . ." Her voice trailed off.

Was Claire still smart and funny? After Julia disappeared and Helen checked out, Lydia had taken over the mothering responsibilities. She was the one who made sure Claire got to school on time, had lunch money and clean clothes. She was the one Claire had always confided in. They were best friends until Paul had forced them apart.

She told Rick, "She's quiet. She hates confrontation. She'll walk halfway around the world to avoid an argument."

"So, she's adopted?"

Lydia slapped his arm. "Trust me, she was very sneaky. It might look like she was agreeing with you, but then she'd run off and do whatever the hell she wanted." Lydia waited for another comment, but Rick held his tongue. She said, "Before the rift, I used to think that I was the only person in the world who really understood her."

"And now?"

Lydia tried to remember exactly what Claire had told her in the cemetery. "She said I don't know a damn thing about her. And she's right. I don't know Claire with Paul."

"You think she's changed that much?"

"Who knows?" Lydia said. "She was thirteen when Julia went missing. We all dealt with it in our own way. You know what I did, and what happened to my mom and dad. Claire's response was to make herself invisible. She just agreed with everybody—at least on the surface. She never caused any problems. She made solid grades in school. She was co-captain of the cheerleading team. She tagged along with all the popular girls."

"That doesn't sound invisible to me."

"I'm saying it wrong, then." Lydia searched for a better way to explain. "She was always holding herself back. She was co-captain, not captain. She could've dated the quarterback, but she dated his brother instead. She could've been top in her class, but she'd purposefully turn in a paper late or miss an assignment so she'd fall closer to the middle. She would know about Mauna Kea, but she would say Everest because winning would bring too much attention."

"Why?"

"I don't know," Lydia said, not because she didn't know, but because she didn't know a way to explain it that made sense. No one understood striving for second place. It was un-American. "She just wanted peace, I guess. Being a teenager is so hard. Julia and I had two great parents growing up. All Claire had was turmoil."

Rick asked, "So, what did she see in Paul? He wasn't exactly in the margins. His obituary made him out to be a pretty success-ful guy."

Lydia had seen the photo in Paul's obit. Claire had somehow managed to put pearls on the proverbial pig. "He wasn't that way when she met him. He was an obnoxious grad student in thick glasses. He wore black socks with sandals. He laughed through his nose. He was really, really smart, maybe even a genius, but he was maybe a five and Claire's always been a solid ten."

Lydia remembered the first time she'd met Paul Scott. Her only thought was that Claire could do so much better. But the fact was that Claire had never wanted to do better.

Lydia said, "She always flirted with the good-looking, popular guys, but she went home with the geeky ones who practically slobbered with gratitude. I think they made her feel safe."

"What's wrong with feeling safe?"

"Because the way Paul made her feel safe was by pushing everybody else out of the way. He was her savior. He made her think that he was all she needed. She stopped talking to her friends. She stopped calling me as much. She didn't go home anymore to visit Mom and Dad. He isolated her."

"Sounds like a classic abuser."

"As far as I know, he never hit her or even raised his voice at her. He just *kept* her."

"Like a bird in a gilded cage?"

"Sort of," Lydia said, because it was more than that. "He was obsessed with her. He'd look at her through the window when she was in class. He'd leave notes on her car. She'd come home and there would be a rose on her doorstep."

"That's not romantic?"

"Not if you do it every single day."

Rick didn't have a response to that.

"When they were out in public, he was always touching her—stroking her hair, holding her hand, kissing her cheek. It wasn't sweet. It was creepy."

"Well," Rick put on his diplomatic tone, "maybe she liked the attention. I mean, she married him and stayed married to him for almost twenty years."

"It's more like she gave in."

"To . . .?"

"The wrong type of guy."

"Which is . . .?"

"Someone she could never be passionate about or lose sleep over or worry about running around. He was safe because she would never really give all of herself to him."

"I dunno, babe. Twenty years is a long time to put up with somebody you don't like."

Lydia thought about how devastated Claire had looked at the cemetery. She certainly seemed to be grieving. Then again, Claire was always really good at behaving exactly the way people expected her to behave—not out of duplicity, but out of self-preservation.

She said, "Back when I was thin and beautiful, guys like Paul were always hanging around. I made fun of them. I teased them. I used them, and they let me use them because being around me meant that they weren't losers."

"Damn, babe. That's harsh."

"It's the truth. I'm sorry to be blunt about it, but girls don't like guys who are doormats. Especially pretty girls, because there's no novelty to it. Guys are hitting on them all of the time. They can't walk down the street or order a coffee or stand on a corner without some idiot making a comment about how attractive they are. And the women smile because it's easier than telling them to go fuck themselves. And less dangerous, because if a man rejects a woman, she goes home and cries for a few days. If a woman rejects a man, he can rape and kill her."

"I hope you're not giving Dee this excellent dating advice."

"She'll learn it on her own soon enough." Lydia could still remember what it felt like back when she was fronting the band. Men had fought for the privilege of accommodating her. She never had to open a door for herself. She never had to buy a drink or a bump or a baggie. She said she wanted something and it was placed in front of her before she could finish the sentence.

She told Rick, "The world stops for you when you're pretty. That's why women spend billions on crap for their faces. Their whole life, they're the center of attention. People want to be around them just because they're attractive. Their jokes are funnier. Their lives are better. And then suddenly, they get bags under their eyes or they put on a little weight and no one cares about them anymore. They cease to exist."

"You're using a mighty broad brush to paint a whole bunch of people."

"Back in high school, did you ever see a guy get shoved into a locker? Or watch someone slap a lunch tray out of his hand?"

Rick said nothing, probably because he had been the one terrorizing the poor kid.

"Imagine if that guy dated the homecoming queen. That's what it was like when Paul started dating Claire. You could totally see what he was getting out of it, but what was in it for her?"

Rick stared at the muted television as he thought it over. "I guess I see your point, but there's more to people than how they look."

"But you only get to know somebody because you like what you see."

He smiled down at her. "I like what I see."

Lydia wondered how many chins she had from lying on her

back and whether or not her roots showed in the glow of the television. "What on earth could you possibly see?"

"The woman I want to spend the rest of my life with." Rick put his hand on her stomach. "This belly you're always complaining about? This is where Dee spent the first nine months of her life." He pressed his palm to her chest. "This heart is the kindest, gentlest heart I've ever known." He let his fingers trace up toward her neck. "And this is where your beautiful voice is made." He lightened the pressure as he touched her lips. "These are the softest lips I've ever kissed." He touched her eyelids. "These eyes see straight through my bullshit." He stroked back her hair. "This head is full of thoughts that surprise me and enlighten me and make me laugh."

Lydia guided his hand back to her breasts. "What about these?"

"Hours of pleasure."

"Kiss me before I say something stupid."

He leaned down and kissed her mouth. She wrapped her hand around the back of his neck. Dee was spending the night at Bella's. Tomorrow was Sunday. They could sleep in. Maybe have a second go round.

Her cell phone chirped in the other room.

Rick knew better than to ask her to ignore the phone when Dee was away.

She told him, "Keep going without me. I'll catch up."

Lydia picked her way past the dogs and a pile of laundry as she made her way into the kitchen. Her purse was in a chair. She dug around in the bag for several seconds before spotting her phone on the counter. There was a new text.

"She all right?" Rick was standing in the doorway.

"She probably forgot her math book again." Lydia swiped her thumb across the screen. There was a text from a blocked number. The message listed an unfamiliar address in Dunwoody.

Rick asked, "What's wrong?"

Lydia stared at the address, wondering if the text was sent by mistake. She ran a small business. She didn't have the luxury of clocking out. The voicemail at work gave her cell phone number. The work number was on the side of her van alongside a photo of a giant yellow Lab that reminded her of the dog her father had rescued after Julia was gone.

"Liddie?" Rick said. "Who is it?"

"It's Claire," Lydia said, because she felt it with every ounce of her being. "My sister needs me."

SEVEN

Claire sat in her office because she couldn't stand being in Paul's anymore. Her desk was an antique Chippendale secretary that she'd had painted a soft eggshell white. The walls were pale gray. The rug on the floor was patterned with yellow roses. The over-stuffed chair and ottoman were covered in a muted lilac velvet. A simple chandelier hung overhead, but Claire had replaced the clear crystals with amethysts that spotted the wall in a purple prism when the sun hit it just right.

Paul never came into her space. He only stood at the doorway, afraid that his penis would fall off if he touched anything pastel.

She looked down at the note Adam Quinn had left on the car.

I really need those files. Please don't make me do this the hard way. AQ

Claire had stared at the words so long that she could see them when her eyes were closed.

The hard way.

That was certainly a threat, which was surprising because Adam had no reason to threaten her. What exactly was the hard way? Was he going to send some goons around to rough her up? Was there some sort of sexual innuendo intended? Her dalliances with Adam had been a little rough sometimes, but that was mostly because of the illicit nature of their affair. There had been no romantic hotel rooms, just quickies up against the wall at a Christmas party, a second time at a golf tournament, and once in the bathroom inside the Quinn + Scott offices. Honestly, their clandestine phone calls and secret texts had been more titillating than the actual acts.

Still, Claire couldn't help wondering which files Adam meant—work files or porn files? Because Adam and Paul had shared everything, from a dorm room in college to the same insurance agent. And Claire supposed she belonged on that list of shared items, but who the hell knew whether Paul had figured that out?

Then again, what exactly had Claire figured out?

She had looked at the movies again—all of them this time. Claire had rigged up Paul's laptop in the garage so she wouldn't have to sit in his office. Halfway through the first series of movies, she'd found herself somewhat anesthetized to the violence. Habituation, Paul would've explained, but fuck Paul and his stupid explanations.

With her new-found distance, Claire was able to see that each movie series told the same linear story. At first, the chained girls were fully clothed. Subsequent installments revealed the masked man slowly cutting or slicing away their clothing to reveal leather bustiers and crotchless panties that they had obviously been forced to wear. Sometimes, their heads were covered in a black hood made of a light fabric that showed their desperate inhalations as they gasped for breath. As the story progressed, the violence ramped up. There was beating, then whipping, then cutting, then burning them with a branding iron, then the cattle prod.

The girls were unmasked toward the end. The first woman's face was exposed for two of the movies before she was butchered. The girl who looked like Anna Kilpatrick was hooded until the very last movie on Paul's secret hard drive.

Claire had closely studied the girl's face. There was no way of telling whether or not she was looking at Anna Kilpatrick. Claire had even pulled up a photo from the Kilpatrick family's Facebook page. She had positioned them side by side and still been unsure.

Then she had clicked the PLAY button and watched the last movie all the way through. Claire had the sound on at first, but she couldn't take the screaming. The man entered wearing the same unnerving rubber mask. He had the machete, but he didn't use it to kill the girl. He used it to rape her.

Claire had nearly been sick again. She'd had to take a walk down the driveway and up again just to get air back into her lungs.

Was it real?

Captain Mayhew had claimed there was a wire running down the girl's side that controlled the release of fake blood. Claire had found a magnifying glass in one of Paul's drawers. All that she could see at the girl's side were pieces of flayed skin sticking out like broken glass. There was certainly no wire on the floor, and surely if there was an operator standing off-camera with a control unit, the wire would have to be connected somehow.

Next, Claire had searched the Internet for information on squibs, but as far as she could tell, all of them were remotely controlled. She had even done a general search for snuff porn movies, but Claire had been terrified to click on any of the links. The descriptions were too unsettling: live beheadings, cannibalism, necrophilia, something called "death rape." She'd tried Wikipedia, but gathered that most recorded murders were frenetic and amateurish, not carefully framed and following a set progression.

So, did that support Mayhew's assertion that the movies were fake? Or did it mean that Paul had found the best snuff porn the same way he found the best golf clubs or the best leather for his custom-made office chair?

Claire hadn't been able to take any more. She had left the garage. She had gone inside the house. She had taken two Valium. She had held her head under the kitchen faucet until the cold water had numbed her skin.

If only she could numb her brain. Despite the pills, her mind would not stop racing with conspiracies. Were these awful movies the files that Adam wanted? Was he in cahoots with mustachioed Captain Mayhew? Was that why Adam was at the police station? Is that why Mayhew had been so strange at the end of their meeting, going out of his way to confirm that there were no more copies of the movies when he'd just told Claire that they weren't real and she shouldn't worry about them?

What if they really were fake, and the girl wasn't Anna Kilpatrick, but an actress, and Adam was at the police station tonight because he had a key to the house and Mayhew knew about the Law of Truly Large Numbers because he'd seen a special on the Discovery Channel and Claire was some kind of paranoid housewife with nothing better to do than smear the reputation of the man who had spent his every waking moment trying to please her?

Claire looked at the orange prescription bottle on her desk. Percocet. The top was off because she'd already taken one. Paul's name was on the label. The directions said: TAKE AS NEEDED FOR PAIN. Claire was certainly in pain. She used the tip of her finger to topple over the bottle. Yellow pills spilled onto her desktop. She placed another Percocet on her tongue and washed it down with a sip of wine.

Suicides ran in families. She had learned this during a class on Hemingway taught by an ancient professor who seemed himself to have one foot in the grave. Ernest had used a shotgun. His father had done the same. There was a sister and brother, a grand-daughter, maybe others whom Claire could not recall but she knew that they'd all died by their own hands.

Claire looked at the Percocet spilled across her desktop. She moved the pills around like pieces of candy.

Her father had ended his life with an injection of Nembutal, a brand of pentobarbital used to euthanize animals. Death by respiratory arrest. Before the injection, he had swallowed a handful of sleeping pills with a vodka chaser. It was two weeks before the six-year anniversary of Julia's disappearance. He'd had a mild stroke the month before. His suicide note was written in a shaky hand on a torn-off sheet of notebook paper:

To all of my beautiful girls—I love you with every piece of my heart. Daddy

Claire recalled a long-ago weekend spent at her father's dismal bachelor apartment. During the day, Sam had done all the things that recently divorced fathers do with their children: bought her clothes he couldn't afford, taken her to a movie her mother had forbade her to see, and let her eat so much junk food that she'd almost been comatose by the time he'd finally brought her back to the sickly pink room with pink sheets that he'd decorated especially for her.

Claire had been well past her pink years. Her room at home was painted robin's-egg blue with a multicolored wedding quilt on the bed and absolutely no stuffed animals but one, which she kept sitting in the rocking chair that had belonged to her mother's father.

Around midnight, the hamburgers and ice cream had commenced an ungodly battle inside Claire's stomach. She had run to the bathroom only to find her father sitting in the tub. He wasn't taking a bath. He was wearing his pajamas. He had his face buried in a pillow. He was sobbing so uncontrollably that he barely noticed when she turned on the lights.

"I'm sorry, Sweetpea." His voice had been so soft that she had to bend down to hear it. Oddly, as she'd knelt by the tub, Claire had imagined that this was what it might be like one day when she bathed her own children.

She'd asked, "What is it, Daddy?"

He'd shaken his head. He wouldn't look at her. It was Julia's birthday. He had spent the morning at the sheriff's office going through her case file, looking at photographs of her old dorm room, her bedroom at the house, her bike that sat chained outside the student center for weeks after she was gone. "There are just some things you can't unsee."

Every argument between her parents featured some variation of Helen telling Sam to just move on. Given the choice between her seemingly cold mother and her broken hull of a father, was it any wonder that later in life, Claire's court-appointed therapist had accused her of not being forthcoming with her feelings?

Her father overflowed with feeling. You couldn't stand near him without absorbing some of the sorrow that seemed to radiate from his chest. No one who looked at him saw a whole human being. His eyes were perpetually weepy. His lips trembled from dark thoughts. He had night terrors that eventually got him evicted from his apartment complex.

Toward the end when Claire would stay with him—honestly, when her mother forced her to stay with him—Claire would lie in bed and press her hand to the thin wall between their bedrooms and feel the vibrations as her father's screams filled the air. Eventually, he would wake himself up. She would hear him pacing the room. Claire would ask him through the wall if he was okay and he would always say he was okay. They both knew this was a lie, just like they both knew she wouldn't go in there to check on him.

Not that Claire was completely heartless. She'd checked on him dozens of times before. She'd run into his room with her heart in her mouth and found him writhing in bed with the sheets tangled around him. He was always embarrassed. She was always conscious of how useless she was to him, how Helen should've really been there, but this was the reason that Helen had left in the first place.

"Kind of makes me love your mom less to hear that," Paul had said when Claire finally told him what life was like after Julia.

Paul.

He had always been Claire's biggest champion. He always took her side. Even the day he'd bailed her out of jail when everything that had happened was clearly a shitstorm of her own making, Paul had said, "Don't sweat it. We'll get a lawyer."

Eighteen years ago, Lydia had told her that the problem with Paul Scott was that he didn't see Claire as a normal, imperfect human being. He was blind to her faults. He covered her missteps. He would never challenge her or scare her or infuriate her or stir up any of those fiery emotions that made it worthwhile to put up with a man's bullshit.

"Why are you saying all of that like it's a bad thing?" Claire had demanded, because she was desperately lonely, and she was tired of being the girl whose sister had disappeared, or the girl whose sister was an addict, or the girl whose father had killed himself, or the girl who was too pretty for her own good.

She wanted to be something new—something that she chose to be on her own. She wanted to be Mrs. Paul Scott. She wanted a protector. She wanted to be cherished. She wanted to be clever. She certainly didn't want someone who made her feel like the ground could shift under her feet at any moment. She'd had quite enough of that in her early life, thank you very much.

Besides, it wasn't like Lydia had found a better alternative. She thrived on insecurity. Every part of her life had been tied up in being popular. She'd started taking pills because all the cool kids were into them. She'd snorted coke because a boyfriend told her that all the fun girls snorted coke. Time and again, Claire had watched her sister ignore the nice, normal guys so she could throw herself at the flakiest, best-looking assholes in the room. The more they ignored her, the more she wanted them.

Which is why it was not surprising to Claire that a month after they had stopped talking to each other, Lydia had married a man named Lloyd Delgado. He was very handsome in a snaggle-toothed kind of way. He was also a cokehead from South Florida with a series of petty arrests on his record. Four months after they married, Lloyd was dead of a drug overdose and Lydia had a court-appointed guardian assigned to protect her unborn child.

Julia Cady Delgado was born eight months after that. For almost a year, they lived in a homeless shelter that offered daycare. Then Lydia got a job at a vet's office cleaning cages in the back. Then she got promoted to grooming assistant and was able to afford a hotel room that she rented by the week. Dee went to private preschool while Lydia skipped lunch and sometimes dinner.

After two years as an assistant, Lydia got promoted to head groomer. Almost a full year later, she was able to buy a reliable car and rent a one-bedroom apartment. Three years after that, she opened her own grooming business. At first, she would go to clients' houses in a dilapidated Dodge van with red duct tape for taillights. Then she got a better van and turned it into a mobile grooming venture. Eight years ago, she opened her own store-front. She had two employees. She had a small mortgage on a small ranch house. She dated her next-door neighbor, a man named Rick Butler who looked like a younger, less sexy version of Sam Shepard. She had several dogs and a cat. Her daughter attended Westerly Academy on a scholarship arranged by an anonymous donor.

Well, not really anonymous anymore, because according to the paperwork Claire had found in Paul's office, he'd been using a shell organization to foot the thirty grand a year for Julia "Dee" Delgado to attend Westerly Academy.

Claire had found Dee's scholarship essay in the same set of files along with thirty other entries from students all over the metro area. Obviously, the contest was rigged, but Dee's paper was remarkably cogent compared to the others. Her thesis dealt with how difficult the state of Georgia made life for convicted drug felons. They were denied food and housing assistance. They couldn't vote. They faced employment discrimination. They were denied scholarship opportunities. They often had no family support system. Considering they had served their time, paid their fines, completed parole and paid taxes, didn't they deserve the right to full citizenship like the rest of us?

The argument was compelling, even without the benefit of the photographs Claire had on her desk in front of her.

And thanks to the private detectives Paul had hired to track Lydia over the years, there were plenty of photographs for Claire to choose from.

A frazzled-looking Lydia carrying Dee in one arm and a bag of groceries in the other. A clearly exhausted Lydia standing at the bus stop outside the vet's office. Lydia walking a pack of dogs down a tree-lined street, her face relaxed for a brief moment in time. Climbing into the beat-up Dodge van with the red tape on the taillights. Behind the wheel of the Ford van with the mobile grooming equipment inside. Standing proudly in front of the new storefront. The photo was clearly taken on grand opening day. Lydia was using a giant pair of scissors to cut a yellow ribbon while her daughter and hippie boyfriend proudly looked on.

Dee Delgado. Claire put the pictures in order. Lydia's child looked so much like Julia that it took Claire's breath away.

Paul must have thought the same thing when he saw the photographs. He'd never met Julia, but Claire had three scrapbooks full of family photos. She wondered if it was worth putting them side by side and doing a comparison. And then she worried that she hadn't opened the scrapbooks in years, and if she did so now, would she find something that told her Paul had looked at the scrapbooks, too?

She decided there was no way he hadn't. Clearly, Paul was obsessed with Lydia. Every September for the past seventeen and a half years, he'd hired a private detective to check in on her. He'd used different agencies each time, but they had all delivered the same type of detailed reports, cataloging the minutiae of Lydia's life. Credit reports. Background checks. Tax returns. Court orders. Parole reports. Court transcripts, though the legal side had dried up fifteen years ago. There was even a separate note detailing the names and types of animals she owned.

Claire had had absolutely no idea that he was doing this. She imagined that Lydia was likewise clueless, because she knew without a doubt that Lydia would die before she took one red cent from Paul.

The funny thing was that over the years, Paul had occasionally suggested that Claire try to get in touch with Lydia. He'd made noises about how he wished he had family left he could talk to. How Helen wasn't getting any younger and it might be good for Claire to heal old wounds. Once, he'd even offered to try to look for her, but Claire had said no because she wanted to make it clear to Paul that she would never forgive her sister for lying about him.

"I will never let another person come between us," Claire had assured him, her voice shaking with the righteous indignation she felt on behalf of her wrongly accused husband.

Had Paul manipulated Claire with Lydia the same way he'd manipulated her with the computer passwords and bank accounts? Claire had easy access to everything, so she felt compelled to look for nothing. Paul had been so very, very cunning, hiding all of his transgressions in plain sight.

The only question now was how many more transgressions was she going to find? Claire stared at the two heavy file boxes she'd carried down from Paul's office. They were made of a milky white plastic. The outside of each box was labeled. PERSONAL-1 and PERSONAL-2.

Claire couldn't bring herself to go through the second box. The first had contained enough hell to end her day on. The file folders inside were color-coded. The tabs were neatly labeled with women's names. Claire had zeroed in on Lydia's for obvious reasons, but she had closed the box on the dozens of other files that had dozens of other women's names because she had already glimpsed quite enough of Paul's personal shit. She could not force herself to go looking for more.

Instead, she opened the flip phone by the overturned Percocet bottle. Claire had bought a pay-as-you-go cell phone, which she knew was called a burner phone. At least if you could believe *Law & Order*.

Lydia's cell phone number was in Paul's reports. Claire had sent her a text from the burner. There was no message, just the Dunwoody address. Claire had wanted to leave it up to chance. Would Lydia dismiss the address as a scam, something along the lines of a deposed Nigerian president seeking her bank details? Or would she dismiss it when she realized it had come from Claire?

Claire deserved to be ignored. Her sister had told her that a man had tried to rape her and Claire's response had been to believe the man.

And yet, Lydia had texted back almost immediately: *I'm on my way.*

Since the robbery, Claire had been leaving the security gate open. She had secretly hoped the burglars would come back and kill her. Or maybe not kill her, because that would be cruel to Helen. Perhaps they could just beat her senseless so she could go into a coma and wake up a year from now when all of the dominos had stopped falling.

Here was the first domino: It was easy to say that a person who watched films of rape was not necessarily interested in real-life rape, but what if there was an instance in that person's past when someone had accused him of trying to commit that very crime?

Second domino: What if that long-ago attempted rape accusation was true?

Third domino: Statistically, rapists didn't just rape once. If they got away with it, they generally kept raping. Even if they didn't get away with it, the recidivism rate was so high that they might as well put a revolving door on every prison.

How did Claire know this statistic? Because she'd volunteered at a rape crisis hotline a handful of years ago, which would have been a hilarious bit of irony if someone had told her this story at a party.

Which brought her to the fourth domino: What was really inside the Pandora's boxes labeled PERSONAL-1 and PERSONAL-2? Any thinking person could guess that the files with women's names were exactly like the file with Lydia's name: surveillance reports, photographs, detailed lists of the comings and goings of women that Paul had targeted.

Fifth domino: If Paul had really tried to rape Lydia, what had he really done to the other women?

Thank God she had never had children with him. The thought made her head spin. Actually, the whole room was spinning. The wine and pills were not playing well with each other. Claire was feeling that familiar, overwhelming sickness again.

She closed her eyes. In her mind, she made a list, because writing things down felt too dangerous.

Jacob Mayhew: Was he lying about the authenticity of the movies? In keeping with his mantle of the hardboiled detective, was he the type of man who would lie to a woman in order to protect her delicate feelings?

Adam Quinn: What files did he really want? Was he as good as

Paul had been at hiding his true nature, even when he was having sex with her?

Fred Nolan: Why was this creepy asshole really at the house the day of the funeral? Was it because of the movies or did he have something worse waiting for Claire around the corner?

Paul Scott: Rapist? Sadist? Husband? Friend? Lover? Liar? Claire had been married to him for almost half of her life but she had no idea who he really was.

She opened her eyes. She looked down at the spilled Percocet and contemplated taking another. Claire didn't understand the appeal of being drugged. She had thought the purpose was to make you numb, but if anything, she was feeling everything much too intensely. She couldn't shut down her brain. She felt shaky. Her tongue was too thick for her mouth. Maybe she was doing it wrong. Maybe the two Valium she'd taken an hour ago were counteracting the effects. Maybe she needed more Percocet. Claire took her iPad out of her desk drawer. Surely she could find some kind of instructional video posted by a helpful drug addict on YouTube.

The burner phone vibrated. Claire read Lydia's message: *I'm here.*

She pressed her palms on the desktop and pushed herself up. Or at least she tried to. The muscles in her arms wouldn't respond. Claire forced her legs to stand and nearly fell over when the entire room made a quarter-turn to the left.

The doorbell rang. Claire shoved all of Lydia's photos and reports into her desk drawer. She took a sip of wine, then decided to take the glass with her.

Walking came with its own challenges. The wide-open spaces

of the kitchen and family room presented few obstacles, but she felt like she was inside a pinball machine as she bumped against the walls in the main hallway. She finally had to take off her heels, which she'd only left on because they always took off their shoes inside the house. All of the rugs were white. The floor was bleached oak. The walls were white. Even some of the paintings were muted whites. She wasn't living in a house. She was occupying a sanitarium.

The handles on the front doors telescoped out of her reach. She could see the outline of Lydia's body through the frosted glass. Claire spilled her wine as she grabbed at the door handle. She felt her lips smiling, though none of this was particularly funny.

Lydia knocked on the glass.

"I'm right here." Claire finally pulled open the door.

"Jesus Christ." Lydia leaned in to look at Claire's eyes. "Your pupils are the size of dimes."

"I don't think that's possible," Claire said, because surely a dime was larger than her entire eyeball. Or was it closer to a quarter?

Lydia came into the house without being asked. She dropped her purse by the front door. She kicked off her shoes. She looked around the entrance foyer. "What is this place?"

"I don't know," Claire said, because it didn't feel like home anymore. "Did you have an affair with Paul?"

Lydia's mouth dropped open in surprise.

"Just tell me," Claire said, because she knew from Paul's reports that Lydia had had a child and that Paul was paying for the girl's education. An affair that produced a love child was so much more palatable than all the other terrible explanations for why Paul would insert himself into her sister's life.

Lydia still had her mouth open.

"Did you?"

"Absolutely not." Lydia looked worried. "What did you take?"

"Nembutal and Ambien with a vodka back."

"That's not funny." Lydia snatched away the glass of wine. She looked for somewhere to put it in the stark entryway and settled on the floor. "Why did you ask me that about Paul?"

Claire kept the answer to herself.

"Was he cheating on you?"

Claire hadn't framed the optics through that lens. Was it cheating to rape someone? Because, to be clear, that's the direction in which all the dominos were falling. If Paul had truly tried to rape Lydia, then he had probably tried and succeeded with someone else, and if he had gotten away with it once, then he had probably tried again.

And hired a private detective to follow them around for the rest of their lives so that he could still exert control over them from his lair over the garage.

But was that cheating? Claire knew from her training at the crisis center that rape was about power. Paul certainly liked controlling things. So, was raping women the equivalent of turning all the cans in the pantry label-out or loading the dishwasher with mechanical precision?

"Claire?" Lydia snapped her fingers very loudly. "Look at me."

Claire tried her best to look at her sister. She'd always thought that Lydia was the prettiest of all of them. Her face was fuller, but she'd aged more gracefully than Claire would've thought. She had laugh lines around her eyes. She had a beautiful, accomplished daughter. She had a boyfriend who was a recovering heroin addict who listened to talk radio while he worked on an old truck in his driveway.

Why did Paul need to know that? Why did he need to know anything about Lydia at all? Was it stalking if you hired someone else to do it? And wasn't watching someone without their knowledge another form of rape?

Lydia asked, "Claire, what did you take?" Her voice softened. She rubbed Claire's arms. "Sweetpea, tell me what you took."

"Valium." Claire suddenly wanted to cry. She couldn't remember the last time someone had called her Sweetpea. "Some Percocet."

"How many?"

Claire shook her head because it didn't matter. None of this mattered. "We had a cat named Mr. Sandwich."

Lydia was understandably perplexed. "Okay."

"We called him Hammy, like ham in a sandwich. He was always between us. On the couch. In the bed. He only purred when we were both petting him."

Lydia tilted her head to the side like she was trying to understand a crazy person.

"Cats know people." Claire was sure her sister understood this. They had grown up surrounded by animals. None of them could walk through a parking lot without attracting a stray. "If Paul had been a bad person, Hammy would've known." Claire knew she was offering a weak defense, but she couldn't stop herself. "Isn't that what you hear, that bad people hate animals?"

Lydia shook her head in confusion. "I don't know what you want me to say, Claire. Hitler loved dogs."

"*Reductio ad Hitlerum*." Claire couldn't stop quoting Paul. "It's when you compare someone to Hitler to win an argument."

"Are we arguing?"

"Tell me what happened between you and Paul."

Lydia let out that heavy sigh again. "Why?"

"Because I've never heard it before."

"You wouldn't let me tell you before. You refused to listen."

"I'm listening now."

Lydia glanced around the foyer, making the point that Claire had barely invited her past the front door. What her sister didn't understand was that Claire could not bear the thought of seeing the cold, soulless house through Lydia's eyes.

"Please," Claire begged. "Please, Pepper. Tell me."

She threw up her hands, as if to dismiss this entire exercise as not worth her time. Still, Lydia said, "We were in his car. The Miata. He put his hand on my knee. I slapped it away."

Claire realized she was holding her breath. "That was it?"

"You really think that's it?" Lydia sounded angry. Claire supposed she had every right to be. "He kept driving, and I thought, Okay, we're just going to ignore that my sister's loser boyfriend put his hand on my knee. But then he took a turn onto a road I didn't know, and we were suddenly in the woods." Lydia's voice had gone soft. Instead of looking at Claire, she was staring over her shoulder. "He pulled over. He turned off the engine. I asked him what was going on, and he punched me in the face."

Claire felt her own fists clench. Paul had never hit anyone in his life. Even in the alley when he was fighting the Snake Man, Paul hadn't managed to land a punch.

Lydia said, "I was dazed. He started to climb on top of me. I tried to fight back. He punched me again, but I turned my head." She turned her head slightly, an actor trying to convince the audience. "I reached for the door handle. I don't know how I managed to get it open. I fell out of the car. He was on top of me. I brought up my knee." She paused, and Claire remembered a self-defense class she had taken. The instructor had drilled it into them that you couldn't count on disabling a man by kneeing him in the groin because it was more likely you would miss the mark and piss him off even more.

Lydia continued, "I started running. I got about twenty, maybe thirty feet away before he tackled me. I fell flat on my face. And he got on top of me." She looked down at the floor. Claire couldn't help but wonder if she was doing it to look more vulnerable. "I couldn't breathe. He was crushing me. I could feel my ribs bending like they were going to break." She put her hand to her ribs. "And he kept saying, 'Tell me you want this.'"

Claire felt her heart stop mid-beat.

"I still have nightmares about the way he said it—whispering, like it was sexy, when it was just so fucking creepy." Lydia shuddered. "Sometimes, I'll fall asleep on my stomach, and I'll hear his voice in my ear and . . ."

Claire opened her mouth so that she could breathe. She could almost feel the flex in her own ribs from when Paul had pressed her into the brick wall. He had whispered, *Tell me you want this,* into Claire's ear. She'd thought it was silly at the time. Paul had never talked to her like that before, but he hadn't let up until Claire had said the exact words back to him.

She asked Lydia, "What did you do next?"

Lydia gave a half-shrug. "I didn't have a choice. I told him that I wanted it. He ripped down my pants. I still have scars on my leg where his nails gouged the skin."

Claire put her hand on her own leg where Paul had scraped away the skin. "And then?"

"He was undoing his belt buckle. I heard whistling, like really loud, whistling. It was a couple of guys. They were walking in the woods and they thought we were making out. I started screaming for my life. Paul jumped up. He ran back toward the car. One of the guys chased after him and the other helped me up. They wanted to call the police, but I told them no."

"Why?"

"I'd just gotten bailed out of jail for the billionth time. Paul was an upstanding grad student with two jobs. Who would you believe?"

She knew whom Claire had believed. "The two guys—"

"Were gay men looking for a hook-up in a South Alabama forest. The cops would've known that the minute they opened their mouths." She shook her head at the futility of it all. "And I didn't really care about me at that point. My only concern was getting him away from you."

Claire put her hand to her forehead. She felt feverish. They were still standing in the foyer. She should've invited Lydia in. She should've taken her to her office and sat with her. "Do you want a drink?"

"I told you, I'm in recovery."

Claire knew that. Paul's detectives had sat in on Lydia's meetings and recorded her every word. "I need a drink." Claire found her wine glass on the floor. She swallowed the dregs in one go. She closed her eyes and waited. There was no relief.

Lydia asked, "Do you have a problem with drugs and alcohol?"

Claire struggled to return the glass to the floor. "Yes. The problem is that I don't like them very much."

Lydia opened her mouth to respond, but light filled the entryway as a car came up the driveway. "Who's here?"

Claire turned on the video keypad by the door. They watched the screen as a black Crown Victoria parked at the mouth of the front walkway.

"Why is a huckleberry here?" Lydia sounded panicked. "Claire?"

Claire was grappling with her own panic. She was more worried about *which* huckleberry it was. Mayhew come to make sure she hadn't made copies of the movies? Nolan with his inappropriate remarks and creepy looks and maddening questions that gave no explanation as to why he was here in the first place? Or was it her parole officer? He had warned Claire that he could turn up and drug-test her without notice.

She told Lydia, "I'm on parole. I can't have drugs in my system." Claire's thoughts raced against the Valium. She remembered another detail from Paul's files. Back when she was using, Lydia had pled guilty to a felony drug charge in order to avoid a prison sentence. Claire tried to push her down the hallway. "Pepper, move! I'm not allowed to associate with felons. They could take me back to jail."

Lydia didn't move. She was trapped in place. Her mouth

worked silently, as if there were too many questions running through her brain to pin down just one. Finally, she said, "Turn down the lights."

Claire didn't know what else to do. She pressed the ambient button on the keypad. All of the lights on the ground floor dimmed, which would hopefully hide the state of her pupils. They both looked at the video screen, their faces inches apart. Lydia's panicked breathing matched Claire's. A man got out of the car. He was tall and solidly built. His brown hair was neatly parted on the side.

"Fuck," Claire groaned, because her brain wasn't sharp enough right now to deal with Fred Nolan. "It's the FBI."

"What?" Lydia's voice almost squeaked with fear.

"Fred Nolan." Claire's skin crawled at the sound of his name. "He's an asshole special agent from the downtown office."

"What?" Lydia looked terrified. "Did you commit a federal crime?"

"I don't know. Maybe." There wasn't enough time to get into it. Claire switched the video screen to the front-door camera. The image showed the top of Nolan's head as he climbed the steps.

"Listen to me." Lydia kept her voice low. "Legally, you don't have to answer any of his questions. You don't have to leave with him unless he arrests you, and if he does arrest you, don't say a Goddamn word. Do you understand me, Claire? None of your bullshit jokes or funny asides. Just keep your fucking mouth shut."

"Okay." Claire could feel her mind clearing, probably from the rush of adrenalin coursing through her body.

They both looked at the front door and waited.

Nolan's shadow loomed large behind the frosted glass. He reached down and pressed the doorbell.

They both flinched at the sound.

Lydia indicated that Claire should stay silent. She was making Nolan wait, which was probably a good idea. At the very least, Claire could take the time to get her breathing under control.

Nolan pressed the doorbell again.

Lydia lifted her feet and made a walking sound. She opened the door a crack and stuck out her head. Claire could see her on the video screen. She had to look up at Nolan because he was so tall.

"Good evening, ma'am." Nolan tipped an imaginary hat. "I'm here to speak to the lady of the house."

Lydia's voice still sounded squeaky and afraid. "She's sleeping."

"She's not standing behind you?" Nolan pressed his hand against the door until Lydia had to open it or fall over. He smiled at Claire. The bruise around his eye had started to yellow. "Funny thing about frosted glass—doesn't really hide anything."

Lydia asked, "What do you want?"

"That's a loaded question." Nolan kept his hand on the door so Lydia couldn't close it. He looked up at the night sky. There was no shelter over the front porch. Paul had said it would ruin the line of the house.

Nolan said, "Looks like the rain's passing."

Claire and Lydia didn't respond.

"Me, I like the rain." Nolan stepped inside the house. He glanced around the entryway. "Great time to sit back and read a book. Or watch a movie. You like movies?"

Claire tried to swallow. Why was he talking about movies? Had he spoken with Mayhew? Was there a tracker on the computers? Claire had used Paul's laptop to access the wi-fi. Had Nolan monitored all of her activity?

"Mrs. Scott?"

Claire managed to take a shallow breath. She forced herself not to ask him point-blank if he was here to arrest her.

"That your truck out there?"

Lydia stiffened. Nolan was talking to her now.

He held out his hand. He didn't have to reach far. He was standing so close to Lydia that he barely had to bend his elbow. "We haven't been introduced. Agent Fred Nolan, FBI."

Lydia didn't shake the offered hand.

"I could get your parole officer over here." He was looking at Claire again. "Setting aside that knowingly and willfully lying or materially misleading a federal agent is punishable by five years in prison, you're technically not allowed to ignore your PO's questions. Terms of your parole. No right to remain silent." He leaned forward and studied Claire's eyes. "No right to get stoned."

Lydia said, "My name is Mindy Parker. The truck is a loaner from my mechanic. I'm a friend of Claire's."

Nolan gave Lydia a careful once-over, because Lydia didn't look like one of Claire's friends. Her jeans were more spandex than denim. Her black T-shirt had a bleach stain at the hem and her gray cardigan was raveled at the edges as if an animal had chewed on it. She didn't even look like the housekeeper of one of Claire's friends.

"Mindy Parker." Nolan made a great show of pulling out a

spiral-bound notebook and pen. He wrote down Lydia's fake name. "Trust but verify. Isn't that what Reagan said?"

"Why are you here?" Lydia demanded. "It's almost midnight. Claire's husband just died. She wants to be left in peace."

"Still wearing her funeral clothes." Nolan let his eyes travel up and down Claire's body. "Not that you don't look great in them."

Claire smiled reflexively, because that's what she always did when she was complimented.

Nolan said, "I'm wondering, Mrs. Scott, if your husband's business partner has been in touch?"

Claire's mouth went dry as salt.

"Mrs. Scott? Has Mr. Quinn been in touch?"

Claire forced herself to answer. "He was at the funeral."

"Yeah, I saw. Nice of him to be there, considering." He pitched up his voice in a bad imitation of Claire. "'Considering what, Agent Nolan?' No, please, call me Fred. Do you mind if I call you Claire? 'No, not at all, Fred.'"

Claire made her expression as hard as she could.

Nolan said, "I'm assuming you knew your husband was embezzling money from the company?"

Claire felt her mouth open in surprise. She had to repeat Nolan's words back in her head before she could divine their meaning. Even then, she couldn't believe what the man was saying. Paul was mind-numbingly fair with money. She'd once suffered through a thirty-minute round trip when he'd realized a cashier at a country store had given him too much change.

She told Nolan, "You're lying."

"Am I?"

Claire wanted to slap his smug face. This was some kind of trick. Nolan was working with Adam and Mayhew, or he was working on his own, and all of it had something to do with those wretched movies. "Whatever game you're playing, it's not working."

"Ask Adam Quinn if you don't believe me." Nolan waited, as if Claire would run to the telephone. "He's the one who called in the feds. One of the company accountants found a three-million-dollar wire into a shell company called Little Ham Holdings."

Claire clenched her jaw shut so she wouldn't scream. Little Ham had been another one of their nicknames for Mr. Sandwich.

Nolan said to Lydia, "That's a lot of money, right? Three mill? People like you and me, we could retire on that."

Claire's knees felt weak. Her legs were shaking. She had to get Nolan out of here before she had some sort of nervous break-down. "I want you to leave."

"I want my wife to stop fucking my neighbor." Nolan chuckled as if they were all in on the joke. "You know, Claire, the funny thing is that kind of dough is a drop in the bucket for a guy like your husband." He told Lydia, "Paul's worth twenty-eight million on paper. Or *was* worth that much. How much is the insurance policy you have on him?" This question was for Claire, but she didn't answer because she had no idea. "Another twenty million," Nolan provided. "Which means you're worth almost fifty million bucks now, Widow Scott." He paused to let the information sink in, but Claire was past the point at which she could make sense of anything.

Nolan said, "It was nice of Adam Quinn to settle out of court instead of letting me toss your husband into the federal pen." He gave Claire a lecherous look. "I guess he found his own way to get your husband back."

The implied insult knocked her out of her stupor. "What gives you the—"

"Shut up, Claire." Lydia stood directly in front of her. She told Nolan, "You need to leave."

Nolan smiled his crocodile smile. "Do I?"

"Are you here to arrest her?"

"Should I be?"

"Number one, back the fuck away from me."

Nolan took a very deliberate step back. "I can't wait to hear what number two is."

"It's this, asshole: If you want to interrogate her, then call her lawyer to set it up."

Nolan smiled like a gargoyle. "You know what, Mindy Parker? Now that I'm looking at you, I'm thinking you look a lot like Claire. It's almost like you two gals could be sisters."

Lydia didn't let him get to her. "Get the fuck out."

Nolan held up his hands in surrender, but he didn't give in. "It's just curious, you know. Why is it that a guy worth all those Benjamins steals three mill from his own business?"

Claire felt a sharp pain in her chest. She couldn't breathe. The ground was moving again. She reached for the wall behind her. She had felt this same way yesterday when she'd fainted.

Nolan said, "Well, I'll let you ladies get back to enjoying your evening." He stepped out onto the porch and looked up at the night sky. "Sure is a nice night."

Lydia slammed the door. She bolted the French lock. She covered her mouth with both hands. Her eyes were wide with fear. They both watched the video display as Fred Nolan shuffled his way down the stone steps and slowly made his way to the car.

Claire looked away. She couldn't watch anymore, but she couldn't stop hearing him. The soft click of his car door opening, the loud bang of it being closed. The rumble of the car's engine. The mechanical groan of the power steering as he turned around and drove back down the driveway.

Lydia dropped her hands. She was breathing as hard as Claire. "What the fuck, Claire?" She stared at Claire with open shock. "What the fucking *fuck*?"

Claire had lost the fuck two days ago. "I don't know."

"You don't know?" Lydia was practically screaming. Her voice echoed off the polished concrete floors and bounced up the metal and glass spiral staircase. "How the *fuck* can't you know, Claire?" She started pacing back and forth across the entryway. "I can't believe this. I can't believe any of it."

Claire couldn't believe it, either. The movies. Mayhew. Nolan. Paul's collection of folders—the ones she knew about, the ones she couldn't force herself to read. Whatever was going on with Adam Quinn. And now she had been told that Paul was a thief. Three million dollars? Nolan's estimate of Paul's net worth was off by several million. He'd only quoted what was in the bank. Paul didn't believe in the stock market. The house was paid off. The cars were paid for. There was no reason for Paul to steal anything.

She laughed at herself because that was all that she could do. "Why can I believe that Paul is a rapist but not a thief?"

The question stopped Lydia cold. "You believe me."

"I should've believed you years ago." Claire pushed herself

away from the wall. She felt the guilt of dragging Lydia into this mess. She had no right to jeopardize her sister, especially after all that had happened. "I'm sorry I asked you to come here. You should go."

Instead of answering, Lydia looked down at the floor. Her purse was a brown leather bag the size of a feedsack. Claire wondered if Paul had a photo of her buying it. Some of the pictures had obviously been taken with a telephoto lens, but others were close enough to read the text on the coupons she always used at the grocery store.

Lydia could never find out about Paul's surveillance. Claire could at least do that for her sister. Lydia had a seventeen-year-old daughter whose school tuition Paul was anonymously paying. She had a boyfriend. She had a mortgage. She had a business with two employees she was responsible for. Knowing that Paul had been there every step of the way would destroy her.

Claire said, "Pepper, really, you need to go. I never should've asked you to come here."

Lydia picked up her purse. She hefted the strap over her shoulder. She put her hand on the door but she didn't open it. "When's the last time you took a shower?"

Claire shook her head. She hadn't bathed since the morning of Paul's funeral.

"What about food? Have you been eating?"

Claire shook her head again. "I just . . ." She didn't know how to explain it. They had taken a cooking class a few months ago and Paul wasn't half bad, but now, every time she thought about her husband in the kitchen holding a knife, all she could think about was the machete from the movies.

"Claire?" Lydia had obviously asked her another question. Her purse was back on the floor. Her shoes were piled where she'd left them. "Go take a shower. I'll cook you something to eat."

"You should go," Claire told her. "You shouldn't get involved in this . . . this . . . I don't even know what it is, Liddie, but it's bad. It's worse than you could ever imagine."

"So I gathered."

Claire spoke the only truth she was certain of. "I don't deserve your forgiveness."

"I don't forgive you, but you're still my sister."

EIGHT

Lydia had texted Rick that she would be home in an hour. She would make sure Claire was bathed and fed, and then she would stand over her sister while she called Helen to come take care of her. Lydia had filled in for her mother twenty-four years ago and she wasn't going to do it again.

Especially with the FBI involved.

Just the thought of Fred Nolan made her nerves pulse with fear. The man obviously knew things about Paul that Claire did not know. Or maybe Claire knew them and she was just a very good actress. In which case, was Claire lying when she said she finally believed Lydia about Paul attacking her? If she wasn't, then what changed her mind? If she was, then what was her motivation?

There was no figuring it out. All the sneakiness her sister had exhibited as a child had been honed to adult perfection, so that

Claire could be standing right in front of an oncoming train and still insist that everything was going to be fine.

Actually, the more Lydia interacted with this adult Claire, the more she understood she hadn't grown up to be a Mother. She had grown up to be *their* mother.

Lydia stared blankly around the kitchen. She had thought that cooking Claire something to eat would be the easy part, but as with the rest of the house, the kitchen was too sleek to be practical. All of the appliances were concealed behind shiny white laminate doors that looked so cheap they had to cost a million bucks. Even the cooktop blended in with the polished quartz countertop. The whole space was part kitchen showroom, part *Jetsons*. She couldn't imagine that anyone would actually choose to live here.

Not that Claire was doing much living. The refrigerator was filled with unopened bottles of wine. The only food was a half-carton of eggs that expired in two days. Lydia found a new loaf of bread in one of the pantries. There was also a coffee machine, which Lydia only recognized because there was a label on it that said COFFEE MACHINE, followed by what she assumed was the installation date.

The laminated set of directions beside the machine was clearly Paul's handiwork. Lydia knew that her sister couldn't be bothered doing something so tedious and stupid. She pressed various buttons until the machine whirred to life. She slid an espresso cup under the spout and watched it fill.

"You figured it out," Claire said. She was dressed in a light blue button-down shirt and faded jeans. Her hair was slicked back to dry. For the first time, Lydia actually saw a woman who looked like her sister.

Lydia handed Claire the cup of coffee. "Drink this. It'll help sober you up."

Claire sat down at the counter. She blew on the steaming liquid to cool it. The counter stools were white leather and shiny chrome. The backs were low. They matched the couch and chairs in the family room that opened onto the kitchen. Wall-to-ceiling glass framed the back yard, where a pool that looked like it was carved from a giant slab of white marble served as a centerpiece for the barren landscape.

There was no part of this house that felt inviting. Paul's cold, calculating hand could be seen behind every choice. The concrete on the entryway floor was polished to a dark mirror straight out of *Snow White*. The spiral stairs looked like a robot's asshole. The endless white walls made Lydia feel like she was trapped inside a straitjacket. The sooner she was out of here the better.

Lydia found a frying pan in the drawer under the cooktop. She poured some oil in the pan and dropped in two slices of bread.

Claire asked, "Are you making me egg bread?"

Lydia fought a reflexive smile, because Claire sounded like she was thirteen again. Egg bread was Lydia's way of getting out of whisking eggs. She just threw it all into a pan and cooked it until the shininess was gone.

Claire said, "I'm on parole because I assaulted somebody."

Lydia almost dropped the carton of eggs.

"We're not supposed to call it assault, but that's what it was." Claire rolled the espresso cup between her hands. "Allison Hendrickson. My doubles partner. We were warming up for a game. She was talking about how she felt like a Holocaust survivor after the Liberation because her last kid was going off to college and she was finally going to be free."

Lydia cracked two eggs into the pan. She hated this bitch already.

"And then Allison started telling me about this friend of hers who had a daughter who went to college last year." Claire put down the cup. "Smart girl, always made good grades. And then the girl gets to college and goes crazy—starts screwing around, missing classes, drinking too much, all the stupid things you hear about kids doing."

Lydia used a spatula to stir the eggs around the bread. She was more than familiar with those stupid things.

"One night, the girl went to a frat party. Somebody slipped a roofie into her drink. Fast-forward to the next day, she wakes up naked in the basement of the frat house. She's battered and bruised, but she manages to find her way back to her dorm, where her roommate shows her a video that's been posted on YouTube."

Lydia froze. Every nightmare she had about Dee going off to college involved some variation on this theme.

"The guys at the frat house filmed everything. It was basically a gang rape. Allison went into great detail about it, because apparently, everyone on campus watched the film. And then she says to me, 'Can you believe that?' And I say no, but of course I can believe it, because people are horrible. And then Allison says, 'That stupid girl, getting drunk like that around a bunch of frat boys. It was her own fault for going to the party.'"

Claire looked as disgusted as Lydia felt. When Julia had first disappeared, people kept asking why she'd been at the bar, what she was doing out that late, and exactly how much alcohol she had consumed, because obviously, it was Julia's own fault that she was abducted and most likely raped and murdered.

Lydia asked, "What did you say?"

"I didn't say anything at first. I was too angry. But I didn't know I was angry, you know?"

Lydia shook her head, because she always knew when she was angry.

"I kept repeating Allison's words back in my head, and the anger just built up and built up. I could feel the pressure of it in my chest, like a tea kettle coming to a boil." Claire clasped together her hands. "Then the ball came over the net. It was clearly on her side, but I went for it. I remember pulling my arm across my body—I've still got a killer backhand—and I watched the racket cut through the air, and at the last minute, I took this tiny lunge forward and I smashed the edge of the racket into the side of her knee."

"Holy shit."

"She fell flat on her face. Broke her nose and two teeth. Blood was everywhere. I thought she was going to exsanguinate. I dislocated her knee, which is apparently very painful. She ended up needing two operations to get it back into place." Claire looked remorseful, but she didn't sound it. "I could've said it was a mistake. I can actually remember standing there on the court with all these excuses running through my head. Allison was writhing on the ground, screaming bloody murder, and I opened my mouth to say what a horrible accident, that I was an idiot, that I hadn't been looking where I was going and it was all my fault and blah-blah-blah, but instead of apologizing, I said, 'It's your own fault for playing tennis.'"

Lydia felt the shock of the act reverberate through the cold kitchen.

"The way the other women looked at me . . ." Claire shook her head, as if she still couldn't believe it. "I've never had people look at me like that before. There was this wave of revulsion. I could feel their disgust to my very core. And I've never told anyone this, not even Paul, but it felt so fucking good to be bad." This, at least, Claire sounded sure of. "You know me, Liddie. I never let loose like that. I usually just hold it all in because what's the point of letting it out, but something about that day made me just—" She held up her hands in surrender. "I was absolutely euphoric right up until I was arrested."

Lydia had forgotten about the egg bread. She moved the frying pan off the eye. "I can't believe they let you off with parole."

"We bought our way out of it." Claire shrugged the shrug of the extremely wealthy. "It took our lawyer a couple of months and a shit-ton of money to bring the Hendricksons around, but they finally told the prosecutor they were okay with parole and a lesser charge. I had to wear an ankle bracelet for six months. I have six more sessions with a court-appointed therapist. I'm on parole for another year."

Lydia didn't know what to say. Claire had never been much of a fighter. Lydia was the one who always got in trouble for giving Indian burns or holding Claire down and dangling spit into her eye.

Claire said, "Ironically, the monitoring bracelet was taken off the same day that Paul was killed." She took the plate of egg bread. "Or is that just coincidence, not irony? Mother would know."

Lydia had spotted the only coincidence that mattered. "When were you arrested?"

Claire's tight smile made it clear that she hadn't missed the connection. "The first week of March."

Julia had gone missing on March 4, 1991.

"So, that's why I'm on parole." Claire picked up the bread with her hands and took a bite. She had told the story of her arrest as if she was relating a funny thing that had happened at the grocery store, but Lydia could see that she had tears in her eyes. She looked exhausted. More than that, she looked scared. There was something about Claire that was so vulnerable. They could just as well be sitting at the kitchen table at their parents' house three decades ago.

Claire asked, "Do you remember the way Julia used to dance?"

Lydia was surprised by how clearly the memories came back. Julia had loved dancing. She would hear the faintest trace of music and throw herself completely into it. "Too bad she had such shitty taste in music."

"It wasn't that bad."

"Really, Menudo?"

Claire gave a surprised laugh, as if she had forgotten all about her crush on the boy band. "She was just so joyful. She loved so many things."

"Joyful," Lydia repeated, relishing the lightness of the word.

When Julia had first disappeared, everyone talked about how tragic it was that something bad had happened to such a good girl. Then the sheriff had floated his theory that Julia had just walked away—joined a hippie commune or run off with a guy— and the tone had changed from sympathetic to accusatory. Julia

Carroll was no longer the selfless girl who volunteered at the animal shelter and worked at the soup kitchen. She was the strident political activist who'd been jailed at a protest. The pushy reporter who alienated the entire staff of the school newspaper. The radical feminist who demanded the university hire more women. The drunk. The pothead. The whore.

It wasn't enough for Julia to be taken away from the family. All the good things about her had to be taken away, too.

Lydia told Claire, "I lied about where I was the night she disappeared. I was passed out in the Alley."

Claire looked surprised. The Alley was a seedy passageway that connected the Georgia Bar to the Roadhouse, two Athens dives that catered to underage townies. Lydia had told the sheriff she was practicing with the band in Leigh Dean's garage the night Julia went missing, when in actuality, she'd been just a stone's throw away from her sister.

Instead of pointing out the proximity, Claire told her, "I said I was studying with Bonnie Flynn, but actually, we were making out."

Lydia choked on a laugh. She had forgotten how good Claire was at tossing out shocking statements. "And?"

"I liked her brother better." Claire picked up a piece of egg between her thumb and finger, but she didn't eat it. "I saw you on the road this afternoon. I was parked in front of the McDonald's. You were stopped at the light."

Lydia felt the hair on her neck go up. She remembered stopping at a red light by the McDonald's on the way to the cemetery. She'd had no idea that someone was watching her. "I didn't see you."

"I know. I followed you for about twenty minutes. I don't know what I was thinking. I wasn't surprised when you ended up at the cemetery. It seemed fitting—a bookend. Paul split us apart. Why wouldn't he bring us back together?" She pushed away the plate. "Not that I think you'll ever forgive me. And you shouldn't, because I was never going to forgive you."

Lydia wasn't sure forgiveness was in her wheelhouse. "What made you believe me after all this time?"

Claire didn't answer. She was staring at the half-finished food on her plate. "I loved him. I know you don't want to believe that, but I really, truly, giddy, heartbreaking, longing, achingly loved him."

Lydia said nothing.

"I'm so angry with myself, because it was all right in front of me and I never thought to question it."

Lydia got the distinct feeling that the conversation had shifted to something else. She asked a question that had been fermenting in the back of her mind. "If Paul's business partner settled out of court, why is the FBI still bothering you? There's no criminal case. It's over."

Claire's jaw worked. She was gritting her teeth.

"Are you going to answer me?"

"This is the part that's dangerous." She paused. "Or maybe not. I don't know. But it's almost midnight. I'm sure you want to go home. I had no right to ask you over in the first place."

"Then why did you?"

"Because I'm selfish, and because you are the only person left in my life who was ever capable of making anything better."

Lydia knew that Paul had been the other person. She didn't

appreciate the association. "What did he do to you, Claire?"

Claire looked down at the counter. She wasn't wearing make-up, but she wiped underneath her eyes in the careful way you did when you were wearing mascara. "He was watching these movies. Not just porn, but violent porn."

The only thing that surprised Lydia was that Claire actually cared. "I'm not taking up for him, but men watch all kinds of weird shit."

"It wasn't weird, Liddie. It was violent. And graphic. A woman is murdered, and this man in a leather mask rapes her while she's dying."

Lydia covered her mouth with her hand. She was speechless.

"There are twenty short films. Vignettes, I guess, of two different women. They're both tortured and electrocuted and burned and branded like cattle. I can't even describe the other things that are done to them. The first girl is murdered." She gripped her hands together. "The second girl looks like Anna Kilpatrick."

Lydia's heart quivered like a harp string. "You have to call the police."

"I did more than that. I took all of the movies to the cops, and they said they were fake, but—" She looked up at Lydia, her face a study in devastation. "I don't think they're fake, Liddie. I think the first woman was really killed. And the girl . . . I'm not sure. I just don't know anymore."

"Let me see them."

"No." Claire vehemently shook her head. "You can't watch them. They're awful. You'll never be able to unsee them."

The words reminded Lydia of her father. Toward the end of his life, he'd often said that about Julia, that there were just some things that you couldn't unsee. Still, she had to know. Lydia insisted, "I want to see the girl who looks like Anna Kilpatrick."

Claire started to argue the point, but she obviously wanted a second opinion. "You can't play the movie. You can only look at her face."

Lydia would play the damn movie if she wanted to. "Where is it?"

Claire reluctantly stood from the bar. She led Lydia to the mudroom and opened the side door. There was a piece of wood where the window should've been.

Claire explained, "There was a break-in on the day of the funeral. Nothing was taken. The caterers stopped them."

"Were they looking for the movies?"

Claire turned around, surprised. "I never even considered it. The police said there's a gang that trawls obituaries looking for houses to rob during funerals."

Lydia had a vague recollection of hearing something similar on the news, but it was still a weird coincidence.

They walked across the large motorcourt toward the garage, which was twice the size of Lydia's house. One of the bay doors was already open. The first thing Lydia saw was a cabinet on its side. Then a set of broken golf clubs. Hand tools. Machinery. Paint cans. Tennis rackets. The garage had been completely ransacked.

"This is my own apeshittery," Claire said, not elaborating. "The burglars didn't make it into the garage."

"You did this?"

"I know," Claire said, as if they were gossiping about another person.

Lydia stepped carefully because her shoes were back inside the house. She braced her hand against a BMW X5 as she stepped over the toppled cabinet. There was a beautiful charcoal Porsche that looked like someone had taken a hammer to it. The silver Tesla had pockmarks on the hood. She was fairly certain that even in their damaged states, any one of these cars could pay off her mortgage.

Claire jumped right into the story. "There was a Thunderbolt cable that went upstairs. Paul drilled a hole in the floor so it could plug directly into his computer."

Lydia looked up at the ceiling. The Sheetrock had been broken open.

Claire said, "I couldn't stay up there anymore. Paul's MacBook was in the Tesla's front trunk. I got it out and put it here, and then got the cable out of the wall so I could plug it in." She was almost breathless, the same way she used to get when she was little and wanted to tell Lydia something that had happened at school. "I did a search on the laptop to see if there were any more movies. I didn't find anything, though who knows? Paul was very good with computers. Then again, he never really bothered to hide anything because he knew that I would never look." She told Lydia, "I trusted him."

Lydia followed the destruction to a silver MacBook Pro that was set up on the workbench. Claire had used a hammer to punch out the Sheetrock, which Lydia knew because the hammer was still stuck in the wall. A thin white cable hung down like a piece of string. Claire had plugged it into the laptop.

"Look back there." Claire pointed behind the workbench. "You can see the light from the external hard drive."

Lydia had to push up onto her toes to see what she meant. She craned her neck. There was the flashing light. The drive was embedded in the wall. The niche was professionally built out, including a trim detail. If Lydia stared long enough, she could almost see the schematic in her head.

"I had no idea it was there. All of this . . ." Claire indicated the garage. "This entire building was designed to hide his secrets." She paused, studying Lydia. "Are you really sure you want to see it?"

For the first time, Lydia felt real trepidation about the movies. Back in the house, what Claire had described sounded terrible, but Lydia had somehow convinced herself that they couldn't be that bad. Rick and Dee loved watching horror movies. Lydia assumed the vignettes couldn't be any worse. Now, faced with the level of Paul's deception, she understood that Claire was probably right: The movies were far worse than anything Lydia could imagine.

Still, she said, "Yes."

Claire opened the laptop. She turned the screen away from Lydia. She moved her finger along the trackpad until she found what she was looking for, then she gave it a click. "This is the best view of her face."

Lydia hesitated, but then she saw the girl on the screen. She was chained to a wall. Her body was torn up. There was no better way to describe what had been done to her. Skin was rent. Burns gaped like open sores. She had been branded. There was a large X burned into her belly, slightly off-center, just below her ribs.

Lydia tasted fear in her mouth. She could practically smell the burning flesh.

"It's too much." Claire tried to close the laptop.

Lydia stopped her hand. Every part of her body was responding to the unnatural acts on the screen. She felt ill. She was sweating. Even her eyes hurt. This was not like any horror movie she had ever seen. The signs of torture weren't meant to scare the viewer. They were meant to arouse.

"Liddie?"

"I'm okay." Her voice was muffled. At some point, she'd put her hand over her mouth. Lydia realized that she'd been so over-whelmed by the violence that she hadn't even looked at the girl's face. At first glance, she looked an awful lot like Anna Kilpatrick. Lydia stepped closer. She leaned down and almost touched her nose to the display. There was a magnifying glass by the laptop. She used it to take an even closer look.

Finally, Lydia said, "I can't tell, either. I mean, yes, she looks like Anna, but lots of girls that age look alike." Lydia didn't tell Claire that all of Dee's friends looked the same. Instead, she put down the magnifying glass. "What did the police say?"

"He said it wasn't Anna. Not that I asked the question, because I didn't pick up on the similarity until I was at the police station. But now that it's in my head, I can't get it out."

"What do you mean, you didn't ask the question?"

"It never occurred to me that she looked like Anna Kilpatrick, but that was the first thing Captain Mayhew said when I showed him the movie: It's not Anna Kilpatrick."

"The guy in charge of the Kilpatrick case is named Jacob Mayhew. He's got a Huckleberry mustache. I saw him on the news tonight."

"That's him, Captain Jacob Mayhew."

"Anna Kilpatrick's all over the news. Why would the guy in charge of finding her stop everything to work on a house robbery?"

Claire chewed her lip. "Maybe he assumed I was showing him the movie because I knew he was investigating the Kilpatrick case." She met Lydia's gaze straight on. "He told me that she's dead."

Lydia had assumed as much, but having it confirmed didn't make it any easier. Even with Julia, who had been gone so long that it wasn't possible she was still alive, Lydia always held out a tiny sliver of hope. "Have they found her body?"

"They found blood in her car. Mayhew said the volume was too much, that she couldn't live without it."

"But the news didn't say that." Lydia knew she was grasping at straws. "Her family's still making pleas for her safe return."

"How many years did Mom and Dad do the same thing?"

They were both quiet, both probably thinking their own thoughts about Julia. Lydia could still remember Sheriff Huckabee telling her parents that if Julia hadn't walked away on her own, she was most likely dead. Helen had slapped him across the face. Sam had threatened to sue the sheriff's department into oblivion if they even thought about suspending the investigation.

Lydia felt a lump in her throat. She struggled to clear it. There was more that Claire wasn't telling her. She was either trying to protect Lydia or trying to protect herself. "I want you to start from the beginning and tell me everything that's happened."

"Are you sure?"

Lydia waited.

Claire leaned against the workbench. "I guess it started when we got back from the funeral."

Claire ran it down for her, from finding the movies on Paul's computer, to Nolan's intrusive questions, to her decision to hand everything over to the police. Lydia asked her to repeat herself when she described Mayhew's less-than-casual curiosity about whether or not Claire had made copies of the movies. And then she got to the part about Adam Quinn leaving the threatening note on her car, and Lydia couldn't keep silent anymore.

She asked, "What files is he talking about?"

"I'm not sure. Work files? Paul's secret files? Something to do with the money Paul stole?" She shook her head. "I still can't understand that. Nolan was right about us being flush. Why steal something you don't need?"

Lydia held back her response—why try to rape someone when you had a beautiful, willing girlfriend back home? Instead, she asked, "Did you check Paul's laptop for a 'Work in Progress folder'?"

Claire's blank expression answered the question. "I was just worried about finding more movies." She leaned over the MacBook and started searching the drive. The Work in Progress folder came up immediately. They both scanned the file names.

Claire said, "These extensions are for an architectural software. You can tell by the dates that Paul was working on them the day that he was murdered."

"What's an extension?"

"It's the letters that come after the period in a file name. They tell you what the file format is, like .jpeg is for photographs and .pdf is for printed documents." She clicked open each of the files. There was a drawing of a staircase, some windows, elevations. "Conceptual drawings. They're all for work."

Lydia considered their options. "Make copies of the files for Adam Quinn. If he leaves you alone, then you know he's not involved."

Claire seemed astonished by the simple solution. She opened the door to the Tesla and grabbed a set of keys that had been tossed onto the dashboard. "I bought Paul this keychain when Auburn went to the BCS bowl. There's a USB drive inside."

Lydia wondered if her sister knew how light her voice sounded when she talked about her life with Paul. It was almost like Claire was two different people—the woman who loved and believed in her husband and the woman who knew he was a monster.

Lydia told her, "I don't want you seeing Adam alone. Text him that you'll leave it in the mailbox."

"That's a good idea." Claire was trying to pry open the split metal keyring with her thumbnail. "I have a burner phone in the house."

Lydia didn't ask her why she had a burner phone. Instead, she went to the laptop and clicked all of the architectural files closed. She stared at the paused movie on the computer screen. The girl's eyes were wide with fear. Her lips were parted as if she was about to start screaming. Part of Lydia was tempted to play the movie out, to see just how bad it would get.

Lydia closed the movie.

The Gladiator drive showed in the finder. She studied the file names, which were numbers, just as Claire had said. "There has to be a pattern to these."

"I couldn't figure it out. Fuck." Claire had split her fingernail on the metal ring.

"Aren't there a million tools in here?"

Claire scrounged around until she found a screwdriver. She sat cross-legged on the floor while she jammed apart the keyring with a metal file.

Lydia studied the file names again. There had to be a code that would explain the numbers. Instead of offering a solution, she said, "Agent Nolan made a point tonight about watching movies. If he meant Paul's movies, how would he know about them?"

Claire looked up. "Maybe he's into them, too?"

"He seems like the type," Lydia said, though she was only guessing. "Why was he here for a house robbery?"

"That's the big question. No one wanted him here. Mayhew clearly can't stand him. So what was Nolan looking for?"

"If Mayhew is involved—"

"Then why put pressure on me?" Claire sounded exasperated. "I don't know anything. Why Paul watched the movies. Who else watched them. What Mayhew knows. What Nolan knows. Or doesn't know. I feel like I'm running around in circles."

Lydia felt the same way, and she'd only been doing this for a few hours.

Claire said, "Nolan flirts with me, right? The way he looked at me tonight, like he was checking me out. You picked up on that?"

"Yes."

"He's creepy, right?"

He was beyond creepy, but Lydia just said, "I guess."

"Ha." Claire stood, holding up the separated keytag in triumph. The plastic medallion was imprinted with the orange and blue logo of Auburn University. Claire pulled it apart, then shoved the USB connector into the laptop. She clicked open the drive. Lydia saw that it was empty save for the software folder.

She breathed a sigh of relief. "Thank God."

"No kidding." Claire copied the Work in Progress folder onto the drive. "I hope these are the files Adam was talking about. I don't think I can take it if they're not."

Lydia noticed a striking similarity between the way she talked about Paul and the way she talked about Adam Quinn. And then she remembered something Nolan had intimated as they all stood at the front door. "You were sleeping with Adam Quinn."

Claire shrugged with feigned innocence. "My court-appointed therapist would say I was trying to fill a hole."

"Is that what you call your vagina?"

Claire chuckled under her breath.

"Unbelievable," Lydia muttered, though history told her it was completely believable.

When Rick had asked Lydia to tell him about Claire, she had left out the part about her sister being sexually liberated. Not that Claire was sloppy about it. She was remarkably adept at compartmentalizing everyone in her life. Her townie friends never met her college friends. Her cheerleading friends never mixed with her track club friends and hardly anyone knew she was on the tennis team. None of them would've ever guessed she was sleeping around. Especially whichever man she was dating at the time.

"Finished." Claire ejected the USB drive. "All right. That's at least one thing that's done."

Lydia didn't care about Adam Quinn anymore. Some component in the back of her brain had been working the puzzle of Paul's code, and she finally understood what he'd done. "The movie names. They're coded dates." She turned to Claire. "Like, if a file was named 1-2-3-4-5, the code would be 1-5-2-4-3. You take the first number, then the last number, then the second number, then the second-from-last number, and work your way into the middle until they're all accounted for."

Claire was already nodding. "So, November 1, 2015, is 11-01-2015, which would make the code 1-5-1-1-0-0-1-2."

"Exactly."

She pointed to the screen. "The last file on the list is the first movie with the girl who looks like Anna Kilpatrick."

Lydia translated the date. "It was made a day after she went missing."

Claire leaned heavily on the workbench. "This is how it's been for the last two days. Every time I convince myself the movies aren't real, something else comes along and I think maybe they are."

Lydia had to play devil's advocate. "I'm not taking up for Paul, but so what if it's real? There's all kinds of shit on the Internet showing people being shot or beheaded or raped or whatever. It's disgusting to watch it, and if Paul knew it was Anna Kilpatrick, he should've reported it to the police, but it's not illegal to just shut up and watch it."

Claire seemed battered by the brutal truth behind Lydia's words. She tucked her chin down the same way Dee did when she didn't want to talk about something.

"Claire?"

She shook her head. "If it's not illegal, then why does Nolan keep coming here? And why did Mayhew act so weird when he asked me if I made any copies?"

"Maybe Nolan's just a prick and he can't stand it that Paul got away with breaking the law." Lydia had to give Captain Mayhew's part a bit more thought. "Mayhew could be trying to protect you. That's what men do around you. They always have. But let's say the movies are real. So what?" Saying those two words a second time made Lydia realize how awful she sounded, because these women were human beings with families. Still, she had to push on. "Worst-case scenario, Mayhew was trying to keep you from thinking your husband is morally bankrupt."

"Paul *was* morally bankrupt." Claire spoke with deadly cold conviction. "I found more files. Paper files."

Lydia felt panic wind up inside of her chest like a watch.

"Paul kept them upstairs in his office. Two big boxes of files and God knows what else. I recognized one of the names on the labels." Claire's gaze shifted to the side the same way it did when she was little and she was trying to hide something.

"What name did you recognize?"

Claire looked down at her hands. She was picking the cuticle on her thumb. "The woman's name was familiar to me. I saw her on the news. A story, I mean, not actually her. She came forward because normally the news wouldn't print, I mean, interview—"

"Claire, use your words."

Claire still would not look up. "Paul was collecting information on a lot of women, and I know that at least one of the women was raped."

"How do you know?"

Claire finally looked her in the eye. "I saw her name on the news. I don't know her. Paul never mentioned her to me. She's just this stranger who's been raped, and Paul has a file on her. And he has a lot of files on other women, too."

Lydia felt a sudden cold come over her body. "What kind of information was he collecting?"

"Where they work. Who they date. Where they go. He hired private detectives to follow them without their knowledge. There are pictures and reports and background checks." Claire obviously felt cold, too. She stuck her hands deep into her front pockets. "From what I saw, he checks in on them once a year, the same time every year, and I keep asking myself why would he have them followed if not for a reason, and what if that reason is that he raped all of them?"

Lydia felt like a hummingbird was trapped in her throat. "Does he have a file on me?"

"No."

Lydia studied her carefully. Claire had always held on to secrets like a cat. Was she lying? Could Lydia trust her about something so important?

"They're in my office." Claire hesitated. "Not that I'm saying you should look at them. I mean . . ." She shrugged. "I don't know what I mean. I'm sorry. I'm sorry I've pulled you into this. You can still go. You should probably go."

Lydia looked down the driveway. Rick's truck was parked in a turn-around by the front of the house. He wouldn't let Lydia drive the van until he changed the wiper blades, which kindness she had returned by letting a special agent with the FBI record his license plate number.

Rick had crossed paths with the various law enforcement agencies during his time as a heroin addict, because he'd managed to sell almost as much as he'd used. Nolan would need to block out a few hours to read his rap sheet. And then what would he do? Go to the gas station and harass Rick until his boss had to let him go? Swing by the house to interrogate him, and maybe run a check on his neighbors and find out that Lydia lived next door?

And then Dee would be pulled into it, and the Mothers would find out, and the people who worked at Lydia's shop would be harassed, and maybe her clients, who would make lame apologies about how they couldn't let a woman being investigated by the FBI give their poodle a sanitary shave because it was too complicated.

"Pepper?" Claire had her arms crossed low on her waist. "You should go. I mean it this time. I can't involve you in this."

"I'm already in it up to my neck."

"Pepper."

Lydia climbed her way back through the garage. Instead of going down the driveway, she headed toward the house. She had dealt with her share of cops, too. They were sharks looking for blood, and by the sound of it, Claire had two boxes of chum in her office that might just get Agent Fred Nolan off all of their backs.

NINE

Claire slumped down into the overstuffed chair in her office as she watched her sister go through Paul's collection of files. Lydia seemed energized by the prospect of uncovering more lurid details, but Claire felt as though she was suffocating under the weight of every new revelation. She couldn't believe that only two days ago, she had watched Paul's coffin as it was lowered into the ground. Her body might as well have been buried along with him. Her skin felt desiccated. She had a deep chill in her bones. Even blinking was a challenge, because the temptation to keep her eyes closed was almost too much to resist.

She stared at the burner phone in her hand. At 12:31 in the morning, Adam had responded to her text about the files with a short, "Okay."

Claire didn't know what that "okay" meant. The USB drive

was waiting for him in the mailbox. Was Adam reserving his judgment until he saw what was on it?

She dropped the phone on the side table. She was sick of all these unanswered questions, and angry that instead of grieving for her husband, she was questioning her own sanity for loving him in the first place.

Lydia clearly had no such reservations. She was sitting on the floor going through the plastic boxes, her expression the same as every Halloween night they'd shared as kids. She had the colored folders stacked by name on the floor in front of her. The colors corresponded to years, which meant that over the last six years, Paul had paid to have eighteen women stalked.

Or worse.

Claire did not tell Lydia that this was likely the tip of the iceberg. While they were out in the garage, she had remembered the storage room in the basement under the main house. Claire had forgotten about the room because she'd only seen it once when they first moved in. This fact would probably sound unbelievable to Lydia, but the basement was huge. There was a screening room, a full gym, a locker room with sauna and steam room, a massage room, a wine cellar, a billiards room with both a pool table and a ping-pong table, a guest suite with full bath, a caterers' kitchen at the base of the elevator, a stocked bar, and a seating area large enough to comfortably accommodate twenty people.

Was it any wonder that Claire had forgotten about a room the size of a jail holding area?

Paul was too organized to be called a hoarder, but he liked to keep things. Claire had always chalked up his collections to having lost everything when his parents died, but now she was seeing a more sinister motivation. He'd built shelves downstairs in the storage closet to hold the many plastic file boxes that he'd been filling since his time at Auburn. When they'd first moved into the house, he'd shown Claire the artifacts he'd kept from their early years—the first birthday card she'd ever given him, a note scribbled on paper that recorded the first time she'd ever written him the words "I love you."

At the time, Claire had found his collection awfully sweet, but now all she could think about was that there were dozens of boxes down there, and that three women a year for the last eighteen years would mean fifty-four more folders filled with fifty-four more unspeakable violations.

There was one file that Lydia would never see. Her sister was disturbed enough by the contents of the folders. If she found out that Paul had done the same to her, there would be no going back.

"Are you all right?" Lydia looked up from the report she was reading. "Do you want to go lie down?"

"I'm fine," Claire said, but her eyelids felt heavy. Her body was so tired that her hands were trembling. She had read somewhere or heard somewhere that criminals always go to sleep after they confess their crimes. Concealing their bad acts took up so much energy that having the truth laid bare brought on a deep, sweet sleep.

Had she confessed to Lydia? Or had she just shared a burden?

Claire closed her eyes. Her breathing got deeper. She was awake—she could still hear Lydia greedily thumbing through pages—but she was also asleep, and in that sleep, she felt herself dipping into a dream. There was no narrative, just fragments of a typical day. She was at her desk paying bills. She was practicing the piano. She was in the kitchen trying to come up with a grocery list. She was making phone calls to raise money for the Christmas toy drive. She was studying the shoes in her closet, trying to put together an outfit to wear to lunch.

Through all of this, she could feel Paul's presence in the house. They were very independent people. They'd always had their own interests, done their own things, but Claire always felt reassured when Paul was close by. Light bulbs would be changed. Faults would be cleared from the security system. The remote control would be deciphered. Trash would be taken out. Clothes would be folded. Batteries would be charged. Big spoons and little spoons would never mingle in the silverware drawer.

He was such a sturdy, capable man. She liked that he was taller than she was. She liked that she had to look up at him when they were dancing. She liked the way she felt when his arms were around her. He was so much stronger than Claire. Sometimes, he would pick her up. She would feel her feet lift off the ground. His chest felt so solid against hers. He would tease her about something silly, and she would laugh because she knew that he loved hearing her laugh, and then he would say, "Tell me you want this."

Claire jerked awake. Her arms flew up as if to ward off a blow. Her throat felt scratchy. Her heart clicked against her ribs.

Morning sun streamed into her office. Lydia was gone. The plastic boxes were empty. The files were gone.

Claire lunged toward her desk. She opened the drawer. Lydia's file was still hidden inside. Claire's relief was so pronounced that she wanted to cry.

She touched her fingers to her cheek. She *was* crying. Her tear ducts were on constant standby for anything that would send them over. Instead of giving in to it, Claire shut the drawer. She wiped her eyes. She stood up. She straightened her shirt as she made her way to the kitchen.

She heard Lydia's voice before she saw her. She was obviously talking on the phone.

"Because I want you to stay at Rick's tonight." Lydia paused. "Because I said so." She paused again. "Sweetheart, I know you're an adult, but adults are like vampires. The older ones are much more powerful."

Claire smiled. She had known Lydia would be a good mother. She sounded just like Helen before Julia disappeared.

"All right. I love you, too."

Claire stayed in the hallway long after Lydia had ended the call. She didn't want her sister to have any fears about being overheard. If Claire was going to continue to lie about knowing every single detail of Lydia's life, she could at least do a good job.

She smoothed down the back of her hair as she walked into the kitchen. "Hey."

Lydia was sitting at the bar. She was wearing reading glasses, which would've been funny if Claire wasn't a couple of years away from needing them herself. Paul's files were scattered across the kitchen island. Lydia had Claire's iPad in front of her. She took off the reading glasses as she asked, "Did you sleep all right?"

"I'm sorry." Claire didn't know what she was apologizing for; there were so many things to choose from. "I should've helped you go through all of this."

"No, you should've gotten some sleep." Lydia started to lean back in the chair, but she caught herself before she fell over the low back. "These are the stupidest chairs I've ever sat in."

"They look good," Claire said, because that was all that had ever mattered to Paul. She went to the video screen on the kitchen wall. The flashing time read 6:03. She pulled up the mailbox camera. Adam hadn't been by yet. Claire didn't know what to make of that, because she still didn't know which files Adam was after.

She told Lydia, "The USB drive is still in the mailbox."

"You have a camera in your mailbox?"

"Doesn't everybody?"

Lydia gave a sour look. "What was the name of the woman you saw on the news?"

Claire shook her head. She didn't understand.

"In the garage, you said that you recognized a woman's name from one of the files because you had seen her on the news. I looked them all up on your iPad. Only two had news items."

Claire spitballed an explanation. "She was in Atlanta."

"Leslie Lewis?" Lydia pushed an open file folder across the counter so that Claire could see the woman's photograph. She was blonde and pretty and wearing thick black glasses. "I found a story about her in the *Atlanta Journal* archives. She was staying in a hotel during Dragon Con. She thought she was opening her door for room service, but a guy pushed his way in and raped her."

Claire looked away from the woman's photo. Quinn + Scott's downtown offices were near the convention site. Last year, Paul had sent her pictures of drunken people dressed like Darth Vader and the Green Lantern clogging the street.

Lydia slid over another file: another pretty, young blonde. "Pam Clayton. There was a story in the *Patch*. She was jogging near Stone Mountain Park. The attacker dragged her into the woods. It was after seven, but it was August so it was still light out."

Paul's tennis team occasionally had games in the park.

"Look at the dates on the files. He hired the detectives to follow them on the anniversaries of their rapes."

Claire took her word for it. She didn't want to read any more details. "Did the attacker say anything to either of them?"

"If he did, it wasn't in the articles. We need the police reports."

Claire wondered why Paul hadn't asked the private detectives to track down the reports. Lydia's file contained her arrest records and all the ancillary paperwork. Maybe Paul figured it was a bad idea to tip his hand by asking all of these different detectives to check up on all of these women who had been raped. Or maybe he didn't need the reports because he already knew exactly what had happened to them.

Or maybe he was getting the reports from Captain Jacob Mayhew.

"Claire?"

She shook her head, but now that she had the thought in her mind, she couldn't get rid of it. Why hadn't she studied Mayhew's expression while he watched the movies? Then again, what good would it do? Hadn't she learned enough about Paul's duplicity to realize that her judgment could not be trusted?

"Claire?" Lydia waited for her attention. "Did you notice something about the women?"

Claire shook her head again.

"They all look like you."

Claire didn't point out that that meant they looked like Lydia, too. "So, what now? We're holding these women's lives in our hands. We don't know if we can trust Mayhew. Even if we did, he didn't take the movies seriously. Why would he investigate the files?"

Lydia shrugged. "We can call Nolan."

Claire couldn't believe what she was suggesting. "Better these women than us, you mean?"

"I wouldn't put it like that, but now that you—"

"They've already been raped. You want to sic that asshole on them, too?"

Lydia shrugged. "Maybe it'll give them some peace knowing that the man who attacked them isn't around anymore."

"That's a bullshit excuse." Claire was adamant. "We know firsthand what Nolan is like. He probably won't even believe them. Or worse, he'll flirt with them like he flirts with me. There's a reason most women don't go to the cops when they're raped."

"What are you going to do, write them a check?"

Claire walked into the family room before she said something she would regret. Writing some checks didn't sound like a bad idea. Paul had attacked these women. The least she could do was pay for therapy or whatever else they needed.

Lydia said, "If Paul had actually raped me, and I found out that every September for almost eighteen years, he'd been stalking me, taking pictures of me, I would want to grab a gun and kill him."

Claire stared at the Rothko over the fireplace. "What would you do if you found out that he was already dead and there was nothing you could do about it?"

"I would still want to know."

Claire felt no temptation to reveal the truth. Lydia had always blustered about how tough she was, but there was a reason she was already numbing herself with drugs at the age of sixteen.

Claire said, "I can't do it. I won't do it."

"I know you don't want to hear it, but it makes me glad to know he's dead. And to know how he died, even though it must have been rotten for you."

"Rotten," Claire repeated, thinking the word was borderline insulting. *Rotten* was being late for a movie or losing a great parking space. Watching your husband get stabbed and bleed to death in front of your own eyes was fucking excruciating. "No. I won't do it."

"Fine." Lydia started grabbing folders and stacking them together. She was clearly angry, but Claire wasn't going to back down. She knew what it was like to be the focus of Fred Nolan's interest. She couldn't unleash that on Paul's victims. There was already enough guilt on her conscience without throwing these poor women into the lion's den.

She walked farther into the family room. The sunlight was blinding. Claire closed her eyes for a moment and let the heat from the sun warm her face. And then she turned away because it seemed wrong to enjoy something so basic considering all of the misery they had uncovered.

Her gaze traveled to the area behind one of the couches. Lydia had spread out some paperwork on the floor. Instead of more private detective reports, Claire was surprised to recognize her father's handiwork.

Sam Carroll had devoted an entire wall in his apartment to

tracking down leads about Julia. There were photographs and note-cards and torn sheets of paper with phone numbers and names scribbled across them. In all, the entire collection took up around five by ten feet of space. He'd lost his deposit for the apartment because of all the holes the thumbtacks had left in the Sheetrock.

She asked Lydia, "You kept Dad's wall?"

"No, it was in the second file box."

Of course it was.

Claire knelt down. The wall had defined her father for so many years. His desperation still emanated from every scrap of paper. Vet school had taught him to be a meticulous note-taker. He had recorded everything he'd read or heard or witnessed, combined police reports and statements, until the case was as imprinted on his brain as the structure of a dog's digestive system or the signs of feline leukemia.

She picked up a sheet of notebook paper that had her father's handwriting on it. In the last two weeks of his life, Sam Carroll had developed a slight palsy after a minor stroke. His suicide note had been barely legible. Claire had forgotten what his original penmanship looked like.

She asked Lydia, "What's it called?"

"The Palmer Method." Lydia was standing behind Claire. "He was supposed to be left-handed, but they made him use his right hand."

"They did that to me, too."

"They made you wear a mitten so you wouldn't use your left hand. Mom was furious when she found out."

Claire sat down on the floor. She couldn't stop touching the only pieces she had left of her father. Sam had handled this picture of a man who talked to another man who had a sister who maybe knew something about Julia. He had touched this matchbook from the Manhattan, the bar where Julia was last seen. He had written notes on this menu from the Grit, her favorite vegetarian restaurant. He had stared at this photograph of Julia leaning against her bike.

Claire stared at the photograph, too. A gray houndstooth fedora was in the handlebar basket. Julia's long blonde hair cascaded around her shoulders in a soft perm. She was wearing a man's black suit jacket and white dress shirt with tons of silver and black bangles on her wrists and white lace gloves on her hands because it was the late 1980s and every girl they knew back then wanted to look like either Cyndi Lauper or Madonna.

Claire said, "I want to tell myself that Paul kept all of this because one day, he thought I might want to see it."

Lydia lowered herself to the floor beside Claire. She pointed to the photo of Julia. "That's my locket she's wearing. It had a cursive L on the front."

They both knew that Julia was still wearing the gold locket when she disappeared. Claire said, "She was always stealing your things."

Lydia bumped her shoulder. "You were always stealing mine."

Claire was suddenly struck by a thought. "Did Paul have a file on me?"

"No."

She studied her sister, wondering if Lydia was lying to her for the same reason that Claire was lying to Lydia.

Lydia asked, "What about Dad's journals?" Sam had started

keeping a diary after Helen left because there was no one left to confide in. "They weren't in Paul's boxes."

"Maybe Mom has them?" Claire shrugged. She had felt so disconnected from her father at the time of his death that she hadn't asked for any of his belongings. It was only later, when she thought of things like his glasses or his books or his collection of animal-themed ties, that she wished she'd been more present.

She told Lydia, "I used to read his journals. Probably because he tried to hide them from me. Bonus points to Paul." She leaned back against the wall. "The last section I read was about six months before he died. They were written like letters to Julia. Things that he remembered about her growing up. How we had all changed without her. He didn't act like it, but he was pretty tuned in to our lives. He knew exactly what we were up to."

"God, I hope not."

"He and Mom still got together. Even after she remarried."

Lydia nodded. "I know."

Claire saw another photo of Julia that she had forgotten about. She groaned as she got up on her knees to retrieve it. She'd torn her meniscus five years ago and it still felt like it was looking for any excuse to crack back open. "Are your knees as bad as mine?"

"Not as bad as Allison Hendrickson's."

"Fair point." Claire looked down at the picture. Julia was sunning herself on the front lawn in a blue two-piece bathing suit. Her pink skin glistened with baby oil. Lydia was probably behind the camera. They never let Claire sunbathe with them. Or go out with them. Or breathe near them. "God, look at how red her skin is. She would've had all kinds of skin cancer."

"I had a spot removed last year." Lydia pointed to the side of her nose.

Claire was momentarily grateful for being left out. "I bet she would've had tons of kids."

"Future young Republicans."

Claire laughed. Julia had feigned a stomach-ache so she could stay home from school and watch the Iran–Contra hearings. "She would've home-schooled her kids to keep them from being brain-washed by the public education machine."

"And made them eat so much soy that their testicles never dropped."

Claire shuffled around some of her father's notes. "Oh, no, she wouldn't have boys. That's giving in to the patriarchy."

"Do you think she would've vaccinated?"

Claire barked a laugh, because even in 1991, Julia had doubted the veracity of the government-backed pharmaceutical industrial complex. "What's this?" She picked up a stapled stack of papers from the Oconee County Superior Court.

Lydia squinted at the document. "I found it in a separate folder. It's a deed for a property in Watkinsville."

Paul had grown up in Watkinsville, which was just outside of Athens. Claire turned to the second page to find the name and address of the legal owner.

"Buckminster Fuller," Lydia said, because of course she'd already seen it. "Why does that name sound familiar?"

"He was Paul's favorite architect." She handed Lydia the pages because she couldn't look at them anymore. "Paul grew up on a farm in Watkinsville. He told me that everything was sold when his parents died."

Lydia stood up from the floor. She retrieved her reading glasses and Claire's iPad from the kitchen island and sat back down beside her.

Claire felt the building wave of nausea that always accompanied uncovering another one of Paul's lies.

Lydia slid on her glasses and started to type. Claire stared at the back of the white leather couch. She wanted to rip open the leather with her fingernails. She wanted to break the wood frame, find some matches, and burn down this entire fucking house.

Not that it would burn. Paul had installed the most comprehensive residential fire-suppression system that the county building inspector had ever seen.

Lydia said, "The online records only go back ten years, but Buckminster Fuller's property taxes are up to date."

Claire thought about the painting in Paul's office. His childhood home. She had spent hours getting the shadows and angles just right. He had cried when she'd given it to him for their anniversary.

She told Lydia, "Paul said the guy who bought the property tore down the house so he could farm the land."

"Did you ever drive by to look at it?"

"No." Claire had asked several times. In the end, she had respected his need for privacy. "Paul said it was too painful."

Lydia went back to work on the iPad. This time, Claire made herself watch. Lydia pulled up Google Earth. She typed in the Watkinsville address. Acres of plowed fields showed on the screen. Lydia zoomed in closer. There was a small house on the property. Claire easily recognized Paul's childhood home. The white wood siding ran up and down instead of across. The barn had been torn down, but there was a car in the driveway and a child's swingset in the large patch of back yard that separated the house from the farmer's field.

Lydia said, "There's no street view. The road doesn't even have a name." She asked, "Do you think he's renting it out?"

Claire put her head in her hands. She didn't know anything anymore.

"There's a phone number." Lydia got up again. She was reaching for her cell phone on the counter when Claire stopped her.

"Use the burner phone. It's by the chair in my office."

Lydia disappeared down the hallway. Claire stared out at the back yard. The windows were clouded with condensation. Mist was coming off the pool. She would need to have the heater turned down. They rarely used the pool in the winter anyway. Maybe she should have it covered. Or filled in with concrete. The marble coping was a bitch to keep clean. In the summer, the decking got so hot that you had to wear sandals or risk third-degree burns. Paul had designed the pool to be beautiful, not usable.

If there was a better metaphor for their lives, Claire didn't know what it was.

She picked up the iPad. The satellite image of the Buckminster Fuller homestead had been taken during the summer months. The field behind the house was lush with fruit vines. The small single-story house still had the same white wood siding that Claire had so carefully tried to render in Paul's anniversary painting. Board-and-batten siding, he had told Claire it was called—large, vertical planks of wood with smaller strips to cover the seams. There were bright green asphalt shingles on the roof. The yard was neatly trimmed. The swingset at the rear of the lot looked sturdy and overbuilt, two things that Paul always strived for in residential construction.

At least Claire knew that Paul hadn't lied about the accident that killed his parents. He didn't like to talk about it, but Claire had heard all of the details from her mother. Despite the 30,000 students attending the University of Georgia, Athens was still a small town, and the main library, like every library in America, was the center of the community. What Helen hadn't read in the newspaper she'd gleaned from local gossip.

The Scotts were driving home from a church function when a tractor-trailer hit a patch of ice and jackknifed across the Atlanta Highway. Paul's father had been decapitated. His mother had lived for several seconds. At least that's what bystanders reported. They had heard the woman screaming as the car was engulfed in flames.

Paul was terrified of fire. It was the only thing Claire knew of that ever scared him. His burial instructions had specifically stated that he shouldn't be cremated.

"What is it?" Lydia asked. She had the burner phone in her hand.

"I was just thinking about Paul's burial instructions." They hadn't been laminated, but they were similar to all the other instructions Paul had made for Claire's benefit. She had found the list inside a folder in her desk that was labeled: IN CASE OF EMERGENCY.

He wanted to be buried in his family plot. He wanted a headstone that was similar in size and composition to the ones for his parents. He didn't want make-up or hair gel or to be embalmed or to have his body placed on view like a mannequin because he deplored the artifice surrounding death. He wanted Claire to pick out a nice suit for him, and good shoes, though what did it matter if he wore shoes, good or otherwise, and how would she know if they had put them on him anyway?

Paul's last request on the list was the one that was most heart-breaking: He wanted to be buried with his wedding ring and Auburn class ring. Claire had been inconsolable, because she had wanted so badly to honor his wishes, but both rings had been taken by the Snake Man.

"Claire?" Lydia was holding out the phone. She had already dialed in the number listed for Buckminster Fuller.

Claire shook her head. "You do it."

Lydia turned on the speakerphone. The ringing sound filled the room, bouncing off the stark walls. Claire held her breath. She didn't know what she was expecting until the phone was answered.

There was a clicking sound like an old answering machine whirring to life. The recording was scratchy, but the voice was unmistakably Paul's.

He said, "You have reached the Fuller residence. If you're looking for Buck . . ."

Claire put her hand to her throat. She knew what was coming next because their own voicemail message followed the same script.

A chirpy woman's voice said, ". . . or Lexie!"

Paul finished, "Please leave a message at the—"

A long beep blared from the burner phone's speaker.

Lydia ended the call.

"Lexie," Claire nearly spat out the word. She sounded younger than Claire. And happier. And stupider, which should've been a consolation but Claire was too consumed with jealousy to care.

Claire stood up. She started pacing.

"Claire—"

"Give me a minute."

"You can't really be—"

"Shut up." Claire turned on her heel and walked back across the length of the room. She couldn't believe this. And then she chastised herself for not believing it because, really, at this terrible point in her life, what difference did it make?

Lydia pulled the iPad into her lap. She started typing again.

Claire kept pacing from one side of the room to the other. She was well aware that her anger was misdirected, but she had proven on more than one occasion that her anger was fairly uncontrollable.

Lydia said, "I'm not finding a Lexie Fuller, Alex Fuller, Alexander Fuller . . . Nothing in the county records." She kept typing. "I'll try in Madison, Oglethorpe—"

"No." Claire pressed her hand against the wall, wishing she could push down the house. "What if we find her? Then what?"

"We tell her that her husband's dead."

"Why do you keep wanting to dump my problems onto other people?"

"That's not fair."

Claire knew she was right, but she didn't care. "So, I knock on this Lexie's door and introduce myself, and if she doesn't tell me to fuck off, which is what I would do in her shoes, I tell her, 'Oh, by the way, in addition to Paul being a polygamist, he's a thief and probably a rapist and absolutely a stalker and he got off on watching women being tortured and murdered'?" She pushed away from the wall and started pacing again. "Trust me. She doesn't want to know."

"Wouldn't you want to know?"

"Absolutely not." Claire was surprised by her decisiveness. She flashed back to the first time she'd sat in front of Paul's computer.

Red pill/blue pill.

If she could go back, would she choose to live in ignorance? Adam might have eventually told her about the stolen money, but the movies and files would've probably remained hidden. Would Claire have gone through the storage area in the basement? Paul was the one with an emotional attachment to silly love notes and the ticket stubs from the first movie they'd ever seen. She had already decided that she couldn't live in Paul's dream house without Paul. Claire would've probably moved to a smaller house, maybe a condo downtown. She could easily imagine her alternate self calling a shredding service to destroy everything rather than pay to have it put into storage or moved.

Lydia asked, "Was Paul away on business trips a lot?"

She shook her head. "Only for a few days at a time, and he usually took me with him." Claire figured she might as well say what they had both thought when they saw the swingset in the front yard. "If he had a kid, then he's a really shitty father."

Lydia said, "Watkinsville is less than fifteen minutes from a campus filled with coeds." She waited for Claire to turn around. "What if there are more folders? More women?"

Claire's mind went to an even darker place. "Is there a basement in that house?"

Lydia didn't move for several seconds. Finally, she started typing on the iPad again. Claire knelt down beside her. Lydia pulled up the tax records for the Watkinsville address. She traced her finger down the descriptions as she read, "Single family home. Wood siding. Built in 1952. Forced air heating. City water. Septic system. No attic square feet. Basement square feet—none." She looked at Claire. "No basement."

Claire slid back down to the floor. She stared out the windows. Sunlight bleached the already-bleached room. "The masked man—that's not Paul. I know his body."

"Is it Adam?"

The question hit Claire like a punch to the heart. Adam was around the same height as the masked man. He also had the same light coloring. As far as the rest, she didn't know. Claire hadn't been in love with Adam Quinn. She hadn't spent hours lying beside him, touching and kissing his skin, memorizing his body. "We fucked three times. We never took off all of our clothes. It was always standing up."

"How romantic." Lydia put down the iPad. "You're sure that's Paul's voice on the answering machine?"

Claire nodded, because Paul's soft, southern drawl was unmistakable. "What should we do?" She amended, "I mean, what should *I* do?"

Lydia didn't answer. She just stared out into the back yard the same way Claire had done before.

Claire joined her, absently watching a lone squirrel hop across the decking and drink saline water from the pool. Asking what to do next was a loaded question, because what it all boiled down to was whether or not Claire wanted to know more. This was past red pill/blue pill. This was skinning the proverbial onion.

They both jumped when the phone rang.

Claire checked the burner, but the screen was blank.

Lydia said, "It's not my cell."

The phone rang a second time. Claire crawled toward the cordless handset on the table beside the couch. The phone rang again. She started to get that familiar sick feeling, even before she heard Fred Nolan's voice.

"Claire," he said. "Glad I caught you."

His voice was as loud and clear as a church bell. Claire held the phone away from her ear so that Lydia could hear, too.

He said, "I think I'm going to take you up on that offer to talk to you and your lawyer."

Claire's eardrums filled with the pounding of her own heartbeat. "When?"

"How about today?"

"It's Sunday." She hadn't realized what day it was until now. Almost a full week had passed since Paul had been murdered.

Nolan said, "I'm sure you've got enough money to pay the Colonel's weekend rate."

The Colonel. That was what they'd called Wynn Wallace, the lawyer who'd helped Claire get out of the assault charge. Paul had called him the Colonel because he was the same type of arrogant prick as Jack Nicholson's character in *A Few Good Men*.

"Claire?"

How would Nolan know their private nickname? Had Paul used the Colonel to get out of the embezzlement charges, too?

"Hello?"

She looked at Lydia, who was shaking her head so hard that she was probably going to give herself whiplash.

Claire asked, "Where?"

Nolan gave her the address.

"I'll be there in two hours." Claire ended the call. She put the receiver back in the cradle. When she took her hand away, she saw that her palm had left a sweaty mark.

Lydia asked, "You're going to give him the files?"

"No. I'm not going downtown." Claire stood up. "I'm going to Athens."

"What?" Lydia stood up, too. She followed Claire into the mudroom. "You just told Nolan you were—"

"Fuck Nolan." Claire picked up her purse. She slid her feet into her tennis shoes. She didn't know why, but she had to see Lexie Fuller. She wasn't going to talk to her or drop a bomb on her life, but Claire needed to see the other woman with her own two eyes.

She said, "Listen, Lydia, I really appreciate—"

"Shut up. I'm coming with you." Lydia disappeared into the house.

Claire checked the mailbox on the video keypad by the door. The Auburn USB drive was still there. It was 9:13 on a Sunday morning. Was it a good or bad thing that Adam Quinn was sleeping in? Or had he left the drive for someone else to pick up? Was Jacob Mayhew on his way? Would Fred Nolan consider Claire's absence in two hours a form of willfully misleading a federal agent? Would she return home tonight to her own bed, or would she be spending the next few years of her life in prison?

Lydia returned with her purse. She had her iPhone in one hand and the burner in the other. "I'm driving."

Claire didn't argue because Lydia was older and she always got to drive. She opened the mudroom door and left it unlocked. At this point, Claire welcomed the burglars to return. She would've left cookies out for them if she'd had the time.

Claire unplugged the Tesla. The keyfob was on the bench where she'd left it. She threw it into her purse and got into the car. Lydia climbed in behind the wheel. She reached down and adjusted the seat. She moved the mirrors. She frowned at the glowing seventeen-inch touchscreen that ran down the middle of the dashboard.

"This is electric, right?" Lydia sounded annoyed. She'd always been angry around new things. "Athens is an hour away."

"Really? I've never noticed that the eleventy billion times I've driven this very same car to Mom's house and back." At least she had before the ankle monitor limited her movements. "Can we just go?"

Lydia still looked annoyed. "Where does the key go?"

"Tap the brake to turn it on."

Lydia tapped the brake. "Is it on? I can't even hear it."

"Are you three hundred years old?" Claire demanded. "Jesus Christ, it's still a car. Even Grandma Ginny could figure it out."

"That was really mean." She put the gear in reverse. The video screen switched to the rear camera view. Lydia huffed in disgust as she inched back the car and turned it around.

The gate was still open at the bottom of the driveway. Claire felt like ten years had passed since she sat in the back of the limousine with her mother and grandmother. She tried to remember how she'd felt. The purity of her grief had been such a luxury.

There was another woman in Watkinsville who might be feeling those same pure emotions of grief. Paul had been gone for almost a week. She would've called hospitals and police stations and the highway patrol and whoever else would listen. And she would be told by everyone who did even the slightest bit of research that Buckminster Fuller, the father of the geodesic dome, had died in 1983.

Claire wondered what story Paul had given the woman to explain his absences. Traveling salesman. Government agent. Roughneck working an oil rig. Pilot.

Paul had trained for his pilot's license in college. He was rated for light jets, which meant that whenever they hired a charter, he was always up in the cockpit talking tailwinds and altimeters with the pilots. Claire used to feel sorry for the poor men who were trying to keep the plane in the sky.

Should she feel sorry for Lexie Fuller? And did she have a right to keep the other woman in the dark about Paul? Claire of all people knew the kind of hell that knowing the truth would rain down. Could she do that to another human being?

Or maybe Lexie already knew about Claire. Maybe the young little bitch was completely fine with sharing another woman's husband, with raising the man's bastard child—or children— while he kept another wife.

Claire closed her eyes. What an awful thing to say about the other woman. She was turning Lexie into a monster when Paul had likely fooled them both. Even if Lexie was complicit in polygamy, there was no way she knew about the dreadful shit that Paul was into.

"Dyadic Completion," Paul would've told Claire. "The human brain tends to assume that, if there's a victim, there has to be a villain."

Was that how Claire was thinking of herself now, as just another one of Paul's victims?

"Claire?" Lydia had relaxed her stranglehold on the steering wheel. "I think we need more information."

Just the thought made Claire cringe. "What do you mean?"

"The county's online records only go back ten years. Has Paul always owned the house?"

"Does that matter?"

"I just wonder if there were other Mrs. Fullers."

Claire stared at the road. The problem with being around Lydia was that she easily thought the worst of Paul. "You think he buried them in the back yard?"

"I didn't say that."

"You didn't have to." Claire leaned her head into her hand. She didn't want Lydia here, but she couldn't imagine doing this without her. She had forgotten how annoying it was to have a sister.

Lydia signaled to merge onto the interstate. By way of an olive branch, she offered, "Dad always hated driving on Sundays."

Claire didn't want to, but she smiled. When her father was teaching her to drive, he'd warned her that Sunday was the most dangerous day to be on the road. He'd said that people were tired and grumpy from sitting in church for hours in scratchy clothes, and that they drove like bats out of hell when they were finally released.

Lydia asked, "What were you doing at the McDonald's yesterday?"

Claire told her the truth. "Wondering if it would be impolite to throw up in the bathroom without ordering something."

"I think they're used to it." Lydia accelerated into the fast lane. For someone who had complained so much about the car, she seemed to be enjoying the ride. "What do you think Nolan's going to do when you don't show up at his office?"

"I guess it depends. If what he's doing is legitimate, then he'll put out an APB on me. If it's not, then he'll start calling me again, or go by the house."

"You left the garage door open. All he has to do is go inside and look at Paul's laptop."

"Let him." Claire couldn't see the point of trying to hide the movies. She was the one who'd turned them over to the police in the first place. "The same rules apply. If Nolan is there legitimately, then he'll have a search warrant. If he's not, then he can take the hard drive and shove it up his ass."

"Maybe he'll be there when Adam picks up the USB drive."

"Great. They can watch the movies and jerk off together."

Lydia didn't laugh. "Can I ask you something?"

Claire studied her sister. She wasn't the type to ask for permission. "What?"

"What do you do all day? Do you have a job or what?"

Claire sensed a loaded question. Lydia probably assumed she sat around all day eating bon-bons and spending Paul's money. To be fair, sometimes she did, but other times Claire felt she made up for it. "I volunteer a lot. The humane shelter. The food bank. The USO." She might as well be making a list of all the things that were important to her father. "I was helping at the Innocence Project for a while, but a case came through with Ben Carver's name on it." Ben Carver had been one of two serial killers who had strung their father along. "I took French and German to travel on. I still play the piano. I cut the grass if it needs it and it's not too hot. I used to play tennis three or four hours a day, but for some reason no one will play with me anymore." She asked Lydia, "What about you?"

"I work. I go home. I go to sleep. I get up and work again."

Claire nodded as if she didn't know otherwise. "You dating anybody?"

"Not really." Lydia darted around a slow-moving Mercedes. "Does Mom know you've talked to me?" She acted like the question was spontaneous, but the rawness in her voice gave her away.

"I didn't tell her," Claire admitted. "But only because I was upset, and I knew if I called her she would hear it in my voice and get the truth out of me."

"What's the truth?"

"That you weren't lying, and that the fact that you weren't lying meant that Paul was, which means that my eighteen-year marriage was complete and utter bullshit and my husband was a psychopath."

Lydia tucked her chin into her neck, but for once, she kept her mouth closed.

Claire realized, "I haven't apologized to you for what I did."

"No, you haven't."

"I'm sorry," she tried, but the two words seemed so small compared with the enormity of what she'd taken away. "I should've believed you." Claire knew that wasn't quite right, either. She couldn't imagine a scenario at that point in their lives where she might have trusted Lydia. "Even if I didn't believe you, I should've never let you go."

Lydia had her head turned away. She sniffed.

Claire looked down at her sister's hand. She didn't know whether or not to touch her. "I'm sorry, Pepper. I abandoned you. I made Mom abandon you."

"You couldn't make Mom do anything she didn't want to do."

"I'm not so sure about that." For the first time, Claire considered the full implications of what she had actually done. She hadn't just cut Lydia out of her own life. She had excised her from what was left of her family. "Mom was terrified of losing another child. I knew that and I worked it in my favor because I was so angry at you. I forced her into a Sophie's choice." Claire thought this might be the only situation where that phrase was even mildly applicable. "I was wrong. I'm so profoundly sorry for what I did to you. To our family."

"Well," Lydia wiped away tears, "I was pretty messed up back then. Everything you said was true. I stole from all of you. I lied all of the time."

"But you never lied about something like that, and I should've seen it." Claire laughed at the gross understatement. "Obviously, I didn't see a lot of things."

Lydia's throat worked as she fought back more tears.

Claire didn't know what else to say. That she was proud of her sister for getting clean and pulling herself up from dire poverty? That her daughter was beautiful and accomplished and clearly amazing? That her boyfriend obviously worshipped her?

Everything she knew about Lydia's life had come from Paul's private detectives.

Which meant that even though Claire had bared the dark, rotted soul of her marriage, Lydia still didn't trust her with the truth about her own life.

"So." Lydia was obviously ready to change the subject. She waved her hand at the touchscreen. "Does this thing have a radio?"

"It can play any song you want." Claire touched the media icon. "Just say out loud what you want to hear and it'll find it on the Internet and play it."

"No way."

"Welcome to the one percent." Claire split the display. She felt like the eager young kid at the Tesla dealership as she swiped through the different screens. "You can read your email, see how much battery power you have left, go on the Internet."

Claire stopped. When she'd touched the Internet icon, the system reloaded the last page Paul had looked at. Feedly.com was a news aggregator that operated along the same lines as Google alerts, but with news stories.

Paul had entered only one name into the search engine.

Lydia asked, "What's wrong?"

"Pull over."

"Why?"

"Pull over."

Lydia gave a heavy sigh, but she still did as Claire ordered. The rumble strips roared inside the car as they coasted to a stop on the side of the interstate.

Lydia asked, "What's wrong?"

"Paul set an alert for any news on Anna Kilpatrick. The last one came in two minutes ago."

Lydia grabbed her purse and pulled out her glasses. "What are you waiting for?"

Claire tapped her finger on the most recent alert, a link from Channel 2, an Atlanta ABC affiliate.

The top of the home page showed a black box for streaming video. The red banner read: "LIVE! Breaking News in the Anna Kilpatrick Case." A spinning circle indicated the video was buffering. Claire turned up the sound. They both waited, eyes focused on the screen.

The Tesla shook as a brown UPS truck drove by.

Lydia said, "This is taking forever."

Finally, the video loaded, but there wasn't much to see. Captain Mayhew was standing behind a podium. Congressman Johnny Jackson, never one to miss a media opportunity, was standing behind him, slightly to the right so that he'd still be in the camera frame. They were both looking at a closed door off to the side. There were flashes of light from the cameras and shuffling sounds as the reporters grew impatient.

A voiceover explained, "We've been told that the parents arrived in the building five minutes ago." The reporter did a recap of the Kilpatrick disappearance, going back to the police finding the girl's car in the parking lot of Lenox mall.

Claire could remember doing press conferences with her family. Back then, there were really only three news stations, so the conferences were held in the small front lobby of the sheriff's station. Claire and Lydia were told to look devastated, but not too devastated. Helen had worried that Julia's abductor would see her last two daughters and want to take them, too. The sheriff had told them to address their comments to Julia, because he adamantly believed she was out there in some run-down hotel laughing at her parents making fools of themselves on the evening news.

Lydia said, "Here they come."

On the screen, the side door opened. Anna Kilpatrick's parents made their way up to the stage and stood on Mayhew's left. He nodded at them as if to say, *We'll get through this.* They did not nod back. They both looked like death-row inmates awaiting execution.

Lydia said, "They found the body."

Claire shushed her, but seconds later, Mayhew confirmed her guess.

He said, "The remains of a young woman were found at approximately four a.m. this morning on a jogging trail off the BeltLine."

The BeltLine ran through Midtown. Claire had some friends who jokingly referred to it as the Rape Line because of the large number of sexual assaults that happened on the trail.

Mayhew continued, "The Dekalb County crime lab was able to identify the remains based on photographs and fingerprints. The Kilpatricks confirmed the findings an hour ago."

Claire asked, "They let them see the body?"

"Wouldn't you want to?"

Claire wasn't so sure anymore.

Mayhew said, "At this moment, we have no additional leads. We would ask that anyone who recognizes the man from this sketch please call the hotline." He held up the police sketch of the man who'd been seen near Anna's car. "The Kilpatricks would like to thank everyone who helped search for—"

Claire muted the sound, because she knew what was coming next. The reporters would ask questions. Mayhew would not give them answers. She watched Mayhew gesture to Bob Kilpatrick, Anna's father. The man had the same weepy, broken expression that she had seen countless times on her father's face.

Lydia had seen it, too. "He reminds me of Dad."

Claire forced herself to look away from Eleanor Kilpatrick. The woman was clinging to her husband like they were lost at sea. And they *were* lost—even if they made it back to land, they would always be on unsteady ground.

Lydia held Claire's hand. She felt the comfort of her sister's touch spread through her like warm water. They sat in the car, listening to trucks whir by. Would Claire want to see Julia's body? It would be different after all these years. There would just be bones, but the bones would mean so much because they would have something to bury, some place to leave their grief.

"What's happening?" Lydia was not posing an existential question. She was pointing to the touchscreen. Eleanor Kilpatrick had pushed Mayhew out of the way. She gripped the microphone in her hand.

Claire turned up the volume.

Eleanor Kilpatrick's angry voice screeched from the speakers: "—was branded like a Goddamn animal!"

The feed was cut. The Channel 2 news anchor came on-screen. "We'd like to apologize to our viewers for the language you just heard."

"Find the uncensored feed," Lydia ordered. "Find it!"

"I'm looking." Claire had already pulled up the search page. The newsfeed had updated again. There were a dozen more sites carrying the press conference. Claire picked the sketchiest one. The rainbow wheel in the center of the screen started to spin.

Lydia said, "Try another one."

"Give it time." Claire gripped her hands together so she wouldn't grab the screen. She was about to give up when the page finally loaded.

Mayhew was frozen, the microphone in front of him. Jackson stared straight ahead like a good soldier. Claire pressed the PLAY button. He said, "The remains of a young woman—"

"It's at the beginning." Lydia had obviously been paying attention. She scrubbed her finger along the bottom of the video until it got to Eleanor Kilpatrick's outburst.

"This is bullshit!" the woman screamed.

Johnny Jackson skillfully stepped out of the frame, leaving the damage control to Jacob Mayhew.

"Mrs. Kilpatrick." Mayhew covered the mic with his hand.

"No!" Eleanor Kilpatrick tried to push away his hand. She was a small woman. She couldn't move him, so she turned to the reporters and yelled, "My daughter was cut up!"

They responded with a strobe of flashing lights.

Mayhew repeated, "Mrs. Kilpatrick."

She grabbed the mic away from him. "Her breasts were mutilated! She was branded like a Goddamn animal!"

Mayhew tried to get the mic. She jerked away from him. He tried again but Bob Kilpatrick sucker-punched him in the stomach.

"She was our baby!" Eleanor cried. "She was just a child!"

Two uniformed cops pinned down Bob Kilpatrick. His wife kept screaming, even as he was dragged away. "What kind of animal would do that to our little girl? What kind of animal?"

Mayhew wiped his mouth with the back of his hand. He was clearly furious. In front of all the reporters, he grabbed Eleanor Kilpatrick around the waist and carried her across the stage. The mic dropped when it ran out of cord. Mayhew practically threw the woman through the open doorway. The door slammed closed. The camera stayed on it for a few seconds before cutting to black.

Both Claire and Lydia stared at the screen.

Lydia asked, "Did you see what she did?"

"Yes." Claire reloaded the page. They waited for the video to load. Instead of skipping forward, she played the press conference from the beginning. First Mayhew, then Eleanor Kilpatrick. As soon as the video finished, she reloaded the page so they could watch the news conference a third time.

The reporter's voiceover. Mayhew at the podium. The Kilpatricks entering the room.

Neither Claire nor Lydia could stop watching. They were both transfixed by Eleanor Kilpatrick's outburst, the way she traced an X on her belly when she said her daughter had been branded.

Claire paused the video. Eleanor Kilpatrick froze on the screen. Her mouth gaped open. She had her right hand pressed to the left side of her belly, slightly off-center, just below her ribs.

Lydia said, "Her breasts were mutilated."

"I know."

Pretty Girls

"Her stomach was branded with an X."

"I know."

Exactly like the second girl in Paul's movies.

The one who looked like Anna Kilpatrick.

iv.

Do you remember that article you wrote for the school newspaper when Timothy McCorquodale was executed? He was sentenced to death in the 1970s for murdering a white girl he'd seen talking to a black man in a Midtown Atlanta bar. You were hard pressed to understand why a white girl talking to a black man engendered so much rage. I was both proud and hopeful that you didn't understand this insipient sort of racism. Your mother and I grew up during the last gasps of Jim Crow. We marched for equal rights, but that was easy to do when all of our friends and fellow students were marching right alongside us.

I remember talking to your mother about your article, in which you editorialized that while McCorquodale deserved to be punished, society did not have the right to put him to death. We were so proud of you for believing the things that we believed. We, too, shared your outrage at the thought of a man being electrocuted for kidnapping, raping, torturing, and eventually murdering a seventeen-year-old girl.

I was thinking about your article this morning when I drove to the Georgia Diagnostic and Classification Prison. You might recall from your research on your story that this is the location of Georgia's death row. I'm not sure why your article came into my mind as I drove through the front gate, and while I am still proud of you, I have understandably changed my mind about the death penalty. The only reservation I have now is that I feel the parents should be given the option of flipping the switch.

A few years after you disappeared, a postal worker named Ben Carver was sentenced to death for murdering six young men. (He is a homosexual, which, according to Huckleberry, means he is not attracted to murdering young women.) Rumors have it that Carver cannibalized some of his victims, but there was never a trial so the more salacious details were not made public. I found Carver's name in the sheriff's file ten months ago, the fifth anniversary of your disappearance. The letter was written on Georgia Department of Corrections stationery and signed by the warden. He was informing the sheriff that Ben Carver, a death-row inmate, had mentioned to one of the prison guards that he might have some information pertaining to your disappearance.

Huckleberry made a note that he followed up on the lead, but Carver told me himself that the sheriff never paid him a visit. Of course, I visited Ben Carver. In fact, I have been to the prison a total of forty-eight times in the last ten months. I would visit him more, but death-row inmates are only allowed visits once a week.

Sweetheart, I am sorry I haven't told you about the visits until now, but please keep reading and maybe you will understand why.

On visiting day, Ben Carver and I sit across from each other like fish in a tank separated by a wire mesh between us. There are tiny holes in the mesh. The visiting room is loud. There are roughly eighty men on death row and for many of them, their only contact with the outside world is their mothers. You can imagine that much emotion is on display. Ben Carver's mother is too elderly to visit him anymore, so it's just me he sees. I have to bend down and put my lips close to the metal, even though I can see the black grime from where thousands of mouths have been before mine.

AIDS, I think. *Hepatitis B. Herpes. Influenza. Mononucleosis.* And still I put my mouth to the screen.

Carver is a charming man with a soft voice. He is courteous and attentive, which I wonder about, because is this his natural disposition, or has he read too many novels about Hannibal Lecter?

Regardless, he always expresses great concern for my well-being. "You look tired today," he'll say, or, "Are you eating enough?" or, "You might want to talk to your barber about your hair."

I know he flirts with me because he is lonely, just as I flirt back because I want to know what he knows.

So, we talk about everything but you.

He has almost perfect recall for movie dialogue. *Casablanca. Gone with the Wind. Midnight Cowboy.* Monty Python. Then there are the books he's read—most of the classics, Anne Rivers Siddons for the Atlanta connection, Barbara Cartland for romance, Neil Gaiman for fantasy. I have had more conversations about *The Celestine Prophecy* than I care to mention.

I do not tell your mother about these conversations, and not just because she thinks *The Bridges of Madison County* is sentimental tripe. She has held firm to her refusal to hear about what I call my extracurricular activities and what she calls my fruitless quest. Absent this subject, there is very little for us to talk about anymore. We can only rehash for so long old memories of agonizing camping trips and Tooth Fairy adventures and heated parent–teacher conferences. Your sisters have started their own lives. They have found their own friends, started to build their own families outside of us. Your mother has my (inferior) replacement and I have? . . .

Can I admit to you that I am lonely? That every morning I wake up to a sparse, empty bedroom and stare up at a yellow popcorn ceiling and wonder if it's worth it to get out of bed? That I can't bear the thought of seeing my toothbrush standing alone without your mother's? That I have two plates, two spoons, two forks, and two knives not because I need that many but because I could only find them in pairs? That I have lost my job? That I have finally lost your mother? That I have stopped asking your sisters to visit because every conversation feels like I am dragging them down underneath the ocean?

So maybe you can understand why discussing movies and literature with a convicted serial killer became such an important part of my life. Here is a reason to bathe. Here is a reason to put on shoes. Here is a reason to leave the house, drive the car, go somewhere else other than my one-bedroom apartment that feels as much like a prison cell as anything you could find at the Georgia Diagnostic and Classification Prison.

I know Ben is stringing me along, just like I know that I am letting myself be strung. It baffles me that the only times lately that I don't think about you are the times I am debating Joyce with a likely cannibal. Isn't the point of my visits to find out what Carver knows? To track down whatever rumor he has heard so that I can finally know what happened to you?

But I have this nagging feeling that he knows nothing about you.

And I have an even deeper nagging feeling that I do not care.

So this is what I do: I tell myself I am studying him. Is this the sort of man who took you? Was your abductor as kind to you in the beginning as Ben Carver is kind to me? Did he take you because he wanted you all to himself? Or did he take you because he wanted to hurt you?

Then I ask myself what would happen if that grimy metal mesh were taken away. What would a man like Ben Carver do to me if there were no guards posted, no barrier between us? Would he explicate Spenser's *Faerie Queene* or would he cut me open and sample a sliver of my pancreas?

I realized today that I will never know the answer—not because the scenario is impossible, but because I have been barred from visiting Ben Carver again. I immediately suspected the hand of Huckleberry, but the warden soon put me straight. It seemed only fitting. He was the man whose report had brought me to Ben Carver in the first place.

This is how it happened: Instead of being herded into the waiting room for visitation, I was led down a long hallway by a plump guard who kept sucking his teeth. The sound echoed off the polished tiles on the floor. The hallways are long and wide in prison, likely so you can run but not hide. There are large fish-eye mirrors at every corner. Video cameras follow your every move.

If only downtown Athens had been so secure, perhaps you would've come home to us.

The warden's office was all cheap paneling and institutional green furnishings. As Ben would've said, "Think *Cool Hand Luke*." Every surface was either metal or fake wood. The warden was fat with a buzz cut and rolls of flesh almost obscuring his collar. His white shirt was short-sleeved and outfitted with a red and black clip-on tie. He smoked a cigarette as he studied me across his desk. I sat in front of him holding a worn copy of Dr. Seuss's *You're Only Old Once!* A gift from Ben sent via the warden. The last communication Carver the Cannibal would have with me. He had revoked my visitation rights. I wasn't allowed in the prison anymore.

"Dr. Carroll," the warden said, his voice sounding like Foghorn Leghorn, "Ben Carver is a psychopath. He's incapable of empathy or remorse. If you see something human in him, that's only because he's playing the part."

I flipped through the book. My hands were sweating. The pages stuck to my fingers. It's hot in prison, no matter what time of year it is. It reeks of sweat and sewage and desperation from the men who are stacked in cells like chattel.

The warden said, "Obviously, Carver's gotten out of you whatever he wanted. He's finished with you. Don't take it personally. Count yourself lucky that you got away unscathed."

Unscathed.

I let the word roll around in my head. I said it aloud as I was escorted back down the long hall. I repeated it in the car as I sat with the book still clutched in my hands.

You're Only Old Once! A Book for Obsolete Children was an adult picture book. Several years ago, you and your sisters had given me a copy of this same book on my birthday, because younger people always think it's funny when older people get even older. I don't recall ever telling Ben about the book, but it seemed like something I would've told him early on when I was trying to trap him into revealing a clue about you.

The conversation would've gone like this:

Ben: Tell me, Sam, what have you been reading lately?

Me: I found a book that Julia and the girls gave me for my birthday. *You're Only Old Once!* by Dr. Seuss.

Ben: You know, my favorite birthday gift was when I was sixteen and my mother gave me my own set of keys to her car. What was your first car, Sam? I bet it was an old jalopy. You would've been pulling in the girls like crazy.

That was what he was like. He always changed the subject with flattery. He was usually more artful. It's hard to describe how someone has manipulated you because you're generally not aware of it when it's happening. You don't exactly take notes, is what I am saying.

I am sure that during my visits, Ben gathered far more information about me than the other way around. I have to admit that he was working at a level I did not even know existed. And he *was* a psychopath, I knew that, but he was an interesting psychopath and he gave me something to do one day a week, every week, for ten months when my only other alternative was to cut open my wrists and watch the blood swirl down the bathtub drain.

I should've mentioned the scalpel when I cataloged the items in my silverware drawer. It has been there for almost a year now—shiny metal with a surgically sharpened blade. I have seen how easily it slices open flesh and dreamed about how easily it would cut into mine.

I think what happened was this: Ben knew he had helped me climb out of that depression, and that it was time to let me go. Not because he wanted to end our contact, but because, if I kept visiting, he would be too tempted to destroy what he had worked so hard to build back up.

So, while the warden was right about my strange friend being a psychopath, he was wrong about Ben Carver's lack of empathy. I have proof of it right here in my hands.

I don't know how he managed to get a copy of *You're Only Old Once!* while living on death row, but I do know that Ben was very resourceful. He had many fans on the outside. The guards gave him the respect of an old-timer. Even in prison, Ben could get almost anything he wanted. And he never wanted anything unless there was a good reason. The reason this time was to send me a message.

This is the inscription Ben wrote inside the book:

"First you must have the images. Then come the words."

Robert James Waller.

Images.

I had seen that word before—at least six times before on my annual reading sojourn to the sheriff's office. The word was connected to a deed and the deed was connected to an act and that act had been committed by a man and that man, I now understood, was connected to you.

You see, sweetheart?

Ben Carver knew something about you after all.

TEN

Lydia stood in front of the Arch in downtown Athens. She looked down at her phone. She reloaded the search page to refresh the links. There were no new details in the Anna Kilpatrick case. That didn't stop the news outlets from regurgitating the story. They were milking the press conference for every bit of emotion they could squeeze out. Eleanor's heartbreaking outburst had busted the coverage wide open. MSNBC, Fox, CBS, ABC, and NBC had all abandoned their Sunday-morning political recaps. CNN had brought in a shrink to discuss Eleanor and Bob Kilpatrick's state of mind. The fact that the doctor had never met the dead girl's parents or even worked on a case where a child was abducted and murdered did not mar his qualifications to speak as an expert on national television.

Lydia was more qualified to know their state of mind. Their sixteen-year-old daughter was dead. She had been tortured and branded and abandoned on the BeltLine, a joke of a recreational path that was more like a criminal hunting ground. At the moment, the Kilpatricks were probably looking for the most expedient way to join their only child.

They had likely suspected all along that Anna was dead, but there was thinking it might be true and then there was having actual confirmation. They had seen her body. They had borne witness to her degradation. Was knowing exactly what had happened better than whatever horrors they had spun in their imaginations?

Like the Carroll family, they were caught between two guns.

Lydia wiped sweat from her brow. The temperature had dropped overnight, but she felt hot, probably from shock or stress, or a combination of the two. She climbed the stone steps up to the iron Arch that had stood at the North Campus entrance since the Civil War. Her father had told them stories about toilet-papering the Arch after football games. Julia had almost been arrested here during a protest against the first Gulf War. On the last night of her life, she had walked past the Arch with her friends on the way to the Manhattan.

And after the Manhattan, they had never seen her again.

Lydia wanted her daughter. She wanted to hold her in her arms and kiss her head the way Dee only let her do when she was sick or feeling sad. When Dee was a baby, she had loved being held. Lydia's back constantly ached from carrying her around the kitchen while she cooked or resting her on her hip while she did laundry. When Rick came along, Dee would drape herself across them like a blanket, her feet in Rick's lap and her head in Lydia's. Rick and Lydia would look at each other and smile because they had such a perfect little girl between them. And Lydia would feel such relief because the only time she truly knew that Dee was safe was when she was close enough to count her daughter's breaths.

She put her head in her hands. She closed her eyes. She gave in to the images of Eleanor Kilpatrick that were burned into every fold of her brain. The way the mother had screamed with such damaged intensity. Her haunted expression. The X she had drawn over the left side of her abdomen.

Eleanor was obviously right-handed. She had to reach across her belly to draw the X. She hadn't chosen that exact spot by coincidence.

Lydia looked across Broad Street. Claire was sitting outside the Starbucks where she'd left her. Her posture was ramrod straight as she stared into empty space. She had the dazed look of a catatonic. There was an unnerving stillness about her. She had always been so hard to read, but right now, she was impenetrable.

Lydia stood up. The thirty yards between them wasn't going to help her magically divine Claire's thoughts. She walked back across Broad, lingering at the median though there was no traffic. Georgia had beaten Auburn last night. The town was sleeping off the win. The sidewalks were sticky from spilled beer. Trash littered the streets.

Claire didn't look up when Lydia sat down at the table, but she asked, "Does it look different?"

"It looks like an outdoor shopping mall," she said, because the campus had turned from that of a quaint southern university into a sprawling corporate behemoth. "It's almost suburban."

"The only thing that's really changed is the length of the khaki shorts."

"Didn't the Taco Stand used to be here?"

253

"We parked right in front of it." Claire indicated the direction with a tilt of her head.

Lydia craned her neck. She saw more tables and chairs crisscrossing the sidewalk. No one was sitting outside because it was too cold. There was a woman standing with a broom and dustpan, but instead of sweeping up the debris left over from the night before, she was checking her phone.

Claire said, "He never asked me for anything weird."

Lydia turned back to her sister.

"I remember when I first saw the movie on his computer—just the beginning of it with the girl chained up—I had this strange feeling, almost like a betrayal, because I wanted to know why he didn't bring it to me." She watched a jogger slowly cross the street. "I thought, If that's what he's into, chaining people up and leather and blindfolds and that kind of thing, even though I'm not particularly into it, why didn't he ask me to give it a try?" She looked at Lydia like she expected an answer.

Lydia could only shrug.

"I probably would've said yes." Claire shook her head as if to contradict herself. "I mean, if that's what he really wanted, then I would've tried it, right? Because that's what you do. And Paul knew that. He knew that I would've tried."

Lydia shrugged again, but she had no idea.

"He never asked me to dress up like a maid or pretend to be a schoolgirl or whatever else it is you hear about. He never even asked for anal, and every man asks for anal eventually."

Lydia glanced around, hoping no one could hear.

"She was younger than me," Claire continued. "The first woman—when I saw her, I had this split-second thought that she was younger than me, and that hurt, because I'm not young anymore. That's the one thing I couldn't give him."

Lydia sat back in her chair. There was nothing she could do but let Claire talk.

"I wasn't in love with him when I married him. I mean, I loved him, but it wasn't . . ." She waved the emotions away with her hand. "We were married for less than a year, and Christmas was coming up. Paul was working on his masters and I was answering phones for a law office and I just thought, I'm out of here. Being married felt so pointless. So tedious. Mom and Dad were so full of life before Julia. They were such passionate, interesting people. Do you remember that? How they were before?"

Lydia smiled, because Claire had somehow unlocked the memories with that one question. Even twenty-two years into their marriage, Sam and Helen Carroll had acted like teenagers who couldn't keep their hands off each other.

Claire said, "They went dancing and to parties and out to dinner and they had their own interests and they loved talking to each other all the time. Remember how we weren't allowed to interrupt them? And we didn't want to interrupt them, because they were so fascinating." Claire smiled, too. "They read everything. They saw everything. People vied to spend time with them. They'd have a party and strangers would show up at the door because they'd heard the Carrolls were so much fun."

Lydia felt it all come rushing back—Helen spraying cheese on celery stalks and Sam singeing his eyebrows off at the grill. Games of charades. Heated political debates. Lively discussions about books and art and movies.

Claire continued, "They were always kissing each other. Like, real kissing. And we'd say it was gross but wasn't it nice, Pepper? Didn't you see them and think that's what love was all about?"

Lydia nodded. She felt intoxicated by the long-forgotten memories.

"That first year with Paul, that's what we didn't have. At least, I didn't think we had it." Claire swallowed so hard that her throat moved. "So I rode my bike home from work that night thinking that I was just going to be honest and tell him it was over. Rip off the Band-Aid. Don't wait for all the Christmas parties and New Years to come and go. Just say it." She paused. Tears rolled down her face. "But I got home, and Paul was in bed. I thought he was taking a nap, but he was covered in sweat. I could hear him wheezing. His eyelids fluttered every time he blinked. I made him get up and I took him to the hospital. He'd had a cold for weeks, but it turned into walking pneumonia. He could've died. He almost did." She wiped away her tears. "But here's the thing: I was terrified. I couldn't think about my life without him. Hours before, I was ready to leave him, but then I realized that I couldn't." She shook her head vehemently, as if someone had asked her to. "He was in the hospital for almost three weeks, and I never left his side. I read to him. I slept in the bed with him. I bathed him. I had always known that Paul needed me, but I never realized until I almost lost him that I really, really needed him."

Claire stopped to take a shallow breath. "That's when you fall in love with somebody. The lust and fucking like rabbits and letting your life fall to shit so you can be around him—that's passion. It's borderline obsession. And it always burns itself out. You know that, Liddie. That high never, ever lasts. But being in that hospital, taking care of him, I started to realize that what I had with Paul, what I thought I had, *that* was more than love. That was *being* in love. It was so tangible I could almost touch it with my hands. I could bite it with my teeth."

Lydia would've never articulated it that same way, but she knew from Rick what her sister was talking about. There was so much of her self that was wrapped up in him: lover, companion, best friend, foil. All of this time she'd been focused on what it would feel like to lose Dee, but losing Rick would be devastating in so many different ways.

Claire said, "Paul knew how it felt for me to lose Julia. I told him everything. *Everything*. I didn't hold back one detail. I can't recall a time in my life when I've ever been that honest with a man. I laid it all out—what it was like when Mom turned into a ghost and Dad turned into Don Quixote. How much I needed you to help me get through the day." She made sure that Lydia was looking at her. "You saved me, Pepper. You were the only thing I had to hold on to when the bottom dropped out."

Lydia felt a lump in her throat. They had saved each other.

"That's probably why Paul had to drive us apart, don't you think? He knew how important you were to me. More important than Mom, even, because I trusted you to be there no matter what."

Lydia shook her head. There was no way to tell what had been in Paul's mind.

"He knew from me what Anna Kilpatrick's family was going through, and he watched those horrible movies despite that. Maybe because of it, because I think that he got off on knowing that Anna wasn't the only one in pain. There were all these other layers of pain rippling through the family, through the community, and even to us—you, me, Mom, Grandma Ginny. He was constantly asking me about Anna Kilpatrick, or referring to the case, and gauging my reaction. He even brought it up the night he died." She gave a dry laugh. "I thought he was asking because he cared about me, but now I can see that it was all part of his game. It's the same kink as raping those women, then having them followed for so many years."

Lydia didn't disagree, but she asked, "Why do you think that?"

"Because it's about control. He controlled me for years by making me think I had everything I wanted. He controlled you by isolating you away from the family. He controlled Mom by making her think he was the perfect son-in-law. He controlled those women in his files by knowing exactly where they were. Hell, he even controlled Grandma Ginny, because she would've been in a state nursing home without his money. For all her noble, impoverished-widow bullshit, she loves having a private apartment and weekly maid service. One way or another, we were all under his thumb."

Lydia gripped together her hands on the table. Why had Claire never seen any of this when Paul was alive? Was he really that good at hiding his darker nature?

Claire said, "God only knows what this Lexie Fuller woman is going through. Maybe he never asked me to do anything weird because he was doing it with her." She laughed again. "Actually, part of me hopes that he did, because that would mean that I wasn't completely crazy, because he was so Goddamn normal. I know you saw through him, but you were the only person in his entire life who thought that something was wrong with him. Even Dad was fooled. I told you I read his journals. The worst thing he ever said about Paul is that he loves me too much."

Lydia doubted her father had paid much attention to Paul. Claire was just getting serious about him when Sam Carroll took his life. Lydia had always assumed the tragedy had escalated their relationship.

Claire told her, "Paul chose to show you that bad side of himself. He worked his ass off to keep it from everybody else, but he showed it to you because he knew that it would split us apart."

"You *let* him play you." Lydia didn't realize how angry she still was until she said the words. Why did Claire just get to pick up where they left off? She was confiding in Lydia like the last eighteen years hadn't happened, like she hadn't been the sole reason Lydia had been shoved out into the cold. She told her sister, "You chose a boy over me."

Claire held Lydia's gaze. "You're right. I did. And I don't know that we'll ever get past it, because it's truly unforgivable."

Lydia was the first one to look away. She had to remind herself who the real villain was. Paul had dedicated his life to manipulating people. Claire had been a naïve and vulnerable teenager when they'd met in college. Helen was still a mess. Sam was on the verge of suicide. Lydia was in and out of jail. Was it any wonder that Paul was able to sink his teeth into her?

And yet, Lydia still could not find within herself the ability to forgive.

Claire asked, "Do you think I should call Captain Mayhew?"

"For what?" Lydia couldn't keep the alarm out of her voice.

The abrupt change in subject slapped her like a cold wind. "He lied to you about the movies. He said they were fake."

"Maybe he lied because he didn't want me to leak them to the press?"

"No, he would've filed an injunction. Or arrested you for interfering with an active investigation. Or just told you to keep quiet."

"I'm not going to take this to Agent Nolan," Claire said. "Who else is left? Huckleberry?" She waved her hand in the general direction of the sheriff's office. "He did a bang-up job with Julia. I'm sure he'd get right on top of this."

Lydia felt like they were letting their imaginations get the best of them. "What do we actually know, Claire? That Paul watched the movies. That's it."

"The movies are real."

"We *think* they're real." Lydia tried to play devil's advocate again. "We *think* that girl looked like Anna Kilpatrick. We *think* that she was mutilated in the same way, based on what her mother said and did during a press conference. But are we one hundred percent certain? Or are we just talking ourselves into it?"

"Confirmation bias." Claire scowled at her own words. "What's the downside of calling Mayhew?"

"Because he lied to you about the movies. Because he's supposed to be working the biggest case in the city right now and he stopped everything to go to your house and investigate an attempted burglary. Because he's a cop and if you piss him off, he can make your life a living hell."

"What is my life now?" Claire held out her hand. "Give me the burner phone."

Lydia studied her sister. There was something different about her. She had stopped sounding like a confused bystander and started acting like the person in charge.

Lydia asked, "What are you going to say to him?"

"That he needs to be straight with me. That he needs to explain to me again why the movie isn't real when, according to Eleanor Kilpatrick, her daughter was abused in the same way as the girl in the movie."

"That's a fantastic idea, Sweetpea." Lydia layered on the sarcasm. "You believe that a high-ranking police officer might possibly be covering up a murder, or maybe is somehow involved in it, or filming it, or distributing images of it, or maybe all of the above, and you're just going to call him up and say, 'Hey, man, what's the what up?'"

"I hadn't planned on sounding like J. J. Walker, but that's the gist."

"Claire."

She held out her hand for the phone.

Lydia knew her sister's mind was set. She rummaged through her purse for the phone. The back of her hand hit the bottle of Percocet she'd taken from Claire's desk. Lydia had told herself she was keeping the pills from Claire, but she had a niggling suspicion that she was keeping them for herself.

"Did you bring it?"

"Yes, I brought it." Lydia pulled out the phone and handed it to Claire. She snapped her purse closed.

Claire easily found Jacob Mayhew's business card in her wallet. She dialed the number and pressed the phone to her ear.

Lydia's body tensed. She counted rings that she could not

hear. Her palms were sweaty. The sound of rushing blood pulsed into her ears. She hadn't been inside a jail house in years, but she was still terrified of the police.

Claire shook her head. "Voicemail."

Lydia exhaled a long breath as Claire ended the call.

"He'd probably just lie to me anyway." Claire put the phone down on the table. "Other than you, I don't know who to trust anymore."

Lydia stared down at her hands. Her palms had left wet streaks on the cold, meshed metal. She didn't want to be here. She shouldn't be here. She should go back home to Dee. If they left now, Lydia could be back at the house in time to make her family a late breakfast.

"He was at school in March of ninety-one."

Lydia looked back up at her sister.

"Paul was living at Lyman Ward Academy when Julia went missing."

Lydia didn't realize the question had been in her mind until Claire had answered it. "Are you sure?"

"It's just outside of Auburn. He took me to see the campus one day. I didn't know why he wanted to go. He hated every minute he was there. But then we got to the school and I realized he wanted to show me off, which was fine, because I like being shown off, but it was a boarding school, and it was very small and very religious and incredibly strict."

Lydia had made the drive from Auburn to Athens many times before. "Julia went missing at around eleven on a Monday night. It's only three hours between here and Auburn."

"Paul was fifteen years old. He didn't have a license, let alone a car, and they checked on the boys two or three times a night. Most of them were there because their parents couldn't control them."

"Is that why Paul was there?"

"He told me that he won a scholarship." Claire shrugged. "It kind of made sense. His father did a stint in the Navy during Vietnam. Paul was planning on following in his footsteps, at least getting college paid for, until he read a book on architecture and changed his mind."

Lydia didn't buy it. "Paul was really smart. Maybe genius-level smart. If he really wanted to be in the Navy, he would've gone to NAPS or West Point Prep, not some ultra-strict, conservative Christian boarding school in the middle of Asshole, Alabama."

Claire closed her eyes for a moment. She nodded in agreement.

Lydia asked, "Are you sure he didn't sneak out?"

"As sure as I can be," Claire admitted. "He had perfect attendance the whole time. His picture was still in the trophy case by the headmaster's office, so there's no way he skipped class or got disciplined for being off-campus, and Spring Break was a week later."

"How do you know?"

"Because he went to the Kennedy Space Center to watch the shuttle launch. There was some kind of technical problem, so it didn't go up. I've seen the pictures. He's standing in front of a big banner with a date on it and you can see the empty launch pad in the distance, and I remember the date was during the second week of March because of—"

"Julia." Lydia looked back at the woman with the broom. She

was scraping chairs across the sidewalk as she put together the tables.

Claire said, "That skeevy jackass who got Dad arrested still runs the place."

Lydia could vividly recall her mother talking about Sam's arrest in her librarian voice, a furious whisper that could freeze an open flame.

Claire said, "It's weird, I miss Daddy more when I'm with you. I guess because you're the only person I can really talk to who knew him."

The door to the Starbucks opened. A group of kids tumbled out onto the sidewalk. Each carried a steaming cup of coffee. They were visibly hungover as they fumbled for their packs of cigarettes.

Lydia stood up. "Let's get out of here."

The Tesla was parked in front of the Taco Stand. Lydia glanced through the restaurant's front windows. The decor had been considerably updated. The chairs were padded. The tables looked clean. There were napkin dispensers on the tables instead of rolls of cheap paper towels.

Claire asked, "We're still going to the house, right?"

"I guess." Lydia didn't know what else to do but keep moving forward.

She got behind the wheel of the Tesla again. She tapped the brake to start the engine. Rick would enjoy hearing details about the car. The touchscreen. The way the steering wheel vibrated if you crossed the yellow line. She would use the information to soften him up, because when Lydia told him what she and Claire had been up to, he was going to justifiably have a fucking fit.

"Go back up the Atlanta Highway." Claire entered the Fuller address into the touchscreen. "I remember dancing to 'Love Shack' with Julia at one of Mom and Dad's Christmas parties. Do you remember? It was three months before she went missing."

Lydia nodded, though her mind was still on Rick. Unfortunately, they didn't have one of those relationships where they hid things from each other. They laid it all out, no matter the consequences. He would probably stop speaking to her. He might even see her crazy road trip as the final straw.

"This is the way Julia went." Claire pointed through the Arch toward the Hill Community, where Julia had lived during her freshman year. "The dorms are air-conditioned now. Mom says they've got free cable and wi-fi, a gym, and a coffee bar."

Lydia cleared her throat. She had gone from thinking that Rick was going to be mad at her to being mad at Rick for telling her what to do, which was crazy because none of the conversations had actually taken place anywhere but inside her own head.

Claire said, "The Manhattan's still over there. It's completely different now."

"Does Mom still walk the path on the anniversary?"

"I think so. We don't talk about it much."

Lydia chewed the tip of her tongue. She wanted to ask if Helen and Claire ever talked about her, but she was too afraid of the answer.

Claire said, "I wonder what's wrong with her."

"With Mom?"

"With Lexie Fuller." Claire twisted in her seat to face Lydia. "Paul obviously chose me because of Julia. I was so vulnerable after she disappeared. He was drawn to my tragedy. Don't you see it?"

Lydia hadn't seen it until now.

"When we first met, Paul pretended he didn't know about Julia, but of course he knew. His parents lived fifteen minutes away from where she disappeared. The farm wasn't self-supporting. His father did seasonal work with the campus grounds crew. His mother did bookkeeping downtown. Missing posters with Julia's face were everywhere. The story was all over the newspaper. Even without that, people in Auburn knew. There were a lot of students from Athens. You were there. You saw it for yourself. We didn't tell a soul, but everybody knew."

"Then why did you believe him when he said he didn't know?"

"Part of me didn't. I just thought he was trying to be polite, because it was kind of like gossip." She leaned the side of her head against the seat. "That's the only instance I can think of when I didn't believe him about anything."

Lydia slowed the car as the GPS alerted her to an upcoming turn. Strangely, she got no pleasure from Claire finally seeing the problems that Lydia had spotted eighteen years before. Maybe Claire was right. Lydia had only seen the dark side of Paul because he had chosen to show it to her. If that moment in the car had never happened, it was just as likely that she would've tolerated him all these years as an annoying brother-in-law who for some reason made her sister happy.

And he had clearly made Claire happy. At least while he was alive. Knowing how the bastard worked, wooing Claire had probably been part of a long game that started before they even met. Lydia wouldn't put it past him to have a thick file somewhere on

Claire Carroll. Was he at Auburn because he knew that Claire would follow Lydia to the university? Was he only working in the math lab because he found out she was flunking trig?

Lydia could still remember the breathless way Claire had told her about the new guy she had just met in the lab. Paul had discovered the perfect way into Claire's psyche—he hadn't praised her good looks, which she'd been hearing about practically from infancy. He had praised her mind. And he had done it in such a way that it seemed like he was the only man on the planet who recognized she had more to offer than her face.

Lydia pulled the car over to the shoulder. She slid the gear into park. She turned to Claire and told her something that she should've told her all along. "I have a seventeen-year-old daughter."

Claire looked surprised, but apparently not for the reason Lydia was thinking. "Why are you telling me that now?"

"You already knew." Lydia wanted to kick herself for being so stupid, and then she wanted to throw up because the idea of Paul paying a stranger to follow her was so deeply unsettling. "Why didn't you tell me Paul had a file on me?"

Claire looked away. "I was trying to protect you. I thought if you knew what Paul had done, you would—"

"Abandon you like you abandoned me?"

Claire took a deep breath and slowly let it go. "You're right. Every time I say that you should stay out of this, I find a way to drag you back in because I want my big sister to make it all better." She looked at Lydia. "I'm sorry. I know it sounds trite, but I really am."

Lydia didn't want another one of her apologies. "What else do you know about me?"

"Everything," she said. "At least everything that we know about Paul's other victims."

Victim. If she hit that nerve any harder, Lydia was going to need a root canal.

She asked Claire, "Did you know about it?"

"Absolutely not. I didn't know about any of them."

"How long was he having me followed?"

"Almost from the moment we stopped talking to each other."

Lydia saw her life flash before her eyes. Not the good things, but the shameful things. All the times she'd walked out of the grocery store with stolen food shoved down the front of her shirt because she couldn't afford to buy anything. The time she'd switched tags on a jacket at the outlet store because she wanted Dee to have the cute one that all the popular girls were wearing. All the lies she'd told about the check being in the mail, the rent money being at work, loans that would soon be repaid.

How much had Paul seen? Pictures of Lydia with Rick? Dee on the basketball court? Had he laughed at Lydia struggling her way out of poverty while he sat in his lifeless air-conditioned mansion?

Claire said, "I know you don't want to hear it, but I am profoundly sorry. I wasn't going to tell you, but then you told me about your daughter, and it felt wrong to pretend."

Lydia shook her head. It wasn't Claire's fault, but she still wanted to blame her.

"She's beautiful," Claire said. "I wish Daddy was still around to meet her."

Lydia felt a current of fear ripple through her body. She had been so focused on what it would feel like to lose her daughter that she had never considered what it would do to Dee if she lost her mother.

Lydia realized, "I really can't do this."

"I know."

She didn't think Claire could possibly understand. "It's not just me. I have a family to think about."

"You're right. I honestly mean it this time. You should go." Claire unbuckled her seatbelt. "Take the car. I can call Mom. She'll get me back to Atlanta." She reached for the door handle.

"What are you doing?"

"This is the road Paul lived on. The Fuller house is around here somewhere."

Lydia didn't bother to hide her irritation. "You're just going to walk down the street and hope to find it?"

"I seem to have a real knack for landing in shit." Claire pulled on the handle. "Thank you, Liddie. I mean that."

"Stop." Lydia felt certain Claire was hiding something again. "What are you not telling me?"

Claire didn't turn around. "I just want to see Lexie Fuller for myself. Lay eyes on her. That's it."

Lydia felt her eyes narrow. Her sister had the carefree air of someone who'd made up their mind to do something stupid. "Why?"

Claire shook her head. "It doesn't matter, Pepper. Go home to your family."

Lydia grabbed her for real this time. "Tell me what you're going to do."

She turned to face Lydia. "I really am proud of you, you know. What you've done with your life, the way you've raised such a smart, talented daughter."

Lydia brushed away the flattery. "You think Lexie Fuller is another one of his victims, don't you?"

Claire shrugged. "We're all his victims."

"This is different." Lydia tightened her grip on Claire's arm. She felt a sudden flare of panic. "You think she's locked inside the house, or chained to a wall, and you're going to go in there all Lucy Liu and save her?"

"Of course not." Claire looked out at the road. "Maybe she has information that will lead us to the masked man."

Lydia's flesh crawled. She hadn't seen that part of the movie, but Claire's description was terrifying. "Do you really want to meet that guy? He murdered a woman with a machete. And then he raped her. Jesus, Claire."

"Maybe we've already met him." Claire shrugged, like they were talking unlikely hypotheticals. "Or maybe Lexie Fuller knows who he is."

"Or maybe the masked man is in that house with his next Anna Kilpatrick. Did you consider that possibility?" Lydia was so frustrated that she wanted to bang her head on the steering wheel. "We're not superheroes, Claire. This is too dangerous. I'm not just thinking about my daughter. I'm thinking about you and me and what could happen to us if we keep digging up Paul's secrets."

Claire sat back in the seat. She stared down the long, straight road ahead of them. "I have to know."

"Why?" Lydia demanded. "He's dead. You know enough

about him now to view that as divine justice. The rest of this we've been doing—it's just asking for trouble."

"There's another video out there that shows Anna Kilpatrick being murdered."

Lydia didn't know what to say. Again, Claire was ten steps ahead of her.

Claire said, "That's the whole point of the series, to ramp it up to a crescendo. The movies show a progression. The final step is murder, so there must be a last movie that shows Anna being killed."

Lydia knew that she was right. Whoever abducted the girl wouldn't get rid of her without having his fun first. "Okay, let's say by some miracle we find the movie. What would it show us other than someone who might be Anna Kilpatrick being murdered?"

"Her face," Claire said. "The last movie with the other woman showed her face. The camera actually zoomed in on it."

"Zoomed in?" Lydia felt like the inside of her mouth had turned into sandpaper. "Not auto-focus?"

"No, it zoomed into a tight frame so you just saw her from the waist up."

"Someone else has to be working the camera to make it zoom."

"I know," Claire said, and Lydia could tell from her dark expression that her sister had been skirting around this possibility for a while.

"Lexie Fuller?" Lydia tried, because she knew that suggesting Paul as an active participant would be the thing that finally broke Claire in two. "Is that what you're thinking, that Lexie was behind the camera?"

"I don't know, but the movies follow the same script, so we can assume that the last Anna Kilpatrick movie zooms in on her face."

Lydia chose her words carefully. "You really think if this Lexie person is behind the camera zooming in on a murder, she's going to confess that she's an accomplice and hand over the recording?"

"I feel like if I see her, look her in the eye, I'll know whether or not she was involved."

"Because you're such a fucking great judge of character?"

Claire shrugged off the observation. "The masked man is out there somewhere. He's probably looking for his next victim. If Lexie Fuller knows who he is, maybe she can help stop him."

Lydia said, "Let me get this straight: You get Lexie Fuller to give you a copy of a movie that you think shows Anna Kilpatrick being murdered. Let's set aside the fact that Lexie's incriminating herself. Who would you give the movie to? Mayhew? Nolan?"

"I could put it on YouTube if someone would show me how."

"They'd take it down in two seconds, and the FBI would arrest you for disseminating obscene material, and Nolan would testify against you at the trial." Lydia thought of something far more horrible. "You think the masked man's just going to let all that slide?"

Claire kept staring out at the road. Her chest rose and fell with each breath. She had that same look of focused intensity on her face that Lydia had seen back at the coffee house.

Claire asked, "What if, twenty-four years ago, two women had information about what happened to Julia—who took her, exactly what was done to her—and they kept their mouths shut because they were too afraid to get involved?"

Lydia tried to give an honest answer. "I hope I would understand that they had to think about their own safety."

"Because you're so understanding?" Claire shook her head, likely because she had known Lydia all of her life and she knew better. "Look at what not knowing did to Dad. Do you want Bob Kilpatrick's suicide on your conscience? Do you want to carry around Eleanor Kilpatrick's misery on your shoulders?" Her tone had become strident. "I have nothing to lose, Liddie. Literally—nothing. I don't have children. I don't really have any friends. My cat is dead. I own a house I don't want to go back to. There's a trust to take care of Grandma Ginny. Mom will survive because she always survives. Paul was my husband. I can't just walk away from this. I have to know. There isn't anything left in my life except finding out the truth."

"Don't be so damn dramatic, Claire. You still have me."

The words hung between them like weighted balloons. Did Lydia really mean them? Was she here for Claire, or was this ludicrous road trip really about proving that Lydia had been right about Paul all along?

If that was the case, then her point had been made long ago.

Lydia closed her eyes for a second. She tried to get her thoughts in order. "We'll go by the house."

"Now who's being dramatic?" Claire sounded as irritated as Lydia felt. "I don't want you to do this. You're not invited."

"Tough." She checked the mirrors before pulling back onto the road. "We're not going in."

Claire didn't put her seatbelt back on. The warning started to chime.

"Are you going to jump out of a moving car?"

"Maybe." Claire pointed up ahead. "That must be it."

The Fuller house was thirty yards past a shiny silver fire hydrant. Lydia tapped the brake. She coasted the car past the white clapboard house. The roof was new, but the grass in the yard was winter brown. Weeds shot up through cracks in the driveway. There were weathered sheets of plywood nailed across all the doors and windows. Even the mailbox had been removed. A lone four-by-four post stuck up like a broken tooth at the mouth of the driveway.

Of all the things Lydia expected to find, this was not it.

Claire sounded just as puzzled. "It's abandoned."

"For a long while, it looks like." The plyboards had started to peel apart. The paint was chipping from the vertical wood siding. The gutters were full.

Claire said, "Turn back around."

The road was sparsely traveled. They hadn't seen another car since Lydia had pulled over ten minutes ago. She executed a three-point turn and drove back toward the house.

Claire said, "Pull into the driveway."

"It's private property. We don't want to get shot."

"Paul's dead, so technically, it's my property."

Lydia wasn't so sure about the legalities, but still she made a wide turn into the driveway. There was something sinister about the Fuller house. The closer they got, the stronger the sensation got. Every bone in Lydia's body was telling her to go back. "This doesn't feel right."

"How is it supposed to feel?"

Lydia didn't answer. She was looking at the large padlock on the metal garage door. The house was isolated. There wasn't another structure for miles. Large trees forested the areas on either side of the house. The back yard was about fifty feet deep, and beyond that were acres of empty rows waiting for spring planting.

Lydia told Claire, "I have a gun." As a convicted felon, she could've gone to jail for possessing a weapon, but Lydia had been a single mother living in some very sketchy neighborhoods when she'd asked a guy at work to get one for her. "I buried it under my back porch steps when we moved into the house. It should still work. I put it in a Ziploc bag."

"We don't have time to go back." Claire drummed her fingers on her leg as she gave it some thought. "There's a pharmacy off Lumpkin that sells guns. We could buy one and be back here in thirty minutes."

"They'll do a background check."

"Do you think anyone's watching background checks? Mass murderers buy machine guns and enough ammo to take down twenty schools and no one bats an eye."

"Still—"

"Crap, I keep forgetting I'm on parole. I'm sure my PO put my name in the system. Where's the NRA when you need them?"

Lydia looked at her watch. "You were supposed to meet Nolan over an hour ago. He's probably put out a BOLO on you."

"I have to do this before I lose my nerve." Claire opened the door and got out of the car.

Lydia let out a string of curses. Claire went up the stairs to the front porch. She tried to see between the cracks in the plywood covering the windows. She shook her head at Lydia as she walked back down the steps. Instead of returning to the car, she walked around the back of the house.

"Dammit." Lydia took her cell phone out of her purse. She should text somebody that they were here. And then what? Rick would panic. She couldn't get Dee involved. She could post it on the Westerly Academy Parents' Bulletin Board but Penelope Ward would probably hire a private helicopter and fly down to Athens for the story.

And then Lydia would have to explain why she was sitting in the car like a coward while her baby sister tried to break into her dead husband's secret house.

She got out of the car. She jogged around the side of the house. Weeds as high as Lydia's waist had taken over the back yard. The sturdy-looking swingset was covered in moss. The ground crackled under her feet. The storms had not yet made their way over from Atlanta. The vegetation was as dry as kindling.

Claire was standing on the small back porch. She had her foot braced on the side of the house and her fingers curved under the sheet of plywood nailed over the back door. "There's no basement, just a crawlspace."

Lydia could see that for herself. Claire had kicked in the access panel to the enclosed area under the house. There was less than two feet between the dirt and the floor joists. "What are you doing?"

"Ruining my manicure. There's a pry bar in the trunk."

Lydia didn't know what to do but go back to the car. She opened the trunk and found what looked like MacGyver's secret stash. A first-aid kit. Emergency water and food. Two warming blankets. A safety vest. An ice scraper. A small tool kit. Flares. A bag of sand. An empty gas can, though the car was electric. Two reflective roadside warning triangles. A large pry bar that you could probably use to take off someone's head.

This was a wrecking bar, not a pry bar. One end had a gigantic hammer head and sharp claw. The other end had a curved edge. The thing had a heft to it, solid steel, about two feet long, and easily weighing just shy of ten pounds.

Lydia didn't stop to consider why Paul would drive around with this kind of thing in his trunk, and as she rounded the corner into the back yard, she tried really hard not to think about the dark joke Claire had made about finding more Mrs. Fullers buried in the overgrown back yard.

Claire was still trying to work the board away from the window. She'd managed to get her fingers between the plywood and the trim around the door. Her skin had broken open. Lydia saw streaks of blood on the weathered wood.

"Move." Lydia waited for her to get out of the way and jammed the flat end of the bar into the crack. The rotting wood came away like a banana peel. Claire grabbed the edge and yanked the board clean off the house.

The door was the same as every kitchen door Lydia had ever seen. Glass at the top, a thin panel of wood at the bottom. She tried the doorknob. Locked.

"Stand back." Claire grabbed the pry bar and busted out the glass. She racked the bar around the frame to make sure all the shards were gone, then stuck her hand inside the door and opened the lock.

Lydia knew it was a bit late, but she still asked, "Are you sure you want to do this?"

Claire kicked open the door. She walked into the kitchen. She turned on the lights. The fluorescent bulbs flickered to life.

The house felt empty, but Lydia still called, "Hello?" She waited a few seconds, then repeated, "Hello?"

Even without an answer, the house felt like it was ready to scream out its secrets.

Claire tossed the pry bar onto the kitchen table. "This is so weird."

Lydia knew what she meant. The kitchen looked like a brand-new late-1980s dream kitchen. The white tiled countertops were still in good shape, though the grout had yellowed with age. The two-toned cabinets had veneered walnut exteriors and white-painted doors and drawers. The white refrigerator was still running. The matching gas stove looked brand-new. The laminate tile on the floor was a parquet pattern of fake red and brown bricks. There was no grime in the corners or crumbs of food lost under the toekicks. In fact, there was very little dust on any of the surfaces. The kitchen felt clean. Despite the house being boarded up, there was no musty odor. If anything, it smelled of Pine-Sol.

Lydia said, "It feels like the Huxtables are about to walk in."

Claire knocked the dish soap and the sponge into the sink like a bored cat. She opened cabinets. She pulled out drawers too far so that they dropped onto the floor. Silverware clanged. Grill utensils and tongs clattered. Her fingers were still bleeding. Every surface she touched was streaked red.

Lydia asked, "Do you want me to get the first-aid kit out of the car?"

"I don't want anything that was Paul's."

Claire walked into the next room, which was obviously the den.

The plywood boards over the windows and front door blocked out any light. She turned on table lamps as she walked around the room. Lydia saw a large couch and a love seat, an easy chair and a television that was the old console kind, more like a piece of furniture. A top-loading VCR sat on a wooden shelf above the TV. The time was not flashing the way every VCR flashed in Lydia's memory. There were VHS tapes stacked beside the player. Lydia scanned the titles. All the movies were from the eighties. *Batman. The Princess Bride. Blade Runner. Back to the Future.*

There were tracks in the thick carpet under their feet where someone had recently vacuumed. Lydia ran her fingers through the light smattering of dust on the table behind the couch. If she had to guess, she would say the place hadn't been cleaned in a week, which was around the same time Paul had died. "Did he come to Athens a lot?"

"Apparently." Claire took out the videotapes and checked that the labels matched the boxes. "He worked long hours. He could easily drive here and back in a day without me ever finding out."

"Can you check the GPS in his car?"

"Look." Claire had found the answering machine on the table beside the couch. It was ancient, the kind that required two cassette tapes—one for the outgoing message and one for incoming calls. The red LED flashed that there were four messages. There was a tape beside the machine labeled MARIA. Claire popped open the cassette player. The outgoing cassette tape was labeled LEXIE.

"Two different tapes," Lydia said. "Do you think it's a code? You call in and one says you're safe and the other says you're not?"

Instead of guessing, Claire pressed the PLAY button for received messages. The machine clicked and whirred to life. The first message was static, followed by heavy breathing. There was a short beep, then the second message played. More of the same, until the fourth message played. Lydia could hear a groan on the other end of the line. She remembered now that Claire had groaned when the message tape had finished.

Claire must've recognized the sound, too. She pressed the STOP button. She looked around the family room. "He kept everything the same," she said, and Lydia knew she meant Paul. "His parents died in ninety-two. Sometime in January. I guarantee you this is exactly how they left it."

"Why would Paul lie about keeping the house?"

Claire didn't answer, likely because there was no answer. "There's no Lexie Fuller, is there?"

Lydia shook her head. Maybe there had been a woman who pretended to be Lexie Fuller, but considering what Paul was into, there was no telling what had happened to her.

Claire looked around the room. "This feels bad."

"The whole house feels bad."

There were two hallways leading off the den. One went to the left toward what were probably the bedrooms. The other went to the right toward the garage. The door was closed at the end of the hall. There was no padlock, just a hollow-core door with a polished brass knob that required a key.

Claire went to the left, turning on all the lights as she stomped through the house with a determination that Lydia had never seen in her sister. This was the Claire who had kneecapped a woman on her tennis team and destroyed every item in her garage. She pulled open drawers and kicked over boxes and rifled bedroom closets. Bottles were toppled. Lamps were broken. She even upended a mattress. Everything she found indicated people were living here, but only if those people hadn't aged since the first Bush lived in the White House.

Paul's boyhood room was a mixture of train sets and heavy metal posters. He'd slept in a twin bed with a dark red quilt neatly draped across the footboard. Every drawer in the bureau was hand-labeled. UNDERWEAR & SOCKS. T-SHIRTS & SHORTS. GYM CLOTHES. As with the den, there was very little dust in the room. The carpet was striped from a recent vacuuming. Even the ceiling fan blades were wiped clean.

The same neatness could be found in the tiny spare bedroom, which had a sewing machine in front of the boarded-up window that overlooked the front yard. There was a McCall sewing pattern laid out on a small folding table. Squares of fabric were beside it, ready to be cut.

The master bedroom was filled with a king-sized bed that had a blue satin quilt. The ghosts of Paul's parents permeated the space. The crocheted doily on the back of a wooden rocking chair. The well-worn, steel-toed boots lined up beside one-inch pumps in the tiny closet. There were two bedside tables. One had a hunting magazine in the drawer. The other contained a plastic case for a diaphragm. The paintings on the wall were the sort of thing you got at a flea market or a starving artist sale: pastorals with lots of trees and a too-blue sky looking down on an unreal tableau of grazing sheep and a contented sheep dog. Again, there were vacuum tracks in the blue shag carpet.

Lydia echoed Claire's earlier observation. "It's like he was keeping a shrine to his childhood."

Claire went into the bathroom, which was as small and tidy as the other rooms. The flowered shower curtain was already pulled back. A bar of green soap was in the soap dish. Head and Shoulders shampoo was on a hanging rack underneath the showerhead. A used towel had been left to dry over the towel bar. The two shag rugs on the floor were neatly aligned, separated by the same amount of space all around.

She opened the medicine cabinet. She pulled out all of the items and tossed them onto the floor. Sure deodorant. Close-Up toothpaste. She held up a prescription bottle.

"Amitriptyline," Claire read. "It was prescribed for Paul's father."

"It's an older antidepressant." Lydia was intimately familiar with popular drugs from the late twentieth century. "Pre-Prozac."

"You'll be surprised to hear that Paul never mentioned anything about depression." Claire threw the bottle over her shoulder. "Are you ready to go into the garage?"

Lydia realized she'd been putting it off, too. She tried, "We could still leave."

"Sure we could." Claire brushed past Lydia and headed back toward the den. She went into the kitchen. When she returned, she was gripping the pry bar in her hands. She walked down the narrow hallway toward the garage. The distance was around fifteen feet, but Lydia felt like everything was moving in slow motion. The pry bar arced over Claire's head. It hung in the air for a few moments before coming down on the brass knob. The door opened into the garage.

Claire reached in and felt for the light switch. Fluorescents sputtered on.

She dropped the pry bar.

Lydia couldn't move. She was ten feet away, but she could still clearly see the wall opposite the doorway—the empty chains bolted to a concrete-block wall, the edge of a dirty mattress, discarded fast-food bags on the floor, photographer's spotlights, a camera on a tripod. The ceiling had been altered so it looked like the room was in a basement. Wires hung down. Plumbing pipes went to nowhere. Chains dangled onto the concrete floor. And there was blood.

Lots of blood.

Claire stepped back into the hall, pulling the door closed behind her. The knob was broken off. She had to wrap her fingers around the spindle. She kept her back to the door, blocking the way, keeping Lydia out of the garage.

A body, Lydia thought. *Another victim. Another dead girl.*

Claire spoke in a low, controlled tone. "I want you to give me your phone. I'm going to use the camera to document the room while you go to the road and use the burner phone to call the FBI. Not Nolan. Call the number in Washington, DC."

"What did you see?"

Claire shook her head once. Her color was off. She looked ill.

"Claire?"

She shook her head again.

"Is there a body?"

"No."

"What is it?"

She kept shaking her head.

"I'm not fucking around. Tell me what's in there."

Claire tightened her grip on the door. "Video cassettes. VHS."

Lydia tasted bile in her mouth. VHS. Not DVDs. Not digital files. VHS tapes. "How many?"

"A lot."

"How many is a lot?"

"Too many."

Lydia found enough strength to start walking. "I want to see."

Claire barred the door. "This is a crime scene. This is where Anna Kilpatrick died. We can't go in there."

Lydia felt Claire's hand on her arm. She didn't remember walking down the hallway, moving toward the thing her sister was trying to keep her away from, but now she was close enough to smell the metallic tinge of coagulating blood.

She asked the only question that mattered. "How far back do the VHS tapes go?"

Claire shook her head again.

Lydia felt her throat turn into barbed wire. She tired to push Claire aside, but Claire would not move. "Get out of my way."

"I can't let you—"

Lydia grabbed her by the arm. Her grip was tighter than she meant it to be, but then her other hand flew up and suddenly, she was engaged in a full-on struggle with her sister. They shoved each other back and forth up and down the hallway the same way they used to fight over a dress or a book or a boy.

The three-year difference in their ages had always worked to Lydia's advantage, but this time it was an extra thirty pounds that helped her prevail. She pushed Claire so hard that she stumbled backward. Her tailbone hit the floor. Claire huffed as the breath was knocked out of her.

Lydia stepped over her sister. Claire made one last grab for her leg, but it was too late.

Lydia pushed open the garage door.

Wooden shelves took up one section of a wall. Eight rows went from floor to ceiling, each approximately eight feet wide and a foot deep. VHS tapes were stacked tightly together. Their colored cardboard sleeves divided them into sections. A familiar number sequence was written by hand on the labels. Lydia already knew the code.

The dates went back to the 1980s.

She stepped down into the room. There was a tremor in her body, almost like she was standing too close to the edge of a cliff. Her toes tingled. Her hands shook. She was sweating again. Her bones vibrated beneath her skin. Her senses sharpened.

The sound of Claire crying behind her. The odor of bleach cutting into the back of her nose. The taste of fear on her tongue. Her vision tunneling to the six VHS tapes given a place of prominence on the middle shelf.

A green rubber band held together the green cardboard-sleeved videotapes. The handwriting was angular and clear. The number sequence was easy to decipher now that Lydia knew the key.

0-1-3-9-0-9-4-1.

03-04-1991.

March 4, 1991.

ELEVEN

Claire opened her mouth to tell Lydia not to touch anything, but the words never came out because there was no point anymore. She had known from the minute she saw the wall of videotapes that there was no turning back, just as she'd known that this had all been inevitable. Paul had been obsessed with Claire for a reason. He had been the perfect husband for a reason. He had manipulated their lives together for a reason.

And all the while, Claire had refused to see what was right in front of her.

Maybe that's why she wasn't feeling shocked. Or maybe she was incapable of feeling shocked anymore, because every time Claire thought she'd seen the worst of Paul, some new detail emerged and she was struck not just by the horror of his deeds, but by her own willful blindness.

There was no telling what Lydia was feeling. She stood

completely still in the middle of the cold garage. Her hand was reaching toward the six videotapes, but she had stopped just shy of touching them.

Lydia said, "March fourth, 1991."

"I know." Claire's eyes had locked straight onto the labels the second she'd opened the door.

"We have to watch it."

Again, Claire did not tell her not to. There were so many reasons to leave this place. There were so many reasons to stay.

Red pill/blue pill.

This was no longer a philosophical exercise. Did they want to know what had happened to Julia or not?

Lydia obviously had her answer. She slowly became unstuck. She grabbed the stack of green VHS tapes with both hands. She turned around and waited for Claire to get out of her way.

Claire followed her sister back into the den. She leaned against the wall as she watched Lydia load a tape into the ancient VCR. She had chosen the last tape in the series because that was the only one that mattered.

There was no remote control for anything. Lydia pulled the button to turn on the TV. The tube popped on. The picture faded from black to snow. She twisted the volume dial to turn down the staticy noise. The console had two knobs—one for VHF and one for UHF. Lydia tried channel three. She waited. She tried channel four.

The screen went from snow to black.

Lydia rested her thumb on the big orange PLAY button. She looked at Claire.

Red pill? Blue pill? Do you really want to know?

And then her father's voice: *There are some things you can't unsee.*

Maybe it was Sam's warning that haunted her most, because Claire had seen the other movies. She knew there was a script to the abuse that the girls endured, just as she knew what she would see on the last tape, the tape that Lydia was waiting to play on the VCR.

Julia Carroll, nineteen years old, naked and chained to the wall. Bruises and burns riddling her body. Electrocution marks. Branded flesh. Skin ripped apart. Mouth open, screaming in terror as the masked man walked in with his machete.

"Claire?" Lydia was asking for permission. Could they do this? Should they do this?

Did they really have a choice?

Claire nodded, and Lydia pressed PLAY.

There was a white zigzag down the black screen. The image rolled too quickly to make out any details. Lydia flipped open an access panel and adjusted the tuner.

The image snapped into frame.

Lydia made a noise somewhere between a groan and a gasp.

Julia was spreadeagled against a wall, her arms and legs shackled apart. She was naked except for the silver and black bangles she always wore on her wrists. Her head was down. Her body was lax. The only thing holding her upright was the chains.

Claire closed her eyes. She could hear Julia's soft whimpers through the console TV's single speaker. The place Julia had been held was different, not the staged basement but the inside of a barn. The slats were dark brown, obviously the back wall of a horse stall. Hay was on the floor. There were droppings of animal feces at her bare feet.

Claire remembered the Amityville-looking barn from the picture she had painted. She wondered if Paul had torn it down out of disgust or if, in his typical, efficient way of thinking, he'd found it more expedient to keep everything under one roof.

On the TV, her sister started to whimper.

Claire opened her eyes. The masked man had entered the frame. Claire had seen photos of Paul from 1991. He was tall and lanky with too-short hair and a painfully straight posture that had been drummed into him by the instructors at the military academy.

The masked man was tall, but not lanky. He was older, probably in his late forties. There was a pronounced curve to his shoulders. His belly was softer. He had a tattoo on his biceps, an anchor with words Claire could not read but obviously signified that he'd been in the US Navy.

Paul's father had been in the Navy.

Slowly, deliberately, the masked man took one step, then another, toward Julia.

Claire told Lydia, "I'm going to go outside."

Lydia nodded, but didn't look back.

"I can't stay in here, but I'm not leaving you."

"Okay." Lydia was transfixed by the television. "Go."

Claire pushed away from the wall and walked into the kitchen. She stepped over spilled cutlery and broken glass and kept walking until she was outside. The cold air pinched her skin. Her lungs flinched at the sudden chill.

Claire sat on the back steps. She hugged her arms to her body.

She was shaking from the cold. Her teeth hurt. The tips of her ears burned. She had not seen the worst of the video, but she had seen enough, and she knew that her father was right. All of her happy memories of Julia—dancing with her to *American Bandstand* in front of the TV every Saturday, singing with her in the car as they drove to the library to pick up Helen, skipping along behind Sam and Lydia as they all went to the campus clinic to see a new batch of puppies—that was all gone.

Now, when she thought of Julia, the only image that came to mind was that of her sister spread against that rough-sawn wall in a stall where animals were kept.

Inside the house, Lydia called out a strangled cry.

The sound was piercing, like a sliver of glass slicing open Claire's heart. She dropped her head into her hands. She felt hot, but her body would not stop trembling. Her heart shuddered inside her chest.

Lydia began to wail.

Claire heard an anguished sob come from her own mouth. She covered her ears with her hands. She couldn't stand the sound of Lydia's keening. They were two rooms apart, but Claire could see everything that Lydia had seen: the machete swinging up, the blade coming down, the blood flowing, the convulsions, the rape.

Claire should go back inside. She should be there for Lydia. She should bear witness to the last few seconds of Julia's life. She should do something other than sit uselessly on the back porch, but she could not force herself to move.

She could only look out at the vast, empty field and scream—for her murdered sister, her exiled sister, her fractured mother, her shattered father, her decimated family.

Claire was overcome with grief, but still she screamed. She fell to her knees. Something broke open inside her throat. Blood filled her mouth. She slammed her fists into the dry red clay and cursed Paul for everything he'd taken away from her: holding Lydia's baby, maybe carrying her own, watching her parents grow old together, sharing her own life with the only sister she had left. She raged against her scam of a marriage—the eighteen years she'd wasted loving a sick, twisted madman who had tricked Claire into thinking she had everything she wanted when really, she had nothing at all.

Lydia's arms wrapped around her. She was crying so hard that her words stuttered. "S-she was . . . s-so . . . s-scared . . ."

"I know." Claire grabbed onto her sister. Why had she ever believed Paul? How had she ever let Lydia go? "It's okay," she lied. "Everything is going to be okay."

"S-she was terrified."

Claire squeezed her eyes shut, praying the images would leave.

"A-all alone. S-she was all alone."

Claire rocked Lydia like a baby. They were both shaking so hard they could barely hold on. The devastation of what they'd been through opened like a blister.

"S-she knew what was coming and s-she couldn't move and there was no one to—" Her words were cut off by a strangled cry. "Oh, God! Oh, God!"

"I'm sorry," Claire whispered. Her voice was hoarse. She could barely speak. Lydia was trembling uncontrollably. Her skin felt cold. Every breath rattled in her lungs. Her heart was pounding so hard that Claire could feel it against her own chest.

"My God," Lydia cried. "My God."

"I'm sorry." This was all Claire's fault. She should've never called Lydia. She had no right to bring her into this. She was selfish and cruel and deserved to be alone for the rest of her life. "I'm so, so sorry."

"Why?" Lydia asked. "Why did he choose her?"

Claire shook her head. There was no explanation. They would never know what it was about Julia on that night at that time that made her a target.

"She was so good. She was so fucking good."

The refrain was achingly familiar. Sam and Helen had asked the same question over and over again: Why *our* daughter? Why *our* family?

"Why did it have to be her?"

"I don't know." Claire had questioned herself, too. Why Julia? Why not Claire, who sneaked away with boys and cheated off her friends in math class and flirted with the gym teacher so she wouldn't have to do sprints?

Lydia shuddered, her body racked with grief. "It should've been me."

"No."

"I was such a fuck-up."

"No."

"It wouldn't have hurt as much."

"No, Liddie. Look at me." Claire pressed her hands to either side of Lydia's face. She had lost her father to this same kind of thinking. She wasn't going to lose her sister again. "Look at me, Lydia. Don't say that. Don't you ever say that again. Do you hear me?"

Lydia said nothing. She wouldn't even look at her.

"You matter." Claire tried to keep the absolute terror out of her voice. "I don't want you to ever say that again, okay? You matter. You matter to Rick and to Dee and to Mom. And you matter to me." Claire waited for an answer. "Okay?"

Lydia's head was still trapped between Claire's hands, but she managed a short nod.

"I love you," Claire said, words she hadn't even told her husband when he was dying in her arms. "You are my sister, and you are perfect, and I love you."

Lydia held on to Claire's hands.

"I love you," Claire repeated. "Do you hear me?"

Lydia nodded again. "I love you, too."

"Nothing is ever going to come between us again. All right?"

Again, Lydia nodded. Some of her color was coming back. Her breathing had slowed down.

Claire gripped both of Lydia's hands in her own. They looked down at the ground because seeing the house and knowing its awful history was too much to bear.

Claire said, "Tell me what it was like when Dee was born."

Lydia shook her head. She was too upset.

"Tell me," Claire begged. The world was falling around them, but she had to know what else Paul had taken away from her. "Tell me what I missed."

Lydia must have needed it, too—some light in this dark grave they had buried themselves inside. "She was tiny." Her lips quivered with a faint smile. "Like a doll."

Claire smiled because she wanted Lydia to keep smiling. She needed to think of something good right now, something that would take away the images of the other Julia in her head.

"Was she an easy baby?"

Lydia wiped her nose with her sleeve.

"Did she sleep all the time?"

"God, no."

Claire waited, willing Lydia to talk about anything but what they had seen on the television. "She was fussy?"

Lydia shrugged and shook her head at the same time. She was still thinking about their sister, still trapped in that deep, dark hole.

"What was she like?" Claire squeezed Lydia's hands. She worked to make her tone sound lighter. "Come on, Pepper. Tell me what my niece was like. Sugar and spice? Sweet and adorable like I was?"

Lydia laughed, but she was still shaking her head. "She cried all the time."

Claire kept pushing. "Why did she cry?"

"I don't know." Lydia heaved a heavy sigh. "She was hot. She was cold. She was hungry. She was full." She wiped her nose again. The cuff of her shirt was already wet with tears. "I thought I had raised you, but Mom did all the hard stuff."

Claire knew it was childish, but she liked the idea of Helen doing all the hard stuff. "Tell me why."

"Holding you and playing with you, that was easy. Changing your diaper and walking with you at night and all that other stuff—it's hard to do by yourself."

Claire brushed back Lydia's hair. She should've been there. She should've brought her sister groceries and folded laundry and spelled her for as long as she was needed.

"She cried for the first two years." Lydia used her fingers to wipe underneath her eyes. "And then she learned how to talk and she wouldn't stop talking." She laughed at a memory. "She sang to herself all the time. Not just when I was around. I would catch her singing on her own and I would feel so weird about it. Like, when you walk in on a cat and it's purring and you feel bad because you thought it only purred for you."

Claire laughed so that Lydia would keep going.

"And then she got older, and . . ." Lydia shook her head. "Having a teenager is like having a really, really shitty roommate. They eat all your food and steal your clothes and take money out of your purse and borrow your car without asking." She put her hand over her heart. "But they soften you in ways you can't imagine. It's so unexpected. They just smooth out your hard lines. They make you into this better version of yourself that you never even knew was there."

Claire nodded, because she could see from Lydia's tender expression the change that Dee Delgado had brought.

Lydia grabbed Claire's hands and held on tight. "What are we going to do?"

Claire was ready for the question. "We have to call the police."

"Huckleberry?"

"Him, the state patrol, the Georgia Bureau of Investigation." Now that Claire was talking it out, she saw a plan. "We'll call everybody. Tell Homeland Security we saw someone making a bomb. Tell the FBI there's a kidnapped girl inside the house. Call the EPA and say we saw a barrel of toxic waste. Tell the Secret Service that Lexie Fuller is planning to assassinate the President."

"You think if we can get them all here at the same time, no one can cover up anything."

"We should call the news outlets, too."

"That's good." Lydia started nodding. "I can post something about it on the parents' message board at Dee's school. There's a woman—Penelope Ward. She's my Allison Hendrickson without the kneecapping. Her husband is running for Congress next year. They're really connected, and she's like a dog with a bone. She won't let anyone drop this."

Claire sat back on her heels. She knew the name Penelope Ward. Branch Ward was running against Congressman Johnny Jackson for his seat. Jackson was the same congressman who'd started Paul on his road to success. He was also the reason Jacob Mayhew had given Claire for his presence at the house the day of the burglary.

Mayhew had told her, "The Congressman asked me to handle this," and Claire's mind had wandered into kickbacks and fraud because she had assumed Jackson was covering his ass. Was there another reason? If Mayhew was involved, did that mean that Johnny Jackson was, too?

Lydia asked, "What?"

Claire didn't share the revelation. They could let the various state agencies figure this out. Instead, she looked back up at the house. "I don't want Julia's tapes to be part of it."

Lydia nodded again. "What are we going to tell Mom?"

"We have to tell her that we know Julia is dead."

"And when she asks how we know?"

"She won't ask." Claire knew this for a fact. A long time ago, Helen had made a conscious decision to stop seeking out the truth. Toward the end of Sam's life, she wouldn't even let him mention Julia's name.

Lydia asked, "Do you think it's Paul's father in the video?"

"Probably." Claire stood up. She didn't want to sit around trying to figure this out. She wanted to call in the people who could actually do something about it. "I'll get the tapes with Julia."

"I'll help."

"No." Claire didn't want to put Lydia through seeing any part of the video again. "Start making the phone calls. Use the landline so they can trace the number." Claire walked over to the wall-mounted phone. She waited for Lydia to pick up the receiver. "We can put the Julia tapes in the front trunk of the Tesla. No one will think to check there."

Lydia dialed 911. She told Claire, "Hurry. This isn't going to take long."

Claire walked into the den. Mercifully, the picture on the television was black. The videotapes were stacked on top of the console.

She called to Lydia, "Do you think we should drive back into town and wait?"

"No!"

Claire guessed her sister was right. The last time she'd left this to the police, Mayhew had managed her like a child. She pressed the EJECT button on the VCR. She rested her fingers on the cassette. She tried to summon into her brain an image of Julia that wasn't taken from the movie.

It was too soon. All she could see was her sister in chains.

Claire would destroy the videos. Once they were safe, she would spool out all the tape and burn them in a metal trashcan.

She slid the cassette out of the machine. The handwriting on the label was similar to Paul's but not exactly the same. Had Paul found the tape after his father died? Was that what had first sparked his interest? Julia disappeared almost a year before his parents' car accident. Five years later, Paul was wooing Claire at Auburn. They were married less than two months after her father had killed himself. Claire could no longer cling to the idea of coincidences, which begged the question: Had Paul designed all of this from the moment he recognized Julia in his father's videotape collection? Was that what had set him on the path toward Claire?

Absent a written explanation, Claire knew that she would never know the truth. Julia's death had haunted her for the last twenty-four years. Now the mystery of what had really gone wrong with her husband would haunt her for the remaining decades.

She slid the tape back into the cardboard sleeve. She wrapped the rubber band around the stack of cassettes.

She smelled Paul's aftershave.

The scent was faint. She put her nose to the tapes. She closed her eyes and inhaled.

"Claire," Paul said.

She turned around.

Paul stood in the middle of the room. He was wearing a red UGA sweatshirt and black jeans. His head was shaved. His beard had grown in. He had on thick plastic glasses like the ones he'd worn back in college.

He said, "It's me."

Claire dropped the tapes. They clattered at her feet. Was this real? Was this happening?

"I'm sorry," Paul said.

Then he drew back his fist and punched her in the face.

V.

I must confess, sweetheart, that I have been neglecting my wall of clues. My "useless gallimaufry," your mother called it on the one and only occasion she deigned to look at my work. I sagely agreed with her observation but of course I went running to the dictionary as soon as she was gone.

Gallimaufry: a hodgepodge; a confused jumble of various people or things; any absurd medley.

Oh, how I adore your mother.

These last ten months that I have been visiting Ben Carver at the prison, I have gone to bed many times without giving my gallimaufry a second glance. The collection has become so mundane that my mind has turned it into a piece of art, more a reminder that you are gone than a roadmap to getting you back.

It wasn't until I read Ben's inscription inside the Dr. Seuss book that I remembered a note from Huckleberry's files. It's been there from the beginning, or at least since I started my annual reading ritual on the anniversary of your birthday. Why is it that we always neglect the things that matter most? This is a universal question, because through the days and weeks and months and years after your disappearance, I understood that I did not cherish you enough. I never told you that I loved you enough. I never held you enough. I never listened to you enough.

You would likely tell me (as your mother has) that I could rectify this deficit with your sisters, but it is human nature to yearn for the things we cannot have.

Have I told you about Claire's new young man, Paul? He certainly yearns for Claire, though she has made it clear that he can have her. The match is an uneven one. Claire is a vibrant, beautiful young woman. Paul is neither vibrant nor particularly attractive.

After meeting him, your mother and I had some fun at the boy's expense. She called him Bartleby, after the well-known scrivener: "pallidly neat, pitiably respectable, incurably forlorn." I likened him more to some form of rat terrier: arrogant. Easily bored. Too smart for his own good. Partial to ugly sweaters. I opined that he is the kind of man who, absent the right kind of attention, can do great harm.

Is this last sentence revisionist thinking? Because I can clearly remember sharing your mother's Bartleby appraisal the first time we met Paul: annoying and harmless and likely to soon be shown the door.

It is only now that I see the meeting in a more sinister light.

Claire brought him home during the Georgia–Auburn game. In the past, I have always felt slightly sorry for any man Claire brings home. You can see it in their eager eyes that they think this is something—meeting the girl's parents, touring the town where she grew up, just around the corner is love, marriage, the baby carriage, etc. Sadly for these young men, the opposite tends to be true. For Claire, a trip to Athens typically heralds the end of a relationship. For your baby sister, this town is tainted. The streets are tainted. The house is tainted. Perhaps we—your mother and I—are tainted, too.

Pepper had warned us in advance about Claire's new beau. She seldom approves of her sister's boyfriends (likewise, Claire never approves of hers; I feel certain you would have been their tie-breaker), but in this instance, Pepper's description of Paul was not only alarming, but spot-on. I have rarely had such a visceral reaction to a person. He reminds me of the worst kind of student I used to have—the kind who is certain that they already know everything worth knowing (which invariably leads to an animal's unnecessary suffering).

If I am being honest, the thing about Paul Scott that bothered me the most was the way he touched my daughter in front of me. I am not an old-fashioned man. Public displays of affection are more likely to make me smile than blush.

And yet.

There was something about the way this man touched my youngest child that set my teeth on edge. His arm linked through hers as they walked up to the house. His hand stayed at her back as they climbed the stairs. His fingers laced through hers as they walked through the door.

Reading back that last paragraph, it all sounds so innocuous, the typical gestures of a man who is making love to a woman, but

I must tell you, sweetheart, that there was something so deeply unsettling about the way he touched her. His hand literally never left her body. Not once the entire time they were in front of me. Even when they sat on the couch, Paul held her hand until she was settled, then he threw his arm around her shoulders and spread his legs wide as if the girth of his testicles had turned his kneecaps into oppositely polarized magnets.

Your mother and I exchanged several glances.

He is a man who is comfortable airing his opinions, and confident that every single word that comes out of his mouth is not just correct, but fascinating. He has money, which is evident from the car he drives and the clothes he wears, but there is nothing moneyed about his attitude. His arrogance comes from his intelligence, not from his wallet. And it must be said that he is clearly a brilliant young man. His ability to at least sound informed on any subject matter points to a voracious memory. He clearly understands details if not nuance.

Your mother asked about his family, because we are southern and asking about someone's family is the only way we can distinguish the chaff from the wheat.

Paul started with the basics: his father's tour in the Navy, his mother's secretarial schooling. They became farmers, salt-of-the-earth people who supplemented their income with bookkeeping and seasonal work with the UGA grounds crew. (As you know, this latter part-time work is not uncommon. Everyone at some point or another ends up working in some capacity for the school.) There were no other relatives but for a seldom-seen uncle on the mother's side who passed away Paul's freshman year at Auburn.

It was because of his childhood isolation, Paul said, that he wanted a big family—a fact that should have pleased your mother and me but I saw her back stiffen alongside mine, because the tone in his voice indicated just how he would go about achieving that.

(Trust me, sweetheart, there is a reason centuries of fathers have fought brutal wars to protect the concept of Immaculate Conception.)

After relaying the basics, Paul got to the part of his history that made your little sister's eyes glisten with tears. That was when I knew he had her. It seems harsh to say that Claire never cries for anyone, but if you only knew, my sweet girl, what became of us after you disappeared, you would understand that she didn't cry because there were no tears left.

Except for Paul.

As I sat there listening to the story of his parents' car accident, I felt some old memories stirring. The Scotts died almost a full year after you were gone. I remember reading about the pile-up in the newspaper because by that time, I was reading every page in case there was some story that connected back to you. Your mother remembers hearing from a patron at the library that Paul's father was decapitated. There was fire involved. Our imaginations ran wild.

Paul's version of events is far more rosy (he is certainly the boot-strapper in this story), but I cannot fault a man for wanting to own his past, and there is no denying that the tragedy works its magic on Claire. For so many years, people have been trying to take care of your little sister. I think with Paul, she finally sees an opportunity to take care of someone else.

If your mother were reading this letter, she would tell me to get to the point. I suppose I should, because the point is this:

Here is the inscription Ben Carver wrote for me in the Dr. Seuss book:

"First you must have the images. Then come the words."

Robert James Waller.

Images.

Ben had taken and distributed images of his crimes. This was part of his legend, his infamy. There were said to be hundreds of photographs and films on the black market that showed him with various victims. But Ben was already in prison. He was not giving me a clue to his own crimes. He was giving me a clue to his competition.

Images.

I had read that word before—many times before.

As with all the suspects in your disappearance, Huckleberry blacked out one particular man's name, but here are the details I transcribed from a deputy investigator's notes in your case file:

XXXXXX XXXXX peeping Tom. Seasonal gardener for UGA grounds crew, arrested 1/4/89; 4/12/89; 6/22/90; 8/16/91— all charges dropped. Targets older female teens, blonde, attractive (17–20). MO: stands outside ground-floor windows and takes what he calls "images"—photographs or recordings of women in various states of undress. Deceased 1/3/1992 (car accident; wife also deceased; 16 y.o. son in boarding school/Alabama).

Images.

The peeping Tom was alive when you went missing. He sought out young women around your age, around your hair color, around your beauty. Had he stood outside the window to your ground-floor bedroom and taken *images* of you? Had he watched you brush your hair and talk to your sisters and undress for bed? Had he seen you on campus when he was working for the grounds crew? Had he followed you to the Manhattan that night? Had he followed you again when you left the bar?

Had he decided that his *images* were not enough?

You may be wondering how Ben Carver got his hands on a copy of your case file. As I told you earlier, Ben is somewhat of a celebrity, even in prison. He receives correspondence from all around the world. According to the warden, Ben traffics in information. This is how he gets extra meals and protection inside the dangerous walls of death row. He finds out what people want to know and he doles it out to them at his pleasure.

Images.

How did Ben know that this word of all words would jog my memory? That it would send me running back to my wall, shuffling through my stack of notebooks, looking for the words I had transcribed from your file almost six whole years ago?

After ten months, after forty-eight visits, did Ben know my mind that well?

The question will remain unanswered. Ben is the type of psychopath who claims he likes the wind to direct his sails, but occasionally, I have seen him dip his hand into the water, rudder-like, to change the course.

And with that one word—*images*—he changed the course of my life.

The peeping Tom's name was Gerald Scott.

His son is your baby sister's new boyfriend.

TWELVE

Claire opened her eyes. The popcorn ceiling had a brownish tinge. The shag carpet felt damp against her back. She was lying on the floor. A pillow was under her head. Her tennis shoes were off.

She sat up.

Paul.

He was alive!

Claire felt a singular moment of absolute elation before she came hurtling back down to earth. Then her mind filled with questions. Why had he faked his death? Why had he fooled her? Who had helped him? What was he doing at the Fuller house? Why had he punched her?

And where was her sister?

"Lydia?" Claire could barely get out the word. Her throat was on fire. She pulled herself up to standing. She fought a rushing nausea as she stumbled against the television. Her cheekbone sent out small explosions of pain. "Liddie?" she tried. Her voice was still hoarse, but the panic spurred her to scream as loud as she could. "Liddie?"

There was no answer.

Claire ran down the hallway toward the garage. She threw open the door. The videotapes. The chains. The blood. They were all still there, but no Lydia. She pulled the door shut behind her as she ran back down the hallway. She checked the bedrooms, the bathroom, the kitchen, her panic ratcheting higher with each vacant room. Lydia was gone. She was missing. Someone had taken her.

Paul had taken her, just like his father had taken Julia.

Claire ran onto the back porch. She scanned the field behind the house. She jogged around to the front, her heart pounding like a jackhammer. She wanted to scream and cry and rail. How had this happened again? Why had she let Lydia out of her sight?

The Tesla was still parked in the driveway. The car door handles slid out when Claire approached. The system had sensed the keyfob, which had somehow ended up in her back pocket. Both her purse and Lydia's were dumped out on the front seat of the car. The burner phone was gone. A long, orange extension cord snaked from the front porch to the driveway and connected to the cable that charged the Tesla.

Inside the house, the phone started to ring.

Claire ran toward the back. She stopped at the kitchen door. She wanted to go in, to answer the phone, but she found herself paralyzed with fear. She stared at the ringing phone. It was white. The cord hung below, stopping several feet short of the floor. Their kitchen phone in the house on Boulevard had a cord that could stretch into the pantry because that was the only place for years that any of them could talk with a modicum of privacy.

Lydia was gone. Paul had taken her. This was happening. She couldn't stop it. She couldn't hide in her room with her headphones on and pretend the world outside was still spinning blissfully on its axis.

Claire forced herself to go into the kitchen. She pressed her palm against the phone but did not pick it up. She felt the cold plastic under her hand. This was a sturdy, old Princess phone, the kind you used to rent monthly from Southern Bell. She could feel the vibrations of the metal bell ringing through her palm.

The answering machine had been turned off. A pillow had been placed under her head. Her shoes had been removed. The Tesla was being charged.

She knew whose voice she would hear before she even picked up the phone.

Paul said, "Are you all right?"

"Where's my sister?"

"She's safe." Paul hesitated. "Are you okay?"

"No, I'm not okay, you motherfucking piece of—" Claire's voice strangled around the words. She went into a coughing fit that brought up enough blood to spray the back of her hand. Claire stared at the red lines streaking across her pale flesh.

Paul asked, "Is that blood?"

Claire spun around the room. Was he inside the house? Standing outside?

He said, "Look up."

Claire looked up.

"A little to your left."

Claire spotted what looked like an air freshener on top of the refrigerator. There was a stem of green eucalyptus leaves carved on a taupe vase. One of the leaves had been cut all the way through to accommodate a camera lens.

He said, "There are more. All around the house."

"This house or the Dunwoody house?"

Paul didn't answer, which was answer enough. He had been watching her. That was why there wasn't a colored file with Claire's name on the label. Paul wasn't hiring detectives to stalk her one month out of the year. He was stalking her every single day of her life.

She said, "Where is Lydia?"

"I'm calling you from a comsat phone with a scrambler. Do you know what that is?"

"Why the fuck would I know what that is?"

"Comsat is an abbreviation for a series of communication satellites," he explained, his voice maddeningly pedantic. "The phone relays calls through geostationary satellites instead of land-based cell towers. The scrambler masks the number and location, which means this call can't be traced, not even by the NSA."

Claire wasn't listening to his voice. She was listening to the ambient noise. She didn't need the NSA to tell her Paul was in a moving car. She could hear road noises and the sound of wind that always seeped in no matter how expensive the vehicle.

Claire asked, "Is she alive?"

He didn't answer.

Her heart twisted so tight she could barely breathe. "Is Lydia alive?"

"Yes."

Claire stared into the lens of the camera. "Put her on the phone. Now."

"She's unavailable."

"If you hurt her—" Claire felt her throat tighten. She had seen the movies. She knew what could happen. "Please don't hurt her."

"I'm not going to hurt her, Claire. You know I would never do that."

Tears finally came because for just a second, just the tiniest second, she let herself believe him. "Let me talk to my sister right now or I will call every Goddamn law enforcement agency in the book."

Paul sighed. She knew that sigh. It was the one he gave when he was about to give Claire what she wanted. She heard the sound of a car pulling over. There was a rustling noise.

"What are you doing?"

"I'm doing what you asked." The car door opened and closed. She heard other vehicles speeding by. He must be on the Atlanta Highway. How long had Claire been out? How far away had he gotten with Lydia?

She said, "Your father killed my sister."

There was a squeaking sound as a door or a trunk was opened.

"It's him in the video, isn't it?" Claire waited. "Paul, tell me. It's him, isn't it?"

"Yes." Paul said, "Check the phone."

"What?"

"Lydia's phone. It's in the den. I hooked it up to the charger because the battery was low."

"Jesus Christ." Only Paul would kidnap someone and charge their fucking phone.

Claire set the telephone down on the table. She went into the den but instead of looking for the cell phone, she scanned the perimeter of the room. Another air freshener was on top of a veneered cherry bookshelf by the front door. How had she not seen that before? How had she not seen any of this?

Lydia's phone made a chirping sound. Paul had left it plugged in on the table by the couch. The screen showed a text from an unknown number. She swiped the notice and a photo of Lydia came up.

Claire cried out. Lydia's forehead was bleeding. One eye was swollen closed. She was lying on her side in the trunk of a car. Her hands were zip-tied in front of her. She looked terrified and furious and so alone.

Claire looked up at the camera on the bookshelf and stared all of her hate through the wires and straight into Paul's black hole of a heart. "I'm going to kill you for this. I don't know how, but I'm going to . . ." Claire didn't know what she was going to do. She looked back down at the picture of Lydia. This was all Claire's fault. So many times she had told Lydia to leave and she hadn't meant it once. She had wanted her sister to keep her safe, and she'd ended up leading Lydia right into Paul's hands.

She heard a car pull into the driveway. Claire's heart leapt. Lydia. Paul had brought her back. She opened the front door. Plywood. There was a sliver of light around the edge. If Claire craned her neck the right way, she could see through the crack and into the driveway.

Instead of Paul, she saw a brown sheriff's patrol car. Her view was narrow. The front windshield was dark against the afternoon light. She couldn't tell who was inside. The driver stayed behind the wheel for an interminably long time. Claire heard her breath stuttering out as she waited.

Finally, the door was opened. A leg came out and rested on the concrete drive. She saw a tooled leather cowboy boot and dark brown pants with a yellowish stripe going up the side. Two hands grasped the door surround as the man pulled himself out of the car. He stood there for a moment, his back to Claire as he checked the empty road. And then he turned around.

Sheriff Carl Huckabee put on his Stetson hat as he walked up the driveway. He stopped to look inside the Tesla. He took in the charger plugged into the side of the car and followed the extension cord with his eyes to the front porch of the house.

Claire pulled back from the door, though there was no way he could see her. Huckleberry was older and more stooped but he still sported the same finely combed, linear mustache and too-long sideburns that had looked out of date even in the nineties.

He had to be working with Paul. It made a sick kind of sense that the man her parents had run to for help was the same man who strung them along all these years.

Claire ran back to the kitchen. Before picking up the phone, she grabbed a sharp paring knife off the floor. She put the phone to her ear. She held up the knife for Paul to see. "I'll slice open his neck if you don't give me my sister back right now."

"What are you talking about?" Paul demanded. "Whose neck?"

"You know who I—" Claire stopped. Maybe he didn't know. The point of putting cameras on the outside of your house was that people would see them. Paul was only concerned with what was going on inside.

"Claire?"

"Huckabee. He just pulled up."

"Fuck," Paul muttered. "Get rid of him right now or you'll never see Lydia again."

Claire didn't know what to do. "Promise me she'll be okay."

"I promise. Don't hang up the—"

Claire hung up the phone. She turned around and faced the open kitchen doorway. The paring knife went into her back pocket, even as she asked herself what the hell she thought she was going to do with it. Her mind was overwhelmed with fragments of thoughts she couldn't chase away. Why had Paul pretended to be murdered? Why had he taken Lydia? What did he want with her?

"Hello?" Huckabee's heavy footsteps pounded up the porch stairs. "Anybody here?"

"Hi." Claire heard the scratchiness in her voice. There was still blood coming from somewhere inside her throat. She kept thinking about Lydia. Claire had to keep calm for Lydia's sake.

"Miss Carroll." The sheriff's expression had changed from one of curiosity to wariness. "What are you doing here?"

"It's Mrs. Scott," she corrected, hating the sound of the name. "This house belonged to my husband. He passed away recently, so I—"

"Thought you'd ransack it?" He was looking at the mess Claire had made of the kitchen. Silverware, pots and pans, Tupperware, and anything else that had been inside a drawer or cabinet was now littering the floor.

He lifted his foot, which had crunched some of the broken glass from the back door. "You wanna tell me what's really going on here?"

Claire started twisting her wedding ring around her finger. She tried to put some authority in her voice. "Why are *you* here?"

"Got an emergency call, but there wasn't nobody stayed on the line." He tucked his thumbs into his belt. "Was that you?"

"I dialed it by accident. I meant to dial information." Claire stifled a cough. "I'm sorry I wasted your time."

"What's your husband's name again?"

"Paul Scott." Claire remembered that the name on the property deed was different. "The house is held in a trust with his law firm. Buckminster and Fuller."

The sheriff nodded, but he didn't seem satisfied. "Looks like it's been boarded up for a while."

"Did you know my husband?"

"I knew his mama and daddy. Good people."

Claire couldn't stop twisting her wedding ring. And then she looked down at her hand, because the Snake Man had taken her ring. How had it gotten back on her finger?

"Mrs. Scott?"

She squeezed her hands into fists. She wanted to yank off the ring and grind it in the garbage disposal. How had Paul gotten the ring back? Why had he put it on her finger? Why were her shoes off? And the keyfob in her pocket? Why was there a fucking pillow under her head when she woke up from her husband knocking the shit out of her?

And where in God's name was he taking her sister?

"What's this?" Huckabee touched his hand to his own cheek. "Looks like you got a shiner coming up."

Claire started to touch her cheek, but then she ran her fingers through her hair. Panic threatened to consume her. She could feel a physical pain in her skull from the strain of trying to process what had happened and what she needed to do next.

Huckabee asked, "You need to sit down?"

"I need answers." Claire knew that she sounded crazy. "My father-in-law, Gerald Scott. You're sure that he's dead?"

He gave her a curious look. "Saw it with my own eyes. At least, after the fact."

Claire had seen Paul die with her own eyes. She had held him in her arms. She had watched the life drain out of him.

Then she had watched him punch her in the face.

Huckabee leaned his shoulder against the doorjamb. "Something goin' on here I need to know about?"

The phone started to ring. Claire didn't move.

Huckabee shifted on his feet. He looked at the phone, then back at Claire.

Paul wasn't going to hang up. The ringing continued until the sound was like a chisel shaving down her eardrum.

Claire picked up the receiver and slammed it back down.

Huckabee raised one of his shaggy eyebrows. The man who for twenty-four years had insisted that her beautiful nineteen-year-old sister had simply turned her back on her family and joined a hippie commune was suddenly suspicious.

The phone started to ring again.

Claire imagined Paul sitting in a car somewhere on the side of the road watching all of this and being absolutely furious that Claire wasn't doing exactly what he'd told her to do.

He should know her better than that by now.

Claire slid the wedding ring off her finger. She placed it in front of the camera on top of the fridge. She turned around to face the sheriff. "I know what happened to Julia."

Huckabee was a heavy breather, obviously a long-time smoker, so it was hard to tell whether or not he sighed or just exhaled normally. "Did your mother tell you?"

Claire leaned against the fridge so she wouldn't sink to the floor. She felt the shock of his statement, but worked to keep the turmoil off her face. Had Helen known about the tapes all these years? Had she kept it a secret from Claire? Had she hidden the truth from Sam?

She tried to bluff Huckabee again. "Yes. She told me."

"Well, I'm surprised by that, Claire, because your mother said she wasn't ever going to tell you girls, and I'm finding it hard to believe that a woman like that would go back on her word."

Claire shook her head, because this man knew there were videos of her sister being brutally murdered and he was lecturing her like she was twelve and he was disappointed in her. "How could you keep it from me? From Lydia?"

"I promised your mother. I know you don't think much of me, but I honor my word."

"You're talking about your fucking word when I've been haunted by this for twenty-four years?"

"There's no need to use that kind of language."

"Fuck you." Claire could almost see the black hatred spewing from her mouth. "You kept saying she was alive, that she'd just run off, that we'd see her come back one day. You knew all along that she was never coming back, but you gave us hope." She could tell he still didn't understand. "Do you know what hope does to people? Do you know what it's like to see somebody in the street, to chase after them, because you think she might be your sister? Or to go to the mall and see two sisters together and know that you're never going to have that? Or to go to my father's funeral without her? Or to get married without—"

Claire couldn't go down that road, because she had married Paul, and the reason that Lydia hadn't been by her side is because Claire's husband had tried to rape her.

Huckabee said, "Tell me how you really found out. Was it the Internet?"

She nodded because that seemed most believable.

He looked down at the floor. "I always worried the tapes would get put out there."

Claire knew she should get rid of the sheriff, but she couldn't stop herself from asking, "How did you find out about them?"

"Your father's apartment. He had one of 'em loaded on his video player while he did it. I expect that's what made him . . ."

He didn't have to finish the sentence. They both knew what her father had done. Now that Claire knew Sam Carroll had seen the tapes, had been watching them while he put the needle into his arm, she finally understood why. She could very well imagine her father wanting to end his life as he watched Julia's being taken from her. The act had an appealing kind of symmetry.

Was that the reason Helen had concealed the truth? Was she afraid that Claire would find copies of the tapes and end up following in her father's footsteps? And Lydia—poor, fragile Lydia. No one saw it at the time, but her addiction had never been about the high, it had been about the escape. She had been actively seeking ways to destroy herself.

Claire asked the sheriff, "What did you do with the tapes?"

"Handed them over to a buddy of mine was in the FBI. We always wondered was there copies. I guess now we know."

Claire looked down at her hands. She was twisting her finger even without the ring.

Huckabee said, "You ain't gotta try and trick me, gal. She was your sister. I'll tell you the truth."

Claire had never wanted to physically hurt someone so badly in her life. He was acting like he'd been willing all along, when Claire had contacted the sheriff countless times over the years asking if there were any new updates. "Then tell me."

He smoothed down the edges of his mustache as if he needed time to figure out how to go about breaking her heart. Finally, he said, "Fella in the movie was part of some kind of ring that distributed a lotta them videos. My friend, like I said, he was in the FBI, so I got some of the inside scoop on it. He said they already knew about the guy. Name was Daryl Lassiter. Caught him in California back in ninety-four trying to snatch a gal same age, same hair color, same build as your sister."

Claire was confused. Had she been wrong about Paul's father? Was there another murderer out there? Had Paul's father come by the tapes as a collector?

Huckabee said, "Lassiter's dead now, if it helps."

No, there was the barn that had been outside, and the kill room not fifteen feet away from where they stood.

"Jury put him on death row." Huckabee looped his thumbs back through his belt. "There was some kind of scuffle at the jail house. Lassiter got stabbed in the neck about a dozen times. He died around the same time your pa died."

Claire tried to think of what to ask next. "Where did Daddy get the tapes?"

Huckabee shrugged. "No idea."

"You didn't look into it?"

'Course I did." Huckabee sounded offended, as if he was actually good at his job. "But your daddy was always on wild goose chases, one after another. There was no telling which one actually panned out, and he wasn't exactly sharing his information with me."

"You weren't exactly encouraging him to."

Huckabee shrugged again, more "water under the bridge" than "I'm sorry I left your father so alone that he killed himself."

But then again, Helen had left Sam alone, too. And then she had lied to Lydia and Claire for years about everything that mattered. Was there anyone in Claire's life who ever told her the truth? Even Lydia had lied about her daughter.

She asked, "Why would Daddy kill himself before finding out who killed Julia?"

"He left the tape playing out on the machine. He knew we'd find it. I mean, that's what I figured he left it for, and he was right. I turned it straight over to the feds. In less than a week, they connected it to the man who killed your sister."

Claire didn't remind the sheriff that the Carrolls had begged him for years to go to the FBI. "And you never made it public so people would know what happened to my sister?"

"Your mom asked me not to. I guess she was worried you girls would look for the tapes." He glanced over Claire's shoulder into the den. "My thinking is she figured it'd be better to never know than to find out the truth."

Claire wondered if her mother was right. Then she wondered how different her life would've been if she'd known that Julia was really gone. How many times had Claire quietly shut herself into her office and cried because an unidentified body had been found in the Athens area? How many missing girl cases had kept her awake at night? How many hours had she spent searching the Internet for cults and hippie compounds and any word of her missing sister?

"Well, that's all I know." Huckabee shifted uncomfortably on his feet. "I hope it brings you some peace."

"Like it did my father?" She resisted the urge to tell the sheriff that Sam Carroll might still be alive if the sheriff had done his fucking job.

"Anyway," Huckabee glanced around the kitchen again, "I told you what you wanted to know. You wanna tell me why you're standing in the middle of all this mess with a knife in your back pocket?"

"No, I don't." Claire wasn't finished questioning him. There was one more thing she had to ask, though she felt in her gut that she already knew the answer. Paul had a mentor, a man who had single-handedly ensured that Quinn + Scott jumped into the stratosphere, a man who took chartered flights and stayed in expensive hotel rooms thanks to Paul's Centurion American Express card. Claire had always chalked up the hours of golf games together and private phone calls and afternoons at the club to Paul just doing whatever it took to keep the Congressman happy, but now she understood that the connection ran deeper.

She asked the sheriff, "Who was your friend at the FBI?"

"Why's that matter?"

"It's Johnny Jackson, isn't it?" Claire knew the man's bio. She'd sat through enough tedious introductions at countless rubber-chicken-dinner fundraisers. Congressman Johnny Jackson had been an agent with the FBI before entering politics. He had given Quinn + Scott millions, sometimes billions, of dollars' worth of government contracts. He had sent Captain Jacob Mayhew to the Dunwoody house to investigate the robbery on the day of Paul's funeral. He had probably also sent Agent Fred Nolan to rattle the bars on Claire's cage.

Jackson was a very common last name, so common that Claire had never made the connection between the maiden name on her dead mother-in-law's headstone and Paul's generous benefactor.

Until now.

She told the sheriff, "He's my husband's uncle on his mother's side."

Huckabee nodded. "He worked in Atlanta on some kind of special task force."

"Did he ever help Paul get out of trouble?"

Huckabee nodded again, but he didn't elaborate. The man probably did not want to speak ill of the dead. Should Claire tell him that Paul was alive? That her husband had abducted her sister?

The phone started to ring again.

Claire didn't move, but she said, "I should get that."

"You sure there ain't nothin' else you wanna tell me?"

"I'm positive."

Huckabee reached into his shirt pocket and pulled out a business card. "Cell number's on the back." He put the card on the kitchen table, then tapped it once with his finger before leaving.

The phone kept ringing. Claire counted off the seconds as she waited for the sound of the sheriff's car door opening and closing, an engine starting, then the grind of wheels on the driveway as he backed onto the road.

Claire picked up the phone.

Paul said, "What the fuck was that about?"

"Give me back my sister."

"Tell me what you said to Huckleberry."

She hated that he knew that word. It was something that belonged to her family, and this sadist she was talking to was no longer her family.

"Claire?"

"My father was watching the tapes of Julia when he killed himself."

Paul said nothing.

"Did you have something to do with that, Paul? Did you show my father the tapes?"

"Why would I do that?"

"Because you were already working on getting Lydia out of the way, and the last person left in my life who really mattered, who would help me no matter what, was my father." Claire was so distraught that she couldn't catch her breath. "You killed him, Paul. You either did it yourself or you just as good as put the needle in his arm."

"Are you insane?" Paul's voice rose with indignation. "Jesus, Claire. I'm not a fucking monster. I loved your father. You know that. I was a pallbearer at his funeral." He stopped talking for a moment, leaving the impression that he was rendered speechless by her accusation. When he finally continued, his voice was low and calm. "Look, I've done some things I'm not proud of, but I would never, ever do that to somebody I loved. You know how fragile Sam was toward the end. There's no telling what finally pushed him over the edge."

Claire sat down at the kitchen table. She turned the chair so that Paul couldn't see the angry tears rolling down her face. "You're acting like you had nothing to do with any of this, like you were just an innocent bystander."

"I was."

"You knew what happened to my sister. You watched me struggle with it for almost two Goddamn decades, and you could've told me at any time what happened to Julia and you didn't. You just watched me suffer."

"I hated every second of it. I never wanted to see you hurt."

"You're hurting me now!" Claire slammed her fist into the table. Her throat spasmed with pain. The anguish was too much. She couldn't do this. She just wanted to lie down on the floor in a ball and cry herself senseless. An hour ago, she had thought she'd lost everything, but now she understood that there was always more, and that so long as he was alive, Paul was going to be there to take more.

He said, "How was I going to tell you what happened to Julia without giving you the whole story?"

"Are you really saying you didn't know how to lie to me?"

He didn't answer.

"Why did you fake your death?"

"I didn't have a choice." He paused for a moment. "I can't get into it, Claire, but I did what I had to do in order to keep you safe."

"I don't feel very safe now, Paul." Claire struggled against the anger and fear that raged inside of her. "You knocked me out. You took my sister from me."

"I didn't want to hurt you. I tried to be as gentle as I could."

Claire could still feel a pulsing pain in her cheek. She couldn't imagine how badly it would hurt if Paul hadn't held back. "What do you want?"

"I need the rest of the keychain to the Tesla."

Claire felt her stomach clench. She remembered Paul handing her the keys outside the restaurant before he pulled her into the alley. "Why did you give it to me?"

"Because I knew you'd keep it safe."

Adam would've retrieved the keytag from the mailbox by now. They'd transferred the work files in the garage. What else was on the thumbdrive? "Claire?" Paul repeated. "What did you do with it?"

She grasped for something that would throw him off. "I gave it to the cop."

"Mayhew?" Tension filled his voice. "You have to get it back. He can't have it."

"Not Mayhew." Claire hesitated. Should she name Fred Nolan? Would Paul be relieved if she did? Or was Nolan in on it?

"Claire? I need to know who you gave it to."

"It was in my hand." Claire pushed back the terror threatening to cloud her thinking. She had to come up with a believable lie, something that would give her some kind of edge over Paul and buy her time to think. "In the alley, I had it in my hand. The man who killed you—who pretended to kill you—he knocked it out of my hand."

Paul spewed a volley of curses.

His anger spurred Claire on. "The police put it in one of those clear plastic evidence bags." She tried to spot the holes in her story. "I used the spare at the house to drive the Tesla home. But I know the keytag is in evidence because they sent me a list for insurance. I had to forward it to Pia Lorite, our insurance agent."

Claire held her breath and prayed that the story made sense. What was on the USB drive inside the keytag? Back in the garage, she had checked to make sure there were no movies. The only folder contained software. Or at least that's what Paul had made it look like. He had always been exceptionally good with computers.

Paul asked, "Can you get it back?" His words were clipped. She could practically see him clenching and unclenching his fists, her usual sign that her words were hitting their mark. In all the years of their marriage, she had never been afraid that he would use those fists on her.

And now she was struck by the very real threat that he would use them on Lydia.

Claire said, "Promise me you won't hurt Lydia. Please."

"I need that keytag." The underlying threat in his tone had a deadly stillness. "You have to get it for me."

"Okay, but—" Claire started to babble. "The detective—Rayman. Don't you know him? Somebody had to help you plan what happened in the alley. There were paramedics, police officers, detectives—"

"I know who was there."

She knew that he did, because Paul had been right there in the alley alongside Claire. How long had he pretended to be dead?

Five minutes at least, then the paramedics had put the blanket over him and that was the last Claire had seen of her husband.

She said, "Eric Rayman is the detective who's in charge of the investigation. Can't you call him?"

Paul didn't answer, but she could feel his anger as if he was standing right in front of her.

She tried again. "Who helped you do this? Can't you—"

"I want you to listen to me very carefully. Are you listening?"

"Yes."

"There are cameras all over the house. Some you can find, some you'll never see. Lydia's cell phone is tapped. The phone you're on right now is tapped. I'm going to call you on this landline every twenty minutes for the next two hours. That's going to get me far enough away so that I know I'm safe, and it's going to keep you there while I figure out what you're going to do next."

"Why, Paul?" She wasn't just asking about what was happening right now. She was asking about everything that had come before. "Your father murdered my sister. I watched the tape. I know what he did to—" Her voice broke. She felt like her heart was breaking along with it. "I don't—" Claire fought back the agony. "I don't understand."

"I'm so sorry." Paul's voice filled with emotion. "We can get through this. We'll get through it."

She closed her eyes. He was trying to soothe her. And the horrible part was that she wanted to be soothed. Claire could still recall what it had felt like in the den when she woke up and realized that Paul was alive. Her husband. Her champion. He was going to make all of this go away.

"I never killed any of them." He sounded so vulnerable. "I promise you."

Claire put her hand to her mouth so that she wouldn't speak. She wanted to believe him. She so desperately needed to believe him.

"I didn't even know what Dad was doing until after the car accident. I went into the barn and I found all of his . . . stuff."

Claire bit her fist to keep from screaming. He was making it sound so logical.

"I was just a kid on my own. Tuition was due at the academy. I had college to think about. It was good money, Claire. All I had to do was make copies and send them out."

Claire couldn't breathe. She had spent that money. She had worn jewelry and clothes and shoes paid for by the blood and suffering of those poor girls.

"I promise you. It was only a means to an end."

She couldn't take this anymore. She was so close to her breaking point that she could practically feel herself bending.

"Claire?"

She said, "The movies on your computer weren't old."

"I know." He was quiet for another moment, and she wondered if he was trying to think of a lie or already had one and was just pausing for effect. "I was a distributor. I never participated."

Claire struggled with the urge to believe him, to hold on to this one piece of her husband's humanity. "Who is the masked man?"

"He's just a guy."

Just a guy.

"You don't have to worry about him." Paul sounded like he

was talking about an asshole from work. "You're safe, Claire. You're always safe."

She ignored his comforts because her only other alternative was to believe him. "What's on the USB drive?"

He went quiet again.

"Are you forgetting who gave you that Auburn keytag, Paul? I know there's a USB drive inside the plastic disk, and I know you want it back because you put something on it for safekeeping."

He kept silent.

"Why?" She couldn't stop asking the question. "Why?"

"I was trying to protect you."

"Is that some kind of stupid joke?"

"The plan had to be moved up. There were other things in play. I tried my best to keep you out of it. But what happened with that guy in the alley, the sentiment was real, Claire. You know I would lay down my life to protect you. Why do you think I'm still here? You're everything to me."

Claire shook her head. She was dizzy from all of his excuses.

He said, "The people who are into this stuff are not nice people. They're powerful. They have a lot of money and influence."

"Political influence."

He made a surprised sound. "You were always so damn clever."

Claire didn't want to be clever anymore. She wanted to be in control. "It's your turn to listen to me. Are you listening?"

"Yes."

"If you hurt Lydia, I will hunt you down and burn you into the fucking ground. Do you understand me?"

"God, I love you like this."

The phone clicked. He'd ended the call.

THIRTEEN

Lydia stared into the darkness of the trunk as she listened to the hum of wheels on the road. She had already run through all the things you were supposed to do if you ever got locked inside a trunk. Obviously, Paul had run through them, too. There were steel plates bolted to the back of the taillights so Lydia couldn't punch them open and stick out her hand to wave down passing motorists. The emergency release latch had been disabled. There was another thick, steel plate between the trunk and the back seat so she couldn't kick her way to freedom. She was pretty sure the area was insulated for sound, too. She couldn't imagine Paul had padded the trunk for her comfort.

Which meant that he had designed this car specifically to hold a prisoner.

Lydia could hear Paul in the front of the car talking on the phone. There were only a few words she could make out, and they were all useless—yes, no, okay. Paul's tone was brisk, so Lydia assumed he wasn't talking to Claire. His voice was different when he talked to her sister. It made Lydia ill to think about how different it was, because Claire had been right: Paul made a conscious choice when he showed his dark side.

She had seen it on full display when he'd opened the trunk to take Lydia's picture. She had watched him turn the darkness on and off like a light bulb. One minute, he was telling Claire to go check Lydia's phone and the next, his face was so frightening that Lydia was afraid she was going to lose control of her bladder.

He had reached into the trunk and grabbed her face so hard that she felt the bones crushing. "Give me a reason to do to you what my dad did to Julia."

Lydia had been shaking so hard when he closed the trunk that her teeth were chattering.

She rolled onto her back to relieve some of the pressure in her shoulder. Her arms and legs were zip-tied, but she could still move if she was careful. The blood from the cut in her forehead had dried. Her swollen eye was leaking tears. The drumming in her head had subsided to an occasional dull thud.

Paul had hit her with something heavy and solid back at the Fuller house. Lydia wasn't sure what he'd used, but it had pounded into her head like a sledgehammer. She hadn't even heard him coming. One moment, she was standing in the kitchen with her mouth open to give the 911 operator her name, and the next, stars were bursting in front of her eyes. Literally. Lydia had felt like a cartoon character. She tottered back and forth. She tried to brace herself on the kitchen table. And then Paul had punched her again, then again, until she was unconscious on the floor.

Lydia had managed to shout, "No," before she blacked out. Obviously, that wasn't enough to warn Claire. Or maybe she'd gotten the warning but didn't know what to do. Lydia couldn't imagine her baby sister having the wherewithal to fight off Paul. Then again, she couldn't imagine her baby sister kneecapping her tennis partner.

She guessed that Claire was asking herself the same questions that were running through Lydia's mind: Why had Paul faked his death? Why had he taken Lydia? What did he want from them?

She didn't want to dwell on that last question, because Paul Scott was clearly obsessed with the Carroll sisters. His father had kidnapped and brutally murdered one of them. He had married another. And now he had Lydia in the trunk of his car, a trunk that had obviously been prepared well ahead of time.

Was he really going to do the same thing to Lydia that had been done to Julia? Was he going to murder her and rape her while she died?

Julia. Her vibrant big sister. Her best friend. Screaming as the machete cut through her neck and shoulder. Writhing as Paul's father ripped her apart.

Bile burned up into Lydia's mouth. She turned her head and spit as more came up. The smell was noxious in the confined space. She moved closer to the back of the trunk to get away from it. Her stomach felt hollow. She could not clear the image of Julia from her mind.

Lydia heard a whimper come from her mouth. She could handle the sickness, but the grief would kill her before Paul had his chance. Julia. Her innocent, tortured sister. There were six tapes in all, which meant Paul's father had taken time with her.

She had been all alone in that barn, waiting for him, dreading his return, up until the final seconds of her life.

Julia had actually looked at the camera as she was dying. She had stared straight into the lens, straight into Lydia's heart, and mouthed the word *Help*.

Lydia squeezed her eyes shut. She let the feelings come uncensored. She should've been sweeter to Dee on the phone this morning. She should've called Rick to tell him that she loved him instead of texting him that she would explain everything later. And Claire. She should've told Claire that she forgave her, because Paul was not a human being. He was some kind of terrifying aberration who was capable of unspeakable deeds.

Lydia fought back another whimper. She couldn't let herself lose it again. She had to be strong for what was coming next, because Paul had a plan. He always had a plan.

Lydia had a plan, too. She kept flexing her hands and moving her feet to make sure there was enough circulation in her body and clarity in her mind because eventually, Paul would have to open the trunk again. Lydia was heavier than he was. Paul would have to cut the zip ties so she could climb out. That would be the only opportunity she would have to stop him.

She kept going over the steps in her mind: At first, she would act confused. This would buy her eyes time to adjust to the sunlight. Then, she would move slowly and pretend that she was in pain, which wouldn't be a stretch. She would act like she needed help and Paul, impatiently, would push her or shove her or kick her and then Lydia would throw her weight into her shoulder and hit him as hard as she could in the neck.

She wouldn't use her fist because the knuckles might glance

off. She would stretch open her hand and use the webbing between her thumb and index finger, creating an arc that sliced nicely into the base of his Adam's apple.

The thought of hearing his windpipe crack was the only thing that kept her going.

Lydia took several deep breaths and let them go. She worked her hands and feet. She pulled up her knees and stretched out her legs. She rolled her shoulders. Having a plan helped the panic die down to a splinter worrying the back of her brain.

The engine changed speed. Paul was taking an off-ramp. She could feel the car slowing. There was a flash of red light around the steel plates, then a yellow pulse as the turning signal was engaged.

Lydia rolled onto her back. She had gone over the plan so many times that she could practically feel Paul's throat crunching under her hand. There was no telling how much time had passed since he'd put her in the trunk. She had tried to count the minutes from when he took the photo, but she kept losing count. Panic could do that. She knew that the most important thing to do while she waited was to keep her mind engaged with something other than worst-case scenarios.

She grasped for memories that didn't involve Paul Scott. Or Dee and Rick, because thinking about her child and her lover right now in this dark deathtrap of a space would lead her down a path of no return.

She had to go back several years for a memory that didn't somehow involve Paul, because even in absence, he had been such a huge part of her life for such a long time. Lydia was twenty-one when Claire met Paul at the math lab. Two months later, he'd managed to tear Lydia from her family. She had always blamed Paul for her darkest days of addiction, but well before meeting him, she was so deep into self-destruction that the only memories she had were bad ones.

October, 1991.

Nirvana were playing at the 40 Watt Club in downtown Athens. Lydia sneaked out of the house. She climbed through her bedroom window, though no one would've noticed if she'd walked straight out the front door. She bummed a ride with her friend Leigh and she left behind all the misery and despair trapped inside the house on Boulevard.

Julia had been gone for over six months by then. It was too hard to be at home anymore. When her parents weren't screaming at each other, they were so despondent that being around them made you feel like an interloper in their private tragedy. Claire had disappeared so far into herself that she could be in the same room with you for ten minutes before you noticed her standing there.

And Lydia had disappeared into pills and powder and grown men who had no business hanging around teenage girls.

Lydia had adored Julia. Her sister was cool and hip and outspoken and she covered for Lydia when Lydia wanted to stay out after curfew, but now she was dead. Lydia knew it like she knew the sun would come up the next day. She had accepted Julia's death before anyone else in her family had. She knew that her big sister would never be back, and she used it as an excuse to drink more, snort more, screw more, eat more, more, more, more. She couldn't stop, didn't *want* to stop, which was why the day after the Nirvana concert, Lydia was clueless when people started arguing about whether the performance was awesome or dog shit.

The band had been drunk off its ass. They were all out of tune. Cobain had started a mini-riot when he'd ripped down the movie screen hanging over the stage. The audience went nuts. They rushed the stage. Eventually, the band piled their instruments on top of the destroyed drum set and walked out.

Lydia had no memory of any of this. She had been so high during the time of the concert that she wasn't even sure she'd made it to the club. The next morning, she'd woken up in the Alley, which was blocks from the 40 Watt, which made no sense until she stood up and felt the wet stickiness between her legs.

She had bruises on her thighs. She felt raw inside. There was a cut on the back of her neck. She had skin under her fingernails. Someone else's skin. Her lips were tender. Her jaw was tender. Everything was tender until she found a guy packing some equipment into the back of a van and he gave her a bump and she gave him a handjob and she crawled back home in time to get yelled at by her parents—not for being out all night, but for not being home in time to walk Claire to school.

Claire was fourteen years old. She could walk herself to school. The building was so close to the Boulevard house that you could hear the bells ringing for class changes. But back then, all of her parents' anger seemed tied up in Lydia's failure to take care of her last remaining sister. She was setting a bad example for Claire. She wasn't spending enough time with Claire. She should try to do more things with Claire.

Which made Lydia feel guilty, and when she wasn't feeling guilty, she was feeling resentful.

335

Maybe that's why Claire had perfected the art of invisibility. It was a form of self-preservation. You couldn't resent what you could not see. She was so quiet, but she noticed everything. Her eyes tracked the world like it was a book written in a language she could not understand. There was nothing timorous about her, but you got the feeling that she always had one foot out the door. If the situation got too hard, or too intense, she would simply disappear.

Which is exactly what she had done eighteen years ago when Lydia had told her about Paul. Instead of confronting the truth, Claire had taken the easy route and made herself disappear from Lydia's life. She had changed her phone number. She had refused to respond to any of Lydia's letters. She had even moved apartments in order to erase Lydia from her life.

Maybe that was why Lydia hadn't been able to forgive her.

Because, really, nothing had changed in the last eighteen years. For all of Claire's tough talk—her seemingly sincere apologies and blunt confessions—she was still keeping one foot out the door. The only reason Claire had reached out to Lydia last night was because she had started to unravel Paul's lies and couldn't handle it on her own. She had said it herself this morning—she wanted her big sister to make it all better.

What would Claire do now? With Lydia gone, there was no one else to call. Helen couldn't be relied on. Huckabee was useless. Adam Quinn was probably in this thing right alongside Paul. Claire couldn't turn to the police because there was no telling who else was involved. She could turn to herself, but what would she find? A kept woman who was incapable of keeping herself.

The car slowed again. Lydia could feel the terrain turn from asphalt to gravel. She splayed her hands to keep from being jolted around the trunk. A large pothole slammed her into the sheetmetal. The cut in her forehead opened. Lydia blinked away the blood.

She struggled with the bad thoughts that were pinging around her brain. And then she stopped struggling, because what was the point? This was no longer a matter of an unhealed rift between her and Claire. This was life and death.

Lydia's life.

Lydia's possible death.

The brakes squeaked as the car rolled to a stop. The engine idled.

She braced herself, waiting for the trunk to open. No one knew where she was. No one even knew she was missing. If she left this all to Claire, Lydia knew that she would never make it out alive.

It had been like this all of their lives—before Paul, even before Julia.

Claire made a choice, and Lydia was the one who paid for it.

FOURTEEN

Claire listened to the click as Paul hung up the phone. She put the receiver back on the hook. She went outside and sat on the back porch. There was a notebook and a pen beside her leg, but she had given up listing questions when Paul had made it clear that he wasn't going to answer any of them. Every time he called, he waited to hear her voice, then he disconnected the line, and the timer reset for another twenty minutes until he called again.

He had called three times so far, which meant she'd wasted an hour feeling paralyzed. Lydia was in grave danger. Her safety depended on Claire. Paul was always driving when he called Claire on the phone, so she had to think that Lydia was still in the trunk. Whether or not that meant she was all right was debatable, because eventually, Paul would get to wherever he was going.

Claire had no idea what to do. She was good at quick, thought-less reactions, but strategizing had never been her way. Paul was the one who saw all of the angles, and before Paul she had relied on Lydia, and before Lydia there was her father to swoop down and make everything all right.

No one was going to solve this for her. There was no one else she could think of to reach out to, which made her angry because she should be able to depend on her mother, but Helen had made it clear a long time ago that she couldn't be counted on. She had hidden the truth about Julia for almost nineteen years. She could've ended Claire's misery, but she chose not to, probably because she didn't want to deal with the emotional fallout.

Claire looked down at the dirt between her feet. She let her mind run wild in the hopes that somehow she would stumble onto a solution.

The foiled burglary during the funeral. Claire was certain that Paul had hired those men to break into the Dunwoody house. They must have been looking for the keytag. Maybe Congressman Johnny Jackson had sent Captain Mayhew for the same reason. Or Agent Nolan. Or both of them, which would explain why they had behaved like two unneutered cats around each other.

Was Johnny Jackson working for Paul or against him?

The answer was most likely on the USB drive inside the keytag. The damn thing had been in Claire's purse during the funeral. She had switched out the bag she was carrying the day of the murder to a black clutch and thrown in Paul's keys because it was easier than going downstairs and putting them on his little labeled hook inside his mudroom cabinet.

So, she knew what the burglars were looking for, but she had no idea how that could help Lydia.

"Think," Claire chided herself. "You have to think."

She had one more hour before Paul gave her his plan to retrieve the USB drive. Her first impulse had been to call Adam Quinn and tell him she needed the keytag back, but if Paul was really monitoring all of the phones, then she would be giving away that the drive was not sitting in evidence at the police station.

And if he knew Claire didn't have the drive, there was no reason for him to keep Lydia alive.

Claire had to keep Paul believing that the cops had the drive. That could buy her some time, but she didn't know how much time. She could pretend to call Rayman, or even pretend to go to the police station, but there would come a point at which Paul would want to know why she wasn't making progress.

And there was the very real possibility that her continued failure would cause greater harm to come to Lydia. Claire knew full well from the videos that there were things a man could do to a woman that didn't kill her, but made her wish she was dead.

Was Paul telling the truth about his role in the movies? She would be a fool to take him at his word. There was some consolation in knowing that her husband was not the man in the mask. The telltale moles under Paul's left shoulder blade were the giveaway. But someone had zoomed in that camera to get a close-up of the girls. Someone else had been in the room recording, witnessing, every degradation.

That someone had to be Paul. The Fuller house was his house. He had obviously been here. No one else would bother to keep everything so clean and organized.

Which meant that Paul knew the identity of the masked man. Her husband was friends or partners with a vicious psychopath who was stealing girls from their families and committing unspeakable horrors against them.

Claire's body gave a violent, involuntary shudder at the thought.

Was that what Paul had stored on the USB drive—proof of the masked man's identity? Claire broke out into a cold sweat. Paul had said she was safe, but if he was threatening to expose the murderer, then that put everyone in danger.

And it meant that yet again, Claire had caught her husband in another lie.

Rick.

Claire could call Rick Butler for help. He was Lydia's boyfriend. They had been together for thirteen years. He was a mechanic. He looked like the kind of man who would know his way around a bad situation. According to Paul's files, he'd been in and out of jail.

No. If Claire knew anything about her sister, she knew that Lydia would not want Rick involved. Bringing in Rick would mean bringing in her daughter, and then suddenly, Paul went from having one victim to ransom to having three.

And Claire could not help thinking that Dee Delgado looked exactly like the kind of girl who ended up in Paul's movies.

Claire stood up. She couldn't sit anymore. She couldn't go back into the house because everything was monitored. Or maybe it wasn't monitored and Claire was still as gullible as before. She put her hands on her hips and stared up at the sky. Asking herself what Paul would do had gotten her here in the first place. Maybe she should ask herself what Lydia would do.

Lydia would want more information.

When Claire had first opened the door to the garage, her gaze had instantly fallen on the rows of VHS tapes, but she knew there were other things in that room that might give her clues as to what Paul was really up to. There were metal shelves that held various computer-related equipment. There was a worktop in the corner with a large computer screen. That computer was probably connected to the Internet.

She went back inside the house. She tracked the hidden cameras with her eyes—first the one in the kitchen, then the one in the den, then the one mounted on a shelf at the end of the hallway that led to the one-car garage.

Women had been savagely murdered in that garage. Countless damaged women had been defiled while a camera recorded every bit of their agony.

Claire pushed open the door. The stench of blood was overwhelming, but the sight of the room was not. She was already habituated to the violence. Maybe that explained the cavalier way Paul had discussed the movies, as if he was talking about widgets instead of lives. How many women had been murdered in this room over the years before Paul became habituated to death?

How long before the excitement of the kill was programmed into his brain?

Claire stepped down into the garage. She rubbed her arms to fight the chill. She was struck by an intense unease. Her body had a visceral reaction to the evil that had happened inside this room. So many women had lost their lives. But it wasn't just that. The farther she went into the garage, the farther she was from escape. Someone could walk in on her. Someone could shut the door.

Claire looked back at the empty doorway. Her mind flashed

up a terrifying image of the masked man's wet smile filling the computer screen.

And then she saw the mask for herself.

It was hanging on a hook by the door. The eyes and mouth were unzipped. The rubber underwear hung on another hook beside it, and on a shelf underneath both was a large bottle of Johnson's Baby Powder and a small tube of WET personal lubricant. Claire forced herself to look away. The juxtaposition was too unsettling.

Plastic slats took up the rest of the wall by the door. She recognized the tools of torture hanging from metal hooks: the cattle prod, the branding iron with the large X at the end, the machete. They were all hung the same distance apart. The machete blade was cleaned to a mirror finish. The charger for the cattle prod had the cord neatly coiled around the base. She might as well be standing in Paul's garage back home.

A familiar Gladiator workbench was set up in front of the metal garage door. Thick foam insulation panels were stuck to the back of the door. The whole room felt warm despite the chill in the air. She assumed Paul had insulated everything with spray foam, because that was what Paul did.

Claire checked behind a loose black curtain, which could be pulled closed to hide the room from the road when Paul opened the garage door. Leaves had blown in under the lip of the door. It wasn't like her husband to let things like that go.

Then again, maybe it was part of the scene he'd set. The garbage Claire had spied in the first movies was not really garbage. Paul had wadded up fast-food bags and paper cups, but there were no grease stains or moldy dregs of soda. Even the bloodstain on the mattress looked fake, which made sense because the movies Claire had seen always showed the woman chained to the wall.

The wall.

Here it was, less than ten feet in front of her. Dark, burgundy blood had permeated the concrete block. The shackles had bolts on them to hold wrists and ankles. There were no locks because the chains were far apart enough to prevent one hand from freeing the other. Claire stopped herself before she pulled on the chains. Just because things looked fake did not mean they were. The blood on the floor was real. You couldn't duplicate that smell, and if you were just doing it for the appearance of reality, you wouldn't use real blood.

Claire lifted her foot. The toe of her shoe was sticky where she'd accidentally stepped in the blood. She waited for the repulsion to roll over her, but she was too numb to feel anything.

Her sneaker made a Velcro-tearing sound as she walked over to the computer. Bird computer speakers on delicate stands were perched on either side of the monitor. The finish was white, because that complemented the silver bezel around the monitor, just like the white amplifier completed the system.

Claire turned the chair sideways so she could still see the door in her peripheral vision. If she was going to be attacked again, at least she would see it coming this time. She tapped the keyboard, but nothing happened. The large screen was made by Apple, but it looked nothing like the iMacs she was used to. She ran her hand along the back in search of the power button. She guessed the large white cylinder by the monitor was the computer. She pressed her fingers on the buttons until Apple's start-up tone blasted through the speakers. Claire dialed down the sound on the amplifier.

There were cables stuck in the back of the computer, more white Thunderbolts that connected to several twenty-terabyte storage drives daisy-chained together on a metal shelf. She counted twelve drives. How many movies could fit on twelve massive drives?

Claire didn't want to think about it. Nor did she want to stand up and examine the other equipment on the metal shelves. An old Macintosh computer. Stacks of five-inch floppy disks. A duping machine for copying VHS tapes. Multiple external disk drives for burning copies of movies. Typically, Paul was archiving the early artifacts from the family business.

Everything would be Internet-based now. Claire had watched a *Frontline* on PBS that showed the vast, illegal market on the dark web. Most people used the hidden Internet to illegally trade stolen movies and books, but others used it to sell drugs and trade in child porn.

Claire thought about Paul's American Express bills with the mysterious charges they never talked about. How many private charter flights had Paul paid for but never flown? How many hotel rooms had he rented that they'd never stayed in? She had assumed the expenses were bribes to Congressman Jackson, but maybe not. Her husband was meticulous in everything he did. He wouldn't want to raise suspicions by abducting too many girls in his own back yard. Maybe Paul was using the flights and rooms to secretly move women around the country.

And maybe the Congressman was as heavily invested in the business as Paul.

Paul had been a teenager when his father died. He was living at a military boarding school one state over. There had to have been an adult who took over Gerald Scott's business while Paul was getting his education. Which could possibly mean that the Congressman's mentorship had run a parallel track: One side helped Paul establish himself as a legitimate businessman, and the other made certain that the movies would still be made.

And distributed, because there had to be quite a bit of money involved in sending out these movies.

Claire had seen Johnny Jackson and Paul together on countless occasions and never put it together that they were related. Were they hiding their relationship because of the movies? Or because of the government contracts? Or was there something far more troubling that Claire had yet to uncover?

Because there was always something far more troubling with Paul. Every time she thought she'd hit bottom, he found a way to open a trap door and let her sink farther down.

Claire asked herself the obvious question about the masked man's identity. Johnny Jackson was in his seventies. He was vigorous and athletic, but the masked man in the more recent movies was clearly younger, closer to Paul's age. He had the same soft belly, the same hint of muscles that were too infrequently exercised at the gym.

Adam Quinn's body had been toned. Claire hadn't seen it, but she had felt the power in his broad shoulders and the hard muscles in his abs.

Which meant something, but she wasn't clear what.

The computer monitor finally flashed to life. The desktop came up. As with Paul's other computers, all of the folders were stored in the dock that ran along the bottom of the screen. She ran the mouse over the icons.

RAW.

EDITED.

DELIVERED.

Claire left the folders alone. She opened up Firefox and connected to the Internet. She typed in the words "Daryl Lassiter + murder + California." This was the man Huckleberry had told her about, the one he believed had kidnapped and murdered Julia Carroll. At least, that's what FBI agent and future congressman Johnny Jackson had told him.

Yahoo gave her thousands of links for Daryl Lassiter. Claire clicked on the top suggestion. The *San Fernando Valley Sun* had a front-page article about Lassiter's murder during his transportation to death row. There were blurry photos of the three women he'd been convicted of killing, but nothing of Lassiter. Claire skimmed a lengthy bit about the history of California's death penalty, then found the meat of the story.

Lassiter had abducted a woman off the street. A witness had called 911. The woman was saved, but the police had found a "mobile murder room" in the back of Lassiter's van, including chains, a cattle prod, a machete, and various other instruments of torture. They had also found VHS tapes, and on the tapes a "masked Lassiter tortured and executed women." The three women pictured in the article were later identified from missing persons reports.

"Joanne Rebecca Greenfield, seventeen. Victoria Kathryn Massey, nineteen. Denise Elizabeth Adams, sixteen."

Claire read each name and age aloud, because they were human beings and because they mattered.

All of the identified girls were from the San Fernando Valley area. Claire clicked through some more links until she found a photograph of Lassiter. Carl Huckabee had not had the Internet at his fingertips back when Sam Carroll had killed himself. Even if he had, he wasn't likely to seek confirmation of what his friend the FBI agent had told him—that the man on the tape who murdered Julia Carroll was the same man they had caught in California.

Which was why Huckleberry would have no way of knowing that while Daryl Lassiter was tall and lanky, he was also African American, with a tight Afro and a tattoo of the Angel of Death on his muscular chest.

Claire felt the last bit of her heart give way. Somewhere, somehow, she had been hoping against hope that Paul's father had not been the man in the tape, that Julia had been murdered by this stranger with the piercing brown eyes and a dark scar running down the side of his face.

Why couldn't she give up on him? Why could she not reconcile the Paul she had known with the Paul she now knew him to be? What sign had she missed? He was so kind to people. He was so fair about everything. He loved his parents. He never talked about having a bad childhood or being abused or any of the awful things you hear about that make men turn into demons.

Claire checked the time on the computer screen. She had another eight minutes before Paul called. She wondered if he knew what she was doing. He couldn't monitor the cameras inside the Fuller house all of the time. He would be driving just under the speed limit, keeping both hands on the wheel, staying as unobtrusive as he could lest the highway patrol stop him and ask what he was keeping in the trunk.

Lydia would make noise. Claire had no doubt that her sister would raise hell the minute she was given the chance.

Claire just had to find a way to give her sister that chance.

She leaned her elbows on the worktop. She looked at the folders on the dock. She let the mouse hover over the one labeled EDITED. Her finger clicked the mouse. No password prompt came up, likely because if someone was in this room, they had already seen enough to guess what was stored on the computer.

The EDITED folder opened. There were hundreds of files.

The extensions all said .fcpx.

Claire had no idea what that meant, but she didn't recognize .fcpx as anything to do with Paul's architectural software. She clicked on the top file, which had last been opened today. At 4 a.m. this morning, Paul had been sitting at this computer while Anna Kilpatrick's body was being discovered on the BeltLine.

The words FINAL CUT PRO filled the monitor. The software was registered to Buckminster Fuller.

Paul's most recent project loaded onto the screen. There were three panels across the middle section. One showed a list of files. The other showed thumbnails of various frames in the movie. The main panel had only one image: Anna Kilpatrick, chained to the wall, frozen in time.

There was a full assortment of editing options laid out underneath the main image, and below that were long strips of film that Claire assumed were pieces of the last Anna Kilpatrick movie. She recognized the buttons for correcting red eye and softening lines, but the others were a mystery. Claire clicked on some of the tabs. Filtering. Music. Text. Color correction. Stabilization. Reverb. Pitch correction. There were even sound files to layer into the background: Rain Falling. Car Noise. Forest Sounds. Water Dripping.

As with everything else in Paul's life, he had complete control.

Unlike when she'd viewed the movies at home, Claire was able to click on the magnifying glass and zoom into the image. She studied the girl's face. There was no doubt in her mind that she was really looking at Anna Kilpatrick.

And there was no doubt that you didn't need someone standing behind the camera to zoom in the frame.

The buttons to fast-forward, rewind, and play all looked as familiar as the buttons on the VCR. Claire started the movie. The speakers were down low. She could hear Anna crying. As before, the masked man's face suddenly filled the screen. He smiled, his wet lips showing underneath the metal teeth of the zipper.

Claire realized that this was the edited version, the one Paul had sent out to his customers. She closed the file. She went back to the folders on the dock and opened the one that was labeled RAW. The most recent file was dated yesterday. Paul had imported the movie sometime around midnight. At the time, Lydia and Claire were going through Paul's color-coded private detective files at the Dunwoody house.

What heady hours to think that her husband was only a rapist.

She clicked on the file. The same three panels came up on the screen with the editing options below.

Claire pressed PLAY.

The footage started the same way: A wide shot of Anna Kilpatrick chained to the wall. Her eyes were closed. Her head was bent. The masked man came into the camera frame. He had the same build, the same coloring, as the man Claire had seen in all of the other movies, but there was something different about him. His skin tone was lighter. His lips were not as red.

There was also something different about the sound. She realized the footage hadn't been mixed yet. All the ambient noise was still there. Claire heard the whir of a heater. The man's footsteps. His breathing. He cleared his throat. Anna startled. Her eyes opened. She struggled against the chains. The man ignored her. He neatly laid out his tools on a rolling table—the cattle prod, the machete, the branding iron. A metal heating element was wrapped around the X to heat the iron. The short electrical cord was tied to a longer extension cord and plugged into an outlet.

The man squirted a glob of lubricant onto his palm and started to stroke himself. He cleared his throat again. There was something eerily businesslike about the routine, as if he was getting ready for another day at the office.

None of this would make it into the final clip. This was pre-production. These were the mundane details that Paul had edited out.

The masked man turned to the camera. Claire fought the urge to jump out of the way. He put his face close to the lens, which she gathered was something of a trademark, like the lion roaring for MGM. The man smiled for the audience, his teeth flashing against the metal zipper. Then he walked over to Anna.

Anna screamed.

He waited for her to stop. The sound wound down from her throat like a siren.

He used his finger to pry open a wound on her belly. She

screamed again. The man waited again, but he wasn't unmoved. His cock had gotten harder. His skin was flushed with excitement.

"Please," Anna begged. "Please stop."

The man leaned in, his lips close to Anna's ear. He whispered something that made the girl flinch.

Claire sat up in the chair. She used the mouse to rewind the movie. She turned up the sound. She pressed PLAY.

Anna Kilpatrick was begging, "—stop."

The man leaned in, his lips close to Anna's ear. Claire dialed up the sound. She leaned forward, too, her ear as close to the computer speaker as the man's mouth was to Anna's ear.

The masked man whispered in a soft drawl, "Tell me you want this."

Claire froze. She stared blankly at the metal shelves with their ancient equipment. Her vision blurred. She felt a sharp, sudden pain in her chest.

He repeated, "Tell me you want—"

Claire paused the movie. She didn't rewind. Instead, she clicked on the magnifying glass to manually zoom in on the masked man's back.

This was the unedited footage. Paul hadn't yet filtered the light or corrected the sound, nor had he erased any identifying marks, like the constellation of three moles underneath the killer's left shoulder blade.

The kitchen phone started to ring.

Claire didn't move.

The phone rang again.

And again.

She stood up. She left the garage. She pulled the door

closed behind her. She walked into the kitchen and picked up the phone.

"You lied to me," Paul said. "I had one of my people check the inventory from the crime scene. The keytag wasn't on there."

Claire could only hear the words "one of my people." How many people did he have? Were Mayhew and Nolan the tip of the iceberg?

Paul said, "Where is it, Claire?"

"I have it. Hidden."

"Where?"

Claire reached up and turned around the fake air freshener so she was out of view.

"Claire?"

"I'm leaving the house now. You are going to send me a photograph of Lydia every twenty minutes, and if I see that you've touched one hair on her head, I will upload the entire contents of the USB drive to YouTube."

Paul scoffed. "You don't know how to do that."

"You don't think I can walk into any copy store and find some pimply geek to do it for me?"

He didn't answer. She couldn't hear road noises anymore. He had stopped the car. He was pacing. She heard his shoes crunching on gravel. Was Lydia still in the trunk? She must be, because Paul had abducted Lydia for leverage and killing her would take everything away.

Suddenly, Claire was struck by a thought. Why had Paul taken Lydia in the first place? If he was really watching the Dunwoody house, then he knew that Lydia had only entered the scene less than a day ago. Even without that, Claire was the one who knew where the USB drive was. Claire was the one who could get it for him.

So, why hadn't he taken Claire?

She had no doubt in her mind that under even the slightest threat of physical harm, she would've told Paul that Adam had the drive. But Paul hadn't taken Claire. He had made the wrong choice. He never made the wrong choice.

"Listen." He was trying to sound reasonable again. "I need the information on that drive. It's important. For both of us. Not just for me."

"Send me the first picture of Lydia, unharmed, and we'll talk about it."

"I could cut her into a thousand pieces before she dies."

That voice. It was the same tone he'd used with Claire in the alley, the same sinister drawl she'd heard on the speakers before Paul could edit his voice into a stranger's. Claire tasted her heart in her mouth, but she knew she could not show this man any fear.

She said, "You want me to go away with you."

It was Paul's turn to be silent.

She had found his weak spot, but not on purpose. Claire was just now seeing the motivation behind Paul's wrong choice. As usual, the answer had been right in front of her all along. He kept saying that he loved her. He had hit Claire, but not with all of his strength. He had sent the men to break into the house during the funeral so Claire wouldn't be there. He had made the wrong choice and taken Lydia because the right choice meant hurting Claire.

He might be able to punch his wife in the face, but he couldn't torture her.

She said, "Promise me you didn't participate in any of the movies."

"Never." His hope was as tangible as a piece of string between them. "I never hurt them. I promise you on my life."

He sounded so persuasive, so sincere, that Claire might have believed him. But she had seen the uncut movies—the raw footage before Paul changed the sound and edited down the scenes and filtered the skin tones and distorted the voices and slyly altered blemishes so that the true identity of the masked man would remain unknown.

Claire knew what her husband looked like when he neatly laid out his tools for a project. She knew the roll of his hand when he jerked himself off. She knew the three tiny moles under his left shoulder blade that she could feel when she lightly stroked his back with her fingers.

Which is why she knew without a doubt that the masked man was Paul.

Claire told him, "Send the pictures. I'll let you know what we're going to do when I'm ready."

"Claire—"

She slammed down the phone.

vi.

I am sorry my handwriting is so difficult to read, sweetheart. I've had a very minor stroke. I am okay now, so please don't worry. It happened shortly after I finished my last letter. I went to sleep scheming my great plans and woke the next day to find that I could not get out of bed. I will admit only to you that I was frightened (though I am really okay now). I experienced a momentary blindness in my right eye. My arm and leg refused to move. Finally, after a great deal of struggling, I managed to rise. When I called your mother to wish her happy birthday, my speech was so unintelligible that she immediately called an ambulance.

The doctor, who assured your mother that he was, in fact, old enough to shave, said that I had experienced a TIA, which of course further infuriated your mother (she has always been hostile to abbreviation). She coaxed him into speaking English, which is how we found out that a TIA, or mini-stroke, stands for transient ischemic attacks.

Attacks as in plural, your mother clarified with the poor man, which explained some of the weakness and dizziness I've been experiencing for the last week.

Or month, between you and me, because now that I think back on my last visits with Ben Carver, I recall some odd exchanges that indicate there were times when my speech must have been unintelligible with him, too.

So perhaps we have our answer as to why Ben Carver stopped my visits and wrote that inscription in the Dr. Seuss book. His mother suffered a massive stroke a few years ago. He must have been attuned to the signs.

There is kindness in so many unexpected places.

Can I tell you that I am the happiest I have been in a good, long while? That your sisters rushed to my side, that my family surrounded me, enveloped me, and that I was finally reminded of the life we all shared before we lost you? It was the first time in almost six years that we all gathered in a room and did not hurt for the lack of you.

Not that we have forgotten you, sweetheart. We will never, ever forget you.

Of course, your mother has used the TIA as an excuse to berate me for my continued tilting at windmills (her words). Though stress is a contributing factor to stroke, and though I have always had high blood pressure, I believe the fault rests firmly on my own shoulders for not getting enough sleep and exercise. I have been skipping my morning walks. I have been lying awake too late at night, unable to turn off my brain. As I have always told you girls, sleep and exercise are the two most important components to a healthy life. Shame on me for not taking my own good advice.

I suppose you could call it a silver lining that your mother has been by the apartment every day since I got out of the hospital. She brings me food and helps me bathe. (I don't really need help bathing, but who am I to stop a beautiful woman from washing me?) Every day, she says all of the things that she has been saying to me for almost six years: You are a fool. You are going to kill yourself. You have to give this up. You are the love of my life and I cannot watch you draw out your suicide any longer.

As if I would ever choose to leave any of you by my own hand.

I know instinctively that your mother does not want to hear what I've found out about Paul's father. She would dismiss the theory as one of my harebrained and pointless pursuits, like chasing down the man who runs the Taco Stand or pushing Nancy Griggs so hard that her father threatened to file a restraining order. (She graduated summa cum laude, sweetheart. She has a good job, a thoughtful husband, and a flatulent cocker spaniel. Did I tell you that already?)

So I keep my thoughts to myself and let your mother cook for me and bathe me and she lets me hold her and we make love and I think of our lives together after I finally have proof that even Huckleberry will have to believe.

I will win back your mother. I will be the father that Pepper needs me to be. I will convince Claire that she is worth more—deserves more—than the men she has long settled on. I will once again be an example to the women in my life—make them know what a good husband and father can be, and make my girls look for that in the men they choose rather than these worthless pieces of flotsam that continually wash up on their lonely shores.

This is what I will have when all of this is over: I will have my life back. I will have my good memories of you. I will have a job. I will take care of my family. I will take care of animals. I will have justice. I will know where you are. I will finally find you and hold you in my arms and gently lay you down in your final resting place.

Because I know what it feels like to finally have a genuine thread to pull, and I know in my heart that I can pull that thread and unwind the whole story of your life after you were stolen from us.

These are the threads that I am picking at: Gerald Scott was a peeping Tom who looked at girls just like you. He took images of them. He must have stored all of these images away some-where. If those images are still around and if I can gain access to them and if I find one of you, then that could be a solid lead that helps us understand what really happened that night in March that seems not so long ago.

I am not sure whether or not Paul knows about his father's peeping Tom proclivities, but at the very least, I can use the information to get him away from your baby sister.

I feel very strongly about this, sweetheart: Paul is not good for Claire. There is something rotting inside of him, and one day—if not soon, then in five years, ten years, maybe even twenty—that rot will eat its way to the outside and spread into everything he touches.

Though you know that I love you, my life from this point forward is devoted to making sure this terrible, rotting devil never gets the chance to spread his evil to your two sisters.

Do you remember Brent Lockwood? He was your very first "real" boyfriend. You were fifteen. The boys you liked before Brent were the innocuous, asexual types who could pass for any member of whatever boy band you were listening to at the moment. I would drive you on dates in the stationwagon and make the boy sit in the back. I would glare at him in the rearview mirror. I would make monosyllabic grunts when he called me Dr. Carroll or expressed an interest in the veterinary arts.

Brent was different. He was sixteen years old, half boy, half man. He had an Adam's apple. He wore acid-washed jeans and kept his hair high mulletted Daniel Boone-like in the back. He came to the house to ask permission to take you out on a date, because he had a car and he wanted to take you out in that car alone and I would never let anyone do that until I looked him in the eyes and made certain that I had scared the ever-loving shit out of him.

I know you find this hard to believe, sweetheart, but I once was a sixteen-year-old boy. The only reason I wanted a car was so I could get girls alone inside of it. Which was a completely understandable, even laudable, goal to all the boys my age, but felt completely different when I was a man, and a father, and that girl was you.

I told him to get a haircut and get a job, then come back and ask me again.

A week later, he was back at my door. His mullet was lopped. He had just started working at McDonald's.

Your mother cackled like a witch and told me next time, I should be more specific.

You spent hours in your room before that first date with Brent. When you finally opened your door, I smelled perfume and hairspray and all of these strange, womanly smells that I never expected to come from my own daughter. And you were beautiful. So beautiful. I scanned my eyes across your face looking for disagreeable things—too much mascara, too-heavy eyeliner—but there was nothing but a light brushing of color that brought out the pale blue of your eyes. I can't remember what you were wearing or how you had styled your hair (this is your mother's domain) but I do remember this breathless feeling in my chest, as if the alveoli inside my lungs were slowly collapsing, slowly depriving me of any oxygen, slowly depriving me of my little tomboy who climbed trees and ran after me when I went for my morning walks.

I now know what it feels like to have a real stroke, even a mini one, but I was certain when I watched Brent Lockwood drive you away in his car that I was having a full-on heart attack. I was so worried about this one boy, this first boy, that I never realized that there would be others. That some of them would make me long for Brent with his third-hand Impala and the smell of French fries he left in his wake.

Why am I thinking about this boy now? Because he was the first? Because I thought he would be the last?

I am thinking about him because of Claire.

Paul called me on the telephone tonight. He was concerned about my health. He made the right kind of small talk. He said all of the right things. He sounded right in every way, though I know that everything about him is wrong.

He thinks of me as old-fashioned, and I let him think that because it serves my purpose. Your mother is the feisty one, the grumpy old hippie who keeps him on his toes. I am the fatherly type who smiles and winks and pretends that he is everything he makes himself out to be.

I told him the story of Brent Lockwood, the boy who asked permission to date my oldest, now missing, daughter.

As I expected, Paul immediately apologized for not asking me whether or not he could date Claire. He is nothing if not a good mimic of appropriate behaviors. Had we been in person rather than on the telephone, I am certain he would've dropped to bended knee as he asked for my permission. But he wasn't, so it was his voice that conveyed the respect and feeling.

Conveyed.

As your mother has said, Paul could be a belt in a donut factory, he is so good at sticky, emotional conveyances.

On the phone call, I laughed, because Paul's request to date your sister was very late in coming, and he laughed, too, because that was what was expected of him. After an appropriate amount of time had passed, he alluded to a future request, one that would put his relationship with Claire on a more permanent footing, and I realized that though this stranger had been dating my daughter for only a few weeks, he was already thinking about marriage.

Marriage. That's what he called it, though men like Paul do not marry women. They own them. They control them. They are voracious gluttons who devour every part of a woman, then clean their teeth with the bones.

I'm sorry, sweetheart. Since you were taken, I have gotten so much more leery than I used to be. I see conspiracies around corners. I know that darkness is everywhere. I trust no one but your mother.

So I cleared my throat a few times and inserted some pained emotion into my tone and told Paul that I could not in all good conscience see myself giving any man permission to marry either of my daughters, or to even attend their weddings, until I know what happened to my oldest child.

Like Pepper, and like you for that matter, Claire is as impulsive as she is stubborn. She is also my baby girl, and she would never, ever go against my wishes. There is one thing I know about both of your sisters: They would just as soon break my arms and legs as break my heart.

I know this truth like I know the sound of Claire's laughter, the look she gets on her face when she is about to smile or cry or throw her arms around my shoulders and tell me that she loves me.

And Paul knows this, too.

After I told him about my dilemma, there was a long pause on his end of the telephone line. He is cunning, but he is young. One day, he will be a master manipulator, but two days from now when I get him alone, I will be the one asking questions, and I will not let Paul Scott leave my sight until he gives me all of the answers.

FIFTEEN

Claire clenched her hands around the steering wheel. Panic had almost closed her throat. She was sweating, though a cold rush of wind came in through the cracked sunroof. She looked down at Lydia's phone on the seat beside her. The screen had faded to black. So far, Paul had sent three pictures of Lydia. Each one showed her from a different angle. Each photo brought Claire some amount of relief because there was no further damage to Lydia's face. Claire didn't trust Paul, but she trusted her own eyes. He wasn't hurting her sister.

At least not yet.

She forced her thoughts not to go to that dark place that they were so desperately drawn toward. Claire could find no location or time stamp on the photos. She had a tenuous hold on the belief that Paul was stopping his car every twenty minutes and taking the photographs, because the alternative was to believe that he had taken all the photos at the same time and that Lydia was already dead.

She had to think of a way out of this. Paul would already be strategizing. He was always five steps ahead of everyone else. Maybe he already had a solution. Maybe he was already implementing that solution.

He would have another house. Her husband always bought a back-up. A two-hour drive from Athens could put him in the Carolinas or on the coast or close to one of the Alabama border towns. He would have another house in another name with another murder room with another set of shelves for his sick movie collection.

Claire felt sweat roll down her back. She opened the sunroof a few inches more. It was just after four in the afternoon. The sun was dipping into the horizon. She couldn't think about Paul or what he might be doing to her sister. He had always told her that winners only competed with themselves. Claire had one more hour to figure out how she was going to get the USB drive back from Adam, how she was going to deliver it to Paul, and how in the hell she was going to save her sister in the process.

So far, she had nothing but fear and the nauseating sensation that the hour would pass and she would be just as helpless as when she'd first left the Fuller house. The same problems that had plagued her before were on an endless loop that took up every conscious thought. Her mother: persistently unavailable. Huckleberry: worthless. Jacob Mayhew: probably working for the Congressman. Fred Nolan: ditto, or maybe he had his own agenda. Congressman Johnny Jackson: Paul's secret uncle. Powerful and connected, and duplicitous enough to stand with the Kilpatrick family during press conferences as if he had no idea what had happened to their precious child. Adam Quinn: possible friend or foe.

The masked man: Paul.

Paul.

She couldn't believe it. No, that wasn't right. Claire had seen her husband in front of that girl with her own eyes. The problem was that she couldn't *feel* it.

She forced all the disturbing things she knew about Paul to the forefront of her mind. She knew there was more. There had to be more. Like Paul's color-coded collection of rape files, there had to be countless more movies documenting the girls he abducted, the girls he kept, the girls he tortured for his own pleasure and for the pleasure of countless other despicable, disgusting viewers.

Was Adam Quinn one of his customers? Was he an active participant? As Lydia had said, it wasn't like Claire was the best judge of character. She had been with Adam because she was bored, not because she wanted to get to know him. Her husband's best friend had been a constant in their lives. In retrospect she understood that Paul had kept him at a distance. Adam was there, but he wasn't inside the circle.

The circle had only ever contained Paul and Claire.

Which was why Claire had never given Adam much thought until that night at the Christmas party. He'd been very drunk. He'd made a pass and she'd wanted to find out how far he would take it. He was good, or maybe just different from Paul, which was all that she had been looking for. He could be awkwardly charming. He liked golf and collected old train cars and smelled of a woodsy, not-unpleasant aftershave.

That was the extent of her knowledge.

Adam had told her that he had an important presentation on Monday, which meant that he'd be in the office first thing tomorrow morning. The presentation would take place at the Quinn + Scott downtown offices, where they had a custom-built screening room with theater seating and young girls in tight dresses who served drinks and light snacks.

Adam would have the USB drive on him. The files were too big to email. If he needed the files for work, then he would have to take them to the offices to load them for the presentation. If he needed the keytag because it had incriminating evidence, he would be a fool to keep it anywhere but on his person.

Claire let her thoughts drift back to the latter possibility. Paul could have another circle that encompassed Adam. They'd been best friends for over two decades, well before Claire entered the picture. If Paul had found his father's movies after his parents' accident, surely he would have gone to Adam to talk about it. Had they hatched a plan then to keep the business going? Had they both watched the films together and realized that they weren't repulsed by, but attracted to, the violent images?

In which case, Adam would've already told Paul that he had the USB drive. Claire didn't know what his silence meant. A falling-out? An attempted coup?

"Think," Claire chided herself. "You have to think."

She couldn't think. She could barely function.

Claire picked up Lydia's phone. Lydia didn't have a passcode, or maybe Paul had helpfully bypassed it for Claire. She clicked the button and the most recent photograph came up on the screen. Lydia in the trunk, terrified. Her lips were white. What did that mean? Was she getting enough air? Was Paul suffocating her?

Don't abandon me, Sweetpea. Please don't abandon me again.

Claire put down the phone. She wasn't going to abandon Lydia. Not this time. Not ever again.

Maybe Claire was tackling this from the wrong end. She couldn't think of her own strategy, so the better thing to do was to guess what Paul was planning. Claire was good at predicting Paul's behavior, at least where Christmas presents and surprise trips were concerned.

His first goal was to get back the USB drive. It would cost him nothing to wait. He was keeping Lydia somewhere. She was his leverage over Claire. He wouldn't kill her until he was absolutely certain that he had the drive in his hands.

The thought brought Claire some relief, but she knew full well that there were other things that Paul could do with Lydia.

She wasn't going to think about that.

Paul still had feelings for Claire—at least inasmuch as he was capable of feeling anything. He had put the pillow under her head. He'd slid her wedding ring back on her finger. He had taken off her shoes. He had charged the Tesla. All of these things had taken time, which meant that Paul placed importance on them. Instead of rushing Lydia out the door, he had risked exposure by taking care of Claire.

Which meant she had a slight advantage.

Claire groaned. She could hear Lydia's voice in her head: *So fucking what?*

The car's GPS told her to make a right turn up ahead. Claire didn't dwell on the relief she felt from having someone else tell her what to do, even if it was the onboard computer. Back in Athens, she had been overwhelmed with bad choices. She couldn't go home to her mother, who would only fret and take to her bed. She couldn't go to the police because there was no telling who was in cahoots with Paul. She couldn't go to the Dunwoody house because Nolan was probably looking for her. The only place she could go to was Lydia's.

She was halfway to the house when she realized there was something at Lydia's that could possibly—maybe—help her.

Claire slowed the Tesla as she took in her surroundings. She had been thoughtlessly following the GPS commands. She hadn't realized until now that she was inside the caverns of an older suburban neighborhood. The houses lacked the uniformity of a new subdivision. There were shotgun-style cottages, Dutch colonials, and the brick ranch where Lydia lived.

Claire didn't need the GPS to tell her that she'd reached her sister's home. She recognized the house from the photographs in Paul's files. The yellow numbers on the side of the mailbox were faded, obviously rendered by a child's hand. Claire pictured Lydia standing in the yard watching her young daughter carefully paint the address onto the side.

Lydia's van was parked in the driveway. According to Paul's detectives, Rick had lived next door to Lydia for almost ten years. Claire recognized the garden gnomes by his front door. Rick's truck was parked outside the Dunwoody house, but he had a second car, an old Camaro, parked in front of his garage.

She scanned both houses as she slowly drove by. Lydia's home was dark, but Rick had a few lights on. It was late after-noon on a Sunday. Claire imagined a man like Rick Butler would be watching football or reading a well-worn copy of *The Hitchhiker's Guide to the Galaxy*. Dee was probably at a friend's. According to the women in Claire's tennis team, teenagers were incapable of turning off lights when they left a room.

Claire turned down the next road, a short dead end with a rundown-looking cottage at the end. She parked and got out of the car. She put Lydia's phone in her back pocket because she was owed another photo in nine minutes. As usual, Paul was being punctual. Or he had programmed the phone to send out the pictures ahead of time.

She opened the trunk of the car. She tossed her purse into the back because this was that kind of neighborhood. She found a collapsible snow shovel inside the emergency backpack that Paul had ordered for all of their cars, including Helen's. The shovel snapped open with a metallic clang. Claire waited for a porch light to snap on or a neighbor to call out, but nothing happened.

She scanned the area to get her bearings. Lydia's home was four doors over. Rick's was five. There were no fences in the back yards save for Lydia's. A long stand of trees separated the yards from the houses behind them. It was four thirty in the afternoon. The sun was already going down. Claire easily made her way through the treeline. No one was looking out their back doors, though she wasn't sure whether or not they could see her even if they did. The sky was overcast. It was probably going to rain again. Claire could taste the moisture in the air.

She grabbed the chain-link fence with the idea of bolting herself over, but the metal rod bent beneath her hands. The chain link bent along with it. Claire put her weight into it until the fence was low enough for her to step over. She took in her surroundings.

Lydia's back yard was huge. She must have paid a fortune for the fence to keep the dogs enclosed.

Claire would repair the fence when her sister was back home with her family.

The back of Lydia's home was better kept than the others. The gutters were cleaned. The white trim was freshly painted. Claire imagined Rick took care of these things because the house next door, the house she knew to be his, showed the same obvious signs of care.

Claire liked the idea of her sister living here. Despite the dire circumstances, she felt the happiness that flowed between the houses. She felt the mark of a family, grateful for each other and their place in the world. Lydia had created more than a home. She had created peace.

Peace that Claire had all but destroyed.

The lights were on in what had to be the kitchen. Claire walked toward the large back deck. There were tables and chairs and a stainless-steel grill that was covered in a black canvas cloth.

Claire froze when she saw the floodlights. The motion sensors hung down like testicles. She looked up at the sky. It was getting darker by the minute. She took a tentative step forward, then another. She braced herself with every movement, but the flood-lights did not come on as she climbed the steps.

She looked at the kitchen through a large window over the sink. Papers covered the table. A bag of old tennis shoes was in one of the chairs. Notes were pinned to the refrigerator with colorful magnets. Dishes were stacked in the sink. Paul would call it borderline hoarding, but Claire felt the warmth of a lived-in space.

There was no window in the back door. There were two dead-bolt locks. A large dog door was cut into the bottom. Claire quietly lifted a heavy Adirondack chair and blocked the dog door. Paul's detective report stated that Lydia had two Labs, but that information had been recorded two months ago. Claire couldn't imagine Lydia keeping an overly territorial breed like a shepherd or a pitbull, but any dog's barking might alert Rick, and he would want to know what the hell a strange woman was doing on his girlfriend's back deck with a collapsible shovel.

Claire hefted the shovel in her hands. It was aluminum, but sturdy. She checked Rick's house for signs of life before walking back down the stairs. The ground was damp as she crawled under the deck. She had to keep her head and shoulders bent so she wouldn't scrape the joists overhead. Claire shuddered as she broke through a spiderweb. She hated spiders. She shuddered again, then she chided herself for being squeamish when her sister's life was at stake.

The area beneath the deck was predictably dark. There was a flashlight in the Tesla, but Claire didn't want to go back. She had to keep moving forward. Momentum was the only thing that was keeping her from collapsing into the fear and grief that bubbled under every surface she touched.

She scooted as far as she could go under the back steps. Narrow slats of light cut through the open risers. She ran her bare hand along the tight space below the bottom tread. The dirt had an indentation. This had to be the spot. Claire angled the shovel into the cramped space and picked out a spoonful of dirt.

She worked slowly, quietly, as she moved more dirt out from underneath the step. Finally, she was able to get the tip of the shovel deeper into the ground. She felt the clink of metal on metal. Claire dropped the shovel and used her hands. She tried not to think about spiders and snakes or anything else that might be hiding in the soil. Her fingers found the edge of a plastic bag. Claire let herself experience the momentary elation of actually completing a task. She yanked out the bag. Dirt flew up around her. She coughed, then sneezed, then coughed again.

The gun was in her hands.

Back in the car, Lydia had told her the weapon was buried under the stairs, but now Claire realized that she hadn't really believed that she would find it. The thought of her sister owning a gun was shocking. What was Lydia doing with such an awful thing?

What was Claire going to do with it?

Claire tested the weight of the revolver. She could feel the cold metal through the plastic Ziploc bag.

She hated guns. Paul knew this, which meant that he would not be expecting Claire to pull one out of her purse and shoot him in the face.

That was the plan.

She felt it snap into her head like a slide loading into a projector.

The plan had been there all along, propelling her toward Lydia's home, all the while niggling in the back of her brain while she let herself get wrapped up in the horrors of what her husband had done.

"Proactive interference," Paul would have explained. "It's when previously acquired information inhibits our ability to process new information."

The new information could not be any clearer. Paul was a

cold-blooded murderer. Claire was an idiot if she thought that he was going to let Lydia walk away. She knew too much. She was expendable. She might as well have a timer over her head count- ing down the minutes she had left.

So this was Claire's next step: She was going to retrieve the USB drive from Adam Quinn—either by asking for it or by threatening him with the gun she now held in her hands. Claire had seen what a tennis racket could do to a knee. She could not imagine the damage a bullet could do.

Lydia was right about seeking out as much information as pos- sible. Claire had to find out why the contents of the drive were so important to Paul. Having that information would put the balance of power firmly back on Claire's side.

Carefully, she removed the gun from the bag. The oily metal- lic smell was familiar. Two years ago, she had taken Paul to a gun range for his birthday. Paul had been pleased, but only because Claire had thought to do something so completely out of her comfort range. She hadn't lasted more than ten minutes inside the range. The emotional toll of holding death in her hands had sent Claire out to the parking lot where she had dissolved into tears. Paul had soothed her while he laughed, because it was silly, and Claire knew it was silly, but she had been absolutely petrified.

The guns were loud. Everything smelled foreign and dangerous. Just holding the loaded Glock made her tremble. Nothing about Claire was equipped to use a gun. She didn't have the hand strength to reliably pull back the slide. The recoil was panic- inducing. She was afraid she would drop the gun and accidentally kill somebody or herself, or both. She was afraid the discharged shell would burn her skin. Every time she pulled the trigger, her fear bumped up another notch until she was shaking too hard to keep her fingers wrapped around the grip.

This had all come later. Before they stepped foot on the range, Paul had asked the rangemaster for a thorough explanation of all the weapons. Claire had been surprised by his request because she just assumed that her husband knew everything about everything. The rangemaster had taken them to a glass display that show-cased the guns they could rent by the hour: pistols, handguns, a few rifles, and, most alarmingly, a machine gun.

They had decided on the Glock because the brand was most familiar. The pistol was a nine-millimeter. You had to pull back the slide to load the bullet into the chamber. With a revolver, you just dropped the bullets into the cylinder, clicked the cylinder into place, cocked the firing pin, or hammer, then pulled the trigger.

Of course, the key word here was bullets.

Claire examined Lydia's revolver. Her sister would not be so stupid as to hide a loaded gun under her back porch. Still, Claire checked the cylinder. The five chambers were empty. She did a mental inventory of the cash in her wallet. She could go to a sporting goods store or a Walmart and buy ammunition with cash because a credit card transaction would show up somewhere.

The floodlights came on.

Claire bumped her head on the deck stairs. Her skull clanged like a bell.

Rick Butler leaned down to look at her. "Can I help you?"

Claire put the gun back in the bag. She tried to crawl out from underneath the deck, but she needed both hands. She tossed the bag out into the yard. Rick stepped back like she'd thrown acid at his feet.

"I'm sorry," she apologized, because that was her answer for everything. "I'm Claire Scott, Lydia's—"

"Sister." Rick looked down at the gun. "I thought she got rid of that thing."

"Well." Claire clapped her hands together to clean off the dirt. She tried good manners, because Helen had taught her to always be polite. At least initially. "It's nice to finally meet you."

"Sure," he said. "An explanation would be nice."

Claire nodded, because it would be nice, but she couldn't give him one. She settled on another "I'm sorry." She picked up the gun. She wrapped the bag tightly around the barrel.

"Wait a minute," Rick said, because he could obviously tell she was going to leave. "Where's Lydia?"

As usual, Paul's timing was impeccable. Claire felt Lydia's phone vibrate in her back pocket. He had sent the latest photo. Should she show it to Rick? Should she let him know what was going on with the woman to whom he had devoted the last thirteen years of his life?

Claire said, "I need to go."

Rick narrowed his eyes. Either he was extremely perceptive or Claire was too easy to read. "You're not leaving here until you tell me what's going on."

"I have a gun in my hands."

"Then use it."

They stared at each other. Somewhere, a dog started barking. Almost a full minute passed before Claire said, "I'm sorry."

"You keep saying that, but it doesn't seem like it."

He had no idea how truly sorry Claire was. "I need to go."

"With an empty gun that's been buried in the ground?" Rick

shook his head. He didn't look angry anymore. He looked frightened. "Is Lydia okay?"

"Yes."

"Did she . . .?" He rubbed the side of his jaw with his hand. "Did she slip?"

"Slip?" Claire's mind filled with an image of Lydia slipping and falling on the floor. And then she understood what Rick Butler really meant. "Yes," she said, because Lydia would prefer this terrible lie over the truth. "She slipped. She drank some wine, and then she took some pills, and she wouldn't stop."

"Why?"

Claire had lived with Lydia's addiction for six years before their break. "Does there have to be a reason?"

Rick looked devastated. He was an addict. He knew that addicts could always find a reason.

"I'm sorry." Claire felt like an anvil was on her chest. What she was doing was awful, inexcusable. She could read the anger and disappointment and fear in every line of Rick's face. "I'm so sorry."

"It's not your fault." His voice went up the way men's voices sometimes squeaked when they were trying to hold back emotions. "Why do you—" He cleared his throat. "Why do you need a gun?"

Claire glanced around the back yard as if an easy explanation would present itself.

"You think she's gonna come back here and try to hurt herself?"

The alarm in his tone was heartbreaking. His throat still worked as he tried to quell his emotions. There were tears in his eyes. He looked like such a kind, gentle man. He was exactly the kind of person she had always hoped that her sister would end up with.

And now Claire was breaking his heart.

Rick asked, "Where is she? I want to see her. Talk to her."

"I'm going to check her into rehab. I'll pay for it. The facility is in New Mexico." Claire pressed together her lips. Why had she said New Mexico?

Rick asked, "Is she in your car?"

"The ambulance is taking her to the airport. I'll meet her there." Claire added, "Alone. She told me to tell you to keep Dee safe. She doesn't want you to see her like this. You know how proud she is."

He slowly nodded his head. "I can't believe she lost her sobriety after so long."

"I'm sorry." Claire was out of words. Her brain was so overtaken by Paul's lies that she was incapable of coming up with new ones on her own. "I'm sorry," she kept repeating. "I'm so sorry."

Claire didn't know what else to say. She headed toward the back yard. She counted her footsteps to fill her head with something other than guilt. Five paces. Ten paces.

Rick stopped her at twenty. "Wait a minute."

Claire felt her shoulders hunch. She had never been good at hiding her guilt because with Paul around, she was always so easily forgiven.

"You can't take the gun."

Claire turned around. Rick was closing the gap between them. Her first thought was that she could not outrun him. Her second thought was that she couldn't think of another lie.

She put the problem back on Rick. "Why not?"

"They're not going to let you take it on the plane. You can't just stash it in the car at the airport." He held out his hand. "I'll hold on to it."

Claire forced herself to look him in the eye. He smelled of car exhaust. She could see hard muscles under the sleeves of his flannel shirt. Even with the ponytail, he was a man in every sense of the word. He'd been in prison. He looked like he could handle himself. Claire wanted to let him help her. Every problem in her life had always been fixed by someone else.

And look where that had gotten her.

"What's really going on here?" Rick's posture had changed. He was looking at her differently now. His arms were crossed. His distrust was evident. "Lydia warned me that you were a really good liar."

"Yeah, well . . ." Claire let out a long sigh. "I usually am."

"Is she safe?"

"I don't know." Claire tightened her grip on the gun. She had to get out of here. If she stood in front of this man for too long, she would ask him for help. She would let him take over. She would get him killed. "Take Dee away from here. Tonight. Don't tell me where you're going."

"What?"

She could read shock in every line on his face. "Just take her somewhere safe."

"You need to call the police." His voice had gone up again, this time with fear. "If there's something—"

"The police are involved. The FBI. I don't know who else."

He opened his mouth, then closed it, then opened it again.

"I'm sorry."

"Fuck your sorry, lady. What the hell did you get her caught up in?"

Claire knew she had to tell him something close to the truth. "Something really bad. Lydia is in danger."

"You're scaring me."

"You should be scared." She grabbed Rick's arm. "Don't call the police. They won't help. Take Dee and get her out of here."

"Dee?" He was almost yelling. "What the hell does Dee have to do with this?"

"You need to take her away."

"You said that. Now tell me why."

"If you want to help Lydia, then you'll keep Dee safe. That's all she cares about."

He put his hand over hers so she couldn't leave. "I know what happened between you two. You haven't talked to each other in twenty years and now you're suddenly worried about her daughter?"

"Lydia is my sister. Even when I hated her, I still loved her." Claire looked down at his hand. "I have to go."

Rick didn't let go of her hand. "Why don't I just hold on to you and call the police?"

"Because if you call the police, then Lydia will be dead and the person who has her will come after Dee."

His grip loosened, but more out of shock than acquiescence. "What can I do? Just tell me what—"

"You can keep Dee safe. I know you love Lydia, and I know you want to help, but she loves her daughter. You know that's all that matters to her."

Claire pulled away from him. Rick didn't make it easy. Obviously, he was torn between letting her go and shaking the truth out of her, but he loved Lydia's daughter. Claire knew from Paul's reports that Rick had practically raised her. He was her father, and no father would let harm come to his child.

She picked up the pace as she jogged through the back yard. She jumped over the low fence. Every step she took forward was hounded by the ones she wanted to take back to Rick. She prayed that he would listen to her and take Dee somewhere safe. But what was safe? Paul had countless resources. Congressman Johnny Jackson had even more.

Should she turn around and go back? Rick loved Lydia. He was her family—probably more so than Claire. He would help her.

And Paul would probably kill him.

Claire pulled Lydia's phone out of her back pocket as she ran toward the car. The latest photo showed Lydia lying on her side. The picture was darker, which she hoped meant that Paul had taken it recently rather than an hour and a half ago.

The streetlights came on as Claire got behind the wheel of the Tesla. She put the gun in her purse. She didn't need Rick Butler. The gun was the plan. She would use it to get information from Adam. She would use it to kill Paul. Claire had felt so certain when she first held the weapon under the deck steps. She couldn't falter now that there were other, easier options. She had to go through with this. She had to confront Paul on her own. If she knew one thing about her husband, it was that he would be furious if she involved someone else.

There could be no one else inside the circle.

She started the car. She did a U-turn back onto the main road. She passed Lydia's home. The lights had been turned on in the front rooms. She prayed to God that Rick was packing Dee's things, that he was doing as she asked and taking Lydia's daughter somewhere safe.

Again, she asked herself what was safe. Fred Nolan could run Rick's credit cards. He could track the man's phone. He could probably find him with drones or CCTV or whatever else the federal government employed to spy on persons of interest.

Claire shook her head. She couldn't keep running off on tangents. She had to take this in steps. She had Lydia's gun now. That was the first step. The second step was to get the USB drive from Adam. She would pull over to a payphone and call him. Sunday night. He would be at home with Sheila. Was there such a thing as a payphone anymore? Claire couldn't risk calling Adam on Lydia's phone. She had watched too many episodes of *Homeland* to know better than that. Agent Nolan or Captain Mayhew—or both—could be monitoring Adam's phone for Claire's call.

Blue lights flashed in her rear-view mirror. Claire instinctively slowed to get out of the cop's way, but the cop car slowed, too, and when she signaled to get over, he signaled, too.

"Shit," Claire hissed, because she'd been speeding. The limit was thirty-five and she was doing fifty.

And she had a gun in her purse.

Claire was on parole. She had a weapon. She probably still had traces of drugs in her system. She had violated every single line item in her terms of parole, including ignoring a law enforcement officer's request for a meeting.

The cop behind her made his siren whoop.

Claire pulled over to the side of the road. What was she going to do? What the fuck was she going to do?

The cop didn't park behind her. Instead, he pulled in front and angled his car so that the Tesla was blocked in.

Claire put her hand on the gear. She could go into reverse. She could back up the car and she could hit the gas and she could probably go about ten miles before every police officer in the vicinity was chasing her down the expressway.

The cop got out of the squad car. He put on his hat. He adjusted his belt.

Claire grabbed Lydia's phone. Paul. He would know what to do. Except she didn't have his number. The caller ID always showed it as blocked.

"Shit," Claire repeated.

Maybe Paul already knew what was happening. He'd made it clear that he had friends in law enforcement. He could easily make a phone call and have Claire pulled over and handcuffed and stuffed into the back of a police car that would take her to wherever Paul was hiding.

The cop hadn't come over. He was standing beside his car. He was talking on his cell phone. They were on the outskirts of Lydia's neighborhood. All of the surrounding houses were dark. The cop checked the empty road over his shoulder before walking toward the Tesla.

Claire's fingers took over. She was dialing a number into Lydia's phone as the cop tapped on her window with the back of his wedding ring.

"Hello?" The phone was answered with the usual breathless

panic that always accompanied calls from unknown numbers. Was it Julia? Was it Lydia? Was it more bad news?

"Mom." Claire gulped back a sob. "Please, Mom, I really need you."

SIXTEEN

Lydia hadn't stood a chance against Paul. She had waited and waited for him to get her out of the trunk, but he just kept stopping to take her picture and then driving some more, then stopping again, then driving. He did this a total of five times before she lost control of her senses.

The first sign was a faint dizziness—nothing alarming, and weirdly pleasant. She had yawned several times. She had closed her eyes. She had felt the tension drain from her muscles. And then a big, goofy smile had spread across her face.

The trunk wasn't just padded for sound.

She heard the faint hissing noise as Paul pumped what could only be nitrous oxide into the trunk. Laughing gas. Lydia had used it once at the dentist when she got her wisdom teeth out and she had been haunted for months by the incredible high.

The gas wasn't meant to knock you out completely, so Lydia

could only retrieve fragments of memories from that point on. Paul grinning as he opened the trunk. Slipping a black hood over her head. Tying the bottom of the hood snugly around her neck. Cutting the zip tie holding together her ankles. Muscling her onto the ground. Pushing her to walk. Lydia stumbling through a forest. Hearing birds, smelling cold, fresh air, feeling her feet slide on dry leaves. They walked for what felt like hours until Paul finally pulled her to a stop. He turned her by her shoulders. He pushed her forward. She climbed an endless number of stairs. The sound of her feet echoed like gunshots in her head.

They were still echoing when he pushed her down into a chair. She was incredibly high, but he still didn't take any chances. First, he zip-tied one ankle, then the other, to the legs of the chair. Then he tightened a chain around her waist. Then he cut open the zip tie around her wrists.

Lydia wanted to move. She may have even tried, but despite the hours of planning, she could not get her arms to lift, her hand to arc into the perfect shape of his neck.

Instead, she felt the plastic zip ties cutting into her skin as he bound each wrist to the arm of a chair.

She felt vinyl under her fingers. She felt cold metal against the skin of her legs. She felt her senses slowly roll back into her consciousness. The chair was metal, and sturdy, and when she tried to move it back and forth it didn't budge because he had obviously bolted the legs to the floor. She leaned back her head and felt the cold, solid pressure of a wall. She felt the hood move in and out with each panicked breath.

Like the car trunk, he had prepared the chair for a prisoner.

Lydia stared into the blackness of the hood. The material was heavy cotton, like a beefy T-shirt. There was a drawstring or elastic or both around the bottom. She could feel the material gripping tightly to her neck.

In movies, people who were hooded could always see out. They found a sliver of light underneath the hood or the material was too thin so they could see a billboard or the setting sun or something that let them know exactly where they were.

No light bled through the hood. The cotton was so thick and impenetrable that Lydia had no doubt Paul had worn it himself to test for vulnerabilities before he used it on others.

There were definitely others. Lydia could smell a faint trace of perfume. She never wore perfume. She had no idea what the scent was, but it had the sickly sweet odor of something only a young girl would wear.

How much time had passed since Paul had taken her out of the trunk? Lydia's brief affair with her dentist's laughing gas had lasted around half an hour, but it had felt like days. And that was with the gas mask over her face at all times. She had a clear recollection of the dentist adjusting the dosage up and down to keep her from coming fully awake. Which meant that the gas didn't last long, which meant that she hadn't walked for hours in the forest. She had probably walked a few minutes, tops, because the laughing gas was already wearing off by the time Paul had bound Lydia to the chair.

Lydia pulled at the zip ties. She strained as hard as she could, but the only thing that broke was the skin around her wrists and ankles.

She listened for sounds in the room. There was the distant chirp of a bird. The wind was blowing outside. Occasionally, she could hear the faint whoosh of a breeze cutting through the trees. She strained her ears, trying to pick out anything different: airplanes overhead, cars passing by.

Nothing.

Did Paul have a cabin somewhere that Claire did not know about? There was so much that he had kept from her. He had seemingly endless amounts of money at his disposal. He could buy houses all over the world, for all Claire knew.

Her sister was so fucking clueless. She was probably still at the Fuller house running around in circles like a lost baby bird.

Lydia felt sick again. She was already covered in her own bile. Her bladder was full. She had reached a numbness beyond terror. She tried not to accept the inevitable, that Claire would fuck this up, that she would do something wrong, and that Paul would kill them both.

She wanted so badly to believe that this time would be different, but Claire was reactive. She was impetuous. She wasn't capable of out-thinking Paul. For that matter, neither was Lydia. He had faked his own death. That had taken a great deal of time and planning, which had most probably involved not only the police force, but the ambulance service, the hospital, the coroner's office, and the funeral home. Paul had at least one cop and an FBI agent in his pocket. He'd had so much more time to think this through than either of them.

Whatever "this" was, because Lydia had no idea. She had been so hell-bent on damning Claire and planning her own stupid escape that she had not asked herself why Paul had taken her in the first place. What value did Lydia bring to the table? What did Lydia have that made him choose to take her over Claire?

She heard a door creak open.

Lydia tensed. Someone was in the room. Standing at the door. Looking at her. Watching her. Waiting.

The door creaked closed.

She squared her shoulders, pressed her head back into the wall.

Soft footsteps padded across the floor. An office chair was rolled over. There was an almost imperceptible huff of air as Paul sat down in the chair opposite Lydia.

He asked, "Are you panicking yet?"

Lydia bit her bottom lip until she tasted blood.

"You used Dee's birthday for your iCloud password." His voice was calm, conversational, like they were sitting across from each other at lunch. The chair squeaked as Paul sat back. His knees pressed against the inside of her knees so that her legs were opened even more. "Are you scared, Liddie?" He pushed her legs wider.

Lydia had tensed every muscle in her body. The hood gripped the front of her face as she panted. They weren't out in the open this time where anyone could come along and save her. They were isolated in a room that Paul had prepared ahead of time. He had her pinned to the chair. Her legs were spread open. He could take his time with her. He could do anything he wanted.

Paul said, "I've been tracking Claire with your Find My iPhone app."

Lydia squeezed her eyes shut. She tried the Serenity Prayer, but she didn't get past the first line. She could not accept this thing that she could not change. She was helpless. Claire was not going to save her from this. Paul was going to rape her.

"Claire was at your house. Do you know why Claire would be

at your house?" Even now, he sounded curious, not angry. "Was she trying to warn Rick? Was she telling him that he needs to take Dee and hide?"

Lydia tried not to think about the question, because the answer was obvious: Claire hadn't gone to Lydia's house. She had gone next door to get help from Rick. It wasn't enough for her to fuck up Lydia's life, she had endangered Lydia's family, too.

Paul seemed to read her thoughts. "Every year, I've watched Dee getting older and older." He didn't wait for a response. "Two more years and she'll be Julia's age."

Please, Lydia thought. *Please don't say what I know you're going to say.*

Paul leaned forward. She could feel his breath against the hood. "I can't wait to see what she tastes like."

Lydia couldn't stop the cry that came out of her mouth.

"You're too easy, Liddie. You've always been too easy." He kept pushing against her knees, then letting them go like they were playing a game. "I stayed at Auburn for you. I matched for grad school at MIT, but I stayed for you because I wanted to be with Julia Carroll's sister."

The band around the bottom of the hood soaked up Lydia's tears.

"I watched you. God knows how long I watched you. But you were sloppy and drunk all the time. Your dorm room looked like a pigsty. You didn't bathe. You were flunking out of your classes." Paul sounded disgusted. "I was about to give up on you, but then Claire came to visit. Do you remember that? It was fall of ninety-six."

Lydia remembered. Claire had visited the campus just after

the Summer Olympics. Lydia was embarrassed because her sister was wearing a sweatshirt with Izzy, the stupid Atlanta mascot, on the front.

Paul said, "Claire practically glowed when she walked around the campus. She was so happy to be away from home." His voice had changed again now that he was talking about Claire. "That's when I knew that I could still have Julia Carroll's sister."

Lydia couldn't contradict him, because they both knew that Claire had curled herself up into the palm of his hand.

Still, she tried, "She cheated on you."

"I wouldn't call it cheating." He sounded unconcerned. "She fucked around. So what? I fucked around, too, but we always came back home to each other."

Lydia knew Paul hadn't just fucked around. She had seen the color-coded files. She had seen the murder room in the garage of the Fuller house. She knew that someone had sat behind the camera and zoomed in on the rapes and murders of countless young girls, just like she knew that that someone had to be Paul.

Was he going to finally cross the line into murderer? Was that why he had Lydia bound and hooded?

He said, "You know, the thing about Claire was that I couldn't figure her out." He laughed, like he was still surprised by the fact. "I never know what she's really thinking. She never does the same thing twice. She's impetuous. She has a hellacious temper. She can be crazy and passionate and funny. She's made it obvious that she's willing to try anything in bed, which takes all of the fun out of it, but sometimes holding back can be just as much of a game as letting go."

Lydia shook her head. She didn't want to hear this. She couldn't hear it.

"Every time I think I have her pinned down, she does something exciting." He gave another surprised laugh. "Like, get this: I was sitting in a meeting one day, and I get this call on my cell phone, and the ID said it was from the Dunwoody police station. I thought it had to do with something else, so I go outside and I answer, and there's this recorded message asking if I'll accept a collect call from an inmate at the Dunwoody jail. Can you believe that?"

He waited, but surely he knew Lydia wouldn't answer.

"It was Claire. She said, 'Hi, what are you doing?' She sounded completely normal, like she was calling to tell me to bring her home some ice cream. But the recording said she was an inmate in jail, so I told her, 'The recording said you were in jail.' And she said, 'Yeah, I was arrested about an hour ago.' So I asked her, 'What did you get arrested for?' And do you know what she said?" Paul leaned forward again. He was clearly enjoying this. "She said, 'I didn't have enough money to pay the hookers and they called the police.'"

Paul's laughter was filled with obvious delight. He actually slapped his knee.

He asked Lydia, "Can you believe that?"

Lydia had no problem believing the story, but she was chained up in an isolated cabin with a hood over her head, not talking to her brother-in-law at a barbecue. "What do you want from me?"

"How about this?" He jammed his foot between her legs so hard that her tailbone slammed into the concrete wall. "Do you think this is what I want?"

Lydia opened her mouth, but she didn't let herself scream.

"Liddie?"

He started to grind in his foot, using the treads of his shoe to press her open.

His tone was still conversational. "Do you want me to tell you where Julia is?"

She forced her mouth closed as the treads cut deeper into her.

"Don't you want to know where she is, Liddie? Don't you want to find her body?"

She felt the skin sliding back and forth across her pubic bone.

"Tell me you want to hear what happened."

She tried to mask her terror. "I know what happened."

"Yeah, but you don't know what happened after."

His voice had changed again. He liked this. He liked seeing her squirm. He was absorbing her fear like a succubus. Lydia heard an echo of the last words Paul Scott had ever spoken to her: *Tell me you want this.*

Her whole body shuddered at the memory.

"Are you scared, Liddie?" Slowly, he removed his foot. She had a second of relief, but then his fingers brushed across her breasts.

Lydia tried to jerk away.

His touch got harder as he moved his fingers to her collarbone, then down her arm. He pressed his thumb against her biceps until she felt like the bone was going to snap.

"Please." The word slipped out before she could stop it. She had seen the movies he liked to watch. She had seen his files filled with women he had raped. "Please don't do this."

"How about this?" Paul grabbed her breast.

Lydia screamed. His hand clamped down like a vise. And then he squeezed harder. And harder. His fingers gouged deep into the tissue. The pain was unbearable. She couldn't stop screaming. "Please!" she begged. "Stop!"

He let go slowly, releasing one finger at a time.

Lydia gasped for air. Her breast throbbed from his fingers piercing the flesh.

"Did you like that?"

Lydia was going to black out. He had stopped, but she could still feel his hand twisting her breast. She was panting. She couldn't catch her breath. The hood was too tight. It felt like there was something around her neck. Was his hand around her neck? Was he touching her? She turned her head left and right. She tried to wrench her body from the chair. The chain dug into her stomach. She lifted her hips off the seat.

Clicking.

She heard clicking.

A spring bending back and forth.

Was he bouncing the chair? Was he jerking himself off?

There was the sharp smell of urine. Had she wet herself? Lydia squirmed in the chair. The stench was overwhelming. She tightened herself against the chair. She pressed the back of her skull into the wall.

"Breathe," Paul said. "Deep breaths."

Click. Squeak. Click.

A spray bottle. She knew the sound. The tiny spring in the handle. The sucking noise as the pump pulled up liquid. The click as the handle released.

Paul said, "You're going to want to keep breathing."

The hood was getting wet. The thick cotton was getting heavy against her mouth and nose.

"I like to think of this as my own special form of water-boarding."

Lydia sucked in great gulps of air. It was piss. He was spraying her with piss. She turned away her head. Paul followed her with the spray bottle. She turned the other way. He turned the bottle.

"Keep breathing," he said.

Lydia opened her mouth. He adjusted the nozzle so the spray turned into a stream. The wet cotton molded to her lips. The hood became soaked. The material clogged her nostrils. Claustrophobia took over. She was going to suffocate. She inhaled a spray of liquid. She coughed and sucked in a mouthful of urine. Lydia gagged. Urine washed down her throat. She started to choke. He kept spraying, angling the stream no matter which way she turned her head. He was trying to drown her. She was going to drown in his urine.

"Lydia."

Her lungs were paralyzed. Her heart strangled.

"Lydia." Paul raised his voice. "I put the spray bottle down. Stop panicking."

Lydia couldn't stop panicking. There was no more air. She had forgotten what to do. Her body couldn't remember how to draw breath.

Paul said, "Lydia."

Lydia tried in vain to draw in more air. She saw flashes of light. Her lungs were going to explode.

"Breathe out," he coached. "You're only breathing in."

She breathed in harder. He was lying. He was lying. He was lying.

"Lydia."

She was going to die. She couldn't work the muscles. Nothing was working. Everything had stopped, even the beats of her heart.

"Lydia."

Explosions of light filled her eyes.

"Brace yourself." Paul punched her so hard in the stomach that she felt the metal chair bend into the wall.

Her mouth opened. She huffed out a stream of warm, wet air.

Air. She had air. Her lungs filled. Her head filled. She was dizzy. Her stomach burned. She collapsed forward in the chair. The chain cut into her ribs. Her cheek hit her knee. Blood rushed into her face. Her heart was pounding. Her lungs were screaming.

The wet cotton hood hung down in front of her face. Piss-tainted air flowed into her open mouth and nose.

Paul said, "It's weird how that happens, right?"

Lydia concentrated on pulling air into her lungs and pushing it back out. She had crumbled so easily. He had sprayed piss in her face and she had been ready to give up.

"You're beating yourself up," Paul guessed. "You've always thought you were the strong one, but you're not, are you? That's why you liked coke so much. It gives you this sense of euphoria, like you can do anything in the world. But without it, you're completely powerless."

Lydia squeezed tears out of her eyes. She had to be stronger. She couldn't let him get into her head. He was too good at this. He knew exactly what he was doing to her. He hadn't just been behind the camera zooming in.

He had participated.

Paul said, "Now, Julia, she was a real fighter."

Lydia shook her head. She silently begged him not to do this.

"You watched the tape. You saw how she fought back, even at the end."

Lydia tensed her body. She pulled at the plastic ties.

"I watched you watching her die. Did you know that?" Paul sounded pleased with himself. "I gotta say, that was pretty meta."

The zip ties were ripping into her skin. She could feel the plastic teeth sawing back and forth.

"My mom helped look for her," Paul said. "Dad and I got a big kick out of her slipping on her boots every morning and trudging out into fields and checking streams and putting up fliers. Everybody was out looking for Julia Carroll, and Mom had no idea that she was hanging out in the barn."

Lydia remembered searching fields and rivers. She remembered the way the town rallied around her family, only to turn their backs two weeks later.

"Dad kept her alive for me. She lasted twelve days. If you can call that living." He leaned forward. She could feel his excitement like it was a creature standing between them. "They were all so close, Lydia. Do you want me to tell you how close?"

Lydia clenched her jaw shut.

"Do you want me to tell you what it's like to fuck somebody when they're dying?"

Lydia screamed, "What do you want from me?"

"You know what I want."

She knew what was coming. He had taken Lydia instead of Claire because he had business to finish.

"Do it," Lydia said. He was right about the coke. He was right about everything. She wasn't strong enough to stand up to him. Her only hope was that it would be fast. "Just get it over with."

Paul laughed again, but it wasn't the delighted laugh he saved for Claire. It was the kind of laugh you gave when you thought someone was pitiful. "Do you really think I want to rape a fat forty-year-old?"

Lydia hated herself for feeling the sting of his words. "I'm forty-one, you stupid motherfucker."

She braced herself for another punch or a kick or the spray bottle, but instead, he did something far worse than she could have ever imagined.

He took off the hood.

Lydia closed her eyes against the blinding light. She turned her head away. She hissed fresh air in and out between her teeth.

Paul said, "You can't keep your eyes closed forever."

She squinted, trying to get her eyes to adjust to the light. The first thing she saw was her own hands clutching the green vinyl pads on the arms of the chair. Then the concrete floor. Wadded-up fast-food bags. A stained mattress.

Lydia looked up at Paul. He held out his hands like a magician finishing a trick.

She *had* been tricked.

The ambient sound was coming from a pair of computer speakers. The leaves under her feet were on the floor of the garage. The wall behind her was stained concrete block. They were not in an isolated cabin in the woods.

Paul had brought her back to the Fuller house.

SEVENTEEN

Fred Nolan said, "Tell me about your relationship with your husband."

Claire looked away from his smug face. They were in a cramped interrogation room inside the downtown FBI field office. She had her legs crossed under a cheap plastic table. Her foot was shaking uncontrollably. There was no clock in the room. Hours had passed. Claire had no idea how many, but she knew her self-imposed deadline for telling Paul how to get back the thumbdrive had long passed.

Nolan asked, "Was he a nice guy? Romantic?"

Claire didn't answer. She felt sick with fear. Paul wouldn't be sending pictures of Lydia anymore. There was nothing to keep him in check. Would he be anxious? Angry? Did he know that Claire was talking to the police? Was he taking out his fury on Lydia?

Nolan said, "Me, I try to be romantic, but I always end up doing it wrong. Tulips instead of roses. Tickets to the wrong show."

Claire tasted bile in her mouth. She had seen the violence that Paul was capable of. With Claire on radio silence, what would he do to her sister?

"Claire?"

Tears filled her eyes. Lydia. She had to help Lydia.

"Come on." Nolan waited a full minute before letting out a long, disappointed sigh. "You're just making this harder on yourself."

Claire stared up at the ceiling so her tears would not fall. The clock on the Tesla had read 6:48 when she'd pulled into the parking deck under the FBI building. How long ago had that been? Claire didn't even know whether or not it was still Sunday.

Nolan knocked on the table to get her attention. "You were married to the guy for almost nineteen years. Tell me about him."

Claire blinked away the useless tears. None of this was going to get Lydia back. What could Claire do? Lydia had said it herself: She wasn't a superhero. Neither of them were. She turned her gaze to the large mirror that took up one side of the wall. Her reflection showed an exhausted woman with a dark circle under her left eye. Paul had punched her in the face. He had knocked her out.

What was he doing to Lydia?

"All right." Nolan tried again. "How about this: Was he a Falcons guy or a Braves guy? Did he like sugar in his coffee?"

Claire stared down at the table. She had to get herself under control. Panicking was not going to get her out of this room. Nolan was playing nice for now. He hadn't arrested her for failing to appear at the scheduled meeting. He'd let her voluntarily follow the police officer to the FBI building. Once he had her inside, Nolan had reminded Claire of the terms of her parole, but he hadn't handcuffed her or threatened her with anything more dangerous than calling her parole officer to drug-test her.

So did this mean that Nolan was clean, or that he was working with Paul?

Claire tried to push down her fear about what might be happening to Lydia and concentrate on what was happening in this airless room right now. Nolan wasn't asking any questions about the USB drive or the Fuller house. He hadn't stashed her in a dirty motel where he could beat the information out of her. He wasn't pushing her about Captain Mayhew or Adam Quinn or talking about how much fun it was to watch movies on rainy nights. He was drilling her about her fucking relationship.

Claire asked, "What time is it?"

Nolan said, "Time is a flat circle."

Claire gave an exaggerated groan. She was going to start screaming if she didn't get out of this room. She had Lydia's phone stashed down the front of her bra. Claire had turned it off after calling her mother. She couldn't text or call Paul. She didn't know her lawyer's phone number. She couldn't call Rick after telling him to take Dee and run as far as he could go.

In the last twenty-four years, Claire had never once asked Helen for anything. Why on earth had she thought that reaching out to her now was a good idea?

"Claire?"

She finally looked at Nolan. "This is the fifth time you've asked me a variation on that same question."

"Humor me."

"For how much longer?"

"You're free to go." He indicated the door, and they both knew he meant free to go to her parole officer, because Nolan knew there were drugs in her system. Maybe he even knew that there was a gun in Claire's car. She had stashed the revolver in the driver's-side door pocket because that was slightly less obvious than hiding it in the trunk.

She said, "I need to go to the bathroom."

"I'll get a female agent to escort you."

Claire clenched her jaw. Three times, she had asked to use the bathroom. Three times, a female agent had taken her to the handicapped restroom and watched Claire use the toilet.

She asked Nolan, "Are you scared I'm going to flush myself?"

"Maybe you've got some drugs hidden in your clothes? You've been hanging around your sister a lot lately."

He had played this card already. Claire did not rise to the bait.

"Still, might be worth calling in a female agent to search you." He was silent long enough to make Claire sweat. She didn't care if they found the gun inside the Tesla, but Lydia's iPhone was her only lifeline to Paul.

There was no passcode on the phone. She could practically hear Paul lecturing her on the importance of using passcodes.

Nolan slapped his palms down on the table. "Ya know, Claire, you should really start answering my questions."

"Why?"

"Because I'm with the FBI. My side always wins."

"You keep saying that, but I do not think those words mean what you think they mean."

He nodded appreciatively. "Rockin' a little Inigo Montoya. I like it."

She looked at the mirror, wondering which Great and Powerful Oz was watching them. Johnny Jackson was her first bet. Captain Jacob Mayhew. Maybe even Paul. She could very well see him having the balls to walk into an FBI field office just to watch her squirm. Maybe they had invited him.

Nolan asked, "Would you say that your relationship with Paul was good?"

Claire gave in a little, because stonewalling hadn't worked the last five times. "Yes. I would say that my relationship with my husband was good."

"Because?"

"Because he certainly knew how to fuck me."

Nolan took the baser meaning. "I've always wondered what it'd feel like to climb behind the wheel of a Lamborghini." He winked. "More of a Pinto man myself."

Claire had never found self-deprecating men attractive. She stared at the two-way mirror. "Paul was good friends with Johnny Jackson. Do you know him?"

"The Congressman?" Nolan shifted in his chair. "Sure. Everybody's heard of him."

"He did a lot for Paul."

"Is that right?"

"Yes." She kept her eyes on the mirror. "He gave Quinn + Scott billions in government contracts. Did you know that?"

"I did."

Claire let her gaze travel back to Nolan. "Do you want me to tell you about Congressman Jackson and his relationship with Paul?"

"Sure." Nolan's tone was even. "We could start there."

Claire studied the man closely. She couldn't get a read off him. Was he afraid? Was he eager? "Johnny was an FBI agent back in the early nineties."

"That's true."

Claire waited for more. "And?"

"He was one of the shittiest agents this office has ever seen."

"I don't recall reading that in his official bio."

Nolan shrugged. He didn't seem afraid that Jackson would break through the mirror and strangle him.

Claire said, "He's been all over the press conferences with the Kilpatrick family."

"I said he was a shitty agent, not a shitty politician."

Claire still couldn't read the man's expression. "You don't sound like a fan."

Nolan clasped his hands together on the table. "On the surface, it seems like we're making progress, but when I think back on the last few minutes of our conversation, I get the feeling that you're questioning me instead of the other way around."

"You'll make a great detective one day."

"Fingers crossed." He flashed a grin. "I want to tell you something about the FBI."

"You always win?"

"Sure, there's that, and terrorists, of course. Kidnappers, bank robbers, pedophiles—nasty fuckers—but nuts and bolts, what we at the ol' FBI deal in day to day is curiosities. Did you know that?"

Claire didn't respond. He'd clearly given this speech before.

Nolan continued, "Local cops, they find something curious they can't figure out, and they bring it to us and we either agree that it's curious or we don't. And generally when we agree, it's not just the one curious thing, it's several curious things." He held up his index finger. "Curious thing number one: Your husband embezzled three million dollars from his company. Only three million dollars. That's curious, because you're loaded, right?"

Claire nodded.

"Curious thing number two." He added a second finger. "Paul went to college with Quinn. He shared a dorm room with the guy, and then when they were in grad school together, they shared an apartment, and then Quinn was best man at your wedding, and then they started the business together, right?"

Claire nodded again.

"They've been best friends for almost twenty-one years, and it seemed curious to me that after twenty-one years, Quinn figures out his best buddy is stealing from their company, the one they built together from the ground up, but instead of going to his buddy and saying, 'Hey, what the fuck, buddy?' Quinn goes straight to the FBI."

The way he put it together did seem curious, but Claire only said, "Okay."

Nolan held up a third finger. "Curious thing number three: Quinn didn't go to the cops. He went to the FBI."

"You have domain over financial crimes."

"You've been reading our website." Nolan seemed pleased.

"But lemme ask you again: Is that what you'd do if your best friend of twenty-one years stole a small, almost negligible, amount of money from your zillion-dollar company—find the biggest, baddest stick to fuck him with?"

The question gave Claire a different answer: Adam had turned Paul in to the FBI, which meant that Adam and Paul were not getting along. Either Adam Quinn didn't know about the movies or he knew about the movies and he was trying to screw over Paul.

Claire asked Nolan, "What did you do next?"

"How's that?"

"You investigated Adam's complaint about the money. You must have talked to the accountants. You traced the money back to Paul. And then what?"

"I arrested him."

"Where?"

"Where?" Nolan repeated. "That's a funny question."

"Humor me."

Nolan chuckled again. He was enjoying this. "I arrested him in his fancy office down the street. I put the handcuffs on him myself. Frogmarched him through the front lobby."

"You surprised him." Claire knew the kinds of things Paul left behind when he was surprised. "Did you check his computer?"

"Another funny question."

"You have your curious things, I have my funny questions."

He drummed his fingers on the table. "Yes, I checked his computer."

Claire nodded, but not for the reason Nolan would be thinking. If Adam had known about the movies, he would've made sure that they weren't on Paul's computer when the cops came. The first thing Paul would've done is point the finger back at his partner. Which meant that Fred Nolan had just handed Claire compelling proof that Adam was not involved in Paul's side business after all.

"So, what do you say?" Nolan asked. "Quid pro quo, Clarice?"

They stared at each other again, this time with hope instead of hostility.

Could she trust Fred Nolan? He worked with the FBI. Then again, so had Johnny Jackson. Maybe Nolan's trash talk about the Congressman was meant to draw her out. Give a little/get a little more. Or perhaps Nolan was being truthful. Paul was always telling Claire that she never trusted people, that she held back too much.

She asked, "What do you want to know?"

A smile broke across his face. "Did Paul slip you something before he died?"

The keytag. She almost laughed with relief. This entire dance had been to move them toward the keytag.

Claire chose to sound obtuse. "Are you making some kind of sexual innuendo because of what my husband and I were doing in the alley?"

"No." The question clearly knocked him off his game. "Absolutely not. I just want to know if he slipped you—gave you—something. Anything. It could be small or big or—"

Claire stood up. "You're disgusting."

"Wait." He stood up, too. "I'm not being an asshole."

Claire employed one of Grandma Ginny's quips. "If you have to say you're not doing something, then you probably are."

"I need you to sit down." Nolan wasn't playing around anymore. There was nothing flirty or silly about his tone. "Please."

Claire sat back down, her spine straight in the chair. She could almost feel the power shifting back to her side. Nolan was going to lay all of his cards on the table, and she knew what the first card would be before he even showed his hand.

He said, "He's alive."

Claire asked, "Frankenstein?"

"No." Nolan smoothed down his tie. "Paul. He's not dead."

Claire twisted her face into what she hoped was an expression of disbelief.

"Your husband is alive."

"I am sick of your bullshit, Agent Nolan." She forced some haughtiness into her voice. "I knew you were reprehensible, but I didn't know you were cruel."

"I'm sorry." He held out his hands as if none of this was his fault. "I'm being straight with you. Your husband is alive."

Claire tried to show surprise, but it felt too fake. She looked away. Coldness had always worked to her advantage. "I don't believe you."

"No more bullshit," Nolan said. "We helped him fake his death."

Claire kept her gaze turned away. She had to remind herself that she wasn't supposed to know the extent of Paul's crimes. "You're telling me that the FBI helped my husband fake his death over three million dollars?"

"No, what I told you before is the truth. The embezzlement charges were dropped. That was settled between your husband

and his partner. But we found some other things while we were investigating the initial complaint. Things that were a hell of a lot more curious than some missing cash." Nolan didn't elaborate. "We realized that Paul had information we needed. Volatile information. His life would've been in danger if it got out that he was talking, and we needed him alive to testify at the trial."

Claire's cheeks were wet. She was crying. Why was she crying?

Nolan said, "He was mixed up in some things—bad things—with some bad people."

She touched her fingers to her face. The tears were real. How could that be?

"He asked to go into witness protection." Nolan waited for her to say something. When she didn't, he continued, "My bosses felt like he might be planning to run, so we moved up the day it was supposed to happen. We picked Paul up on his way to see you, taped him up with the squibs—that's like a plastic balloon with fake blood—and told him it was going down in the alley."

Claire stared at her wet fingertips in disbelief. She couldn't be crying for Paul. She wasn't that stupid. Was she crying for herself? For Lydia? For her mother who would never come?

Claire looked up at Nolan. He'd stopped talking. She should say something now, ask a question, make a comment.

She said, "Did you know Paul was going to meet me? That I would see it?"

"That was part of the agreement." This time, Nolan looked away. "He wanted it to happen in front of you."

Claire's hands were shaking again. She longed for a time when nothing on her body shook with rage or fear or whatever mixture of hate and betrayal she was feeling right now. "The paramedics—"

"Were undercover agents. Detective Rayman was in on it, too."

"The man at the funeral home?"

"It's amazing what people will do for you when you threaten to sic the IRS on their financial records."

"They asked me if I wanted to see the body."

"Paul said that you wouldn't."

Claire clenched her fists. She hated that he knew her so well. "What if he was wrong and I asked to see it?"

"It's not like on TV. We show you the image on a screen. The body's usually in another room with a camera pointed on it."

Claire shook her head. She couldn't fathom the level of deceit at play. All to help Paul. All to give him a new life without Claire.

"I'm sorry." Nolan reached into his jacket. He handed Claire a handkerchief. She stared at the neatly folded white cloth. His initials were embroidered in the corner.

She said the things she had wanted to say to Paul. "I watched him die. He was in my arms. I felt his skin go cold."

"A lot can happen in your head when you're in a bad situation like that."

"You think I imagined those things? I saw blood pouring out of him."

"Yeah, we put two squibs on him. Probably could've gotten away with just one."

"But the knife—"

"The knife was fake, too. Retractable. The plastic on the squibs only takes a little bit of pressure."

"The killer." Claire thought of the snake tattoo on the man's neck. "He looked real."

"Yeah, well, he's a real bad guy. One of my confidential informants, a low-level drug dealer who'll do anything to stay out of jail."

Claire put her hand to her head where the Snake Man had nearly ripped open her scalp.

"Yeah, sorry. He got a little carried away. But Paul went off script, and my guy got pissed. That thing at the end where Paul turned into a Ninja Turtle, that was not in the program."

She patted the edge of the handkerchief underneath her eyes. She was still crying. This was crazy. She wasn't in mourning. Why was she crying?

Nolan said, "The ambulance brought Paul to the parking garage downstairs. He was supposed to have some information on him, but surprise, he didn't have it." Nolan was obviously still angry about this part. "He told me it was in his car. We waited until nightfall. Just me and him. Very low key. We were walking down the street talking about next steps—your husband's all about the big picture—then we get to his car and he's rummaging around inside the glove box and I'm thinking, What the fuck? Do I look like a fiddle that needs playing? and he says, 'Here it is,' and I'm thinking he's just being an asshole, because the guy's a real asshole, and he comes outta the car and I've got my hand palm up like some kinda stupid kid thinking he's gonna get some candy and boom, the asshole cold-cocks me."

Claire looked at the yellow-purple swirl around Nolan's eye.

"I know, right?" Nolan pointed to his eye. "Dropped me like a sack of hammers. I was seeing tweety birds and then I was seeing that asshole skipping up the street like a fuckin' schoolgirl. He turns around at the corner and gives me one'a these." Nolan gave two thumbs-ups as he flashed a fake grin. "By the time I manage to peel my sorry ass off the sidewalk, turn the corner myself, he's in the wind." Nolan looked both annoyed and impressed. "I gotta say, it's not the only reason, but it's part of the reason I really, really want to find your husband."

Claire shook her head. This still didn't make sense. Paul asking to be placed in witness protection? He would never hand someone else control over his life. They wouldn't let him be an architect in witness protection. They wouldn't let him draw attention to himself or his career accomplishments. There had to be something else he was trying to get out of the FBI. She was missing a detail or a stray word that would put together the puzzle.

Nolan said, "Look, I know I've been a dick, but I wasn't sure whether or not you knew about your husband's extracurricular activities."

"The embezzling?"

"No, not that. Like I said, the money case is closed as far as we're concerned. I mean the other stuff."

Claire stared in disbelief. How could anyone think she would know about the movies and sit idly by? But Nolan hadn't talked about the movies. He had only talked about Paul knowing some bad people who were mixed up in some bad things.

She asked, "What else was he involved in?"

"Maybe it's good you don't know," Nolan said. "I can tell he kept you in the dark. Think of it as a blessing. I see your hands shaking, the confusion in your eyes. But you need to understand that the man you loved, the guy you thought you were married to, is dead. He doesn't exist anymore. Hell, maybe he never existed."

He wasn't telling Claire anything she did not know. "Why do you think that?"

"We had a shrink take a look at him. Witsec—that's Witness Security with the Marshall's service—they always want a profile of anybody they put into the system. Kind of like a cheat sheet so they can predict behavior."

Claire doubted a stadium full of shrinks could predict her husband's behavior. "And?"

"He's a non-violent, borderline psychopath."

They were wrong about the non-violent part. "Borderline?" she asked. Why did she want to hold on to that word, to think that Paul wasn't a total psychopath because he was still capable of loving her?

Nolan said, "He's been living a parallel life. There's the guy who's married to this beautiful woman and has this successful career and lives in a million-dollar mansion and then there's the real guy who's not very nice."

"Not very nice," Claire echoed. What a massive fucking understatement. "You said they found him non-violent."

"They did, but I'm the dumbass who took a hit in the eye, so I'm bound to think otherwise."

"Why were you helping him if he's such a bad person?"

"Because the real Paul Scott knows the identity of a very bad man who needs to be in prison for a very long time." Nolan glanced back at the mirror. "That's all I can tell you. Straight up, no bullshit. That's how the system works. You do something bad, we let you go if you can point us toward somebody doing worse. And believe me, this is a hell of a lot worse."

Claire looked down at her hands. Clever Paul. He hadn't just fooled Claire with his movie-editing skills. He had fooled the Federal Bureau of Investigation. They had found the disgusting movies on his work computer and he had dangled the identity of the masked man in front of their faces in return for his freedom.

She asked Fred Nolan a question she knew she would eventually ask herself. "You said he wanted to go into witness protection. He was just going to leave me? Just like that?"

"I'm sorry, but trust me, you're better off."

"Did Adam Quinn know about the other stuff Paul was mixed up in? The name of the bad man?"

"No. We grilled the shit out of him. He had no idea." Nolan picked up on her distress. "I can see why you stepped out on your husband. He really didn't deserve you."

Claire agreed, but she had caught Nolan in a lie. "If Paul was planning to run, why would he slip me something before we went into the alley?"

"Back-up plan?" Nolan guessed. "There was no guarantee he'd be able to get the drop on me."

"I want to get this straight." Claire turned around all the cards he'd just laid out so he could see them from her perspective. "You caught Paul doing something bad, something worse than embezzling. He told you that he knows the identity of this boogeyman. You said he was taking you to his car to show you some kind of proof, so I'm going to guess that's a photograph or a document or something electronic, which means it has to be stored on a piece of paper or a disk or a flashdrive or something like that? Something he could fit in his glovebox? Something that could be slipped to me before we went into the alley?"

Nolan shrugged, but she could read him now and she could tell that he was getting nervous.

"You also said that Paul's life would've been in danger if it got out that he was sharing this information about the boogeyman."

"Right."

"So that gives you all the power. Paul needs you more than you need him. I mean, yes, you want to make a case, but Paul wants to live. You said his life was in danger. You're the only one with the resources to protect him. So why is he hiding from you?"

Nolan didn't glance back at the two-way mirror, but he might as well have.

Claire tried to look at the situation from a different angle—Paul's angle.

He'd escaped from Nolan, but he hadn't run off to an island country with no extradition treaty. Claire had no doubt that Paul had a secret stash of money waiting for him somewhere. He'd probably already ordered the Gladiator cabinets for the garage. He'd admitted to her over the phone that the timeline had been pushed up, but that didn't explain why he was sticking around. The FBI couldn't find him, but as Lydia would say, so what? Paul was a free man. He didn't need to go into witness protection. He didn't need the FBI. He didn't need anything.

Except for whatever was on the USB drive.

The door shook as someone pounded a fist against the flimsy wood. "Claire!"

Claire recognized the angry voice of her lawyer on the other side of the door. Wynn Wallace, the Colonel.

"Claire!" Wynn tried the knob. The door was locked. "Keep your Goddamn mouth shut!"

Nolan told Claire, "You can refuse his counsel."

"So you can keep lying to me?"

"Claire!" Wynn yelled.

Claire stood up. "You're asking the wrong question, Fred."

Wynn tried to shoulder open the door. There was a sharp crack.

Nolan said, "Tell me the right question."

"Paul didn't give you the information you wanted, therefore his life isn't in danger. He should be on a beach somewhere. Why is he sticking around?"

Nolan hacked like a dog with a string down its throat. "You've seen him?"

Claire opened the door.

Wynn Wallace stormed into the room. "What the hell is going on here?"

Nolan tried to stand up, but Wynn blocked him, demanding, "Who the hell are you? I want your ID number and your supervisor's name right now."

"Claire," Nolan tried, "don't go."

Claire edged her way out the door. She fumbled for Lydia's phone in her bra. The metal was hot. She pressed the button to power on the phone. She stared at the screen, silently begging for a message from Paul.

"Sweetpea?"

Claire spun around. She wondered if she was hallucinating. "Mom?"

Helen was near tears. "We've been halfway around the state. They wouldn't tell us where you were." She cupped her hand to Claire's face. "Are you all right?"

Claire was trembling again. She couldn't stop. It was like she was standing on the beach in the middle of a hurricane. Everything was slamming into her at once.

"Come with me." Helen took her hand. She pulled Claire down the hallway. They didn't wait for the elevator. Helen led her to the stairs. Claire looked down at the phone as she followed her mother. The signal was strong. No calls. No voicemail. There was one new text: a photograph that had been sent a few minutes after Claire turned off the phone. Lydia was still in the trunk. Her face didn't show any new cuts or bruises, but her eyes were closed. Why were her eyes closed?

Helen said, "Just a little bit farther."

Claire put the phone in her back pocket. Lydia had blinked when Paul took the picture. Or she was tired. She had closed her eyes against the sun. No, it was dark in the photo. Lydia was being contrary. She didn't want Paul to get his way. She was trying to make trouble because that's what Lydia did.

Claire's knees felt weak. She almost stumbled. Helen helped her down another two flights of stairs. Finally, she saw the sign for the lobby. Instead of going through the marked door, Helen took her through the emergency exit.

The sunlight was faint, but Claire still shielded her eyes with her hand. She looked around. They were standing on the corner of Peachtree and Alexander. Traffic was starting to fill the streets.

She asked Helen, "What time is it?"

"Five thirty in the morning."

Claire leaned back against the wall. She had been inside the building for almost twelve hours. What could Paul do to Lydia in twelve hours?

"Claire?"

She waited for her mother to lay into her, to demand an explanation for why she had to find a lawyer and rescue her daughter from the FBI.

Instead, Helen stroked Claire's cheek and asked, "What can I do to help?"

Claire was speechless with gratitude. She felt like decades had passed since someone had offered her something as simple and genuine as help.

"Sweetheart," Helen said, "nothing is so bad that it can't be fixed."

She was so wrong, but Claire forced herself to nod.

Helen stroked back her hair. "I'll take you home, okay? I'll make you some soup and tuck you into bed and you can get some sleep and we can talk this out. Or not. It's up to you, sweetheart. Whatever you need me to do, I'm here."

Claire felt herself start to crack. She turned away from her mother's touch, because the only other option was to fall into her arms and tell her everything.

"Sweetpea?" Helen rubbed her back. "Tell me what I can do."

Claire opened her mouth to tell her mother there was nothing that could be done, but she stopped, because she saw someone familiar standing fifty feet away.

Detective Harvey Falke. She recognized him from the Dunwoody police station. Captain Mayhew had called him in to help connect the massive hard drive to his computer so that he could tell Claire that the movies Paul had been watching were fake.

Harvey was leaning against a railing. His suit jacket was

open, showing his gun. He wasn't being shy about it. He was looking directly at Claire. His lips smiled under his bushy mustache.

"Claire?" Helen sounded even more concerned. She had seen the man, too. "Who is—"

"The Tesla is parked downstairs on the third level." She took the keyfob out of her pocket. "I need you to move it to the Marriott Marquis for me, okay? Visitors' parking. Leave the ticket on the seat and hide the keyfob behind the parking pay machine in the lobby."

Miraculously, Helen still did not demand an explanation. "Is there anything else you need?"

"No."

She squeezed Claire's hand before leaving.

Claire waited until her mother disappeared into the FBI building. She walked down the street. She forced herself not to look over her shoulder as she reached the corner. She crossed against the light, dodging around a yellow taxi. She took West Peachtree toward downtown. She finally looked behind her.

Harvey was thirty yards away. His arms were bent at the elbows as he tried to catch up with her. His jacket billowed out. His gun was dark and menacing against his white dress shirt.

Claire picked up the pace. She regulated her breathing. She tried to keep her heart rate under control. She looked behind her.

Harvey was twenty yards away.

Lydia's phone started ringing. Claire pulled it from her back pocket as she started to jog. She looked at the screen. UNKNOWN NUMBER.

Paul said, "Did you enjoy your time at the FBI?"

"Is Lydia okay?"

"I'm not sure."

Claire crossed the street again. A car screeched to a stop inches away from her hip. The driver yelled out his open window. She asked Paul, "Do you want that USB drive or not?"

"Lydia is fine. What did you tell the FBI?"

"Nothing. That's why they kept me so long." Claire looked over her shoulder. Harvey was closer, maybe fifteen yards away. "A cop is following me. One of Mayhew's guys."

"Get rid of him."

Claire ended the call. She jogged across the street. She knew this area of town because she had worked in the Flatiron Building when they first moved to Atlanta. Claire had hated the job. She took long walks during lunch and came back late and flirted with her boss so he would let her leave early.

She started jogging again. Harvey was quickly closing the gap between them. He was a big man with a long stride. He was going to catch up with her soon.

Claire turned the corner onto Spring Street. She lunged into a full run. She was at the next corner by the time Harvey rounded the building. Claire went halfway down the side street. She checked over her shoulder. Harvey hadn't made the corner yet. She frantically looked for an escape route. The Southern Company's side entrance was the closest option. There were six glass doors and a large revolving door at the far end. She tried the first door, but it was locked. She tried the next one, then the next one. She looked back for Harvey. Still not there, but he would be running now, catching up fast. She tried another door, then wanted to kick herself for not going to the revolving door first. Claire ran full-bore into the open mouth of the door. She pushed so hard against the glass partition that she heard the motor grind.

The lobby was cordoned off by glass turnstiles. The sleepy guard behind the counter was smiling. He had probably watched her try each door.

"I'm sorry." Claire pitched up her voice a few octaves so she sounded helpless. "I know it's awful of me to ask, but can I use your restroom?"

The guard smiled. "Anything for a pretty lady." He reached under the desk and opened one of the turnstiles. "Go straight through to the main lobby on West Peachtree. The bathrooms are on the right."

"Thank you so much." Claire walked briskly through the partition. She looked behind her. Harvey raced past the side-entrance doors.

She had two seconds of relief before he came back.

Claire darted into an elevator alcove. She kept her head turned so she could see him. Harvey started toward the building. He pulled on one of the locked doors. He was clearly winded. His breath fogged the glass. He wiped it away with his jacket sleeve. He cupped his hands to his eyes and peered into the lobby.

The guard mumbled something under his breath.

Claire pressed her back against the elevator doors.

Harvey pushed away from the glass. Instead of leaving, he moved toward the revolving door. Claire tensed herself. She would tell the guard that Harvey was stalking her. Then Harvey would flash his badge. She could run toward the front entrance, dart back into the street.

Or she could stay here.

Harvey hadn't pushed through the revolving door. He was still standing outside. His head was turned to the right. Something on West Peachtree had caught his attention.

Claire held her breath until he ran off toward whatever had distracted him.

She peeled herself away from the alcove. She went back out the glass turnstile. She told the guard, "Thank you."

He tipped his hat. "You have a blessed day."

Claire pushed open the door. She knew better than to think she was safe. She ran back toward Spring Street. She hooked a left onto Williams. Her feet pounded against the cracked sidewalk. There was a mist of rain in the air. Claire scanned the area behind her as she kept running. She tried to orient herself. Staying on the street was not on option. There had to be somewhere to hide, but it was too early for any of the cafes to be open.

Lydia's phone rang. Claire didn't slow as she answered, "What?"

Paul said, "Take a left. Go to the Hyatt Regency."

Claire kept the line open. She took the left. She saw the Hyatt in the distance. Her knees hurt. Her legs were screaming. She was used to running on the treadmill, not up and down hills and over cracks in the concrete. Sweat dripped from her scalp and down her back. The waist of her jeans was starting to chafe. She gripped the phone in her hand as she ran. How was Paul tracking her? Was Mayhew tag-teaming Harvey? Were they trying to funnel her into a location where they could grab her?

The bellhop outside the Hyatt opened the door when he saw

Claire round the drive. If he thought it was odd that a grown woman dressed in jeans and a button-down shirt had gone for a run at six in the morning, he didn't say.

Inside the building, Claire slowed her pace. She followed the signs to the women's restroom. She pushed open the door. She checked the stalls to make sure they were empty.

Claire locked the last stall door. She sat down on the toilet. She was panting for breaths when she said, "Let me speak to Lydia."

"I can let you hear her scream."

Claire put her hand to her mouth. What had he done? Twelve hours. He could have Lydia in Key West or New Orleans or Richmond by now. He could be torturing her and beating her and—

Claire couldn't let herself think of the "and."

Paul asked, "Still there?"

She fought back the overwhelming agony that came from knowing exactly what her husband was capable of. "You said you weren't going to hurt her."

"You said you were going to call me back."

"I will drive over that fucking USB drive with a Mack truck."

Paul had to know that Claire would do it. She had never been averse to burning bridges she was still trying to cross.

He asked, "Where is it?"

Claire tried to think of an area she was familiar with but Paul was not. "It's at the Wells Fargo on Central Avenue."

"What?" He sounded concerned. "That's a very dangerous area, Claire."

"Are you really worrying about my safety?"

"You need to be careful," he warned. "Where is the bank exactly?"

"Near the main post office." Claire had driven to the post office several times to drop off mailers for the Humane Society. "I'll go get it right now. We can meet somewhere and—"

"It's almost six in the morning. The bank won't be open until nine."

Claire waited.

"You can't leave now. You'll get carjacked if you park the Tesla on Central for that long." She could practically hear the wheels turning in his head. "Stay in the hotel. At eight thirty, drive down to Hapeville. That should get you there right when the bank is opening."

"Okay."

"Traffic will be bad coming back. Get on seventy-five and wait to hear from me."

Claire didn't ask how he would know where she was because she was beginning to think Paul knew everything. "Nolan told me what you did."

"Is that right?"

Claire didn't elaborate, but they both knew Nolan had only seen what Paul wanted him to see. "He said you wanted to be in witness protection."

"That wasn't going to happen."

"He said you wanted me to watch you die."

Paul was quiet for a moment. "It had to seem real. I was going to come back for you. You know that."

Claire didn't respond.

Paul said, "I'm going to take care of this. You know I always do."

Claire took a stuttered breath. She couldn't stand the soft, reassuring tone of his voice. There was still an infinitesimal part of her that wanted her husband to somehow make it all better.

But Fred Nolan was right. The Paul she had known was dead. This stranger on the other end of the phone was an imposter. Or maybe he was the real Paul Scott, and her husband, her friend, her lover, had been the lie. It was only when he put on that black leather mask that the real Paul showed his face.

She said, "I want to speak to my sister."

"In a minute," he promised. "The battery on your phone is probably getting low. Did you bring the charger from the house?"

Claire checked the screen. "It's at thirty percent."

Paul said, "Go buy a charger. And you need to juice up the Tesla. There's a charging station at Peachtree Center. I down-loaded the app for you so just—"

"Let me talk to Lydia."

"Are you sure you want to do that?"

"Put my sister on the Goddamn phone."

There was a rustling sound, then the tinny echo of a speakerphone.

"Wake up." Paul said. "Your sister wants to talk to you."

Claire gritted her teeth. He sounded like he was speaking to a child. "Lydia?" she tried. "Lydia?"

Lydia didn't answer.

"Please say something, Liddie. Please."

"Claire." Her voice was so flat, so lifeless, that Claire felt like a hand had reached inside her chest and ripped out her heart.

"Liddie," Claire said, "please, just hold on. I'm doing everything I can."

Lydia mumbled, "It's too late."

"It's not too late. I'm going to give Paul the USB drive, and he's going to let you go." Claire was lying. They all knew that she was lying. She started crying so hard that she had to brace herself against the wall. "Hold on a little while longer. I'm not going to abandon you. I promised you—never again."

"I forgive you, Claire."

"Don't say that now." Claire bent at the waist. Tears fell onto the floor. "Tell me when you see me, okay? Tell me when this is over."

"I forgive you for everything."

"Pepper, please. I'm going to make this right. I'm going to make everything all right."

"It doesn't matter," Lydia told her. "I'm already dead."

EIGHTEEN

Paul was smiling when he put the phone down on the table beside the black hood. Lydia didn't look at the phone, which she could not reach, but at the soaked black hood next to it, which she knew would eventually be wrapped around her head again. The spray bottle was empty for the third time. Paul was drinking filtered water so he could fill it back up again.

When he was ready, he would make her watch him fill up the bottle, then he would put the hood back over her head, then he would start spraying. Seconds before she passed out, he would shock her with the cattle prod or whip her with the leather belt or punch her or kick her until she gasped for breath.

And then he would start the process all over again.

He said, "She sounds good, right? Claire?"

Lydia looked away from the hood. There was a computer on a workbench like the one Paul had in his garage. Metal storage

427

shelves. Old computers. She had cataloged everything in her head because she had been here almost thirteen hours—Paul updated her with the time every half-hour—and the only thing that was keeping her from going insane was reciting the inventory like a mantra while he tried to drown her in his piss.

Apple Macintosh, dot-matrix printer, five-inch floppy disks, duping machine, disk burner.

"I bet you want to know what's on that USB drive, Lydia. I like to call it my 'get out of jail free' card."

Apple Macintosh, dot-matrix printer, five-inch floppy disks, duping machine, disk burner.

"Fred Nolan wants it. Mayhew. Johnny. Lots of other people want it, too. What a surprise. Paul Scott has something that everybody else wants." He paused. "What do you want from me, Liddie?"

Apple Macintosh, dot-matrix printer, five-inch floppy disks, duping machine, disk burner.

"Do you want some Percocet?"

The question pulled her out of her stupor. She could almost taste the bitter pill in her mouth.

He shook the prescription bottle in front of her face. "I found it in your purse. I guess you stole it from Claire." He sat down in the chair across from her. He rested the bottle on his knee. "You were always stealing from her."

Lydia stared down at the bottle. This would be it. She had told Claire that she was already dead, but there was still an ounce of life left inside of her. If she gave in to her desire, if she took the Percocet, that would truly be the end.

"This is interesting." Paul crossed his arms. "I've listened to you beg and plead and squeal like a stuck pig, and this is the line you're drawing? No Percocet?"

Lydia tried to summon the euphoria the pills would bring. She'd read somewhere that if you thought about a food long enough, you wouldn't want it anymore. You would trick yourself into thinking you'd already eaten it. This had never worked with donuts or hamburgers or French fries or— *Apple Macintosh, dot-matrix printer, five-inch floppy disks, duping machine, disk burner.*

"I could force the pills down your throat, but what would be the fun in that?" He stretched her legs wider apart with his knees. "I could put them somewhere else. Somewhere you could more easily absorb them into your system." He took a deep breath and sighed it out. "What would that be like, I wonder? Would it be worth fucking you if I could use my cock to shove all of these pills up your fat ass?"

Lydia's mind started to go blank. This was how it happened. Paul would push her and she would get too scared or too broken and she would just shut down.

His hand went to her thigh. His fingers drilled toward the bone. "Don't you want the pain to go away?"

Lydia was too exhausted to cry out. She wanted him to get it over with—the punch, the jab, the slap, the electric cattle prod, the branding iron, the machete. She had seen what the masked man had done with the tools of his trade. She had seen what Paul's father had done to Julia. She had experienced firsthand the type of torture Paul was capable of and she was certain that his role in the movies had been far from passive.

He was enjoying this. No matter what derogatory things he'd said, Paul was aroused by Lydia's pain. She could feel the hard shaft of his prick when he leaned in close to gorge himself on her terror.

Lydia just prayed that she would be dead by the time he finally got around to raping her.

"New strategy." Paul snatched the pill bottle off his leg. He placed it on the rolling table where he was keeping his tools. "I think you're going to like this."

Apple Macintosh, dot-matrix printer, five-inch floppy disks, duping machine, disk burner.

He stood in front of the metal shelves beside the computer. Her anxiety ramped back up, not because he was going to do something terrible and new but because he was going to mess up the order of the items on the shelves.

Apple Macintosh, dot-matrix printer, five-inch floppy disks, duping machine, disk burner.

They had to stay that way—in that exact order. No one could touch them.

Paul dragged over a step stool.

Lydia nearly cried with relief. They were safe. He was reaching up to the top shelf, past the equipment, past the floppy disks. He pulled down a stack of notebooks. He showed them to Lydia. Her relief dissipated.

Her father's notebooks.

Paul said, "Your parents are quite the prolific letter-writers." He sat down across from Lydia again. The notebooks were in his lap. A stack of letters she hadn't noticed before were on top. He held up an envelope for Lydia to see.

Helen's handwriting—precise and neat and so sorrowfully familiar.

"Poor, lonely Lydia. Your mother wrote you tons of letters over the years. Did you know that?" He shook his head. "Of course you didn't know that. I told Helen I tried to get them to you, but you were homeless and living on the streets or you were in rehab but you checked yourself out before I could get to you." He tossed the letters on the floor. "I actually felt bad every time Helen asked me if I'd heard back from you, because of course I had to tell her that you were still a fat, worthless junkie sucking cock for Oxy."

His words had the opposite effect. Helen had written to her. There were dozens of letters in the pile. Her mother still cared. She hadn't given up.

"Helen would've been a great grandmother to Dee."

Dee. Lydia couldn't even summon her face. She had lost all images of her daughter the second time Paul had electrocuted her with the cattle prod.

"I wonder if she'll check out when Dee goes missing the same way she did after Julia was gone." He looked up. "You wouldn't remember this, but Claire was all alone after Julia."

Lydia remembered it. She had been there.

"Every night, poor little Claire was all by herself in that big house on Boulevard listening to your worthless-piece-of-shit mother cry herself to sleep. No one cared if Claire cried herself to sleep, did they? You were too busy stuffing every hole in your body. That's why she fell so hard for me, Liddie. Claire fell for me because none of you were there to keep her from falling."

Apple Macintosh, dot-matrix printer, five-inch floppy disks, duping machine, disk burner.

"These." Paul held up one of her father's notebooks. "Your

dad didn't care about Claire either. All of his letters were to Julia. Claire read most of them, at least the ones he wrote before she went to college. Think about how that made her feel. Her mother was a borderline alcoholic who couldn't get out of bed. Her father spent hours writing to his dead daughter when his living daughter was standing right in front of him."

Lydia shook her head. It hadn't been like that—at least not entirely. Helen had eventually pulled herself out of her depression. Sam had tried so hard with Claire. He had taken her shopping and to see movies and to visit museums.

"No wonder she didn't want to go see him after he had the stroke." Paul thumbed through the pages. "I made her go. I told her that she would regret it if she didn't. And she listened to me, because she always listens to me. But the funny thing is, I really liked your dad. He reminded me of my own father."

Lydia felt her jaw ratchet down so she wouldn't scream at him.

"You never know with parents, do you? They can be selfish bastards. For instance, I thought Dad and I were close, but he took Julia without me." Paul looked up from the notebooks. He obviously liked what he saw in Lydia's surprised expression. "I gotta say, I was upset about that. I got home from Spring Break and there your big sister was in the barn. He hadn't left much of her for me to enjoy."

Lydia closed her eyes. *Apple Macintosh.* What came next? She couldn't look at the shelves. She had to think of it on her own. *Apple Macintosh.*

He said, "Sam was smart. I mean, a lot smarter than any of us gave him credit for. He would've never found Julia's body, I'm the only person left alive who knows where she is, but your father was on to me. He knew about my dad. He knew that I was somehow involved. Did you know that?"

Lydia had become anesthetized to surprises.

"Sam asked me over to his apartment. He thought he was going to trick me, but I did some reconnaissance before we were supposed to meet." He held up her father's notebooks like a trophy. "My advice: If you're trying to trick somebody, don't leave your playbook lying around."

Lydia gripped the arms of the chair. "Shut the fuck up."

Paul smiled. "There's my little fighter."

"What did you do to my father?"

"I think you know what I did." Paul shuffled through the stack of notebooks. He checked the front pages. He was looking for something. "I arrived at his apartment at the requested hour. I poured us some drinks so we could talk like men. Your father liked doing that, didn't he? Making sure we knew who the men were and who were the boys."

Lydia could hear her father's voice in his words.

"Sam drank his vodka. He called himself a social drinker, but we know he drank himself to sleep at night, don't we? Just like Helen did while poor Claire was sitting alone in her room wondering why no one in her family noticed that she was still alive."

Lydia swallowed. She tasted the sour burn of his piss.

"I guess the vodka masked the sleeping pills I ground up in his drink."

Lydia wanted to close her eyes. She wanted to block him out. But she couldn't.

"I watched his head dip." Paul imitated her father falling into a stupor. "I tied him up with some sheets that I brought with me. They were torn into long strips. His hands were so limp when I tied him up that I was worried he'd died before the fun could start."

Lydia felt every sense lock onto him.

Paul leaned back in the chair with his legs spread wide. Lydia forced herself not to look down because she knew exactly what he wanted her to see. "If you use strips of bed sheets to tie somebody up, then the marks don't show when the coroner gets them. If you're careful, I mean, because of course you have to fold the sheets properly, which I did because I had time with your father. I want you to hear that, Liddie: I had lots and lots of time with your father."

Lydia's mind had gone haywire. It was too much. She couldn't take in what he was saying.

"When Sam woke up, we watched the tape together. You know the tape I'm talking about? The tape with Julia?" Paul rubbed the sides of his face. His beard was growing in. "I wanted us to watch all of the tapes together, but I was worried the neighbors would hear his screams." Paul added, "Not that Sam didn't scream a lot at night anyway, but still."

Lydia listened to the steady in and out of her own breathing. She rearranged his words in her head until they fell into digestible sentences. Paul had drugged her father. He had made her father watch his oldest daughter being brutally murdered.

"At the end, I debated whether or not to tell Sam where Dad and I had dumped Julia's body. What's the harm, right? We both knew he was going to die." Paul shrugged. "Maybe I should've told him. It's one of those questions you still ask yourself years later. I mean, Sam was so tortured, right? All he wanted to know was where she was, and I knew, but I just couldn't bring myself to tell him."

Lydia knew that she should rage against him. She should try to kill him. But she couldn't move. Her lungs were wet with urine. Her stomach was filled. Her body was seized by pain. There were welts on her arms where he'd electrocuted her. The cut on her forehead had been opened. Her split lip had been torn in two. Her ribs were so bruised that she felt like the bones had turned into knives.

He said, "I used Nembutal. You know what that is, right? They use it to put animals out of their misery. And he *was* miserable, especially after he watched the tape." Paul had found the notebook he was looking for. "Here you go." He held up the page so Lydia could see. The bottom half was torn away. "Look familiar?"

Her father's suicide note had been written on a torn off-sheet of notebook paper. Lydia could still see his shaky words in her head:

To all of my beautiful girls—I love you with every piece of my heart. Daddy

Paul said, "I think I chose a good line. Don't you?" He put the notebook back in his lap. "I chose it for Claire, really, because I thought that the line was particularly true about her. All his beautiful girls. You were never really beautiful, Lydia. And Julia—I told you I still visit her sometimes. She's no longer beautiful. It's been sad watching her decay over the years. The last time I checked in on her, she was just rotten bones with long strands of dirty blonde hair and those stupid bracelets she used to wear on her wrist. You remember those?"

Bangles. Julia had worn bangles on her left wrist and a big, black bow in her hair and she'd stolen Lydia's saddle oxfords to complete the outfit because she'd said they looked better on her anyway.

Suddenly, Lydia had too much saliva in her mouth. She tried to swallow. Her throat spasmed. She coughed.

"Don't you want to know where Julia is?" Paul asked. "It's really the one thing that broke you all apart. Not her disappearance, not her probable death, but the never knowing. Where is Julia? Where is my sister? Where is my daughter? The not-knowing completely destroyed every single one of you. Even Grandma Ginny, though the old bitch likes to act like the past is past."

Lydia felt herself start to slip back into that in-between space. There was no use listening to him anymore. She already knew everything she needed to know. Dee and Rick loved her. Helen had not given up. Lydia had forgiven Claire. Two days ago, she would've panicked if someone had told her that she had a finite amount of time to settle all of her affairs, but when she got down to it, her family was really the only thing that mattered.

"I visit Julia sometimes." Paul was studying her face to gauge his words. "If you had a dying wish, wouldn't it be to know where Julia is?"

Apple Macintosh, dot-matrix printer, five-inch floppy disks, duping machine, disk burner.

"I'm going to read you some selections from your father's journals, and then I'm going to waterboard you again in . . ." He looked at his watch. "Twenty-two minutes. All right?"

Apple Macintosh, dot-matrix printer, five-inch floppy disks, duping machine, disk burner.

Paul rested the notebook in his lap on top of the others. He started reading aloud, "'I remember the first time your mother and I walked you through the snow. We wrapped you up like a precious gift. The scarf was wound so many times around your head that all we could see was your little pink nose.'"

His voice. Paul had known her father. He had spent hours with him—even up to his last hours—and he knew how to read Sam's words with the same soft cadence that her father had always used.

"'We were taking you to see your Grandma Ginny. Your mother, of course, was not pleased with this particular errand.'"

"Yes," Lydia said.

Paul looked up from the page. "Yes what?"

"Give me the Percocet."

"Sure." Paul dropped the notebooks on the floor. He unscrewed the top from the spray bottle. "But first you have to earn it."

NINETEEN

Claire sat on the toilet with her elbows on her knees and her head in her hands. She had cried herself out. There was nothing left inside of her. Even her heart labored to beat in her chest. The slow thumps were almost painful. Every time she felt the pulse, her brain silently said the word: Lydia.

Lydia.

Lydia.

Her sister had given up. Claire could hear it in Lydia's voice, which had no tone except the tone of complete and utter surrender. What terrible thing had Paul done that made Lydia believe that she was already dead?

Thinking about the answer to that question would only drive Claire deeper into despair.

She rested her head against the cold wall. Her eyes closed. She was punch-drunk with exhaustion. The God's honest truth was that Claire desperately wanted to give up, too. She felt the desire with every fiber of her being. Her mouth was dry. Her vision was blurred. There was a high-pitched tone ringing in both of her ears. Had she slept inside the interrogation room? Could she count being knocked out by Paul as resting?

All that Claire knew was that she had been awake for almost twenty-four hours. The last time she'd eaten was when Lydia made her egg bread yesterday morning. She had two and a half hours before she was supposed to go to the bank in Hapeville—for what? Adam had the USB drive. He was the one Claire should be talking to. The Quinn + Scott offices were ten blocks away. Adam would be there in a few hours for his presentation. Claire should be waiting in front of the office doors, not sitting on the toilet in the Hyatt. If her Hapeville lie had been designed to buy more time, then she'd bought herself another useless four or five hours.

She still didn't know what she was going to do. Her mind was refusing to run around in the familiar circles. Mayhew. Nolan. The Congressman. The gun.

What the hell was she going to do with the gun? All the certainty from before had drained away. Claire could not rekindle the steely resolve she'd felt when she first held Lydia's revolver. Could she really shoot Paul? A better question might be could she shoot him and actually hit him. She wasn't Annie Oakley. She would have to be close enough to hit him, but not so close that Paul could take the gun away.

And she would have to throw it at his head because she didn't have any fucking bullets.

The bathroom door opened. Instinctively, Claire pulled up her feet and rested her heels on the toilet bowl. She heard the light tread of soft-soled shoes on the porcelain floor tiles. Harvey? Claire assumed such a large man would have a more lumbering tread. A stall door was pushed open, then another, then another, until Claire's locked door rattled.

Claire recognized the shoes. Brown Easy Spirit loafers for walking through the stacks. Light tan pants that wouldn't show dust from old magazines and paperbacks.

"Mom." Claire unlocked the door. "What are you doing here? How did you find me?"

"I looped back around the building after I got rid of your tail."

"You what?"

"I saw that man running after you. I went around the other side of the building and clapped my hands to get his attention and—" Helen was holding on to the door. Her face was flushed. She was breathless. "They let me cut through the main lobby. The guard at the side entrance told me you'd just left. You were running so fast I almost lost you, but then the bellman outside said you were here."

Claire stared in open disbelief. Helen was wearing a colorful blue Chico's blouse with a chunky necklace. She should be hosting a book signing, not running through the streets of downtown Atlanta drawing off a tail.

Helen asked, "Do you still want me to move your car?"

Claire shook her head, but only because she didn't know what she wanted Helen to do.

"I know Paul was accused of stealing money." Helen paused, as if she expected Claire to protest. "That Agent Nolan was at the house yesterday afternoon, and that police captain, Jacob Mayhew, dropped by almost as soon as he left."

"He did it," Claire said, and it felt good to tell her mother even the tiniest bit of truth. "Paul stole three million dollars from the company."

Helen seemed appalled. Three million dollars was a hell of a lot of money to her mother. "You'll pay it back. You'll move in with me. You can get a job teaching art at the school."

Claire laughed, because she made it sound so simple.

Helen pressed together her lips. She obviously wanted to know what was going on, but she only said, "Do you want me to leave you alone? Do you need my help? Tell me what to do."

"I don't know," Claire admitted, another slice of truth. "I have to leave for Hapeville in two hours."

Helen didn't ask why. She simply said, "All right. What else?"

"I need to charge the Tesla. I need to get an iPhone charger."

"I have one in my purse." Helen unzipped her purse, which was brown leather with flowers embroidered around the strap. She told Claire, "You look awful. When was the last time you had something to eat?"

Lydia had asked her that same thing two nights ago. Claire had let her sister take care of her and now she was Paul's captive. His bargaining chip. His victim.

"Sweetheart?" Helen had the charger in her hand. "Let's go to the lobby and get something to eat."

Claire let her mother lead her out of the bathroom the same way she had led her out of the FBI interrogation room. Helen took her deep into the hotel lobby. There were several groupings of large couches and overstuffed chairs. Claire practically fell into the closest one.

Helen said, "Stay here. I'll go to the cafe and get something."

Claire leaned back her head. She had to get rid of Helen. The only reason Lydia was in trouble was because Claire had involved her in Paul's madness. She would not lead her mother down that same path. She had to think of something that would get them all out of this. Paul would want to meet somewhere isolated. Claire should have an alternative space to suggest. Somewhere open with a lot of people around. A mall. Claire knew all of the high-end stores inside Phipps Plaza. She imagined herself walking through Saks with dresses folded over her arm. She would have to try them on because some of the brands were running smaller than usual, or maybe Claire was running larger since she'd stopped playing tennis four hours a day. She wanted to look at the new Prada bags, but the display was too close to the perfume counter and her allergies were acting up.

"Honey?"

Claire looked up. The light had changed. So had the scenery. Helen was sitting on the couch beside her. She had a paperback in her hand. She was using her thumb to mark her place.

She told Claire, "I let you sleep for an hour and a half."

"What?" Claire sat up, panicked. She scanned the lobby. There were more people now. The front desk was fully staffed. Suitcases were being rolled across the carpet. She checked the faces. No Jacob Mayhew. No Harvey Falke.

"You said you had two hours." Helen put the book in her purse. "I charged your iPhone. The Tesla is plugged in one street over on Peachtree Center Avenue. Your purse is right beside you. I put the key in the zippered pocket. There's some clean underwear in there, too." She indicated the coffee table. "The food is still warm. You should eat. It'll make you feel better."

Claire looked down at the table. Her mother had bought her a large cup of coffee and a chicken biscuit.

"Go ahead. You have time."

Her mother was right. She needed to get something of caloric value in her system. The coffee she could handle. Claire wasn't sure about the food. She took the plastic lid off the cup. Helen had poured in enough milk to turn the liquid white, just the way Claire liked it.

Helen opened a napkin and put it on Claire's lap. She said, "You know that revolver takes .38 Special ammunition, right?"

Claire sipped the coffee. Her mother had been inside the Tesla. She would've seen the weapon in the door pocket.

"It's in your purse. It didn't seem safe to leave a gun in your car while it's parked on the street. I couldn't find a place downtown or I would've bought ammunition for you."

Claire put down the cup. She unwrapped the biscuit to give her hands something to do. She expected the smell to turn her stomach, but she realized that she was hungry. She took a large bite.

Helen said, "Huckleberry called me. I know you know about the tape."

Claire swallowed. Her throat still hurt from screaming in the back yard of the Fuller house. "You lied to me about Julia."

"I protected you. There's a difference."

"I had a right to know."

"You are my child. I am your mother." Helen sounded resolute. "I won't apologize for doing my job."

Claire bit back a sharp comment about how refreshing it was to hear that Helen was back on the job.

Helen asked, "Did Lydia show you the tape?"

"No." She wasn't going to let her sister take the blame yet again. "I found it on the Internet. I showed it to her." Lydia's phone. Helen had seen the unfamiliar number on her caller ID. "I took her phone. Mine was stolen during the robbery, and I needed one, so I took hers."

Helen didn't press for a better explanation, likely because she had investigated countless thefts when the girls were growing up. She only asked, "Are you all right?"

"I feel better. Thank you." She looked over her mother's shoulder because she couldn't bring herself to look her in the eye. Claire couldn't tell Helen about Lydia, but she could tell her about Dee. Her mother was a grandmother. She had a beautiful, accomplished grandchild who was hopefully being hidden somewhere that Paul would never find her.

Which meant that, right now, Claire couldn't let Helen find her, either.

Helen said, "Earlier, when Wynn and I were looking for you, I remembered something your father told me." She gripped her purse in her lap. "He said that children always have different parents, even in the same family."

Family. Helen had more than she knew about. Claire felt the weight of her own guilt pressing down on her chest.

Helen continued, "When Julia was little and it was just the three of us, I think I was a pretty damn good mother." She laughed, because the memory obviously made her happy. "And then Pepper came along and she was such a handful, but I loved every frustrating, challenging minute of it because she was so opinionated and strong-willed, and she knocked against Julia all the time."

Claire nodded. She could remember the screaming arguments between her older sisters. They were too much alike to get along for more than a few hours at a time.

"And then there was you." Helen smiled sweetly. "You were so easy compared to your sisters. You were quiet and sweet-natured and your father and I used to sit up at night and talk about how different you were. 'Are you sure they didn't mix up the babies at the hospital?' he would say. 'Maybe we should go down to the county jail and see if our real child has been arrested for being a public nuisance?'"

Claire smiled, because this sounded just like something her father would say.

"You watched everything. You noticed everything." Helen shook her head. "I would see you sitting in your highchair, and your eyes would follow my every move. You were so curious about the world, and so keyed into everybody else—the tempers and the passions and the overwhelming personalities—that I was afraid you'd get lost. That's why I took you on our little outings. Do you remember?"

Claire had forgotten, but she remembered now. Her mother had taken her to art museums in Atlanta and to puppet shows and even participated in an ill-fated pottery class.

Just the two of them. No Pepper to ruin Claire's perfectly formed clay bowl. No Julia to spoil the puppet show by commenting on the patriarchal structure of Punch and Judy.

Helen continued, "I was a really good mother to you for thirteen years, and then I was a really bad one for about five, and I feel like I've spent every day since then trying to find my way back to that place where you see me as a good mother again."

Claire had been either seeking or avoiding this conversation with Helen for the last twenty years, but she knew if they had it now, she would fall apart.

So she asked, "What did you think of Paul?"

Helen twisted the ring on her finger. Paul had been wrong. Claire twisted her own ring because she had seen her mother do it so many times.

She said, "You won't hurt my feelings. I want to know the truth."

Helen didn't hold back. "I told your father that Paul was like a hermit crab. They're scavengers. They don't have the ability to make their own shells, so they cast around until they find abandoned shells, and then they move in."

Claire knew better than anyone that her mother was right. Paul had moved into her shell, the one that had been abandoned by her grief-stricken family.

She told Helen, "I'm supposed to drive to Hapeville in half an hour. To a bank up from the Dwarf House. It needs to seem like I'm there, but I have to be somewhere else."

"What bank?"

"Wells Fargo." Claire took another bite of biscuit. She could tell her mother was desperate for more information. "They're tracking me. I can't go to Hapeville, and I can't let them know where I'm really going."

"Then give me your phone and I'll drive to Hapeville. I should probably take the Tesla. They might be tracking that, too."

The phone. How could Claire have been so stupid? Paul had known she was in the FBI building. He had known her exact location on the street. He had told her to take a left toward the hotel. He was using the Find My iPhone app because he knew that Claire would not go anywhere without her only connection to Lydia.

She told her mother, "I need to be able to answer the phone if it rings. It has to be my voice."

"Can't you use call forwarding?" Helen jabbed her thumb toward the hotel gift shop. "They have a display for pre-paid phones. We can buy you one of those, or I can give you my phone."

Claire was dumbfounded. In less than a minute, Helen had solved one of her biggest problems.

"Here." Helen pulled her car keys out of her purse along with a light blue parking ticket. "You hold on to this. I'll go check on a phone."

Claire took the keys. Ever the cataloger, her mother had written down the floor level and parking space number on the back of the ticket.

She watched Helen talking to the clerk in the store. The man was showing her various models of phones. Claire started to ask herself who this confident and efficient person was, but she knew this person. This was the Helen Carroll she had known before Julia was taken.

Or maybe it was the Helen Carroll who'd come back to Claire after mourning the loss of Julia, because Helen had called Wynn Wallace the second she got off the phone with Claire. She had been searching for Claire all night. She had rescued her from Fred Nolan. She had distracted Harvey Falke so that Claire could get away. And now she was sitting in the lobby of a hotel doing everything possible to offer her aid.

Claire longed to enlist her mother's help in solving her other problems, but she was incapable of coming up with a believable story that didn't reveal the truth, and she knew there was a limit to Helen's restrained curiosity. She couldn't believe how resourceful her mother had already been. She had even looked for ammunition for the gun. Paul would be shocked.

Claire caught herself a moment too late. She wasn't going to tell Paul this story when he got home from work tonight. They would never share a moment like that ever again.

"That was easy." Helen had already taken the phone out of the box. "The battery has a half-charge, but I got a car charger and the nice man behind the counter had a coupon, so you got an extra thirty minutes for free. Inasmuch as paying for something to get something is free." Helen sat back down beside Claire. She was obviously nervous because she was babbling the same way Claire babbled when she was nervous. "I used cash. I'm probably being paranoid, but if the FBI is tracking you, then they might be tracking me. Oh." She reached into her purse and pulled out a wad of cash. "I got this at the ATM while you were asleep. Five hundred dollars."

"I'll pay you back." Claire took the money and stuffed it into her purse. "I can't believe you're doing this."

"Well, I want to make it clear to you that I'm terrified about what you're involved in." She was smiling, but her eyes glistened with tears. "The last time I was terrified about one of my children, I failed everyone in my family. I failed your father and I failed you and Lydia. I'm not going to do that ever again. So, *mea culpa* all the way to federal prison, if that's what it takes."

Claire realized that Helen thought this was about the

embezzled money. The FBI and the police had questioned her. Nolan had brought in Claire for a twelve-hour interrogation. Claire was sending her to a bank in Hapeville. She clearly thought she'd put all the pieces together but she had absolutely no idea what was really happening.

Helen picked up Lydia's phone. "The nice man at the store told me that you go into settings."

Claire took the phone. "It needs the password." She angled the screen so her mother couldn't see the last thing she'd looked at—Paul's photo of Lydia in the trunk. She got rid of the image and pretended to tap in the password before handing the phone back to Helen, then watched in amazement as her mother navigated the software.

Helen entered in the burner phone's number, then exited out of the menu. "Oh, look." She turned the screen toward Claire. "See that funny thing at the top, the image of a phone and an arrow? That means the calls are being forwarded." She seemed impressed. "What a wonderful little device."

Claire didn't trust the funny thing at the top. "Call the number and make sure it's working."

Helen took out her iPhone. She found Lydia's number under recent calls. They both waited. Several seconds passed, then the burner phone started to ring.

Helen disconnected the line. "My mother used to scold me for calling her on the phone. She said, 'It's so impersonal. Why don't you write me a letter?' And I scold you for emailing instead of calling. And all of my friends scold their grandchildren for their illiterate texting. Such a strange gallimaufry of needs."

"I love you, Mom."

"I love you, too, Sweetpea." She cleaned up the mess Claire had left on the coffee table. Helen was trying to appear casual, but her hands were shaking. She still had tears in her eyes. She was obviously conflicted, but she was just as equally determined to do whatever she could to help. "I should get going. How long do I need to stay at the bank?"

Claire had no idea how long it took to access a safety deposit box. "At least half an hour."

"And then?"

"Get back on seventy-five. I'll call you on your phone and let you know." She remembered what Paul had said. "Be careful. That's not a great area, especially in the Tesla."

"The bank will have a security guard in the parking lot." Helen touched Claire's cheek. There was still a slight tremor in her hand. "We'll have dinner after this is over. With drinks—lots of drinks."

"Okay."

Claire checked the time so she didn't have to watch Helen walk away. Adam Quinn had said his presentation was first thing this morning. The offices opened at nine, which meant that Claire had half an hour to walk ten blocks.

The burner phone went into her back pocket. Her purse went over her shoulder. She finished her coffee as she walked back toward the bathroom. Claire's appearance had not improved since she'd seen her reflection in the mirror behind Fred Nolan. Her hair was plastered to her head. Her clothes were a mess. She probably smelled sweaty from running full-bore through the city.

The cut on her cheek was still tender. The dark circle under her eye was turning into a full-on black bruise. Claire touched her fingers to the skin. Paul had punched Lydia, too. He had made her forehead bleed. He had made her eye swell shut. He had done other things, too, things that had made Lydia give up, to believe that no matter what Claire did, she was already dead.

"You are not dead, Lydia." Claire spoke the words aloud for her own sake as much as her sister's. "I am not going to abandon you."

Claire ran water in the sink. She couldn't go to Adam Quinn looking like this. If Adam was clueless as to what Paul was really involved in, then he'd be much more likely to help Claire if she didn't look like a homeless person. She washed her face, and then quickly took a whore's bath. The underwear Helen had bought came up past Claire's belly button, but she was in no position to complain.

She slicked back her hair with water, then fingered it into a soft wave to dry. There was make-up in her purse. Foundation. Concealer. Eye shadow. Blush. Powder. Mascara. Eyeliner. She winced as she patted her finger around the bruise. The pain was worth it, because she felt like she was slowly coming back to herself.

The hour and a half of sleep had probably helped more than the ninety-dollar concealer. She felt her thoughts whirring back awake. She remembered the question she had told Nolan he needed to ask: Why was Paul sticking around?

He wanted the USB drive. Claire was not so narcissistic to think that her husband was waiting around for her. Paul was a survivor. He was risking his safety in order to get the USB drive, and he was telling Claire the things he thought she wanted to hear because keeping her onside was the best way to get it.

Saying he loved her was the carrot. Lydia was the stick.

Nolan thought that Paul was offering evidence of the masked man's identity, but Claire knew that Paul wasn't going to give the FBI evidence against himself. So what did that leave? What information could be on the drive that was so valuable that Paul was risking his freedom?

"His customer list," Claire told her reflection. It was the only thing that made sense. On the phone yesterday, Paul had claimed he got into the family business because he needed tuition. Setting aside that he had graduated years ago, what kind of money were people willing to pay to watch his movies? And just how many names were on his customer list?

Gerald Scott's VHS collection went back at least twenty-four years. There were at least one hundred videotapes in the garage. The archived equipment on the metal shelves pointed to various other means of duplication. Floppy drives for photographs. DVDs for movies. The super Mac to upload edited footage to the Internet. There had to be an international component. Paul had taken Claire to Germany and Holland more times than she could count. He'd said he was going to conferences during the day, but she had no way of knowing exactly what he did with his time.

Paul couldn't be the only man in this business, but if she knew her husband, he was the best. He would franchise the concept to other men in other parts of the world. He would demand top dollar. He would control every aspect of the market.

So long as he had his client list, Paul could operate the business from anywhere in the world.

The bathroom door opened. Two young girls came in. They were giggling and happy and carrying large Starbucks cups filled with sugary, iced concoctions.

Claire drained the water from the sink. She checked her make-up. The bruise still showed in a certain light, but she could easily explain the damage. Adam had seen her at the funeral. He knew that her cheek was scraped.

The lobby was filled with travelers in search of breakfast. Claire looked for Jacob Mayhew and Harvey Falke, but they were nowhere in sight. She knew from movies that FBI agents tended to wear earbuds, so she scanned the ears of all the single men in the vicinity. And then she looked at the women, because women were in the FBI, too. Claire was fairly certain that she was looking at tourists and businesspeople because they were all vastly out of shape and she assumed you had to be fit to work for the FBI.

Her refreshed brain easily jumped to the next conclusion: No one had found her in the Hyatt, which meant that Paul had not given them her location, which meant that Paul was not working with Jacob Mayhew or the FBI, which meant that by extension, he was not working with Johnny Jackson.

Probably.

A quick look outside the hotel revealed that the light mist had turned into a steady rain. Claire went up one floor and took the skybridge, which was part of an eighteen-building, ten-block project to help tourists navigate the convention corridor without passing out in the sweltering summer heat.

Quinn + Scott had worked on two of the skybridges. Paul had given Claire a tour of all eighteen, taking her up and down elevators and escalators to access the glass-enclosed bridges spanning countless downtown streets. He'd pointed out various architectural details and told her stories about the buildings that had been torn down to clear way for new ones. The last part of the tour had ended at the Hyatt skybridge, which was closed off for construction. The sun had been setting over the skyline. The Hyatt's pool had sparkled below. They'd had a picnic on a blanket with chocolate cake and champagne.

Claire looked away from the pool as she walked across the bridge toward the Marriott Marquis. Traffic was clogging the streets as commuters filled the Peachtree Center complex, which was comprised of fourteen different buildings that housed everything from corporate offices to several shopping areas. She felt like her head was mounted on a swivel as she looked for earbuds or Mayhew or Harvey or Nolan or any other face that seemed threatening or familiar. If none of them were aligned with Paul, then all of them would have a reason to use Claire as leverage. She couldn't afford another twelve-hour detour while Lydia was waiting.

Not waiting, because Lydia had already given up.

Claire jogged down another set of escalators as she headed toward the next skybridge. She couldn't let herself dwell on what was happening to Lydia. Claire was making progress. That was what mattered right now. She had to focus on the task at hand, which was getting the USB drive from Adam. She kept reminding herself of something Nolan had revealed during the interrogation: They had checked Paul's computer.

Adam had been the one who called in the FBI in the first place. He would know that they would search Paul's office and computer. Actually, if Adam was part of an operation that produced and distributed snuff porn, no matter how much money Paul stole from him, there was no way in hell he would be stupid enough to involve any law enforcement agencies, let alone the FBI.

She felt some of the weight lift off her shoulders as she made her way up to the skybridge that connected the last AmericasMart building to the Museum Tower. From there, it was just a brisk walk outside to the Olympic Tower on Centennial Park Drive.

Claire darted under awnings to avoid the pelting rain. She usually drove downtown every few weeks to have lunch with Paul. She had a Quinn + Scott ID in her purse, which she used in the main lobby to get through the turnstiles. The office was on the top floor of the tower, overlooking Centennial Park, a twenty-one-acre remnant from the Olympics. As part of a fundraising effort, the Olympic committee had sold personalized engraved bricks that lined the walkways. One of the last presents her father had given her was a brick in the park with Claire's name on it. He'd purchased one for Lydia and Julia, too.

Claire had shown Paul the bricks. She wondered if he sometimes looked down from his penthouse office and smiled.

The elevator opened onto the Quinn + Scott floor. It was 9:05 in the morning. The secretaries and underlings had probably been ten minutes early. They were all bustling around their desks and rushing around with cups of coffee in their hands and donuts stuck in their mouths.

They all came to a stop when they saw Claire.

There were awkward looks and nervous glances, which confused Claire until she remembered that the last time they had seen her, she'd been standing in front of her husband's coffin.

"Mrs. Scott?" One of the receptionists came around the high desk that separated the lobby from the offices. Everything was open-plan and highly designed with satin chromes and bleached woods and no obstructions to the usually spectacular view of the park.

Claire had stood right on this spot while Paul and Adam celebrated their new, larger space with picklebacks and pizza, a disgusting holdover from their college years.

"Mrs. Scott?" the receptionist repeated. She was young and pretty and blonde and exactly Paul's type. Both Pauls, because the girl could be a young Claire.

Claire said, "I need to see Adam."

"I'll buzz him." She reached over the counter for the phone. Her skirt was tight around her ass. Her left foot came up as she bent her knee. "There's a presentation in the—"

"I'll find him." Claire couldn't wait any longer. She walked through the open offices. Every eye followed her across the room. She went down the long hallway that housed the associates who'd earned the luxury of an office door. The presentation room was opposite the conference room, which looked over the park. Paul had explained the reasoning to Claire when they toured the empty shell of the top floor. Wow the customers with the million-dollar view, then take them into the presentation room and wow them with the work.

Presentation Studio. That's what Paul had called it. Claire had forgotten until she saw the sign on the closed door. She didn't bother knocking.

Adam swiveled around in his chair. He was watching a dry run of the presentation. Claire saw a slew of numbers alongside a quote from the mayor boasting that Atlanta was set to surpass Las Vegas for number of convention visitors.

"Claire?" Adam turned on the lights. He closed the door. He took her hands. "Is something wrong?"

She looked down at their hands. She would never feel another man's touch without wondering whether or not she could really trust him.

She told Adam, "I'm sorry to bother you."

"I'm glad you're here." He indicated the chairs, but Claire didn't sit down. "I was shitty to you with that note. I'm sorry I threatened you. I want you to know that I would've never gotten the lawyers involved. I needed the files, but I didn't have to act like a thug."

Claire wasn't sure what to say. Her wariness had returned. Paul was such a good actor. Was Adam a good actor, too? Nolan claimed he'd grilled the shit out of Adam, but Nolan was a spectacular liar. They were all so much better at this than Claire.

She told Adam, "I know about the money."

He winced. "I should've handled that between me and Paul."

"Why didn't you?"

He shook his head. "It doesn't matter. Just know that I'm sorry."

"Please." Claire touched his hand. The touch turned into a stroke, and his demeanor softened as easily as if she had pressed a button.

She said, "I want to know, Adam. Tell me what happened."

"Things haven't been good between us for a while. I guess that's partly my fault. That whole thing with you was crazy." He assured Claire, "Not that it wasn't good, but it wasn't right. I love Sheila. I know you loved Paul."

"I did," she agreed. "I thought you did, too. You've known him for twenty-one years."

Adam went silent again. She touched her fingers to his cheek so that he would look at her. "Tell me."

He shook his head again, but he said, "You know he had his moods, his bouts with depression."

Claire had always thought that Paul was the most even-keeled person she had ever known. She guessed, "He got it from his dad."

Adam didn't disagree with her. "It seemed like lately, he couldn't climb out of it. I guess it's been a year, maybe two, since I felt like we were really friends. He always kept me at arm's length, but this was different. And it hurt." Adam did in fact look hurt. "I acted out. I shouldn't have called the FBI, and believe me, I'm processing through it with my therapist, but something made me snap."

Claire was reminded of one of the reasons she had never seen herself in anything long-term with Adam Quinn. He was constantly talking about his feelings.

He said, "I wasn't just pissed off about the money. It was one more thing on top of the mood swings and the temper tantrums and his need to control everything and—I never meant for it to escalate. When that asshole from the FBI handcuffed him and walked him out of the office, I knew that was it. The look on Paul's face. I've never seen him angry like that. He just kind of turned into this guy I had never seen before."

Claire had seen what that guy was capable of. Adam was lucky Paul had been in handcuffs. "You dropped the charges. Was that because Paul paid the money back?"

"No." He looked away from Claire. "I paid it back."

Claire was sure she'd heard wrong. She had to repeat his words to make sure. "*You* paid back the money."

"He knew about us. The three times."

The three times.

Claire had been with Adam Quinn three times: at the Christmas party, during the golf tournament, and in the bathroom down the hallway while Paul was downstairs waiting for them to join him for lunch.

Fred Nolan had the answer to his first curious thing. Paul had stolen one million dollars for each time Adam had fucked her.

"I'm sorry," Adam said.

Claire felt foolish, but only because she hadn't figured it out on her own. Paul and Adam had always been driven by money. "He took enough money to get your attention, but not enough to make you call the police. Except that you did. You called in the FBI."

Adam nodded sheepishly. "Sheila pushed me into doing it. I was pissed off—I mean, why? And then it snowballed into them arresting Paul and searching his office and . . ." His voice trailed off. "I actually ended up begging him for his forgiveness. I mean, yeah, what I did was wrong, but we're partners and we had to find a way to be able to work together again, so . . ."

"You paid him a three-million-dollar penalty." Claire didn't have the luxury of processing her feelings. "I guess if I'm going to be a whore, at least I'm not a cheap one."

"Hey—"

"I need the USB drive back, the one I left for you in the mailbox."

"Of course." Adam walked over to the projector. His briefcase was open beside it. She supposed this was the last bit of proof she needed that Paul had hidden his sick venture from his best friend. Or former best friend, as seemed to be the case.

Adam held up the keytag. "I already downloaded the files I needed. Can I help you with—"

Claire took the drive out of his hand. "I need to use the computer in Paul's office."

"Sure. I can have—"

"I know where it is."

Claire walked down the hallway with the keytag clenched in her hand. She had Paul's customer list. Claire was sure of it. But she couldn't get Fred Nolan's words out of her head: *Trust but verify.*

The lights were off in Paul's office. His chair was tucked under his desk. The blotter was clear. There were no stray papers. The stapler was aligned to the pencil cup was aligned to the lamp. Anyone would assume that his office had been cleaned out, but Claire knew differently.

She sat in Paul's chair. The computer was still on. She stuck the USB connector into the back of the iMac. Paul hadn't logged out of the system. She could picture him sitting behind his desk when Fred Nolan came to tell him that it was time to fake his death. Paul wouldn't have been able to do anything but stand up and leave.

So of course he had taken the time to slide his chair back under his desk at a precise angle to the legs.

Claire double-clicked on the USB drive. There were two folders, one for Adam's work-in-progress files and the other for the software that ran the USB drive. She clicked open the software folder. She scanned the files, which all had technical-looking names and .exe extensions. She checked the dates. Paul had saved the files onto the drive two days before his staged murder.

Claire scrolled to the bottom of the list. The last file Paul had saved was a folder titled FFN.exe. In the garage two nights ago, Claire had checked the USB drive for movies, but that had been before she discovered the true depth of her husband's depravities. She knew better than to take things at face value now. She also knew that folders didn't require extensions.

FFN. Fred F. Nolan. Claire had seen the man's initials on his handkerchief.

She clicked open the folder.

A prompt came up asking for a password.

Claire stared at the screen until the prompt blurred. She had guessed the other passwords with the notion that she knew her husband. This password had been set by the Paul Scott she had never met—the one who donned a mask to film himself raping and murdering young women. The one who charged his best friend a million bucks a pop to fuck his wife. The one who had found his father's stash of movies and decided to scale up the business.

Paul must have watched the tapes on the same VCR that Lydia and Claire had seen in the Fuller house. Claire imagined her young, awkward husband sitting in front of the television watching his dead father's movies for the first time. Was Paul surprised by what he saw? Was he disgusted? She wanted to think that he'd been outraged, and repulsed, and that habituation and necessity had compelled him not only to sell the tapes, but to try out his father's deviations for himself.

But then less than six years later, Paul was meeting Claire in the math lab. Surely he knew exactly who Claire was, exactly who her sister was. Surely he had watched Julia's movie dozens, maybe hundreds of times by then.

Claire's hands were surprisingly steady on the keyboard as she typed in the password: 03041991.

No mnemonics. No acronyms. March 4, 1991, the day that her sister had gone missing. The day that had started it all.

She pressed enter. The rainbow wheel started to spin.

The folder opened. She saw a list of files.

.xls—Excel spreadsheet.

There were sixteen spreadsheets in all.

She opened the first spreadsheet. There were five columns: Name, email, address, bank routing info, member since.

Member since.

Claire scrolled down the list. Fifty names in total. Some of the memberships went back thirty years. They were anywhere from Germany to Switzerland to New Zealand. Several addresses were in Dubai.

She had been right. Paul needed his customer list. Was Mayhew looking for it, too? Did he want to take over Paul's business? Or was Johnny Jackson sending the police to clean up his nephew's mess?

Claire closed the file. She clicked open all of the other spreadsheets and scrolled through each name because she had paid the price that came with not looking at everything once before.

Fifty names on each spreadsheet, sixteen spreadsheets in all. There were 800 men scattered all over the world who were paying for the privilege of watching Paul commit brutal, cold-blooded murder.

If only Claire had clicked open all of the files on the USB drive back in the garage. Then again, there was no way she would've guessed the same password, because back in the garage, she'd thought her husband was a passive viewer rather than an active participant.

Claire held the mouse over the last file, which wasn't really a file. It was another folder, this one titled JJ.

If the FNF folder contained things that Fred Nolan wanted to get his hands on, she knew that the JJ folder would contain information valuable to Congressman Johnny Jackson.

Claire opened the folder. She found a list of files with no extensions. She scrolled over to the column on the far right.

Kind: JPEG image.

Claire clicked open the first file. What she saw made her gag.

The photo was in black and white. Johnny Jackson was standing inside what could only be the Amityville barn. He was posing with a body that was suspended upside down from the rafters. The girl was trussed up like a deer. Her ankles were tied together with barbed wire that sliced into the bone. She was hanging from a large metal hook that looked like something from a butcher's shop. Her arms dragged the floor. She had been cut open stem to stern. Johnny Jackson held a sharp-looking hunting knife in one hand, a cigarette in the other. He was naked. Black blood covered the front of his body and engulfed his rigid penis.

Claire clicked open the next file. Another man in black and white. Another dead girl. Another bloody scene of carnage. She didn't recognize the face. She kept clicking. And clicking. And then she found what she should've guessed would be there all along.

Sheriff Carl Huckabee.

The photograph was in Kodachrome color. Huckleberry had what could only be called a shit-eating grin under his neatly combed mustache. He was naked but for his cowboy hat and boots. There was a splash of blood on his bare chest. His thick thatch of pubic hair was caked with dried blood. The girl hanging beside him was trussed up like all the others, except this girl wasn't just any girl. Claire immediately recognized the silver and black bangles that hung from her limp wrist.

It was Julia.

Her sister's beautiful blonde hair dragged the dirt floor. Long cuts exposed the white of her high cheekbones. Her breasts had been cut off. Her stomach was sliced open. Her intestines hung down to her face and wrapped around her neck like a scarf.

The machete was still inside of her.

Paul, aged fifteen, was standing on the other side of Huckabee. He was dressed in acid-washed jeans and a bulky red polo shirt. His hair was feathered. He wore thick glasses.

He was giving the man behind the camera two thumbs up.

Claire closed the photograph. She looked out the window. The sky had opened up, sending a deluge of water into the park. The clouds had darkened to an almost black. She listened to the insistent tapping of rain against glass.

She had lulled herself into hoping that Paul would not irreparably harm Lydia because he still wanted to please Claire. The justifications followed a simple pattern: He had obviously terrified Lydia. He had clearly hurt her. But there was no way he would truly damage her. He'd had his chance eighteen years ago. He had paid men to follow her for years. He could've taken her at any point and he had chosen not to because he loved Claire.

Because she was pretty? Because she was smart? Because she was clever?

Because she was a fool.

Lydia was right. She was already dead.

TWENTY

Paul was pacing the room as he talked on the phone. Words were coming out of his mouth, but none of them made sense. Actually, nothing made sense to Lydia.

She knew she was in pain, but she didn't care. She was afraid, but it didn't matter. She pictured her terror as a festering wound below a fresh scab. She knew it was still there, she knew that even the slightest touch could make it open, and yet she could not bring herself to worry.

Nothing could occupy her thoughts for very long except for one exquisite truth: She had forgotten how fucking fantastic it was to be high. The stench of piss had gone away. She could breathe again. The colors in the room were so Goddamn gorgeous. The Apple Macintosh, dot-matrix printer, five-inch floppy disks, duping machine, disk burner. They glowed every time she looked at them.

Paul said, "No, you listen to me, Johnny. I'm the one in control."

Johnny. Johnny Appleseed. Johnny Jack Corn and I don't care.

No, that was Jimmy.

Jimmy Jack Corn and I don't care.

No, it was *Jimmy Crack Corn.*

But did she care?

Lydia vaguely recalled Dee singing the song along with the puppets on *Sesame Street.* But that couldn't be right. Dee was terrified of Big Bird. Probably Claire had sung the song. She'd had a Geraldine doll that said "the devil made me do it" every time you pulled the string. Claire had broken the string. Julia was furious, because the doll had belonged to her. She had gone to Sambo's with her friend Tammy.

Was that right? Sambo's?

Lydia had been there, too. The restaurant's menu had a black-faced child running around a tree. The tigers chasing him were turning into butter.

Pancakes.

She could almost smell her father making pancakes. Christmas morning; it was the only time Helen let him in the kitchen. Her father delighted in taunting them. He made them eat all of their breakfast before they were allowed to open any gifts.

"Lydia?"

Lydia let her head roll to the side. Her eyelids had stars on the inside. Her tongue tasted like candy.

"Oh, Lydia?"

Paul's voice was sing-songy. He was off the phone. He was standing in front of Lydia with the pry bar in his hands. Claire had dropped it on the kitchen table yesterday. The day before? Last week?

He tested the weight of the bar in his hands. He looked at the hammer head, the giant claw on the other end. "This is something that I could find very useful, don't you think?"

Lydia said, *Motherfucker*, but only in her head.

"Watch this." He held the pry bar like a bat on his shoulder. He swung the claw at her head.

He missed.

On purpose?

She had felt the breeze as the metal chopped through the air. She could smell a metallic kind of sweat. Claire's sweat? Paul's sweat? He wasn't sweating now. She only saw him sweat when he was standing over her with that sick grin on his face.

Lydia blinked.

Paul was gone. No, he was sitting at the computer. The monitor was massive. Lydia knew he was looking at a map. She wasn't close enough to make out any landmarks. He was glued to the screen, tracking Claire's progress as she went to the bank, because Paul had told her Claire was hiding the USB drive in the bank. In a safety deposit box. Lydia had been tempted to tell him otherwise, but her lips felt too full, like giant balloons were glued to the skin. Every time she tried to pry her mouth open, the balloons got heavier.

But she couldn't tell him. She knew that. Claire was doing something. She was tricking him. She was trying to help Lydia. She said on the phone that she was going to take care of this, right? That Lydia needed to hold on. That she wouldn't abandon her again. But the USB drive was with Adam Quinn, so what the hell was she doing at the bank?

Adam Quinn has the USB drive, Lydia told Paul, but the words were only in her head because her mouth was taped shut because she had finally managed to say some things to Paul that he did not want to hear.

Claire hates you now. She believes me. She will never, ever take you back.

We are never ever ever getting back together.

Taylor Swift. How many times had Dee played that song after she caught Heath Carmichael cheating?

This time I'm telling you . . .

"Lydia?" Paul was standing beside her. She looked back at his computer monitor. When had he moved? He had been looking at the computer. He was saying something about Claire leaving the bank. How was he standing beside her now when he was at the computer?

She turned her head to ask Paul. Her vision staggered through each frame. She heard the bionic sound like Steve Austin made in the *Six Million Dollar Man*.

Ch-ch-ch-ch . . .

Paul wasn't there.

He was standing in front of the rolling cart. He was replacing the old items with new ones. His movements were slow and precise. *Ch-ch-ch-ch* came the bionic sound as he moved in stop-motion like in *Rudolph the Red-Nosed Reindeer*.

Claire. She hated the Christmas special with the freakishly happy creatures whose movements stuttered one millisecond at a time. Julia made them watch it every year, and Claire would curl into Lydia like a tiny, frightened doll and Lydia would laugh along with Julia because Claire was such a baby but secretly, the creatures scared her, too.

Paul said, "You're going to want to prepare yourself for this."

This sounded important. Lydia felt the scab start to itch. She shook her head. She wouldn't pick at it. She needed that scab to stay on. Instead, she tried to concentrate on his hands, the stilted moves of his fingers as he straightened everything once, then twice, then a third time, then a fourth.

Lydia heard a new mantra come into her head—

Barbed wire. Pry bar. A length of chain. A large hook. A sharp hunting knife.

A moment of clarity broke through the clouds in her mind.

They were close to the end.

TWENTY-ONE

Claire sat with her back to the wall inside the Office Shop across from Phipps Plaza. She had angled herself between the front and back doors so that she would know if anyone came in. She was the only customer in the small storefront. The clerk was working silently at one of the rental computers. Claire held the burner phone in her hand. Helen had been on I-75 for ten minutes.

Paul still hadn't called.

Her head was filling with wild reasons for why the phone had not yet rung. Paul was on his way here. He had already murdered Lydia. He was going to murder Claire. He was going to track down Helen and go to Grandma Ginny's home and then he was going to search for Dee.

Maybe that had been his plan all along, to wipe out her entire family. Claire was nothing more than a calculated first step.

Dating her. Wooing her. Marrying her. Pretending to make her happy. Pretending to *be* happy.

Lies on top of lies on top of more, endless lies.

They were like grenades. Paul lobbed them over the wall and Claire waited an interminable amount of time before the truth finally exploded in her face.

The photographs were a thousand grenades. They were the nuclear explosion that sent her reeling into the darkest place she had ever known.

Paul, fifteen years old, flashing a maniacal grin as he posed for the camera beside the trussed-up body of her sister. He had his thumbs up, the same way he had given Fred Nolan a thumbs-up when he'd given the FBI agent the slip.

Claire stared at the burner phone. The blank screen stared back. She forced herself to come up with less alarming reasons for why the phone was not ringing. The call forwarding wasn't working properly. Mayhew had talked to someone at the phone company who put Paul on to the burner phone. Adam was secretly in on it and he'd alerted Paul so that his men could follow Claire.

None of those things was any less terrifying, because they all led back to Paul.

Claire patted her hand to her purse until she felt the hard outline of Lydia's revolver. At least she'd done one thing right. Buying bullets for the gun had been easy. There was a gun store down the street that had sold her a box of hollow-point ammunition, no questions asked.

The Office Shop offered printing services as well as hourly computer rental. She had been too wrapped up in her own fear to flirt with the geeky boy behind the counter, so she'd bribed him with two hundred and fifty dollars of Helen's cash instead. She had explained her problem in loose terms—she wanted to put something on YouTube, but it was photographs, not movies, and there were a lot of them, along with some spreadsheets, and she needed all of it to work properly because someone was going to try to take them down.

The boy had stopped her there. She didn't want YouTube, she wanted something like Dropbox, and then Claire had shifted her purse on her shoulder and he had seen the box of ammo and the gun and told her that it was going to be an extra hundred dollars and she wanted something called Tor.

Tor. Claire had a vague recollection of reading about the illegal file-sharing site in *Time* magazine. It had something to do with the dark web, which meant it was uncataloged and untraceable. Maybe Paul was using Tor to distribute his movies. Instead of emailing large files, he could send out a complicated website link that no one else could find unless they put in the exact combination of letters and numbers.

She had their email addresses. Should she send Paul's customers his spreadsheets and photographs?

"It's ready." The geeky boy stood in front of Claire with his hands clasped in front of his pleated slacks. "Just jack in the thumbdrive and drag everything you want onto the page and it'll be uploaded."

Claire read his nametag. "Thank you, Keith."

He smiled at her before trouncing back to the counter.

Claire pushed herself up. She sat in the chair in front of the computer, occasionally glancing at the entrance and the exit as she followed the boy's instructions. The store was cold inside, but she was sweating. Her hands weren't shaking, but she felt a vibration in her body, like a tuning fork had touched her bones. She checked the doors again as Paul's files started to upload. She had put the JPEGs at the top so that the first click would open the image of Johnny Jackson. The trick would be making someone want to click.

Claire went to the mail program that Keith had set up for her. She had a new email address that came with the ability to schedule the exact time and date that emails were sent out.

She started to type.

> *My name is Claire Carroll Scott. Julia Carroll and Lydia*
> *Delgado were my sisters.*

Claire felt sick from the betrayal. Lydia was alive. She had to be alive.

She hit the backspace key until the last sentence was deleted.

> *I have posted proof that Congressman Johnny Jackson*
> *has participated in pornographic films.*

Claire stared at the words. This wasn't entirely true because it was more than porn. It was abduction, rape, and murder, but she was worried that listing all of that out would dissuade people from clicking on the link. She was sending this to every media outlet and government agency who listed a contact address on their website. Most likely, the accounts were monitored by young interns who hadn't any idea who Johnny Jackson was or who had grown up around email and therefore knew not to click anonymous links, especially ones that connected to Tor.

Claire opened a new browser window. She found Penelope Ward's email on the Westerly Academy PTO page. Lydia's nemesis looked just as candy-apple fake as Claire would've guessed. The Branch Ward for Congress Exploratory Committee listed the address intern@WeWantWard.com. The site indicated the group was a PAC, which meant they would be looking for any dirt on their opponent that they could find.

The burner phone rang.

Claire headed into the stock room and opened the back door. Rain was still pouring down. The wind had picked up, sending a cold jet of air into the small space. She hoped the background noise was enough to convince Paul that she was driving the Tesla up I-75.

She flipped open the phone. "Paul?"

"Do you have the keytag?"

"Yes. Let me talk to Lydia."

He was silent. She could feel his relief. "Did you look at what's on it?"

"Sure, I used the computer at the bank." Claire funneled all of her anger into the sarcastic response. "Let me speak to Lydia. Now."

He went through the usual steps. She heard the speakerphone turn on.

Claire said, "Lydia?" She waited. "Lydia?"

She heard a loud, desperate moan.

Paul said, "I don't think she feels like talking."

Claire leaned her head back against the wall. She looked up

at the ceiling as she tried to keep her tears from falling. He had really hurt Lydia. Claire had held on to a shred of hope that he hadn't, the same way she'd held on to a shred of hope about Julia for so many years. Her face burned with shame.

"Claire?"

"I want to meet at the mall. Phipps Plaza. How long do you need?"

"I don't think so," Paul said. "Why don't we meet at Lydia's house?"

Claire stopped fighting her tears. "Did you take Dee?"

"I haven't taken her yet, but I know you went to Lydia's house to warn her redneck boyfriend. He took Dee to a fishing shack off Lake Burton. Haven't you figured out by now that I know everything?"

He didn't know about the gun. He didn't know about the Office Shop.

He said, "Drive back to Watkinsville. I'll meet you at my parents' house."

Claire felt her stomach drop. She had seen what Paul did to prisoners inside the Fuller house.

"Still there?"

Claire forced herself to speak. "There's a lot of traffic. It'll probably take me a couple of hours."

"It shouldn't take more than ninety minutes."

"I know you've been tracking me with my phone. Watch the blue dot. It'll take however long it takes."

"I'm just about the same distance away from the house as you are, Claire. Think about Lydia. Do you really want me to get bored waiting around for you?"

Claire closed the phone. She looked down at her arm. The rain had come in through the door. Her shirtsleeve was wet.

There were two more customers in the storefront. One woman. One man. Both young. Both dressed in jeans and hoodies. Neither of them had earbuds. Claire searched their faces. The woman looked away. The man smiled at her.

Claire had to get out of here. She sat back down at the computer. The files had finished uploading. She checked the link to make sure it worked. The monitor was turned away from the other patrons, but she felt a rush of heat as she made sure that the photograph of Johnny Jackson was on the server.

Should she leave it open on the monitor? Should she let Keith find out what he'd unwittingly been a part of?

Claire had already hurt enough people. She closed the photograph. She didn't have time to wax eloquent in her email. She wrote out a few more lines, then pasted the Tor link underneath. She double-checked the scheduled time for the emails to be sent out.

In two hours, anyone with Internet access would know the true story of Paul Scott and his accomplices. They would see it in the pictures of his uncle and father passing down the family's bloodlust. They would see it in the almost one thousand email addresses that gave his customers' true identities and locations. They would know it in their guts when they saw picture after picture of young girls who had been abducted from their families over the course of more than four decades. And they would understand how Carl Huckabee and Johnny Jackson had exploited their law enforcement careers to make sure that no one ever found out.

Until now.

Claire pulled the USB drive out of the computer. She made sure there were no copies left on the computer desktop. The drive went back into her purse. She waved to Keith as she left the store. The sky had opened up again, pouring rain down on her head. She was soaked by the time she got behind the wheel of Helen's Ford.

Claire turned on the windshield wipers. She pulled out of the space. She waited until she was safely down Peachtree Street before she called her mother.

Helen's voice sounded strained. "Yes?"

"I'm okay." She was becoming just as adept at lying as Paul. "I need you to keep driving to Athens. I'm about twenty minutes ahead of you right now, so I need you to go slow. No more than the speed limit."

"Am I going home?"

"No, don't go home. Park at the Taco Stand downtown, then walk to Mrs. Flynn's house. Leave the phone in the car. Don't tell anyone where you're going." Claire thought about the emails that were scheduled to go out. Her mother was on the list of recipients, which was the emotional equivalent of stabbing the woman in the heart. "I sent you an email. It should be there by the time you get to Mrs. Flynn's. You can read it, but don't click on the link. If you haven't heard from me in three hours, I want you to take it to your friend who works at the *Atlanta Journal*—the one who writes books."

"She's retired now."

"She'll still know people. It's very important, Mom. You have to get her to click on the link, but don't look at what she sees."

Helen was obviously scared, but she didn't say anything else but, "Claire."

"Don't trust Huckleberry. He lied to you about Julia."

"I saw what was on the tape." Helen paused before continuing. "That's why I never wanted you to see it, because I saw it myself."

Claire didn't think she was capable of feeling any more pain. "How?"

"I was the one who found your father." She stopped for a moment. The memory was clearly difficult. "He was in his chair. The TV was on. The remote control was in his hand. I wanted to see what he'd been looking at and—"

She stopped again.

They both knew the last images that Sam Carroll had seen. Only Claire guessed that her husband had been the one to show it to him. Had that been the last straw that led her father to take his own life? Or had Paul helped him with that, too?

Helen said, "It was a long time ago, and the man who did it is dead."

Claire opened her mouth to say otherwise, but her mother would know everything when she opened the email. "Does it help? Knowing he's dead?"

Helen didn't answer. She had always been against the death penalty, but something told Claire her mother had no problem with someone other than the government putting to death the man she believed had killed her daughter.

Claire said, "Just don't go to Huckleberry, okay? You'll understand later. I need you to trust me. He's not a good man."

"Sweetpea, I've been trusting you all day. I'm not going to stop now."

Again, Claire thought about Dee. Helen was a grandmother. She deserved to know. But Claire knew it wasn't just a matter of telling her mother. Helen would want details. She would want to meet Dee, talk to her, touch her, hold her. She would want to know why Claire was keeping them apart. And then she would start asking about Lydia.

"Honey?" Helen asked. "Is there something else?"

"I love you, Mom."

"I love you, too."

Claire flipped the phone closed. She tossed it onto the seat beside her. She grabbed the wheel with both hands. She looked at the clock on the dashboard and she gave herself one full minute to let out the grief and despair that she hadn't had the where-withal to express at her father's funeral.

"Okay," she told herself. "Okay."

The grief would help her. It would give her the strength she needed to do what she had to do. She was going to kill Paul for showing her father the tape of Julia. She was going to kill him for what he'd done to them all.

Rain pelted the windshield, almost blinding her, but she kept driving because the only thing she had on Paul was the element of surprise. Exactly how that surprise would play out was still a mystery. Claire had the gun. She had hollow-point bullets that could tear a man in half.

She remembered that long-ago day that she'd taken Paul shooting. The first thing the rangemaster had said was that you should never point a weapon at another person unless you were willing to pull the trigger.

Claire was more than willing to pull the trigger. She just didn't know how she was going to find the opportunity to do it. There was a chance she could get to the Fuller house ahead of Paul. She could park her mother's car in the stand of trees beside the house and walk on foot to the back door. There were several places she could lie in wait: in one of the bedrooms, in the hallway, in the garage.

Unless he was already there. Unless he was lying to her again and he'd been there this whole time.

She had assumed he had another house, but maybe the Fuller house was the only house Paul needed. Her husband liked for everything to stay the same. He was a slave to routine. He used the same bowl for breakfast, the same coffee cup. He would wear the same style black suit every day if Claire let him. He needed structure. He needed familiarity.

There was a chiming sound coming from the dashboard. Claire had no idea what the noise meant. She slowed her mother's car. She couldn't have the engine stall on her. She frantically searched for warning lights on the dashboard, but the only yellow light was the gas can over the fuel gauge.

"No, no, no." The Tesla never needed gas. Paul topped up the tank in Claire's BMW every Saturday. She couldn't remember the last time she'd been to a gas station for anything but Diet Coke.

Claire checked the signs on the interstate. She was forty-five minutes from Athens. Several exits went by before she saw a Hess sign.

She was coasting on fumes by the time she pulled into the gas station. The rain had let up, but the sky was still dark with thunderclouds and the air had turned bitter cold. Claire took the last of Helen's cash into the store. She had no idea how many gallons her mother's Ford Focus took. She handed the guy behind the counter forty dollars and hoped for the best.

A young couple was standing by a beat-up sedan when Claire got back to the car. She tried to ignore them as she gassed up the Ford. They were fighting about money. Claire and Paul had never fought about money because Paul always had it. Their early arguments were mostly because Paul was doing too much for her. There wasn't one need she had that Paul did not meet. Her friends over the years had always said the same thing: Paul took care of everything.

The pump handle clicked.

"Shit." Gas had spilled all over Claire's hand. The smell was noxious. She popped the trunk, because Paul had put the same emergency supplies in Helen's trunk that he'd put in all their cars. She dumped out the backpack and retrieved a packet of hand wipes. There were scissors, but Claire used her teeth to open the foil wrapper. She looked at the spilled contents in the trunk as she scrubbed the gas off her hand.

Early in their marriage, Paul had had a recurring nightmare. It was the only time Claire could think of that she'd actually seen her husband afraid.

No, that was wrong. Paul hadn't been afraid. He'd been terrified.

The nightmare didn't come often, maybe two or three times a year, but Paul would wake up screaming, his arms and legs clawing at the air, his mouth gasping for breath, because he'd dreamed that he was burning alive the same way his mother had burned alive in the car accident that had taken both his parents' lives.

Claire inventoried the contents of the trunk.

Emergency flares. A book of waterproof matches. A four-gallon gas can. A paperback to read while waiting for help.

Paul really did take care of everything.

Now it was Claire's turn to take care of him.

TWENTY-TWO

The rain had not yet touched Athens by the time Claire drove through downtown. Strong winds gusted down the streets. Students were bundled up in scarves and coats as they grabbed lunch between classes. Most of them were running to beat the coming storm. They could all see the darkness on the horizon: heavy black clouds making their way over from Atlanta.

Claire had called Helen to see how much time she had. Her mother was somewhere near Winder, around thirty minutes away. There had been an accident on 75 that bought an extra ten minutes. Fortunately, Helen had told Claire about it immediately, so when Paul called she could tell him truthfully why Lydia's iPhone had stopped moving.

She took the same route to Watkinsville that she and Lydia had taken the day before. Claire almost missed the turn-off to Paul's road. She drove slowly, because it wasn't just Jacob Mayhew and Harvey Falke she had to worry about. Carl Huckabee was still county sheriff. He would have deputies, though there was no telling which side of the law they were on.

He was also intimately familiar with the goings-on at the Fuller house.

Claire knew better than to leave the car out in the open. She angled the Ford off the road and drove into the thick stand of trees. The wheels popped and protested against the rough terrain. The side-view mirrors clapped inward. Metal squealed as pine bark scraped off the paint. She drove as far into the woods as she could go, then climbed out the window because she had trapped herself inside the car. She reached back in for the revolver.

The gun felt heavier somehow. Deadlier.

She left the open box of ammunition on the roof of the car. She picked up one bullet at a time and carefully slotted them into the cylinders.

"For Julia," she said on the first one. "For Daddy. For Mom. For Lydia."

Claire studied the last bullet in the palm of her hand. This one felt heaviest of all—shiny brass with a menacing black tip that would flare out once it hit soft tissue.

"For Paul," she whispered, her voice sounding hoarse and desperate.

The last bullet would be for her husband, who had died a long time ago, back when he was a boy and his father had taken him out to the barn for the first time. Back when he'd told Claire that he'd had a happy childhood. Back when he'd stood in front of the justice of the peace and sworn to love and cherish her for the rest of his life. Back when he'd so convincingly held on to her hand as he pretended to die in the alley.

No pretending this time.

Claire clicked the cylinder into place. She tested the gun, holding the barrel straight out in front of her, curling her finger around the trigger. She practiced pulling back the hammer with her thumb.

This was the plan: She was going to pour gasoline around the Fuller house—just the bedrooms, the front porch, and under the bathroom, because she was betting that Paul was keeping Lydia in the garage and she wanted to stay as far away from her sister as possible. Then she was going to light the gasoline. Then Paul would smell the smoke or hear the flames. He would be terrified, because fire was the only thing that ever really scared him. As soon as he ran out of the house, Claire would be waiting with the gun in her hands and she would shoot him five times, one for each of them.

Then she would run into the house and save Lydia.

The plan was risky and most likely crazy. Claire was aware of both of these things. She also knew that she was literally playing with fire, but there was nothing else she could think of that would get Paul out of the house, taken unaware, long enough for her to act.

And she knew it had to happen quickly, because she wasn't sure that she could pull the trigger if she gave herself too long to think about it.

Claire was not her husband. She could not so casually take another human life, even if that life had been drained of its humanity.

She tucked the gun into the front of her jeans. The barrel wasn't long, but the cylinder dug into her hipbone. She moved it to the center, just along the zip, but that was worse. She finally shifted the weapon to the small of her back. The granny panties her mother had bought bunched up around the cylinder. The barrel went down the crack of her ass, which was mildly unpleasant, but none of her pockets were deep enough and she knew that she would be screwed if Paul saw the gun.

She opened the trunk. She unzipped the backpack and searched for the Mylar emergency blanket. The packet the blanket came in was small, but when she unfolded it, she saw it was the size of a large cape. The waterproof matches were on top of the flares, which were all on top of a thick paperback.

The Complete Poems of Percy Bysshe Shelley.

As Helen might say, poets weren't the only unacknowledged legislators of the world.

Claire wrapped her stash in the foil blanket. She opened the four boxes of water. Her shirt was still damp from running through the rain. Still, she doused herself with water. The chill struck her immediately, but she made sure she covered her head, back, and every inch of her shirtsleeves down to the buttoned cuffs. She poured the rest of the water on the legs of her jeans.

She grabbed the blanket and the four-gallon gas can.

Gas sloshed around inside the large plastic can as she lugged it through the forest. A permanent mist of rain seemed to be trapped under the tree canopy. She heard a distant rumble of thunder, which seemed appropriate given the task she'd laid out. Claire squinted ahead. The sky was getting darker by the minute, but she could make out a powder-blue Chevy parked behind a row of trees.

Claire put down the gas can and blanket. She drew the revolver. She cocked the hammer. She approached the car carefully in case Paul or one of his cronies was inside.

Empty.

She uncocked the gun. She tucked it into the back of her jeans. Habituation. The gun didn't feel so strange anymore.

She pressed her hand to the hood of the car. The engine was cold. Paul had probably been staying at the Fuller house from the moment Claire left.

Why would he go anywhere else? He had the sheriff to protect him.

She retrieved the blanket and gas can and continued her walk toward the house. The brush was thick. Claire felt a moment of panic where she wondered if she'd gotten off course, but then she saw the green roof of the house. She walked in a crouch. The windows were still boarded up with weathered plywood. Claire stayed low anyway, because she knew that there was a slit in the den windows that showed the driveway, so it followed that there would be others.

The overgrown back yard hadn't had time to absorb the slow, sloppy rain. Claire heard dry grass crackle under her feet. The swingset groaned as a strong wind swept through the open field where the Amityville barn had been. Claire kept clear of the area. She used her feet to press down a patch of tall grass to create a staging area for the blanket and its contents.

She studied the back of the house. The plywood board she and Lydia had pried off the kitchen door was leaning up against the side of the house. They had left it on the ground where they'd dropped it. She assumed Paul had neatly leaned up the board beside the door. He had probably straightened up inside the house as well. Or maybe he'd left the silverware strewn across the floor as a sort of alarm so that he would know if someone tried to enter the house.

Claire was more worried about getting Paul out of the house than her going in.

She bent down to the gas can and took the cap off the flexible spout. She started to the left of the small back porch off the kitchen, dripping gasoline down the slats of wooden siding that covered the exterior of the house. Claire worked carefully so that the gas got into the seams between the boards. She raised up the can every time she passed a window, soaking the plywood as much as she could without making too much noise.

Claire's heart was pounding so loudly when she walked up the front porch steps that she was afraid the noise would give her away. She kept her eyes on the garage. She tried not to think about Paul in there with Lydia. The roll-up metal door was still padlocked from the outside. The hasp was secure. His murder room. Lydia was locked inside his murder room.

Claire turned back around. Quietly, she made a half-loop back around the house, double-checking her work underneath the boarded-up windows. By the time she was finished, she'd poured a crescent of gasoline around the left side of the house, covering the front porch, the bedrooms, and the bathroom. Only the kitchen and garage were left untouched.

Step one: complete.

Claire returned to the foil blanket. She knelt down. She was sweating, but her hands were so cold she could barely feel her fingers. She said a silent apology to her mother the librarian as she ripped apart the Shelley collection. She wadded and rolled together the pages into a long wick. She unscrewed the spout from the gas can. She shoved the wick inside, leaving around six inches of exposed paper.

Step two: ready.

There were two long flares from the backpack. Claire kept both in her hand as she walked to the front of the house. She stood underneath the sewing room. The empty street was behind her. At the gas station, she had read the instructions for lighting the flare. It worked the same way as striking a match. You pulled off the plastic cap and struck the sandpaper side to the top of the flare.

Claire pulled off the plastic cap. She looked up at the house. This was the moment. She could stop now. She could go back to her car. She could call the FBI in Washington, DC. Homeland Security. The Secret Service. The Georgia Bureau of Investigation.

How many hours would it take for them to get to the house?

How many hours would that give Paul alone with her sister?

Claire struck the top of the flare. She jumped back, because she hadn't anticipated such an immediate, blazing plume of fire. Sparks dripped at her feet. The flare made a spurting sound like a faucet turned on full blast. She felt a quiver of panic at what she was doing. She'd thought there would be more time, but the fire was rapidly eating away the seconds. The gasoline had caught. Reddish orange flames licked up the side of the house. She dropped the flare. Her heart was in her throat. She had to move quickly. This was happening now. There was no going back.

Claire jogged around to the side of the house. She struck the other flare and dropped it underneath the master bedroom. There was a whooshing sound, a puff of hot wind, and the flames roiled along the gas trail up to the plywood boards covering the window.

The heat was intense, but Claire was shivering. She ran back to her staging ground and wrapped the Mylar cape around her shoulders. The crinkly material barely covered her upper body. She looked up at the sky. The clouds were moving fast. The rain had gone from a fine mist to big, fat drops. Claire hadn't counted on the rain. She watched the side of the house to make sure the fire was taking. White smoke spiraled high into the air. Orange flames licked out from behind the plywood.

Step three: in progress.

Claire grabbed the gas can and walked toward the back porch. She stopped ten feet away, perfectly in line with the steps. She put down the can. She took out the revolver. She held the gun at her side, barrel pointing toward the ground.

She waited.

The wind shifted. Smoke blew into her face. The color had changed from white to black. Claire didn't know what that meant. She recalled a television show where the color difference was an important plot point, but then she also recalled an article that said the color of smoke varied depending on what was burning.

Was anything burning? Claire couldn't see any more flames. There was only a steady plume of black smoke as she waited for Paul to run screaming from the house.

A minute passed. Another. She gripped the revolver in her hand. She swallowed down a cough. The wind shifted back toward the road. Another minute. Another. She listened to the rushing sound of blood in her ears as her heart threatened to beat out of her chest.

Nothing.

"Shit," she whispered. Where was the fire? There wasn't enough rain to wet the grass, let alone snuff out a burning house. Even the emergency road flare was sputtering out.

Claire kept her eye on the back door as she shuffled a few feet over to check out the side of the house. Smoke rolled out from underneath the plywood like a coal fire plant. Was the fire inside the walls? The wood siding was old and dry. The wooden studs had been inside the walls for over sixty years. Claire had seen thousands of diagrams of residential walls: the siding on the exterior, the thin wood sheeting for strength, the thick layer of insulation tucked between the wooden studs, the Sheetrock. There was at least six inches of material between the inside and outside of the house, most of it wood, much of it soaked in gasoline. Why wasn't the fire blazing through the house by now?

The insulation.

Paul had replaced all the windows. He would've pulled the old Sheetrock off the walls and foamed in a fire-retardant insulation because no matter what Claire thought of, Paul was always six fucking steps ahead of her.

"God dammit," she muttered.

What now?

The gas can. She picked it up. There was still a swill of gasoline inside. The paper wick had sucked most of it into the fibers. This was her one and only back-up plan: to light the wick and throw the can on the roof.

And then what? Watch that not burn, either? The point of

directing the fire into a crescent was to send Paul running out the back door. If he heard something on the roof, he could just as easily go out the front or even through the garage door. Or ignore the sound as a fallen tree limb or maybe not hear it at all because he was too busy doing whatever it was that he was doing with Lydia.

Claire put down the gas can. She opened the flip phone. She dialed information and got the home number for Buckminster Fuller. She pressed the key to connect the call.

Inside the house, the kitchen phone started ringing. The sound still felt like an ice pick in her ear. She let the muzzle of the gun tap at her leg as she listened to the rings. One. Two. Three. This time yesterday, Claire was sitting on the back porch like a docile child as she waited for Paul to call her every twenty minutes to tell her whether or not her sister was still alive.

Paul answered the phone on the fifth ring. "Hello?"

"It's me." She kept her voice quiet. She could see him through the broken kitchen door. His back was to her. There was no smoke in the room, no sign of the fire. He had taken off the red sweatshirt. She could see his shoulder blades stretching against the thin material of his T-shirt.

He said, "Why are you calling on this phone?"

"Where is Lydia?"

"I'm really getting sick of you asking about your sister."

The wind had shifted back. Smoke burned her eyes. "I saw the unedited videos."

Paul didn't answer. He looked up at the ceiling. Could he smell the smoke?

"I know, Paul."

"What do you think you know?" He tried to stretch the phone cord to look in the hallway.

A flash of light caught Claire's eye. A single flame fingered its way down from the soffit over the bathroom. She looked back at Paul. The phone was keeping him tethered inside the kitchen. "I know you're the masked man."

Again, he said nothing.

Claire watched the finger of flame turn into a hand. The soffit blackened. The wood grain on the siding laced with soot. "I know you have photographs of Johnny Jackson on the USB drive. I know you want your client list so you can keep the business going."

"Where are you?"

Claire's heart thrilled with excitement as she watched the fire trace up the plywood board covering the bathroom window.

"Claire?"

Paul wasn't talking on the phone. He was standing on the porch looking up at the house. Smoke rolled off the roof. He didn't look terrified. He looked stunned. "What did you do?"

Claire dropped the phone. She still held the revolver at her side. Paul looked down at her hand. He knew that she had a gun. Now was the time to raise it up, point the barrel at him, cock the hammer. She should move quickly. She should widen her stance. She should be ready to pull the trigger before his foot hit the ground.

Paul walked down the three steps. She remembered him walking down the stairs at home, the way he would smile at her in the morning and tell her how beautiful she was, the way he would kiss her cheek, the way he would leave her notes to find in the medicine cabinet and send her funny texts during the day.

He asked, "Did you set the house on fire?" He sounded incredulous and secretly pleased, the exact same way he'd sounded when Claire had called him from the police station to tell him she needed bail money.

"Claire?"

She could not move. This was her husband. This was Paul.

"Where did you get that?" He was looking down at the gun. Again, he seemed more surprised than concerned. "Claire?"

The plan. She couldn't forget the plan. The fire was catching. The revolver was in her hand. She needed to cock the hammer. Point it at Paul's face. Pull the trigger. Pull the trigger. Pull the trigger.

"Lydia's fine." He was standing so close to her. She could smell his musty sweat. His beard was full. He had taken off the thick glasses. She could see the outline of his body underneath his white T-shirt.

She had kissed his body. She had curled her fingers into the hair on his chest.

He glanced back at the house. "Looks like it's spreading fast."

"You're terrified of fire."

"I am when it's close enough to hurt me." He didn't state the obvious: that he was outside, that it was raining, that he had acres of fields he could run to for safety. "Listen, the fire won't hold off like that for long. Go ahead and give me the USB drive, and I'll leave, and you can go inside and untie Lydia." He smiled his sweet, awkward smile that told her everything was taken care of. "You'll see I didn't hurt her, Claire. I kept my promise to you. I always keep my promises to you."

Claire watched her hand go up to touch his cheek. His skin felt cold. His T-shirt was too thin. He needed a jacket.

She said, "I thought—"

Paul looked into her eyes. "You thought what?"

"I thought I chose you."

"Of course you did." His hands gently cradled her face. "We chose each other."

Claire kissed him. Really kissed him. Paul moaned. His breath caught when their tongues touched. His hands trembled at her face. She could feel his heart beating. It was the same as it had always been, which was how she knew that it had always been a lie.

Claire cocked the hammer. She squeezed the trigger.

The explosion shook the air.

Blood splattered up her neck.

Paul dropped to the ground. He was screaming. The sound was feral, frightening. He clutched at his knee, or what was left of his knee. The hollow-point bullet had disintegrated his kneecap and ripped apart his ankle. White bone and strips of tendon and cartilage dangled down like bloody pieces of frayed string.

She told Paul, "That was for me."

Claire shoved the gun down the back of her jeans. She grabbed the foil blanket. She started toward the house.

Then she stopped.

Fire had taken over the left side of the house. Flames were clawing at the kitchen wall. Sparks jumped up at the ceiling. Glass shattered in the intense heat. The telephone had melted. The linoleum was black. Smoke hung like white cotton in the air. Orange and red flames had filled the den as they trudged toward the hallway.

Toward the garage.

It was too late. She couldn't go in. Trying to help Lydia would be madness. She would die. They would both die.

Claire took a deep breath and ran into the house.

TWENTY-THREE

"I'm in the garage!" Lydia pulled uselessly at her restraints as bright red flames licked at the mouth of the hallway. "Help me!"

She had heard gunfire. She had heard a man screaming.

Paul, she thought. *Please, God, let it be Paul.*

"I'm here!" Lydia cried. She strained against the chair. She had given up hope until the phone rang, until the gunshot.

"Help!" she screamed.

Did they know about the fire? Were the police handcuffing Paul when they should be running into the house? He had left the door to the house open. She had a front-row view to the changing nature of the fire. The gentle flicker had turned into white-hot flames that were chewing through the walls. The carpet peeled up. Chunks of plaster melted off the ceiling. Smoke and heat roiled through the narrow corridor. Her hands felt hot. Her knees felt hot. Her face was hot.

"Please!" Lydia screamed. The fire was moving so fast. Didn't they know she was in here? Didn't they see the flames shooting through the roof?

"I'm in here!" she yelled. "I'm in the garage!"

Lydia pulled uselessly at the restraints. She couldn't die like this. Not after what she had survived. She needed to see Rick one more time. She needed to hold Dee in her arms. She had to tell Claire that she had really forgiven her. She had to tell her mother that she loved her, that Paul had killed Sam, that her father had not taken his life, that he had loved them all so much and—

"Please!" She screamed so loudly that she strangled on the word. "Help me!"

There was a figure at the end of the hallway.

"Here!" she yelled. "I'm here!"

The figure got closer. Closer.

"Help!" Lydia cried. "Help me!"

Claire.

The figure was Claire.

"No, no, no!" Lydia panicked. Why was it Claire? Where were the police? What had her sister done?

"Lydia!" Claire was running at a crouch, trying to stay below the smoke. A foil blanket was over her head. Fire roiled behind her—brick-red and orange flames that lapped up the walls and dug chunks out of the ceiling.

Why was it Claire? Where were the firemen? Where were the police?

Lydia frantically watched the door, waiting for more people to rush in. Men in heavy fireproof jackets. Men with helmets and oxygen. Men with axes.

There was no one else. Just Claire. Crazy, impetuous, idiotic fucking Claire.

"What did you do?" Lydia screamed. "Claire!"

"It's all right," Claire screamed back. "I'm going to save you."

"Jesus Christ!" Lydia could see the fire curling the paint off the walls. Smoke was filling the garage. "Where is everybody?"

Claire grabbed the knife off the table. She cut through the plastic ties.

"Go!" Lydia pushed her away. "I'm chained to the wall! You have to go!"

Claire reached behind the chair. She twisted something. The chain fell away like a belt.

For a moment, Lydia was too stunned to move. She was free. After almost twenty-four hours, she was finally free.

Free to burn alive in a fire.

"Come on!" Claire headed toward the open door, but the fire had already consumed their only way out. Flames melted the plastic slats on the wall. The shag carpet curled like a tongue.

"No!' Lydia screamed. "God dammit, no!" She couldn't die like this. Not after living through Paul's torture. Not after thinking she was going to get away.

"Help me!" Claire ran at the roll-up door. The metal made a clanging sound that rattled Lydia's eardrums. Claire tried to run at the door again, but Lydia grabbed her arm.

"What did you do?" she screamed. "We're going to die!"

Claire jerked away her arm. She ran to the wooden shelves. She swept the videotapes onto the floor. She wrested the shelves from their brackets.

"Claire!" Lydia yelled. Her sister had finally gone insane. "Claire! Stop!"

Claire grabbed the pry bar off the floor. She swung it like a bat at the wall. The hammer stuck into the Sheetrock. She wrenched it out and swung again.

Sheetrock.

Lydia watched dumbly as Claire took another swing at the wall. Like everything else in the garage, the concrete-block wall was for show. The actual garage walls were made of Sheetrock and wooden studs and beyond those studs there would be siding and beyond that would be freedom.

Lydia snatched the pry bar out of Claire's hands. Every muscle in her body screamed as she lifted the ten-pound metal bar over her head. She put her full weight into the swing, bringing it down like a hammer. She swung again and again until the Sheetrock was gone and hard pieces of foam chipped out like snow. Lydia took another swing. The foam was melting. The metal bar cut through like butter.

Claire yelled, "Use your hands!"

They both grabbed handfuls of smoldering foam. Lydia's fingers burned. The foam was returning to its liquid state, releasing pungent chemicals into the air. She started coughing. They were both coughing. The smoke was thick inside the garage. Lydia could barely see what they were doing. The fire was getting closer. Heat blistered at her back. She frantically pulled at the boiling insulation. This wasn't going to work. It was taking too long.

"Move!" Lydia backed up as much as she could and ran at the wall. She felt her shoulder crunch against the wood siding. She backed up and ran again, angling her body between the studs so she could get to the outside part of the wall.

Lydia backed up to make another run.

Claire screamed, "It's not working!"

But it was.

Lydia felt the boards crack against her weight. She backed up again. Daylight showed through the splintered wood.

Lydia ran full-bore at the wall. The wall buckled. Something popped in her shoulder. Her arm hung uselessly at her side. She used her foot, kicking with every ounce of her remaining strength until the wooden slats popped off their nails. Smoke funneled toward the fresh air. Lydia turned around to get Claire.

"Help me!" Claire's hands were full of videotapes. The fire was so close that she looked luminescent. "We have to get them out!"

Lydia grabbed her sister by the collar and pushed her toward the narrow opening. Claire couldn't fit through the gap with the tapes. Lydia slapped them out of her hands. She pushed Claire again. Her feet slipped. Her shoes were melting into the concrete. Lydia made one last push. Claire went flying outside. Lydia was right after her. They both landed hard on the driveway.

The sudden fresh air shocked Lydia's system. Her collarbone had cracked against the concrete. She felt like a knife had jammed into her throat. She rolled onto her back. She gasped for air.

Videotapes rained down around her. Lydia swatted them away. She hurt so bad. Everything hurt so bad.

"Hurry!" Claire was on her knees. She was reaching her hands back into the garage, trying to save the videotapes. One of her shirtsleeves caught on fire. She shook out the flame and kept reaching in. Lydia tried to push herself up, but her left arm wouldn't work. The pain was almost unbearable as she lifted herself with her right hand. She grabbed Claire by the shirt and tried to pull her away.

"No!" Claire kept reaching for more tapes. "We have to get them." She used both hands to gather the tapes the same way she used to gather sand to make castles. "Liddie, please!"

Lydia got on her knees beside Claire. She could barely see more than a few inches in front of her. Smoke was furling out the opening. The heat was suffocating. She felt something drop on her head. Lydia thought it was a spark from the fire, but it was rain.

"There's just a few more!" Claire kept pulling out the tapes. "Get them away from the house!"

Lydia used her good hand to toss the videos out into the driveway. There were so many. Her eyes scanned the dates on the labels, and she knew the dates corresponded to missing women, and that the women had families who had no idea why their sisters, their daughters, were gone.

Claire fell backward as flames shot out from the garage. Her face was black with soot. The fire had finally engulfed the garage. Lydia grabbed her collar and pulled her away from the house. Claire stumbled as she tried to stand. Her melted shoes fell off her feet. She banged into Lydia. The jolt sent pain straight up into Lydia's shoulder, but it was nothing like the hacking coughs that wracked her body. She bent at the waist and let out a stream of black water that tasted like piss and cigarette ash.

"Liddie." Claire rubbed her back.

Lydia opened her mouth and let out another foul black stream that made her stomach spasm. Mercifully, there wasn't much more. She wiped her mouth. She stood up. She closed her eyes to fight the dizziness.

"Lydia. Look at me."

Lydia forced open her eyes. Claire stood with her back to the garage. Fire and smoke raged behind her, but she was looking at Lydia, not the fire. She had her fingers pressed to her mouth. She looked stricken.

Lydia could only imagine what her sister was seeing: the bruises, the welts, the electrical burns.

Claire said, "What did he do to you?"

"I'm okay," Lydia said, because she had to be.

"What did he do?" Claire was shaking. Tears cut white tracks into the soot on her face. "He promised he wouldn't hurt you. He promised."

Lydia shook her head. She couldn't do this now. It didn't matter. None of it mattered.

"I'm going to kill him." Claire's bare feet pounded into the ground as she stalked around to the back of the house.

Lydia followed, holding her useless left arm as still as she could. Every step sent her collarbone clashing against the base of her throat. Her joints had filled with gravel dust. Rain had turned the soot on her skin into a wet, black ash.

Claire was just ahead of her. She had a revolver stuffed down the back of her jeans. Lydia recognized the gun, but not the fluid way Claire pulled the weapon, cocked the hammer, and trained the sights at the man crawling on the ground.

Paul had pulled himself about twenty feet away from the house. A streak of dark blood showed his progress through the wet grass. His right knee was a bloody pulp. His ankle was shattered. The bottom half of his leg hung at an unnatural angle. Bone and sinew and muscle glistened in the light from the still-roaring flames.

Claire had the gun pointed at Paul's face. "You fucking liar."

Paul kept moving, using his elbow and hand to pull himself away from the fire.

Claire tracked him with the gun. "You said you didn't hurt her."

Paul shook his head, but he kept crawling.

"You promised me."

He finally looked up.

"You promised," Claire said, sounding petulant and devastated and furious.

Paul managed a shrug. "At least I didn't fuck her."

Claire pulled the trigger.

Lydia screamed. The noise from the gun was deafening. The bullet had torn open the side of Paul's neck. His hand clamped down on the wound. He fell onto his back. Blood seeped between his fingers.

"Jesus Christ," Lydia breathed. It was all she could say. "Jesus Christ."

"Claire." Paul's voice gurgled in his throat. "Call an ambulance."

Claire trained the gun at his head. She looked down at him with an utter lack of emotion. "You lying piece of shit."

"No!" Lydia grabbed Claire's hand just as she pulled the trigger. The shot went wild. She could feel the recoil travel through Claire's hand and up her own arm.

Claire tried to aim the gun again.

"No." Lydia forced her hand away. "Look at me."

Claire wouldn't let go of the gun. Her eyes were glazed. She was somewhere else, somewhere dark and menacing where the only way out of it was to murder her husband.

"Look at me," Lydia repeated. "He knows where Julia is."

Claire wouldn't look away from Paul.

"Claire." Lydia spoke as clearly as she could. "Paul knows where Julia is."

Claire shook her head.

"He told me," Lydia said. "He told me in the garage. He knows where she is. She's close by. He told me he still visits her."

Claire shook her head. "He's lying."

Paul said, "I'm not lying. I know where she is."

Claire tried to move the gun back to his head, but Lydia stopped her. "Let me try, okay? Just let me try. Please. Please."

Slowly, Claire slackened the tension in her arm as she gave in.

Still, Lydia kept an eye on her sister as she struggled to kneel down. The pain nearly took her breath away. Every movement sent a sharp knife into her shoulder. She wiped the sweat from her brow. She looked down at Paul. "Where is Julia?"

Paul wouldn't look at her. He was only interested in Claire. "Please," he begged her. "Call an ambulance."

Claire shook her head.

Lydia said, "Tell us where Julia is and we'll call an ambulance."

Paul squinted up at Claire. The rain was pelting his face. Spraying his face. Streaming into his face.

"Call an ambulance," Paul repeated. "Please."

Please. How many times had Lydia begged him in the garage? How many times had he laughed at her?

Paul said, "Claire . . ."

"Where is she?" Lydia repeated. "You said she was close. Is she in Watkinsville? Is she in Athens?"

He said, "Claire, please. You have to help me. This is serious."

Claire held the gun limply at her side. She was looking back at the house, staring into the fire. Her lips were in a tight line. Her eyes were still wild. She was going to crack. Lydia just couldn't tell which way.

She looked back down at Paul. "Tell me." She tried to keep the begging tone out of her voice. "You said you know where she is. You said you visited her."

. . . rotten bones with long strands of dirty blonde hair and those stupid bracelets . . .

"Claire?" Paul was losing too much blood. His skin had turned a waxy white. "Claire, please—just look at me."

Lydia didn't have time for this. She jammed her fingers into his shattered knee.

Paul's screams pierced the air. She didn't let up. She kept pressing until her fingernails had scraped raw bone.

She said, "Tell us where Julia is."

He hissed air between his teeth.

"Tell us where she is!"

Paul's eyes rolled back in his head. His body started to convulse. Lydia took away her hand.

He gasped for air. Bile and pink blood dribbled out of his mouth. He pressed the back of his head into the ground. His chest was heaving for air. He made a choking sound. He was crying.

No, he wasn't crying.

He was laughing.

"You don't have it in you." Paul's bloody white teeth showed between wet lips. "Worthless fat bitch."

Lydia jammed her fingers into his knee again. She could feel her knuckles bend as they curled around the broken shards of bone. This time, Paul screamed so loud that his voice broke. His mouth was open. Air was passing through his vocal cords, but there was no sound.

His heart would be shaking. His bladder would be releasing. His bowels would be liquid. His soul would be dying.

Lydia knew, because Paul had made her scream the same way inside the garage.

He started to convulse again. His arms were stiff. His grip tightened around the wound in his neck. She saw dark red blood dripping between his fingers.

Claire said, "I have a first-aid kit in the car. We could patch up his neck and make this last longer." Her tone was conversational, almost the same as Paul's had been inside the garage. "Or we could burn him alive. There's some gas left in the can."

Lydia knew that her sister was deadly serious. Claire had already shot him twice. She would've executed him if Lydia hadn't stopped her. Now she wanted to torture him, to burn him alive.

What was Lydia doing? She looked down at her hand. The fingers had all but disappeared inside what was left of Paul's knee. She could feel his tremors resonating straight into her heart.

Into her soul.

She forced herself to withdraw her hand. Taking away his pain was one of the hardest things she had ever done. But no matter what hell Paul Scott had visited on Lydia and her family, she wasn't going to turn into Paul, and she sure as hell wasn't going to let her baby sister.

"Where is she, Paul?" Lydia tried to appeal to what little humanity Paul had left. "You're going to die. You know that. It's just a matter of time. Tell us where Julia is. Do one decent thing before you go."

A thread of blood slipped from Paul's mouth. He told Claire, "I really did love you."

Lydia asked, "Where is she?"

Paul would not look away from Claire. "You were the only good thing I ever did."

Claire tapped the muzzle of the gun against her leg.

He said, "Look at me. Please, just one more time."

She shook her head. She stared out at the field behind the house.

He said, "You know that I love you. You were the only part of me that was normal."

Claire shook her head again. She was crying. Even in the rain, Lydia could see the tears streaming down her face.

"I was never going to leave you." Paul was crying, too. "I love you. I promise, Claire. I love you with my dying breath."

Claire finally looked down at her husband. Her mouth opened, but only to take in air. Her eyes tracked back and forth like she couldn't quite understand what was in front of her.

Was she seeing the old Paul in this moment, the insecure grad student who so desperately wanted her to love him? Or was she seeing the man who had filmed those movies? The man who for twenty-four years had kept the dark secret that had haunted her family?

Paul reached up to Claire. "Please. I'm dying. Just give me this. Please."

She shook her head, but Lydia could tell her resolve was breaking.

So could Paul. He said, "Please."

Slowly, reluctantly, Claire knelt down beside him. She let the gun fall to the grass. She placed her hand over his. She was helping him staunch the wound, helping him stay alive.

Paul coughed. Blood spit between his lips. He tightened his grip on his wounded neck. "I love you. No matter what, always know that I love you."

Claire held back a sob. She stroked his cheek. She brushed the hair out of his eyes. She gave him a sad smile and said, "You stupid asshole. I know you put Julia in the well."

Lydia would have missed Paul's shocked look if she hadn't been watching his face. He quickly rearranged his expression into one of open delight. "My God, you were always so clever."

"I was, wasn't I?" Claire was still leaning over him. Lydia thought she was going to kiss him, but instead, Claire peeled his hand away from his wounded neck. Paul struggled to resist, to stop the flow of blood, but Claire held tight to his hand. She pushed him onto his back. His strength was gone. He couldn't stop the blood. He couldn't stop Claire. She straddled his waist. She pinned down both of his wrists. She kept looking him in the eye, drinking in every change that crossed his face—the disbelief, the fear, the desperation. His heart was frantically pounding. Every beat sent out a fresh spray of arterial blood. Claire did not look away when his mouth gaped open, or when rain thumped the back of his throat. She held his gaze as the spray from his neck turned into a steady flow. As his hands unclenched. As his muscles relaxed. As his body slackened. Even when the only indication that Paul was still alive was the heavy wheeze of his breaths and the pink bubbles between his lips, Claire did not look away.

"I see you," she told him. "I see exactly who you are."

Lydia was dumbstruck. She couldn't believe what was happening right in front of her. What she had allowed her sister to do. They couldn't come back from this. There was no way Claire would ever come back from this.

"Come on." Claire was talking to Lydia. She stood up. She wiped her bloody hands on her pants like she'd just come in from the garden.

Lydia still couldn't move. She looked at Paul. The bubbles had stopped. She could see the flames from the house reflecting in the glassy black of his irises.

A drop of rain hit his eyeball. He didn't blink.

"Liddie."

Lydia turned away. Claire was in the back yard. The rain was really coming down now. Claire didn't seem to notice. She was kicking at the grass, pushing her way through the overgrowth.

"Come on," Claire called. "Help me."

Somehow, Lydia managed to leverage herself up. She was still in shock. That was the only reason the pain didn't stop her. She forced herself to put one foot in front of the other. She made herself ask Claire, "What are you doing?"

"There's a well!" Claire had to raise her voice to be heard

over the rain. She was kicking at the weeds with her bare feet, making wide circles on the ground. "The property taxes said the house was on city water." Her excitement was barely contained. She had the same breathlessness as when she used to tell Lydia a story about the mean girls at school. "I did a painting for Paul. Years ago. It was from a photograph of the back yard. He showed it to me when we were first dating and he said he loved the view because it reminded him of home, and his parents, and growing up on the farm and there was a barn in the picture, Liddie. A big, scary barn and right beside it was a well with a roof over it. I spent hours trying to get the color right—days, weeks. I can't believe I forgot about that fucking well."

Lydia pushed away some tall weeds. She wanted to believe her. She longed to believe her. Could it be that simple? Could Julia really be here?

"I know I'm right." Claire kicked at the ground under the swing-set. "Paul kept everything the same in the house. Everything. So why would he tear down the barn except to hide the evidence? And why would he cover the well if there wasn't something in it? You saw his expression when I said that about the well. She has to be here, Pepper. Julia has to be in the well."

They were all so close, Lydia. Do you want me to tell you how close?

Lydia started kicking through the wet weeds. The wind had changed direction again. She couldn't imagine a time when she would smell anything but smoke. She looked back at the house. The fire was still going strong, but maybe the rain would keep it from jumping into the grass.

"Liddie!" Claire was standing under the swingset. She banged the ground with her heel. A hollow sound echoed up from deep in the earth.

Claire dropped to her knees. She started digging her fingers into the earth. Lydia dropped down beside her. She used her good hand to feel what her sister had found. The wooden cover was heavy, about an inch thick and three feet round.

"This has to be it," Claire said. "It has to be it."

Lydia grabbed handfuls of dirt. Her hand was bleeding. There were blisters from the fire, from the melting foam. Still, she kept digging.

Claire finally moved enough dirt to wedge her fingers underneath the cover. She squatted down like a weightlifter and pulled so hard that the muscles on her neck stood out.

Nothing.

"Dammit." Claire tried again. Her arms shook from the effort. Lydia tried to help, but she couldn't make her arm move in that direction. The rain was doing them no favors. Everything felt heavier.

Claire's fingers slipped. She fell backward into the grass. "Shit!" she screamed, pushing herself back up.

"Try pushing it." Lydia braced her feet against the cover. Claire helped, using the heels of her hands, putting her back into it.

Lydia felt herself slipping. She dug in the heel of her good hand and pushed so hard that she felt like her legs were going to break in two.

Finally, eventually, they managed to move the heavy piece of wood a few inches.

"Harder," Claire said.

Lydia didn't know how much harder she could push. They

tried again, this time with Claire beside her using her feet. The cover moved another inch. Then a few more. They both pushed, screaming out the pain and the effort until the cover had moved enough so that their legs were dangling over open earth.

Dirt and rocks fell into the mouth of the well. Rain splattered against water. They both looked down into the endless darkness.

"Dammit!" Claire's voice echoed back up. "How deep do you think it is?"

"We need a flashlight."

"There's one in the car."

Lydia watched her sister sprint away in her bare feet. Her elbows were bent. She hurdled over a fallen tree. She was so intent on moving forward that she wasn't stopping to look back at what she had left in her wake.

Paul. She hadn't just watched him die. She had taken in his death like a hummingbird drawing nectar.

Maybe that didn't matter. Maybe watching Paul die was the sustenance that Claire needed. Maybe Lydia shouldn't worry about what they had done to Paul. She should be more concerned about what Paul had done to them.

To their father. To their mother. To Claire. To Julia.

Lydia looked down into the gaping blackness of the well. She tried to listen for the rain hitting the water at the bottom, but there were too many drops to follow the path of just one.

She found a pebble on the ground. She dropped it into the well. She counted seconds. At four seconds, the pebble splashed into the water.

How far could a rock travel in four seconds? Lydia reached down into the darkness. She ran her hand along the rough rocks, trying not to think about spiders. The rocks were uneven. Mortar was chipping away. If she was careful, maybe she could get a foothold. She leaned in farther. She swept her hand back and forth. The mortar felt dry. Her fingers brushed across a vine.

Except it was too delicate to be a vine. It was thin. Metal. A bracelet? A necklace?

Carefully, Lydia tried to pick the chain away from the wall. The resistance changed, and she guessed it was stuck on something. She couldn't reach her other hand down to pull it away. She looked back over her shoulder. Claire was in the distance. The flashlight was on. She was running. Her feet were going to be cut up from the forest. She probably couldn't feel it now because of the bitter cold.

Lydia groaned as she leaned farther into the well. She let her fingers walk along the chain. She felt a solid metal piece, almost like a coin, stuck between the rocks in the wall. There was a shape to it, not round but maybe oval. She traced her thumb along the smooth edges. Carefully, Lydia pried out the coin, rocking it gently back and forth until it came loose from the crevice. She wound the chain around her fingers and pulled her arm out of the well.

She looked down at the necklace in her hand. The gold locket was shaped like a heart and engraved with a cursive L. It was the sort of thing a boy would give you in the ninth grade because you let him kiss you and he thought that meant you were going steady.

Lydia couldn't remember the boy's name, but she knew that Julia had stolen the locket from her jewelry box, and that she was wearing it the day she had disappeared.

Claire said, "It's your locket."

Lydia rolled the cheap chain between her fingers. She had thought it was so expensive. He'd probably paid five bucks for it at the Ben Franklin.

Claire sat down. She turned off the flashlight. She was breathing hard because of the run. Lydia was breathing hard because of what they were about to do. Thick smoke rolled across the faint sunlight. The air was frigid. The condensation from their combined breaths mingled together over the locket.

This was the moment. Twenty-four years of searching, longing, knowing, not knowing, and all they could do was sit in the rain.

Claire said, "Julia used to sing Bon Jovi in the shower. Do you remember that?"

Lydia let herself smile. "'Dead or Alive.'"

"She always ate all the popcorn at the movies."

"She loved licorice."

"And dachshunds."

They both made a sour face.

Claire said, "She liked that gross guy with the mullet. What was his name? Brent Lockhart?"

"Lockwood," Lydia remembered. "Dad made him get a job at McDonald's."

"He smelled like grilled beef."

Lydia laughed, because Julia the vegetarian had been appalled. "She broke up with him a week later."

"She let him get to second base anyway."

Lydia looked up. "She told you that?"

"I spied on them from the stairs."

"You were always such a brat."

"I didn't tattle."

"For once."

They both looked back down at the locket. The gold had worn off the back. "I meant what I told you on the phone. I forgive you."

Claire wiped rain out of her eyes. She didn't look like she would ever forgive herself. "I sent out an email—"

"Tell me later."

There were so many more important things to catch up on. Lydia wanted to watch Dee meet her crazy aunt. She wanted to hear Rick and Helen discussing the inherent evil of eBooks. She wanted to hold her daughter. She wanted to gather up her dogs and her cats and her family and be made whole again.

Claire said, "All Daddy ever wanted was to find her."

"It's time."

Claire turned on the flashlight. The light reached down to the bottom of the well. The body had come to rest in a shallow pool of water. The skin had fallen off. No sunlight had bleached the bones.

The locket. The long blonde hair. The silver bangles.

Julia.

TWENTY-FOUR

Claire lay on Julia's bed with her head propped up on Mr. Biggles, Julia's favorite stuffed animal. The ancient, shaggy dog had barely survived their childhood. Jean Naté After Bath Splash suffused his stuffing. His legs had been dipped in Kool-Aid as payback for a purloined book. Part of his nose had been burned off in a stealthy bit of retribution for a stolen hat. In a fit of pique, someone had snipped the fur on his head down to the cotton batting.

Lydia didn't look much better. Her singed hair was growing back, but six weeks out from their ordeal, her bruises were still a nasty black and yellow. The cuts and burns had only recently started to scab. The area around her fractured eye socket was still red and swollen. Her left arm would be in a sling for another two weeks, but she had become remarkably adept at doing almost everything with one hand, including folding Julia's clothes.

They were in the house on Boulevard. Helen was making lunch in the kitchen. Claire was supposed to be helping Lydia pack Julia's things, but she had easily fallen back into the old pattern of letting her older sister do everything.

"Look how tiny she was." Lydia smoothed out a pair of Jordache jeans. She splayed her hand at the waist. Her thumb and pinky finger were only inches from the sides. "I used to borrow these." She sounded astonished. "I thought I was so fat when she died."

When she died.

That's what they were saying now—not *When Julia disappeared* or *When Julia went missing*, because the DNA had confirmed what they had known in their hearts all along: Julia Carroll was dead.

Last week they had laid her to rest beside their father. The ceremony was small, just Claire, Helen, Lydia, and Grandma Ginny, who kept freaking Lydia out by telling her she was just as pretty as she remembered. They had taken Ginny home after the burial and met Dee and Rick at the Boulevard house. Christmas was only a week away. There were presents under the tree. They sat at the long dining-room table and ate fried chicken and drank iced tea and told long-forgotten stories about the departed—the way Sam used to hum every time he ate ice cream and how Julia had forgotten all the notes before her first piano recital. They heard stories about Dee, too, because they had missed seventeen years of her life and she was such an interesting and bubbly and smart and pretty young girl. She was clearly her own person, but she was so much like Julia that Claire still felt her heart skip a beat every time she saw her.

"Hey, lazybutt." Lydia dumped a drawer full of socks on the bed beside Claire. "Make yourself useful."

Claire sorted the socks with a deliberate slowness so that Lydia would get annoyed and take over. Julia had loved little-girl patterns with pink hearts and red lips and various breeds of dogs. Someone would get good use out of them. They were donating their sister's clothes to the homeless shelter, the same shelter she had volunteered for the day Gerald Scott had decided to take her away from them.

And Paul, because the photograph in the barn proved he was an active participant in their sister's murder.

Lydia had relayed all the other details that Paul had confessed to in the garage. They knew about their father's staged suicide. They knew about the notebooks. The letters Helen had written to Lydia that were never delivered. Paul's plans for Dee when she turned nineteen. At some point, Claire had chosen to pull a Helen and stopped asking questions because she did not want to know the answers. There was no difference between the blue pill and the red pill.

There were only degrees of suffering.

Paul had been a violent psychopath. He was a torturer. He was a murderer. His color-coded files had been investigated and he'd been proven to be a serial rapist. The files in the basement storage area had led the FBI to offshore accounts with hundreds of millions of dollars deposited from customers all around the world. Claire had guessed correctly about Paul's franchising the system. There were other masked men in Germany, France, Egypt, Australia, Ireland, India, Turkey . . .

Past a certain point, more detailed knowledge about the

volume of her husband's sins could not make Claire's burden feel any heavier.

"I think this is yours." Lydia held up a white T-shirt with RELAX written in black letters across the front. The collar had been cut out *Flashdance*-style.

Claire said, "I used to wear that with the most amazing pair of rainbow-colored leg warmers."

"Those were my leg warmers, you brat."

Claire caught the shirt Lydia threw at her head. She held it up in front of her. It was a good shirt. She could probably still wear it.

"Have you thought about what you're going to do?"

Claire shrugged. This was a common question. Everyone wanted to know what Claire was going to do. She was living with Helen at the moment, not least of all because her mother's neighbors were much less likely to talk to the press, which is what everyone in Dunwoody who'd ever met Claire or even seen her cross a room was doing. The women on her tennis team sounded devastated for the cameras, yet they all somehow managed to get their hair and make-up professionally done before appearing on film. Even Allison Hendrickson had joined the fray, though no one had yet made the obvious joke about Claire's violent propensity toward kneecaps.

At least no one had but Claire.

Lydia said, "That teaching job at the school sounds nice. You love art."

"Wynn thinks I'll be all right." Claire rolled onto her back. She stared up at the Billy Idol poster taped on the ceiling above the bed.

"You'll still need to get a job."

"Maybe." Paul's assets had been frozen. The Dunwoody house had been seized. Wynn Wallace had explained that sorting out the ill-gotten gains from Paul's legitimate business holdings would take years and likely consume millions in legal fees.

Of course, Paul had obviously considered that when he structured his estate.

Claire told Lydia, "The life insurance policies were owned by an irrevocable trust that Quinn and Scott paid for. There's a clear paper trail. I can draw from it any time."

Lydia stared at her. "You can collect on Paul's life insurance policies?"

"Seems only fair. I'm the one who killed him."

"Claire," Lydia warned, because Claire wasn't supposed to joke about getting away with murder.

And as far as she knew, Claire had certainly gotten away with it. Not to brag—because Lydia wouldn't let her do that, either—but if Claire had learned one thing from her previous sojourn into the criminal justice system, it was that you didn't have to talk to the police unless you wanted to. Claire had sat in an interrogation room and remained silent until Wynn Wallace had arrived at the Georgia Bureau of Investigation's regional office and helped her come up with a legally sound defense for arson and murder.

Good thing, because apparently, committing a felony in the act of a murder generally meant you ended up on death row.

Claire had ended up in the passenger's seat of Wynn Wallace's Mercedes.

Paul had started the fire. Claire had shot him in self-defense.

Lydia was the only witness, but she'd told the investigators that she'd blacked out, so she had no idea what happened.

Between the rain and the firemen who soaked the smoldering embers of the Fuller house, there wasn't a lot of pesky evidence to poke holes in the story. Not that anyone was paying close attention to Claire's crimes by then. Her timed email with the Tor link was already making the rounds. The *Black and Red* had picked it up first, then the *Atlanta Journal*, then the blogs, then the national news stations. So much for her fears that no one would click an anonymously sent link.

Her biggest regret was that she had included Huckleberry in the email list, because according to witnesses, Sheriff Carl Huckabee had been sitting at his computer reading Claire's email when he grabbed his chest and died of a massive heart attack.

He was eighty-one years old. He lived in a nice house that was paid off. He'd seen his children and grandchildren grow up. He'd spent summers fishing and winters at the beach and pretty much enjoyed all of his other twisted hobbies with absolutely no impediments.

If you asked Claire, Huckleberry was the one who'd really gotten away with murder.

"Hey." Lydia threw a sock at Claire to get her attention. "Have you given any more thought about seeing a real therapist?"

"'With a poster of Rasputin and a beard down to his knee?'"

"More like 'Kid Fears.'"

Claire laughed. They had been listening to Indigo Girls on one of the hundreds of mix tapes Julia had kept in a shoebox under her bed. "I'll think about it," she told Lydia, because she knew that the twelve-step program was important to her sister. It was also the only reason Lydia was able to stand there folding Julia's clothes instead of curling into a ball in the corner.

But as Claire had told her court-appointed therapist during their last mandated session, her quick temper had ended up leading them to Julia. Maybe one day, maybe with a real therapist, Claire would work on her anger issues. God knew there was plenty enough to work on, but for right now, she wasn't inclined to get rid of the very thing that had saved them all.

Who the hell would?

Lydia said, "Did you see the news?"

"Which news?" Claire asked, because there was so much that they could barely keep up with it.

"Mayhew and that other detective were denied bail."

"Falke," Claire provided. She didn't know why they were still holding Harvey Falke. He was absolutely a bad cop, but he was just as clueless as Adam Quinn had been about Paul's illegal business. At least that's what Fred Nolan had told Claire after the Big Boys came down from Washington and interrogated both men for three weeks.

Could she believe Fred Nolan? Could Claire ever believe another man for as long as she lived? Rick was nice. Lydia had finally asked him to move in with her. He was taking care of her. He was helping her heal.

And yet.

How many times had Claire done the same thing for Paul? Not that she thought Rick was a bad man, but she'd thought Paul was a good man, too.

At least she was certain on which side of the line Jacob Mayhew fell. His house had been raided. The FBI had searched his computers and found links to almost all the movies that Paul had ever created, plus many of the international ones.

Claire had guessed correctly about the scale of the operation. Between Mayhew's computer, the contents of the USB drive, and the VHS tapes from the garage, the FBI and Interpol were working to identify hundreds of victims who had hundreds of families all over the world who might one day find their way back to peace.

The Kilpatricks. The O'Malleys. The Van Dykes. The Deichmanns. The Abdullahs. The Kapadias. Claire always repeated aloud each of their names from each of the news stories, because she knew what it was like all those years ago when people had opened their newspapers and skipped over Julia Carroll's name.

Congressman Johnny Jackson's name was not one that anyone could avoid. His involvement in the snuff porn ring was still the lead story in every newspaper, webpage, news report, and magazine. Nolan had confided that there was some kind of plea deal being worked out to keep the Congressman off death row. The US Department of Justice and Interpol needed Johnny Jackson to corroborate the details of Paul's business in various courts of law around the world and Johnny Jackson did not want to be strapped to a gurney while a prison doctor jammed a needle into his arm.

Claire was sorely disappointed that she would not be able to sit in the viewing room and witness every single flinch and whimper and sob as Johnny Jackson was put to death by the Great State of Georgia.

She knew what it was like to watch a bad person die, to feel their panic swell to a crescendo, to watch the dawning in their eyes when they realized that they were completely powerless. To know that the last words they would ever hear were the ones you said to their face: that you saw through them, that you knew everything about them, that you were disgusted, that you did not love them, that you would never, ever forget. That you would never, ever forgive. That you would be fine. That you would be happy. That you would survive.

Maybe she really should consider going into therapy sooner.

"Jesus Christ." Lydia grabbed the socks away from Claire and started folding them. "Why are you so distracted?"

"Fred Nolan asked me out."

"Are you fucking kidding me?"

Claire tossed her a stray sock. "It's weird how the guy who seemed like he was into snuff porn was actually the only guy who wasn't into snuff porn."

"You're not going to go out with him?"

Claire shrugged. Nolan was an asshole, but at least she would know it going in.

"Jesus Christ."

"'Jesus Christ,'" Claire mimicked.

Helen knocked on the open door. "Are you two squabbling?"

They both answered, "No, ma'am."

Helen smiled the relaxed smile Claire remembered from her childhood. Even with the press hounding her door, Helen Carroll had finally found peace. She picked up one of Julia's socks from the pile on the bed. There were two kissing dachshunds embroidered around the band. Helen found the match. She folded them together. The Carrolls weren't sock rollers. They paired them together in a drawer and assumed they would manage to stay that way.

Lydia said, "Mom, can I ask you something?"

"Of course."

Lydia hesitated. They had been apart so long. Claire had keenly noticed that their rapport wasn't as easy as it once was.

Helen said, "It's all right, sweetheart. What is it?"

Lydia still seemed hesitant, but she asked, "Why did you keep all this stuff when you knew she wasn't coming back?"

"That's a good question." Helen smoothed Julia's quilt before sitting down on the bed. She looked around the room. Lilac walls. Rock posters. Polaroids stuck in the mirror over the dresser. Nothing had changed since Julia had left for college, not even the ugly lava lamp that everyone knew their mother hated.

Helen said, "It made your father happy to know it was the same, that her room would be waiting for her if she ever came back." Helen rested her hand on Claire's ankle. "After I found out she was dead, I guess I just liked coming in here. I didn't have her body. There was no grave to visit." She invoked Grandma Ginny's words. "I suppose this was the only place where I could come to leave my grief."

Claire felt a lump come into her throat. "She would've liked that."

"I think so."

Lydia sat down beside Helen. She was crying. So was Claire. They were all crying. This was how it had been since they had looked down that well. Their lives had been rubbed raw. Only time could thicken their skin.

Lydia said, "We found her. We brought her home."

Helen nodded. "You did."

"It's all that Daddy ever wanted."

"No." Helen squeezed Claire's leg. She stroked a strand of hair behind Lydia's ear.

Her family. They were all together again. Even Sam and Julia.

"This," Helen said. "This is all your father ever wanted."

vii.

I remember the first time you wouldn't let me hold your hand. You were twelve years old. I was walking you to Janey Thompson's birthday party. Saturday. Warm weather though it was early fall. The sunlight was drumming at our backs. The low heels of your new shoes were clicking against the sidewalk. You were wearing a yellow sundress with thin straps. Too old for you, I thought, but maybe not because suddenly, you were older. So much older. No more gangly arms and lanky legs knocking over books and bumping into furniture. No more excited giggles and pained screams at the injustice of denied cake. Golden hair turned blonde and wavy. Bright blue eyes squinted with skepticism. Mouth no longer so quick to smile when I pulled your pigtails or tickled your knee.

No pigtails today. Stockings covered your knees.

We stopped at the street corner and I instinctively reached for your hand.

"Dad." You rolled your eyes. Your voice was older. A hint of the woman I would never get to meet.

Dad.

Not Daddy anymore.

Dad.

I knew that was it. No more holding my hand. No more sitting in my lap. No more throwing your arms around my waist when I walked through the front door or standing on my shoes while we danced around the kitchen. I would be the bank now. The ride to your friend's house. The critic of your biology homework. The signature on the check mailed away with your college application.

And as I signed that check at our kitchen table, I would remember how I used to drink pretend tea from tiny china cups as you and Mr. Biggles excitedly told me about your day.

Mr. Biggles. That poor, stuffed shaggy dog had survived chicken pox, a spilled glass of Kool-Aid, and an unceremonious toss into the trashcan. He was flattened by your weight, accidentally burned when placed too close to a curling iron, and sheared for reasons unknown by your baby sister.

Me walking into your room as you packed for college: "Honey, did you mean to throw away Mr. Biggles?"

You looking up from your suitcase filled with too-small T-shirts and cut-offs and make-up and a box of tampons that we both chose to ignore.

Dad.

The same annoyed tone you'd used that day on the street corner when you wrenched your hand from mine.

The next times you touched me would be casually—as you grabbed car keys or money or hugged me quickly for letting you go to a concert, a movie, a date with a boy I would never like.

If you had lived past the age of nineteen—if you had survived—would you have married that boy? Would you have broken his heart? Would you have given me grandchildren? Great-grandchildren? Christmas mornings at your house. Sunday dinners. Birthday cards with hearts on them. Shared vacations. Complaining about your mother. Loving your mother. Babysitting your nieces and nephews. Annoying your sisters. Bossing them around. Calling them all the time. Not calling them enough. Fighting with them. Making up with them. Me in the center of all of this, taking late-night phone calls about croup and chicken pox and why won't the baby stop crying and "what do you think, Daddy?" and "why does she do that, Daddy?" and "I need you, Daddy."

Daddy.

I found one of your scrapbooks the other day. You and your sisters spent the fifteenth year of your brief life planning your dream wedding. The dresses and the cake, the handsome grooms and their sophisticated brides. Luke and Laura. Charles and Diana. You and Patrick Swayze or George Michael or Paul McCartney (though he was much too old for you, your sisters agreed).

Last night, I dreamed of your wedding—the wedding you never had.

Who would've been waiting for you at the end of the aisle? Sadly, not that purposeful young man you met at freshman orientation, or the pre-med student who had a ten-year plan. It's more likely you would've chosen that slouchy, feckless boy with the floppy hair who so proudly declared his major was undeclared.

Since this wedding that never happened is *my* fantasy, that boy is clean-shaven on your special day, hair combed neatly, slightly nervous as he stands by the preacher, looking at you the way I always wanted a man to look at you: kind, loving, slightly in awe.

We would both be thinking the same thing, Mr. Feckless and I: *Why on earth did you choose him?*

The music plays. We begin our march. People are standing. There are whispers about your beauty. Your grace. You and I are a scant few feet away from the altar when suddenly, I want to grab you and run back up the aisle. I want to bribe you into waiting a year. Just living with him, though your Grandma Ginny would be scandalized. You could go to Paris and study Voltaire. Visit New York and see every Broadway show. Move back into your room with the posters on the walls and Mr. Biggles on your bed and that ugly lamp you found at a yard sale that your mother was praying you would take with you to college.

Though even in my dream, I know that pushing you one way will send you hurtling in the other direction. You proved as much at the end of your life as you did at the beginning.

And so there I am standing beside you on your phantom wedding day, holding back tears, offering you to the future you will never have. Your mother is in the front row waiting for me to join her. Your sisters are by the preacher, opposite the boy, and they are beaming and nervous and proud and tearful from the romance and also from fear of the changes they know will come. They are both maids of honor. They are both wearing dresses that were fought over long ago. They are both so proud and so pretty and so ready to get out of their tight dresses and pinching heels.

You cling to my arm. You hold on to my hand—tightly, the way you used to do when we crossed the street, when a scary movie was on, when you just wanted to let me know that you were there and that you loved me.

You look up at me. I am startled. Suddenly, quite miraculously, you are a grown-up beautiful woman. You look so much like your mother, but you are still uniquely you. You have thoughts I will never know. Desires I will never understand. Friends I will never meet. Passions I will never share. You have a life. You have an entire world in front of you.

Then you smile, and you squeeze my hand, and even in my sleep, I understand the truth: No matter what happened to you, no matter what horrors you endured when you were taken away, you will always be my pretty little girl.

Acknowledgments

First thanks goes to my stellar editor and Brain's Best Friend, Kate Elton, who makes everything I do so much easier. Victoria Sanders, my literary agent, and Angela Cheng Caplan, my film agent, round out my fantastically supportive team. I would also like to extend a heart-felt thanks to my new friends at Harper Collins—Dan Mallory, Liate Stehlik and Virginia Stanley, among many others. Thanks to Random House UK (Susan Sandon, Jenny Geras, Georgina Hawtrey-Woore and the gang).

Patricia Friedman assisted me with some of the thornier legal issues in the story. The kindly folks at Quickshot Shooting Range familiarized me with various weapons. Lynne Nygaard told me some great stories about her dad, which I was very open about stealing and/or combining with stories about my own wonderful father. Barry Newton helped me with some of the computer stuff (any mistakes are all his fault). The gentlemen at Tesla Marietta walked me through the most awesome car in the world. For many years, I've written about BMW in the hopes of being rewarded (Mr. Musk, a loaded grey metallic P85D with matte obeche wood and grey interior would not go amiss . . .). My Dymo labelmaker has brought me endless pleasure in the order it provides (sorry Dymo, I would rather have the Tesla). Pia Lorite won a "have your name appear in the next Karin Slaughter novel" contest. Abby Ellis should be commended for her accurate recollections of all the bars in Athens (though I was concerned by her less-than-accurate recollections of the campus). Those who went to UGA should keep in mind that this book is fiction. It is neither fact nor travelogue (your first clue: Georgia beats Auburn).

As always, I would like to give special thanks to my daddy, who brings me soup when I am writing and makes sure I do important things like comb my hair and sleep. And lastly to D.A., whose label would read MY HEART.